THOU SHALT NOT

DESIRE

THOU SHALT NOT

DESIRE

A NOVEL

CRAIG S. MORGAN

Silver Creek Farm LLC

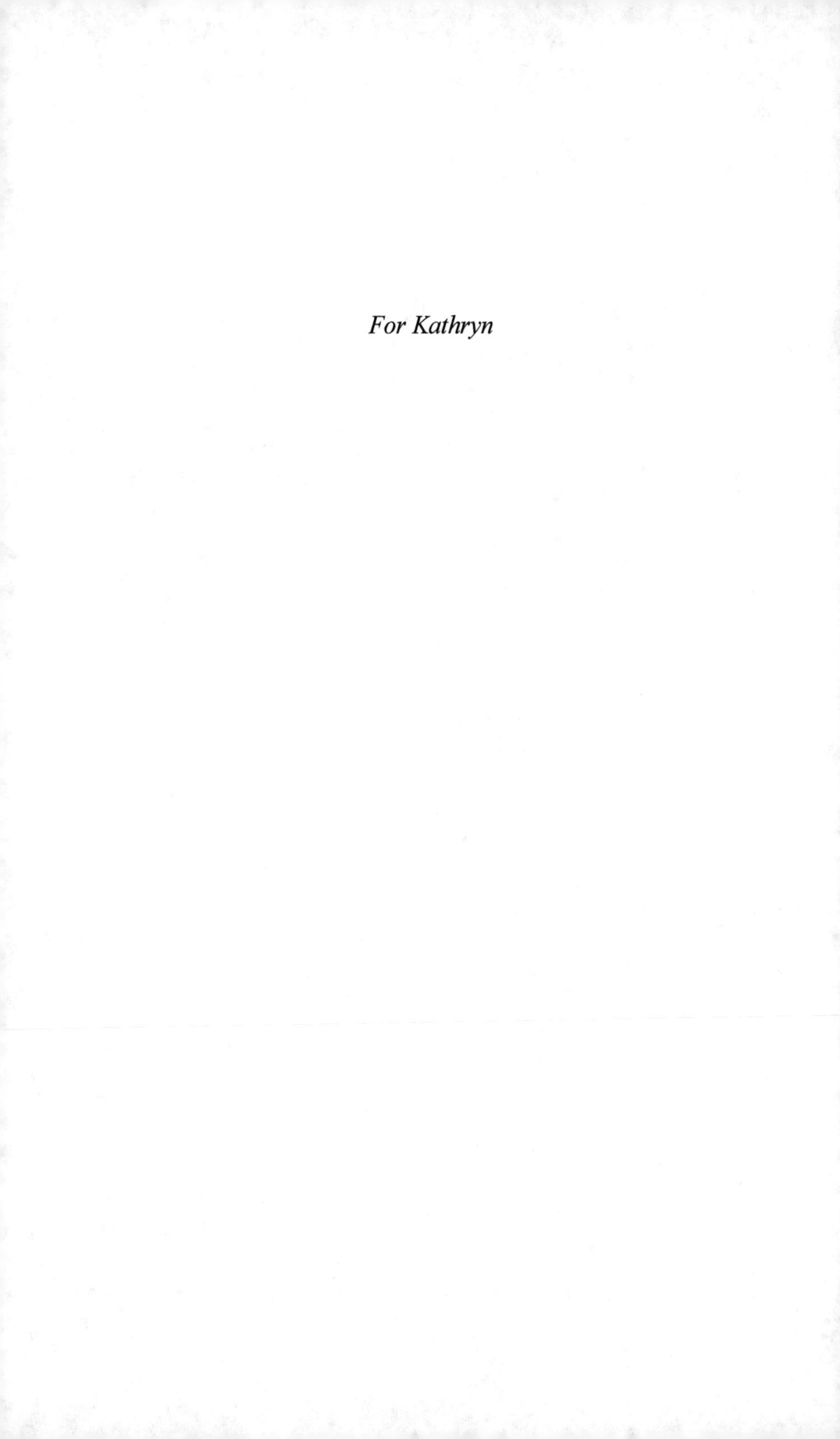

For Kathryn

CHAPTER 1

Having shaved all the areas Reverend Caldwell demanded, Lynnette stepped from the bathroom, engulfed in steam, wearing only a towel on her head. At the bar, she grabbed a tumbler and threw the ice cubes into the glass to maximize the noise. Bent slightly at the waist, standing on her tippy-toes to accentuate her calves, she looked over her shoulder to see if Caldwell had looked up from his iPhone.

Turning toward the bed, she placed one hand on her hip, as she gently traced her bottom lip with the edge of the glass. Clearing her throat, she coughed loudly and took a drink of the whiskey and water. Caldwell was shaking his head as he continued to scroll through the phone.

Moving to the bed, she set the drink on the nightstand, dropped the towel from her head, and ran her hands through her short platinum blonde hair. She slid under a layer of expensive Ritz-Carlton sheets, nudging the iPhone with the top of her head as she kissed Caldwell's neck. She moved a hand down his stomach and inside the elastic waistband of his pajama bottoms.

"Your hair is damp," Caldwell said, holding his phone up to keep from touching her. Supporting his shoulders by folding a pillow in half, he propped the back of his head against the padded headboard. Resting his hands on Lynnette's hip, he dialed Ignatius Selman.

"What is it now?" Iggy answered.

"Iggy, it's Reverend Caldwell."

"I know. What do you want?"

"Uh…I want the grapevine crosses…"

"You can't afford them. Goodbye."

"Wait. Wait. Wait. I've got money."

"Uh-huh"

"…and the gold one. I want the gold one that goes with them as well."

"They're not for sale."

"Iggy! I've got the money. I'll give you twelve thousand for the set." Caldwell moved Lynnette by pushing his left leg under her and directing her hips between his knees. He hit the speaker on his cellphone and placed the phone on the bedstand. Gently running his hands through Lynnette's hair, he moved her part from one side of her head to the other.

"Iggy," he said, after a long pause. "That's a good price. Twelve grand."

"They're worth much more."

"No, they're not. That's a fair price," Caldwell reached over to Lynnette's bedstand with his left hand and grabbed the drink.

"Iggy," he said, taking a large gulp of the whiskey. "I want those god-damned crosses. I'm willing to pay for them this time."

A long silence followed as Caldwell lost track of time. He regained his senses when Lynnette moved up the bed and gave him a kiss on the forehead. Snatching the drink from his hand, she drank the remainder. Setting the tumbler back on the bedstand, she took a seat next to Caldwell.

"You still there Iggy?"

"Yes."

"I'll be in Algier's Point in six weeks, for one night only, Thursday, November 18. You can deliver them to me then. Okay?" Caldwell rolled his legs off the edge of the bed and fell back into Lynnette's lap. "Also, I'm going to need some company for that night." He smiled up at Lynnette, who was brushing his hair gently.

"Company?"

"God, Iggy, company for Christ's sake. Do I need to spell it out?"

"You mean a whore?"

"Hell no, Iggy. Not some skank whore. Who do you think I am? It's New Orleans. Surely there's an escort service."

Lynnette scowled and pushed Caldwell's head off her lap roughly. She left the bed for the bathroom.

"I don't deal with escorts."

"Well, it's about time you upped your game," Caldwell said, laughing.

• • •

Ignatius Selman stared at the phone for several seconds, before pressing the little round button to end the call. He wanted to push his finger through the phone.

Iggy longed for the days of the rotary phone, when he could take the handset and slam it into its stand several times. Banging and screaming, each blow bringing the satisfying, stress relieving sound of the little bell inside, crying out against the attack.

"What a prick," Diamond Olivet said, hugging Iggy around his ample waist from behind him. "So, are you going to sell him the crosses?"

"It's a fair price," Iggy said, pulling Diamond's arms apart. "What on earth was he doing anyway?"

"Sounded like he was getting off." Diamond released Iggy. She pushed him aside and pressed the "release" button on the cash register drawer. "I need a few bucks."

Iggy slammed the drawer shut. "Forget it." He pushed her from behind the counter.

Diamond was wobbly on her four-inch stiletto heels. Catching her balance with a hand on the edge of a display case, she straightened the black, leather mini-skirt down her thin hips. She brushed her hands through a thick mane of shoulder length, overly bleached hair.

"You know I could do it." With exceedingly long fingernails, she picked at her sweater to straighten it across her large breasts. She pulled the sleeves down over her wrists.

"Do what?" Iggy asked. He returned to dusting a large statue of the Madonna with a feather duster.

"I can be the escort," Diamond said, moving back toward the register. "I can make a few bucks, and I could get your precious crosses back. He'll just think he's been robbed by an escort."

"I'm no pimp and you're no escort," Iggy said, without breaking his attention from the mother Mary. "Besides, Caldwell said he didn't want a skank whore."

"God, Iggy do you have to be such a pig!" Diamond reached over the counter, pushed the release button, and grabbed a handful of five-dollar bills. "I hate that!"

CHAPTER 2

Mary Ellen Retinoir sat fifteen feet above Magazine Street, resting her chin and forearms on a wrought-iron railing. The sun was low, setting near Audubon Park, a few miles upriver. Her shadow ran forever off the edge of the balcony, eventually scattering amongst the scraggly limbs of a crepe myrtle.

Moving just her eyes, she tracked Jarrell's progress toward the Balcony Bar. Power lines and internet cables, sporadically decorated with faded Mardi Gras beads, hid her from pedestrians walking below. Patrons at the Rum House, kitty corner across the street, took advantage of the alfresco dining, sitting at multi-color picnic tables loaded with pitchers of margaritas and chips.

Coming from the Lower Garden District on a bicycle, Jarrell took an abrupt left, crossing traffic. Skidding to a stop, he chained the bike to a telephone pole, scanned the street, and ran across, waving up at Mary Ellen.

"You need a drink?" he yelled, when he passed below her.

Standing, she leaned over the rail.

"A rum and coke."

Taking her seat, she pulled a pack of cigarettes from an oversized handbag. The afternoon was cool for New Orleans. Experiencing the first day to drop into the sixties since June, Mary Ellen wore jeans, a white T-shirt, and an unbuttoned flannel shirt with the sleeves rolled up to the elbows.

She was still looking for a lighter when Jarrell stepped onto the balcony with a couple of drinks.

"Here you go."

"Thanks. You got a light?"

Jarrell searched the pockets of his cargo shorts. "Mary Ellen, how would you like to make some serious coinage?" he smiled, nodding as he spoke. Lighting the cigarette, he pulled a wrought-iron chair from the table and took a seat. He patted Mary Ellen's knee with the hand that was holding the lighter. "Well… do you?"

Mary Ellen took a long drag of the cigarette. Placing her purse on the floor, she picked up her drink.

"Jarrell, I'm done dealing. I told you that." She took a drink. "I can't afford to lose my job."

"No. No. I know. Listen, you know that old asshole I work for?"

"Which one? The antiques shop or the pedicab?" Mary Ellen pushed Jarrell's hand off her knee, sat back, and crossed her legs. She brushed the hair out of her face with her free hand.

"The religious relics place in the Quarter." Jarrell sat back, drinking hungrily from a draft beer. "I overheard him and his hooker girlfriend talking about delivering a really, really expensive cross to a preacher that's coming to town this weekend." Jarrell sat forward and placed a hand on Mary Ellen's knee. "He was saying he didn't trust her with it. Anyway, she starts screaming that she's going to be screwing him anyway. She might as well…"

"What are you talking about?"

"Oh, get this. Apparently, this Reverend Caldwell character is a real whore-hound. In addition to the cross, he wants Mr. Selman to set him up with an escort for after the revival," Jarrell said. "I think that's what they were really fighting about. Diamond wants to do the escorting and I don't think my boss wants her to."

"Diamond's the girlfriend?"

"Yeah."

"He must really like her," Mary Ellen said, pushing Jarrell's hand off her knee.

"Either that or he really likes the preacher." He took another swig of beer. "It's hard to tell with that guy. Anyway, she starts screaming that she can do whatever she god-damned well wants to and I jumped in and broke it up and said that I could deliver the cross."

"Okay, so where's the big score?" Mary Ellen asked.

Jarrell's dark eyes flashed with mischief. "You can be the escort."

"You're out of your mind," Mary Ellen said, letting out a little laugh.

"Not really," Jarrell said, smiling. He pushed his chair closer to Mary Ellen. "You favor Diamond. I mean, you have similar features. You're younger and prettier. Well, much prettier. Anyway, Thursday morning, that's when he gets into town, and when I deliver the cross, I'll happen to mention that the escort he requested will be at the revival. I'll describe you and what you'll be wearing. Anyway, during the revival, you find out what trailer he's in, grab the cross, and split before the revival is even over."

"I'm not pretending to be a whore." Mary Ellen crushed out her cigarette.

"Of course not. You're pretending to be an escort."

"Same thing."

"Whatever."

"It's a victimless crime," Jarrell said. "What's he going to do? Call the cops and say an escort robbed him. Not going to happen. And then you can pawn the cross right back to my boss."

Mary Ellen pulled another cigarette from the pack. Jarrell lit it quickly. She finished her drink. "Let me think about it."

CHAPTER 3

Reverend Caldwell practically swallowed the microphone when he made his final plea. The black foam covering the mic was saturated with spit and sweat; the metal beneath it clicked against his front teeth. On a platform beneath the big top, Caldwell's words flowed like a cool stream in a dry land.

"Come, be saved." The words trickled out in a whisper; his voice was destroyed. "The day of salvation is near."

Reverend Caldwell's tent-show revival was nothing like the subdued, reverent worship services he once practiced in a Houston mega-church.

Ten years ago, the climax of the worship service was when they passed the collection plate to 10,000 plus worshipers.

Those were the years of exaltation, when money flowed through Caldwell's hands as fast as his liaisons. The fall had been abrupt and steep.

Mary Ellen Retinoir sat quietly, four rows from the stage. Hidden by a sea of born-again Christians, all jumping, and singing, and basically acting like fools, she grabbed her handbag from below her chair and rested a compact on her knee.

Brushing through her thick, blonde hair, she re-tied her pony tail. A few strands at the temples were left unbound, to frame her pretty, round face. With a little blush and a swipe of a light pastel eye shadow across the lids, her crystal blue eyes were suddenly large and beautiful. When she smeared the mascara at the corners of her eyes with a tissue, she instantly looked as if she had been crying. She looked vulnerable.

Placing everything back into her purse, she shot up from her seat. "Halleluiah!" She shouted toward the stage.

Slipping past a teenager who was sobbing and waving her hands high above her head, Mary Ellen accepted Caldwell's invitation to come forward. It was a calling alright.

A call to action.

She merged into the fluid mass of people. Chairs rattled and hymnals fell to the turf; men and women shuffled toward the stage. The newly saved, with legs too weak to walk, were ushered by the elbow.

Mary Ellen found the strength to walk alone.

Within twenty feet of the stage, she reapplied her lipstick and wiped her nose, being careful not to dry the crocodile tears she was able to shed.

CHAPTER 4

Diamond Olivet scanned the crowd surrounding her, nervously looking over one shoulder then the other. Seated in a hard plastic folding chair next to Ignatius Selman, her legs bounced uncontrollably. To keep her hands from shaking, she picked at the scratchy fabric of her dress, then clasped them as if she were going to pray, then more picking and tweaking.

"I hate this dress," she said, leaning into Iggy.

Acoustic guitars blared over the incessant pounding of drums. Singers wailed their praise to the Lord God Almighty, while Iggy sat forward covering his ears with his hands.

"I hate this dress!" Diamond yelled. "I look like a pilgrim."

Iggy turned toward her and shook his head.

The music reached an ear-splitting crescendo then fell, suddenly, in volume and tempo to a single piano playing softly, reverently. "Come, be saved." Reverend Caldwell said. "The day of salvation is near."

"Thank God," Iggy said.

People, hands waving, tears streaming from their eyes, started moving toward the aisles, striking their legs against Diamond and Iggy's knees as they tried to pass. Iggy and Diamond stood to make passage easier.

"I hate this dress," Diamond said, pulling Iggy next to her. She spoke directly into his ear.

"You've got to look the part, I guess," Iggy said.

"Miss Tessy sent it and told me to wear it. I look like an idiot."

"You look like the rest of the women here."

"You sure, you don't want me to put the good word in with her?" Diamond took a water bottle from her purse and took a couple of drinks of vodka." She offered it to Iggy, who waved her off. "She's going to need someone to pawn the crosses. There's no one better than Selman's Antiques." She smiled.

"I don't know Miss Tessy. I don't trust people I don't know. You can tell her to take her business elsewhere."

"Not a problem."

They both took their seats. Their row was now completely empty.

"So Miss Tessy contacted Caldwell and told him that you would meet him after the revival?" Iggy asked, after Diamond finished her water bottle and threw it on the ground at their feet.

"Yep."

"She talked to Caldwell directly?"

"I guess so."

"And Caldwell, just like that, is going to hook-up with a prostitute. Sight unseen."

"An escort."

"A harlot?" Iggy sat back and ran his hands over this his face and head. "A whore?"

"Yep."

"And what do you get for this?"

"Three hundred dollars. But half of…"

"Three hundred dollars? Are you kidding me?"

"Well, Miss Tessy gets half." Diamond said, pulling a pack of cigarettes from her purse. She crushed the empty box and threw it on the ground.

"Unbelievable."

A young girl moved in front of Caldwell and bowed. Caldwell placed both hands on the side of her head and began whispering directly into her ear. As his hand moved up, lifting her ponytail away from the back of her neck, Iggy saw a barcode tattoo. He shook his head in disgust.

White trash slut.

"One of these days…" Iggy said, stopping short of expressing his complete disgust with the preacher.

"What?"

"Nothing. Just tell Miss Tessy I'm interested in the crosses, if you're actually able to get them."

• • •

Iggy sat quietly, watching the roadies work their magic. After the lengthy altar call, Diamond left to find Caldwell's trailer. During the next half-hour, Iggy nodded off briefly as a never-ending praise song ushered people toward the exits. Although the evening was cool, inside the giant tent, body heat from the crowd had made it balmy. A bead of sweat formed on Iggy's bushy, gray brow.

When the lead guitarist finally unplugged his instrument and pulled the strap over his head, Iggy stood and stretched.

Walking toward the stage, he grabbed the attention of a roadie, who was folding chairs and stacking them on a cart.

"Do you know where I might find Reverend Caldwell?"

The roadie, who was Hispanic, smiled and pointed at the very tall, thin woman standing at the base of the stairs that led to the stage.

Iggy nodded when he saw Lynnette Faust.

He hesitated for a moment, examining her from a distance, trying to see if she was still as potent in real life as she was in his dreams. Memories of the one night they spent together, an intense, scary, sexual encounter that he relived over and over again when he was at his loneliest, crashed in around him and weakened his knees. Lynnette was foreboding. She was perfection.

Moving toward her, Iggy smiled. Yes, she was tall, so wonderfully tall. A half-foot taller than Iggy, her hair was cropped short, over her ears. The closer he got to her, the more he fixated on her magnificent face. Her dark eyes, flashed with authority, darting from one location to another. She barked commands in English and Spanish to a dozen different people. Her lips were thin, her cheekbones hard.

When he was only a few steps away, Iggy stood for a moment, waiting for her to notice him.

"Iggy!"

He gave a weak wave.

"It's so good to see you." She gave him a warm hug and a kiss on the side of his face.

"Lynnette, it's really good to see you," Iggy said, blushing a bit. "I had no idea you were…"

She held up a finger to stop Iggy from talking. "No, Johnny, the table cloths go to the laundry. You don't need to bother folding them. I'm sorry, Iggy."

"I was saying I didn't know you went on the road with Reverend Caldwell."

"Oh sure. It's really the only big money we make any more."

"You guys must be doing pretty good for him to want the grapevine crosses back," Iggy said, giving a wry smile. "I deposited the check this afternoon."

"I told him it was a waste of money, but…"

"No. No. I actually gave him a break. I would have given him a little more of a break, if I knew you were still involved with this get-up."

"That's sweet, Iggy."

"You're sweet. So, is he around?"

"He's busy." She spoke over the top of Iggy. "Yes, yes right there. The laundry bags are stenciled with Aramark."

"But I have the…"

"The what?" she said, suddenly giving Iggy her full attention.

"The…uh…his company?" Iggy said, with a shrug. "You know for after the show."

"Oh that's right," she said. "He's with her now."

"That was fast."

Iggy brushed the thin strands of gray hair, that covered his balding head, back with both hands. He rolled down the sleeves of his long-sleeved cotton shirt, refastening the buttons at the wrist.

"So," Iggy smiled. "How long are you in town?"

"Rolling out tomorrow. We've got one day to set up for a revival in Jackson."

"Any way, you can find time to swing by my place?" Iggy gave a wink.

"Oh that's sweet Igg. Uh…I don't really think so. Not this trip."

"That's cool."

She took his hands in hers and returned the smile.

"See you around," Iggy said, holding Lynnette's hands as long as possible.

CHAPTER 5

M ary Ellen pushed the heavy canvas material to one side with her forearm, and stood in the inverted "V" shaped opening that led outside. Stooping to clear the low edges of the canvas, she looked back over her shoulder and caught a glimpse of Caldwell still grabbing people's heads and blessing them from the stage.

Moments earlier, the stage manager, an extremely tall blonde, stood in the very same inverted "V" and pointed out Caldwell's trailer to her.

Leaving the comfort and safety of the backstage area, Mary Ellen paused a minute under the flap. Finding sound footing was difficult on the uneven pastureland. Her heart jumped a beat when she heard someone moving up behind her.

"I'll hold, senora."

"Gracias."

With the last shred of light casting itself from underneath the tent, she swayed for just a moment in the opening before the flap fell behind her. She was suddenly immersed in total darkness.

The lights of the parking lot, powered by generators scattered throughout the Algiers Point farmland, lit the heavy air above her head. Caldwell's trailer was visible. She walked steadily, across the grassy field that had been trampled by staffers and musicians. Behind her, the sounds of the worship service softened with each step.

As Mary Ellen brushed off her feet on a blanket at the base of the stairs to Caldwell's trailer, she scanned the parking lot behind her. Stepping up onto the metal step, she pushed on the flimsy metal door to Caldwell's trailer, entered, and closed the door behind her.

Scanning the single room, she moved quickly to the desk that sat to the right of the door, positioned under the back window of the trailer.

The top of the desk was cluttered with documents, books, and receipts. She didn't bother searching beneath them.

The top desk drawer was stuffed full of papers. She grabbed a wad of twenty dollar bills that were hidden way in the back and shoved them into her purse. There was nothing in the right side drawers. Opening the middle drawer on the left side, she smiled.

"Bingo."

Reaching in with both hands, she removed the box, that Jarrell had described perfectly, and placed it on the desk.

The wooden box, embossed with an odd-shaped cross, was held closed with a little brass latch. Releasing the latch, she opened the box revealing a set of four small crosses shaped like the one embossed on the lid. Gently, she worked the tray of crosses up from the box, revealing, underneath, a green felt bag.

"Here we go," she whispered, placing the heavy, green felt bag into her purse. As she tried to align the tray of other crosses back into the box with the little brass latch, the door to the trailer shook violently.

Mary Ellen jumped, dropping the tray and letting out a little squeak. Her hands tingled. Her face flushed, as she scanned the room for a hiding place. There was none—no bed to hide under, no closet to dive into. She bolted toward the door as it began to open into the trailer. As the person, a young lady, entered, Mary Ellen spun around the door and jumped to the ground. Taking off in a dead sprint toward the parking area, she kept low, clutching her purse tightly to her chest.

• • •

"What the…" Diamond yelled, as a person bolted past her and pushed her away from the door into the preacher's trailer. Losing her balance, Diamond landed face first into a couch. Dropping to her knees, Diamond watched the figure disappear into the darkness of the Algiers Point fairgrounds. "What the hell?"

Standing, Diamond brushed off her knees and straightened her awful, itchy dress. Without bothering to close the door, she moved to a tiny mini-fridge and grabbed a box of pinot grigio. She emptied the entire box into a red solo cup.

Taking a seat at a little table, she thought briefly of searching for the crosses, but she really didn't know what she was looking for, and Iggy didn't seem that concerned about getting them back. Besides, she wasn't being paid to steal crosses. She was being paid to screw the preacher.

In the next half-hour, Diamond finished the wine, smoked a cigarette, and dropped a handful of roofies in the pitcher of tea that was in the refrigerator.

Finding an ancient bottle of vodka in the back of a little cupboard, she filled her red solo cup and took a seat on the couch. With each drink, she decided to make the preacher's seduction easy. After the first gulp, she pulled the ankle length dress up over her waist, and bunched it behind her. She briefly thought about removing her panties, but she had spent good money on a new silky, red pair and wanted to look classy. After the second gulp, she unzipped the dress from behind and lowered the shoulders to her waist, exposing a tattered, dirty brassiere. By the time, she had finished the vodka, her legs were spread wide, her arms rested along the top of the couch, and the back of her head rested on a throw pillow. The bra sat on the floor in a crumpled mess.

"My goodness," Reverend Caldwell said, when he eventually stepped into the trailer.

"Something wrong preacher?" Diamond asked, displaying a thick southern drawl.

"No, no, I was just…wow."

Caldwell closed the flimsy metal door into his portable home. He latched and chained it.

"Can I get you something to drink?" Caldwell asked. "Some tea?"

"You're out of booze."

"I have some wine."

"I drank that."

"Okay then," Caldwell said, moving to the refrigerator. "Tea?"

"No thanks," Diamond said. "Help yourself."

"I think I will." Caldwell poured a large glass of tea and drank it down in one breath. "So you're a friend of Iggy's?" Caldwell asked, as he poured another glass of tea.

"Uh…"

"Mr. Selman?"

"Oh, yeah. No…I wouldn't say we're friends." Diamond dropped one hand from the back of the couch and began to gently massage between her legs. "You know we've got stuff to do, right?"

Caldwell finished his second glass of tea and took a seat at the table. Sitting back, he rubbed himself over his black preacher pants as he watched Diamond.

"Oh, I like you…" he said, smiling.

"Diamond."

"Diamond, of course." Caldwell sat for several minutes, watching Diamond caress different parts of her body. Eventually he took a seat beside her on the couch, and gently placed his hand on her breast. He kissed her neck. "Diamond, the escort," he whispered, as he moved up to nibble on her ear.

Suddenly realizing that she was not simply hooking, but was a bona fide "Miss Tessy" escort, Diamond turned her face to meet Caldwell and kissed him hungrily—something she would never do on a normal date. She removed her other arm from the back of the couch and shifted her body, pulling him down on top of her.

Grabbing his crotch, she rubbed violently, and hooked her leg around his waist. Moving her lips to his neck, she sucked and kissed, listening for an "Ohh. or Ahh. or That's it baby. or Right there."

But there was none.

Instead, as she continued to rub and kiss and suck and gyrate, she could feel him losing strength in the arm that kept his weight off of her.

"Preacher?" she spoke directly into his neck. "Preacher?"

Suddenly, she felt the full weight of the man as he slumped down into her and began to snore heavily.

• • •

Mechanical advantage, provided by the ingenious murder device, was crucial to ensure that death came with the least amount of physical exertion by the killer. After all, the inventor of the device wanted it to be functional for a feeble old lady or perhaps a ninety-pound weakling, the customer base would be endless.

Small enough to carry in an oversized handbag or in the sleeve of a jacket, it was constructed of four components—the blue nylon cord, a metal rod for the base, a metal rod for the handle, and the tennis ball.

The killer assembled the components seated beside Caldwell, who was incapacitated and lying face down, naked, on the floor of his trailer. One of the four grapevine crosses from the wooden box with the little brass latch was on the floor beside him. The preacher's breathing was smooth and peaceful.

Taking the base, the killer inserted the handle into its designated hole, making the clever device look like a "T". One end of the blue nylon cord was threaded under Caldwell's neck and then through its designated hole in the base. The ends of the blue nylon rope were tied together with a square knot, making a loose loop that encircled the victim's neck. Plenty of slack was needed to ensure the knot did not interfere with the rotation process.

The killer straddled Caldwell and placed a knee between his shoulder blades. Jamming the tennis ball on to the end of the base, the murder device suddenly resembled the front legs of nana's walker.

Placing the tennis ball between their knee and Caldwell's shoulder blade, a simple rotation, using the handle, tightened the nylon cord as it spooled around the base.

Caldwell was smiling, perhaps dreaming sweet dreams, as the murder device, with the mechanical advantage, slowly rotated and removed all the slack in the blue nylon cord loop. As the blue cord lightly touched the circumference of his neck, Caldwell swallowed, unconsciously trying to clear the obtrusive object from his Adam's apple.

With one effortless turn of the base using the handle, taking only the strength of a mouse, the cord ate into the flesh of Caldwell's neck. His breathing ceased. Air was no longer able to pass in or out of his lungs.

Involuntary jerking and convulsing of his chest erupted.

Holding on like a rodeo bareback rider, the killer fought the urge to turn the handle even half a rotation. Caldwell's eyes were already popping out of his head.

Seconds later, Caldwell was calm, lifeless. The handle was turned counterclockwise to release the tension.

Disassembling the device, the blue nylon cord, tennis ball, handle, and base were all placed on the floor so that Caldwell's bulging eyeballs could look at them in death.

A small hammer was the only other tool needed to complete the job.

Spinning on the knee that was still resting on Caldwell's back, the killer placed the tip of the grapevine cross at the intersection of Caldwell's bottom rib and spine. Using the small hammer, the killer struck the end of the cross three times, inserting it two inches into Caldwell's torso.

Although gushing blood was expected, only a tiny trickle appeared.

With the physical work completed, the killer walked to Caldwell's desk. Opening a well-worn Bible to Proverbs, a quick swipe of lipstick around a favorite verse was all that was needed to introduce New Orleans to its newest serial killer.

CHAPTER 6

Gasping for air, Pastor Cooper Dupree's mind began to finalize his delivery—two left jabs, then the right roundhouse kick to the side of Gregor's head. As Dupree sprinted through the turn of his twenty-fourth lap, he could see the finish line. He grabbed his left side; his ribs were tight. The abdominal injury might never heal completely. It had been two months since a couple of 22-caliber slugs had passed clean through him, and now the entry wound was beginning to burn. Favoring his left side, with sweat dripping into his eyes, he pumped his arms and lunged for the imaginary tape.

Gregor Thomson was going down.

At five o'clock, next Wednesday, Dupree's best friend was going to suffer a humiliating and painful defeat, in order to purchase coats for children in Pascagoula's newly constructed government housing complex. Gregor deserved a little pity. After all, he did save Dupree's life. However, the recovering preacher would still rain blows down on his friend, if for no other reason than to shut him up.

"No body-blows?" Gregor had argued. "Dude, you are like taking away the best part of my stuff!"

"Sorry man," Dupree had said when they were negotiating the terms of the upcoming match. He had pulled his shirt up to show the pink scar that ran diagonally under his rib cage. "Doctor's orders."

"You use that excuse too much."

The air was crisp and cool. Dupree leaned over and grabbed the bottom of his trunks. His arms were cut and lean. His hands pulled his shorts down from his waist. Breathing heavily, he stretched his lower back. Sweat dripped from his brow onto the pavement outside of the Christ Church Family Center.

It was Gregor with his "All Out Fight to the Finish Cage Match Challenge" that finally got Dupree moving again. For a month after the preacher's showdown with the psychotic Kenneth Schultz, he was in a funk.

The Pascagoula Police Department had given him more accolades. The Mississippi Press Register ran a full-page article honoring him for the work he did saving a young mother from Schultz. However, the evil of Schultz, coupled with December 21 looming in the near future, brought numbness to his hands and a lethargy that robbed the color from his tan cheeks, leaving a hazy film over his clear, brown eyes.

Dupree brushed a handful of hair out of his eyes, before stretching toward the sky. At six feet, two inches tall, he was built more like a basketball player than a long-distance runner. He took off in a slow jog toward the church.

"Two left jabs and the right roundhouse to the head," he said, smiling.

• • •

The clear November morning was like a poster day for the Pascagoula Mississippi Chamber of Commerce. Live oaks, in their full green regalia, decorated the library. Leaves from other trees littered the streets, rolling here and there, depending on the direction of the cars. A bright, blue sky, scarred with a single vapor stream from a passenger plane en route from Atlanta to New Orleans, expanded infinitely toward the flat, shimmering Gulf of Mexico.

As Dupree rounded the entrance to Christ Church, he noticed Kelly Mitchell's car parked in the visitor space, next to his Toyota Camry.

He let out a deep sigh and slowed his pace. Dupree even looked back over his shoulder toward the running track to see if maybe he should…

"Hey there, handsome!"

Kelly was waving from the front door and she was absolutely beautiful. She should not have been allowed to wear green scrubs.

Her fantastically green eyes, framed by soft auburn hair, made her approachable, desirable.

Dupree forced himself to pick up the pace.

"Looks like you got a good workout. Are you ready for Wednesday?" Kelly asked, as he approached. She puckered up to kiss him. With her eyes closed, craning toward Dupree, he offered his cheek and gave her a distant hug, arms outstretched, butt sticking out.

"Oh, you can hug me, Coop. I don't mind getting a little sweat on me," she said, pulling him close. "Besides, I kind of like…"

"Kelly," Dupree said, pushing back. "Not here. Please. Not… I'm sorry. Just not here."

"Okay."

Dupree stepped past her, into the lobby of Christ Church. The cool air inside matched that from outside. He briefly thought about telling the trustee-on-duty to open all of the windows, but then remembered he had something to handle.

"Kelly, we need to talk."

With four words, Kelly and Cooper were over. When they slipped from his lips, Dupree instantly felt crushing pain and a sense of relief. Part of him wanted to unsay the words, but a bigger part of him was proud that he found the strength to say them.

For two weeks, Dupree struggled to tell Kelly that Sarah, his wife who had been missing for almost three years, still consumed his thoughts. When Dupree held Kelly's hand in public or when he kissed her, he felt guilty.

He couldn't escape the thought that he was cheating on Sarah. He was being unfaithful.

Kelly and Cooper's whirlwind relationship, that was bolstered by working through the trauma of a shooting, and a murder, and a kidnapping, was now simply two very attractive people who were dating. They were a power couple that everyone in the community, all friends and family, wanted to see together forever.

But then Dupree said, "Kelly, we need to talk." And everyone would soon hate the jerk preacher that broke the heart of the nicest, prettiest, most wonderful nurse.

And, although Dupree kept a stern, sorrowful look as they had the "talk", he wanted to explode with happiness. He wanted to shout from the mountain tops, "Kelly, we need to talk!"

• • •

Dupree propped his feet up on his desk and placed his hands behind his head. Gregor Thomson closed the door to the office.

"How do you tell someone that you're not ready to date? I mean it's been three years since…you know since Sarah. Three years is a long time. You would think that I could shake this thing by now," Dupree said.

After Kelly left, with an understanding that "they can still be friends," Dupree showered and shaved, changed into his clergy uniform (sporting the wrap around white collar rather than just the little white square at the throat), and took a couple of painkillers.

"…and Kelly is so wonderful, you know that. And she's unbelievably gorgeous. You should have seen her this morning. I mean, I almost…"

"Dude, you're not into her. It's just that simple," Gregor said. He was seated across the desk. His curly blonde hair was untamed and looked like it had been cut with hedge clippers. He went to prop his bare feet up on the desk, as well.

"Get your nasty feet off my desk," Dupree said, sitting forward and swiping his hand toward Gregor. "Do you ever wear shoes? Seriously."

Gregor jumped up from his seat.

"You better bring more than that, dude," he said, smiling. "I'm bringing the Malibu beat-down." He started jumping around, jabbing at the air. "I'm so pretty! Look at me! Look at my pretty face!"

"Whatever," Dupree said, smiling. "I wouldn't even do this, if it weren't for the kids."

"That's right!" Gregor said, still imitating Mohammed Ali. "I'm gonna' mess up your ugly face for the children. "Because I'm the greatest!!"

"Sit down," Dupree said. "Be serious for one minute. You know she started crying."

"They all cry, dude. It's tough. No one likes to get dumped." Gregor sat down and reached for the candy jar on the edge of the desk.

"I didn't dump her. We're still going to be friends."

"That's getting dumped."

"Whatever. I'm the one with the problem. I mean, it's been three years. You would think…"

"It's not three years until next month."

"Whatever, it's close enough. Three years is a long time to…"

"Dude, three years is nothing. I swear, I think this T-shirt is three years old. Three years…it's nothing." Gregor sat back and crunched down on a peppermint. The room was suddenly filled with a fresh, minty smell. "Besides, Kelly was nice. I mean, she really was. But, dude, you weren't into her. You did her a favor. Let her move on."

"You really think so."

The phone rang.

"I don't know," Gregor said, placing his feet back on the desk.

Dupree answered, sitting forward and studying the calloused bottoms of Gregor's feet. "Our services are at 8:30 and 10:30, and we have Sunday school at 9:30. Sure. We'd love to have you. You're welcome."

"What are you preaching on?" Gregor asked.

"Mark 2," Dupree said, staring at the phone. He brushed the hair out of his eyes. "It's the part where the guys lower a paralytic through the roof to see Jesus."

"Okay, just make it short," Gregor said, smiling.

"Whatever."

Dupree reached for the phone. "I should call her."

"I wouldn't do it, man. It's a bad idea."

Dupree dropped the phone and turned away from Gregor. The window behind his desk was bright. The sun was low enough to make him want to lower the blinds. "Maybe you're right," Dupree said. "Maybe, I'm just not into her. Maybe, I'll never be into anyone ever again."

"Well, don't think like that," Gregor said. "It's not like Sarah was the only one you were crazy for."

"What are you talking about?" Dupree spun back toward Gregor.

"Dude, you already told me about that girl you dated at Southern. What was her name?"

"When did I tell you about that?"

"Remember. We were sailing and I told you that I had mixed the margaritas a little strong and you…"

"I remember you poisoned me," Dupree said, smiling.

"Whatever, but you told me that you and what's-her-name were all gaga and that…"

"Regina. Her name was Regina Welsh. Did I tell you she was drop-dead gorgeous?"

"You kept talking about her legs."

"Yeah, that was Regina," Dupree said, searching his memory for an image of Regina's legs. "Did I tell you she was a ballet dancer?"

"About a thousand times. And, if memory serves me right, you started ballet lessons soon after you recovered from our sailing trip. Now, that's being into someone."

Dupree's face flushed, as he turned back toward the window. He ran his finger inside his collar, which suddenly seemed confining.

"I started those lessons because of Sarah. I told you that."

"I'm just jerking your chain, man," Gregor said. "All I'm saying is you'll know when you want to date someone. You'll feel it." Gregor walked around the desk and grabbed the back of Dupree's chair. Spinning him around, he slammed his knee into Dupree's thigh, bringing out a groan. Dupree retaliated by throwing a punch toward Gregor's abdomen. Blocking it with his forearm, he pinned Dupree into the chair with his leg.

"So, this is what you do," Gregor said, getting into Dupree's face. "You call up this Regina, find out what she's up to."

"She's married."

"Separated. You told me she was getting a divorce."

"Same thing."

"Like hell it is. Where does she live?"

"I don't know."

"We'll find her. Go on Facebook or google her or something. Find her and…"

The phone interrupted the conversation. Dupree twisted in the chair and answered. Gregor moved back a step.

"Pastor Dupree. Yes. Yes ma'am. I see."

Dupree slid a notepad across the desk and started writing.

"Rod Webster? Okay…and he's the lead detective? Yes ma'am. Algiers Point? Do you have an address? I can be there around, let's see…I can be there around two, maybe a little before. Yes ma'am. Thanks, goodbye."

"What was that all about?" Gregor asked.

Dupree spun and gave a stiff right jab deep into Gregor's thigh.

"Ugh, what the…"

"That was the New Orleans Police Department," Dupree said, as a wry smile flashed briefly across his face. He took another swing, missing wide, as Gregor jumped back. "They wanted to see if I was available to review a crime scene."

"New Orleans?" Gregor said, hobbling toward his chair. "That's big time. Is it a murder?"

"She didn't say, but it sounded like it," Dupree said, rubbing his hands together. His mind flashed with a thousand things that needed to be done.

Gregor was saying something. His voice rattled around in Dupree's head like white noise.

"Sounds like I need to leave right away," Dupree said, almost unconsciously, as he slipped into prayer.

I need guidance. Help me, Lord Jesus.

"Do you need me to watch Red?" Gregor asked.

"What? Oh yeah, can you watch Red for me?" Dupree asked, grabbing the phone. "I should be back by Sunday. I've got to preach Sunday, so…I'll be back. Can you watch him?"

"Sure, no problem."

• • •

27

Sitting in the shade of a Chevron station in Diamondhead, Mississippi, Dupree's finger rested over the send button of his iPhone. Behind him, Interstate 10 hummed with a steady flow of semi-trucks. The oak trees surrounding the parking lot were holding onto their leaves, thankful to have experienced a summer free of hurricanes. He reread the message.

"Hey! Guess who? Joey told me that you're in Nola. Hope all is well. Coming into town for a day, but may be busy. If possible, okay to touch base? Cooper D."

Dupree erased the part that said, "It would be great to see you again."

Taking in his surroundings from the driver's seat of his car, he took a deep breath of the sweet air that circled the gas pumps. Diamondhead was rebuilding. The gas station and the Dairy Queen looked even better than they did before the hurricane. The storm surge didn't make it this far north. Waveland Mississippi did a great job throwing itself in the path and sacrificing every man-made structure to save the pristine country club community.

Dupree looked back at the message.

He had spent the last hour heading west at 75 miles per hour and, as the mile markers fell toward zero, his mind flashed with a thousand images of crime scenes and break-up scenes and Sarah and preaching and fighting and…

Regina.

Gregor was very intuitive. The night after Dupree's first ballet lesson, he found Regina Welsh-Brandingham. A conversation with a mutual friend gave Dupree all the information that he needed to make contact. Too bad the conversation didn't give him the guts to follow through.

Dupree's stomach knotted as he touched the green button.

He immediately started pushing buttons and searching the options menu of his phone to find the "cancel" or "retrieve" or "stop transmission".

But there was no such button. The message had been sent.

CHAPTER 7

egina Welsh-Brandingham stood in the marbled foyer of her Lower Garden District home; the screwdriver she found on the bureau looked large in her thin, delicate hands. The floor was cold on her bare feet. She retightened her robe, slipping the screwdriver into the tie wrap like a sword. She flipped up her collar.

The sun, shining through the beveled glass panels of the front door, warmed her cheek.

Lining the walls of the foyer were cardboard boxes that had been professionally sealed with packing tape and labeled with master bedroom, dining room, kitchen, etc. They stood six feet high in several rows, making it easy for the movers to use the front door to load the truck. The packers would be back at noon to finish packing the bathrooms, living room, den, etc.

Looking into the study, Regina grimaced at her reflection in the glass door; another gray hair had sprouted overnight.

"Marta!" she yelled toward the back of the house. Taking the ponytail holder from her hair, she placed it in her mouth and started reworking her dark, shoulder length hair, with her hands.

"Dis is re-dicurous," she said, trying not to drop the rubber band from her lips.

Rebinding her hair and combing her bangs to the side, she patted her cheeks and stretched her face in the reflection. Her eyes were dark, her face thin. Regina was blessed with beauty. With strikingly hard facial features and a perfect complexion, the only make-up she really needed was to flash a smile. But with the hurricane and Cecil's antics, she had run out of smiles and desperately needed a makeover.

"Marta!" she yelled. Her reflection was projected deep into the study.

"Yes, ma'am."

Regina jumped. Marta was behind her.

"Oh my god, Marta, you scared me to death," she said, turning her attention to the housekeeper. "Marta, I need you to run some errands. Can you go to Rite-Aid and pick up my prescription, and I need you to run by Martin's to get a case of wine I ordered before all this came up. It's just going to be another thing we'll need to move."

"Yes ma'am."

"Oh," Regina said, turning toward the front door. She started studying the street. "You should pick up something for the packers for lunch, since the kitchen is out of commission. When you're at Martin's get a tray of those little muffalettas and we can set them up a cooler with Gatorade."

"Should I get chips and snacks?"

"Yes, that's perfect. Get something sweet, like cookies or Little Debbie cakes. Do you need to write this down?"

"No ma'am."

"I'm expecting Mr. Brandingham, this afternoon," she said, turning to address Marta. Her expression turned grim. "I definitely need you back before he gets here."

"Yes ma'am," Marta said. "I'll be back. So, Rite Aid and Martin's?"

"That should do it," Regina said, looking back toward the street. "Thanks. And take my car. It needs to be run, anyway. Okay?"

"Yes Miss Regina."

As soon as Marta had safely backed out of the driveway, Regina turned her attention to the matter at hand.

At one time, the study of the Brandingham residence was filled with financial statements, ledgers, computer files, spreadsheets, and all sorts of accounting things that are essential to document wealth. The forensic accountants hired by Regina's divorce lawyer found none of it. Cecil had expertly scrubbed any trace of the true value of their net worth.

As Regina grabbed the handle and instinctively looked in every direction for Cecil, she imagined that she would be able to find those things that the accountants could not. First, she would look in the easily accessible file drawer marked "important papers". From there, she would move to the one marked "Stuff I don't want Regina to see, especially if she plans to divorce me".

As she pushed on the door, the smell of wood, books, and lemon Pledge sifted through the crack. In fifteen years of marriage, Cecil had never invited her into his office. Until this morning, Regina had never really wanted to encroach on her ex-husband's private space.

The idea that Cecil actually had his own private place suddenly infuriated her.

The floors were polished and buffed. Light filtered through the real-wood plantation blinds, creating a notebook effect, complete with lines and margins. Regina saw Cecil's private stories of take-overs, tax evasions, and infidelity written on the over-stuffed chairs, framed prints, and computer equipment. Her stomach was suddenly uneasy; her bowels growled as she stepped inside and closed the door.

The room had no visible filing cabinets. The books that lined the shelves behind his desk were unread and in perfect order.

Regina took a seat at the desk. She pulled gently on the handle of the top drawer, almost expecting it to easily slide open and fall into her lap. It was, however, locked. She tugged harder with each locked drawer. When she reached the final drawer, at the bottom left, she screamed curses as she shook it violently against its lock.

"Open, damn you, open," Regina yelled, into the room. She pulled the screwdriver from her robe and shook it at the drawer. "You want me to use this? Is that what you want?"

Trying to calm down, she spent a couple minutes exploring locations for hidden keys. Finding none, she sat crossed-legged on the floor, grabbed her screwdriver, and began to pry on one of the drawers.

"Oh my god!" Regina yelled, as the screwdriver slipped, causing the back of her hand to smash against the drawer. Splinters from the gouged mahogany mocked her, as she rubbed the knuckles of her right hand. She tossed the screwdriver across the room; it came to rest along the baseboard under the window.

"This is impossible." She rolled up to all fours. Her head dangled from her slumped shoulders.

Looking up, she crawled for one small stride and placed her upper body under the desk. "Hello." Her voice amplified in the confined space. "Echo." It would be so much fun to lie down underneath the desk and hide from her life.

Regina backed out and took a seat in the enormous leather chair. She wheeled herself up to the desk and took a business posture, clasping her hands together in front of her.

"Now listen up. We have a lot of important business to get done today and it's going to take a team effort," she said, to no one. She looked very comfortable at her desk, wearing a business suit of terry cloth.

Cecil's appointment book rested in the center of the desk; she pulled it onto her lap. The date was nine months ago.

Flipping through the calendar, Regina reviewed Cecil's old appointments. She was circling a Wednesday lunch meeting with someone named CPA, when her cellphone rang. It was Cecil. Sitting forward, she answered on the third ring.

"Hello," Regina said, as she continued to flip through the appointment book.

"Hey, Regina," Cecil Brandingham said. His voice was cold, matter-of-fact.

"Oh my god, Cecil, this is amazing," Regina said, placing the appointment book on the desk. "You will never guess where I am."

"At home packing, I hope."

"No, I mean, yes, I'm at home, but you'll never guess where," Regina said.

"Regina, I don't have time…"

"I'm in your precious office. I have infiltrated your sanctuary," she said, laying back in the chair and propping her feet up on the desk.

"Good for you," Cecil said, not sounding at all alarmed.

"I'm also going to look through all of these locked drawers and show my attorney everything those stupid accountants couldn't find."

"Regina, there's nothing in the drawers. I know you don't want to believe it, but the report on our assets was correct."

"Give me a break, Cecil,"

"It's true sweetheart; you got the lion's share of nothing. The most valuable thing in that office is the desk itself."

"We'll see." Regina looked down at the damaged drawer and shrugged. "So what time are you coming in?"

"That's why I called. I'm not going to the closing. I've got an interview and I can't..."

"What?!" Regina yelled. She dropped her feet to the floor. "The closing is at three o'clock and we have to close because I have the movers coming tomorrow and I..."

"Regina!"

"...if we don't go, then they'll charge me rent for the..."

"Regina, we're still closing at three," Cecil yelled over the top of her rant. "I've already sent my power-of-attorney to Jim Hopkins and he's..."

Regina hung up the phone. Her ears rang; her head was pounding. Tears began to well in her eyes. Cecil was not done issuing heartaches. Abandonment, infidelity, divorce—none of it was enough. Now he was going to heap bankruptcy onto the pile of dung that was her life for the last four years. She swept her hand across the top of the desk and knocked the appointment book onto the floor.

Dropping to her knees, she crawled toward the screwdriver. She collapsed half-way there. Sobbing heavily, lying in the morning sunlight, she covered her face with the lapel of her robe. She couldn't bring herself to even look at the text message that beeped on her cellphone.

• • •

Fortuna's wheel had completed its first cycle in the life of young, eloquent Regina Welsh-Brandingham. The fragile victim of circumstance now faced the final stage—acceptance. Tomorrow, when the moving van pulled up to the front of her house on Camp Street, she would realize that the past was gone.

She had no kingdom.

The crystal ball of her imagination saw her sitting on the front stoop, watching years of acquisition, being toted off on the sweaty shoulders of New Orleans' day-laborers. And she wouldn't even shed a tear.

Although Regina likened her life to that of a ball bearing in a pinball machine, she was actually held solidly to Lady Fortune's wheel. As a talented dancer, her potential was limitless. Exquisitely beautiful, with dark penetrating eyes and full pouty lips, she moved with purpose and grace.

In the innocent days of her youth, Regina was in the first stage of the wheel.

She would reign.

If Regina were the ball bearing, a random strike by the flipper might have directed her to follow her first true love, Cooper Dupree. He was, after all, her equal in beauty. But his future was on a course directed away from the mystic; he would not be directed by a pinball flipper or Fortuna's wheel. He had a calling to follow his spirituality; he was going to seminary to become a Christian pastor. No. Regina was on the wheel and she must be queen. Cooper Dupree would never reign, having given up any rights to his kingship to a savior.

So, Regina Welsh moved aggressively to the second stage of Fortuna's wheel by moving on from "college Cooper" and becoming Regina Brandingham. With her talent and beauty, and Cecil Brandingham's unlimited funds, Regina accepted her crown.

She reigned.

Years of opulence and travel, red carpet treatment, and "A" list connections suited Regina well. Everyone wanted to be photographed with the young socialite, as she was spotted in Vail,

Cannes, and New York. It was in her newly adopted home of New Orleans, that she attained the status of royalty.

But Fortuna's wheel cannot be stopped. There are no rods that can be jammed into the spokes.

The wheel will only be driven by beauty for so long, a dozen years at the most. And, Cecil was not pretty enough to make it last longer.

Although Cecil was a master at making money, he did not possess classic beauty. His eyes were light. Were they hazel? It wasn't green or blue or light blue. He was prematurely bald, making him look mature beyond his years. He wore a scruffy beard, which Regina never liked. This meant that they rarely kissed, and if they did, it was always in public.

The marriage was over when Cecil realized he and his lover kissed exclusively in private.

That was nearly two years ago. Now, in her house filled with boxes, Regina was ending the third stage of the wheel.

She had reigned.

And as she stared deeper into the crystal ball of her mind, she contemplated what would power her back to the top of the wheel. With the failure of beauty, what would give her the impetus to want to reign once again—money, love, commitment, duty?

The answer rested in the "inbox" of her cellphone.

• • •

A Bach concerto floated throughout the Brandingham home, filling every nook and cranny with a lilting "ba-da-dum, ba-da-dum". The packers had finished the house and were working in the garage. A supervisor for the moving company was taking inventory. In the study, Regina had to sign a release form, stating that the damage to the mahogany desk was present before the move.

She was only able to open one drawer, which contained papers with a wealth of information about nothing.

Walking along the rail at the top of the stairs, Regina floated with the sound of violins above the foyer. Propelled by the intricate counterpoint—light upticks mixed with the notes of heavy dissonance—found her falling like an angel with one measure, only to ascend to higher peaks, darker emotions, with the next.

Regina felt inspired; she wanted to dance.

She looked down from her loft.

Marta darted from the living room, past the front door, to the study.

For the last two years, Regina had been imprisoned in 150-year-old brick and heart-cut timber. Now, she was motivated.

To do what? Dance? Certainly not dance.

Oak staircases, silk wallpaper, and hand-carved molding had killed her resolve; money and opulence had robbed Regina of purpose. She wore gold handcuffs. But, with the sale of the house, she could find a new purpose.

If not dancing, then what? Revenge?

Ridding the world of Cecil could be her new calling.

"Maybe he'll die," Regina asked, in response to the first product of her inspiration.

Regina looked down at the marbled foyer; she envisioned Cecil's body lying in a heap.

Did he bounce when he landed?

"How would I know?" Regina said, concentrating on the image of her dead husband.

You were right behind him when it happened.

"Yes, but he fell," she said, letting out a little laugh. "I didn't tell him to lean out so far over the edge."

The concerto ended. Maybe there was a better purpose.

Regina walked elegantly down the stairs holding the banister with her left hand. She projected each foot out over the next step before allowing her back knee to bend, thereby falling another six inches. At one time, her ankles and feet could point in a perfectly straight line in any direction, including twelve o'clock. However, the years had not been kind to her flexibility.

Once in the kitchen, she grabbed a muffin from a bakery box. She tugged a small piece off and placed it gently in her mouth.

Silence followed for what seemed an eternity. Regina stared out of the kitchen window toward the garden. Antonio was working on his knees weeding a small group of flowers for the last time. He was a small man with several children. Living in a house full of smiling faces, he went home to a dinner of rice and beans. Dark and warm, Antonio was always drenched in sweat. He smelled like labor and peppers.

Regina was brushing her hands off over the sink, when a text message notification came from her purse.

Grabbing the cellphone, she read the message from her real estate agent, confirming the three o'clock closing.

Scrolling down, she read a message from her sister and a friend and a...

"Mississippi?"

Regina recognized the area code.

"Who would text me from..."

Her heart instantly skipped a beat as the message flashed in front of her eyes.

"Oh my god!" she said, holding a hand over her mouth. She reread the message aloud. "I'm coming into town for a day, but may be busy. If possible, okay to touch base? Cooper D."

CHAPTER 8

Detective First Class Rod Webster stepped out of the Canal Street entrance of the 23rd Precinct, into a crisp New Orleans mid-morning. Stretching his arms over his head, he pulled in a massive breath of deliciousness. Eleven o'clock was lunchtime in the Crescent City and Rod smiled for the first time that day.

The smell of cayenne pepper and onions rolled down the street from Shirley's next door. Rod turned his nose upwind; he could taste the air. Taking in another huge breath, the thick bristly hair of his mustache pushed into his nose and brought a tear to his eyes.

Rod moved his thumbs under his belly and around the inside of his belt. The stretch had completely disheveled Rod's attire. Having stressed the seams of his white oxford shirt to its limits, he managed to pull the shirt tail completely out of his pants. After tucking in his shirt, Rod straightened his tie and badge.

The waistband of his new suit pants had stretched as much as his backlog of cases; for every unsolved murder, Rod gained another ten pounds. The suit he purchased for his interview with chief Warren was already getting tight in the arms and around the waist. The only loose part was in the rear end, from the daily butt-chewing his lieutenant dished out to his over-worked detective staff.

Even though Rod exceeded the BMI for being morbidly obese, he was still a handsome man. With lighter skin than other African Americans and deep green eyes, his ancestry of Creole Louisiana was evident. His frame held extra weight easily, giving him the look of an offensive lineman.

"You sure you want to go to Mother's?" Singleton asked. "You look like you could go for Shirley's"

"No, I had Shirley's yesterday, and I had my heart set on a debris po-boy."

"It's six blocks from here. Shirley's got a roast beef po-boy."

"It's not the same," Rod said, as he turned toward the river on Canal. Singleton followed. "Besides, I'm grabbing a few ham biscuits for dinner. You ever had their baked ham?"

"Of course," Singleton said, stepping ahead of Rod and directing him to cross into the neutral ground. "At least we'll take the streetcar to the end of Canal."

The two detectives began the thirty-foot trek to the Canal Street streetcar stop. The ride would cut the walk down to two blocks each way.

"You sure this is a good idea?" Singleton asked.

"Of course, their debris is the best in the city."

"No, I mean, taking off like this without a car," Singleton said. "I can't be gone long; I'm meeting with forensics at noon."

"A man's got to eat."

"Tell me about it. And, I've been going at it since five thirty this morning."

"It'll be fine," Rod said. "Nothing ever happens at lunch. You know that." He positioned himself next to an attractive young woman holding a bag of groceries. "Good morning."

"Good morning officer," she smiled.

"Would you like me to hold that while we wait?"

"That's okay. Thanks."

• • •

Rod and Singleton stepped off the streetcar at the foot of the World Trade Center Building. Rod was immediately hit with a temptation that could have ruined his po-boy lunch experience—Popeye's Chicken.

"Come on, big fella," Singleton said, grabbing his arm and turning him toward Poydras Street. "We can get Popeye's anytime."

"Thanks Singleton."

The sun was bright, the air fresh, as two of New Orleans' finest

39

walked side-by-side along the palm-lined street. Circling Ceasar's casino on uneven sidewalks, Rod studied the pavers that rushed toward him under his protruding belly.

Rod caught his reflection in the plate glass of a law office. To stand upright, he tilted slightly backwards at his lower back, his shoulders and head counter-balanced the weight of his stomach. His chin rested on the knot of his necktie, as he scanned the upcoming terrain, looking from the bottom of his eyes.

He pushed Singleton aside as he filled the entrance to Mother's Restaurant.

"Ah, Detective Rod!" the hostess said, as he entered. "...and Detective Gary. So good to see you both."

"Suzy," Rod said, holding two fingers up.

"Just the two of you. Right this way," she said. "Iced tea?"

"Yes, please," Singleton replied.

Rod nodded as he sat. He grabbed a menu from the center of the table and began studying the starters when his phone began ringing. He looked at the number. It was his lieutenant.

"Uh oh," he said, before answering. "Webster."

"Rod!"

"Yes, Lieutenant," he said, pulling the phone away from his ear.

"Rod, where the hell are you? I thought I told you you've got to..."

"I'm at lunch. I'm at Mother's."

"I thought I told you to mark out when you leave! I've been looking all over and I had to go all the way down to the front desk for them to tell..."

"Lieutenant, what's up?"

"Is Singleton with you?"

"Yes," he said, shrugging his shoulders toward Singleton. "What is it?"

"I need you to go out to Algiers Point right now. They've got a stiff that's been waiting for a detective to show for about an hour now. Madere called in sick and no one told me. So, I've been looking all over for him for about twenty minutes and then..."

"Lieutenant?" Rod interrupted. "Where in Algiers point? Singleton and I will head that way." Both men instinctively rose and headed toward the front door. Singleton threw a couple dollars on the table to cover the tea.

"No, hell no. Tell Singleton that he needs to get his butt back here. I need you to go to the fairgrounds out by the Naval base. The CSI unit is already there. The victim was found in a trailer. He's a tent show preacher that had something going on last night. His name is Caldwell. I want you to head that way ASAP."

"Yes sir."

"Also, be on the lookout for a preacher that I've called in to review the crime scene."

"A preacher?"

"Yes, he's coming over from Pascagoula. His name is Cooper Dupree. Make sure everything stays intact until he shows. You got it?"

"Yes sir."

"And, tell Singleton that if he doesn't get back in my office in ten minutes, he'll be working traffic patrol at Ceasar's this weekend."

"I'll let you tell him," Rod said, handing the phone to Singleton, as they stepped onto the street. "He wants to talk to you."

• • •

When Rod Webster stepped off the aluminum landing attached to the bottom of the crime scene, the whole trailer rocked back and forth so violently that the crime scene technician inside had to grab the walls to catch his balance. Rod took in a deep breath and stretched his arms out. The sun was high and bright, the air crisp. Being inside the tiny trailer made him claustrophobic; having a dead preacher stinking up the place didn't help matters either.

Rod saw everything he needed to start his investigation. Caldwell was strangled with a blue nylon cord, either before or after being stabbed with a weird cross. He was naked and possibly raped.

There were no witnesses, the place wasn't ransacked, and

nothing appeared to be stolen. There was no evidence of a struggle. The lock on the door was not compromised.

"So what do you think?" Marshall asked, stepping out behind Rod onto the flattened pasture land. Marshall was the lead technician. He had spent the last hour dusting for fingerprints, collecting samples of hair, and bagging swatches of blood-soaked carpet and fabric.

"Well, it looks like a hit to me." Rod wrote the tag numbers of Caldwell's truck and trailer in his notepad. "But, hit men rarely leave calling cards."

"You mean the cross?"

"Yeah, and they're also a little more merciful." Rod scanned the fairgrounds.

"What's the deal with the tennis ball?" Marshall asked, almost laughing. He started loading his equipment into the trunk of an unmarked CSI pool-car. "The whole scene is freaking me out."

Rod waved his hand over his head to get the attention of a young man walking across the pasture.

"Hey!" Rod started walking toward him. As he moved closer, the young man looked behind himself to see if the detective was actually addressing him. "Yeah, you, what's your name?" Rod asked, approaching quickly.

"Flacko."

"Flacko, who's in charge today?"

"Miss Lynnette."

"And where is Miss Lynnette?"

Flacko pointed toward a white Ford pickup truck. "Miss Lynnette!"

"Thank you, gracias," Rod said, heading toward the truck. He waved toward Lynnette when she turned toward him.

"Miss Lynnette, can I have a word with you?"

"Lynnette Faust," she said, offering her free hand. In her other hand, she held a computer tablet.

"Detective Webster." Rod released her hand after only a light squeeze.

Rod stood only an inch taller, than the stunning Miss Faust. She wore a baseball cap that shaded her dark eyes and picturesque nose. Her hair was blonde. Rod couldn't tell if it was long and pulled into the cap or cut very short. She wore no make-up, although physical exertion and the cool afternoon air had given her fair complexion a little color.

"Detective," Lynnette said, giving a confident smile. "What can I do for you?"

"Are you in charge of this operation now? I mean now that Reverend Caldwell is no longer with us."

"Yes. I'm in charge now. Was before also." She leaned back against the hood of the truck. She crossed her arms, clutching the tablet to her chest. "I'm the road manager. I run the day-to-day operation of Reverend Caldwell's revivals."

"I see," Rod said, taking notes. "So you're the one who knows what goes on around here?"

"Sure do," Lynnette said. "And I know, that today I've got to layoff fifteen workers when they've loaded up everything. Then, I've got to find a new job."

"Uh-huh."

"I know that it isn't right, what they did to Reverend Caldwell."

"They?" Rod asked.

"Whoever it was," Lynnette said, struggling with her words. "I can't get the image out of my mind."

"So, you found him?"

"Yes, about 10:30 this morning." She stared down at the ground and kicked the tip of her work boot into the beaten down grass. "I was worried about him because he never sleeps in late and then there was the young lady that was with him last night. Usually, I'm the one that has to make sure she gets off without anyone seeing her. Although everyone knows that…"

"Hold up," Rod said, shaking the hand with the pen. "What young lady?"

"I don't know her personally. She was at the revival last night. She was an escort…a professional…if you know what I mean?"

Rod nodded as he wrote.

"Anyway, she was sent by this lady, Miss Tessy."

"Who's Miss Tessy?"

"I suppose she's a madam or pimp or something. I really don't know how it all works," Lynnette said. "She called me on my cellphone around 5:00 yesterday afternoon and told me she was sending a young, blonde, blue-eyed girl."

"Did you get a name?"

"Yes, Diamond." Lynnette let out a little laugh. "Like that's her real name. Anyway, she said Diamond was twenty-eight years old and STD free and…this she repeated about five times…she was going to cost $500 for the evening."

"Can I have that number?"

Lynnette pulled the number from her "recent" calls. "601-555-1104."

"Mississippi number," Rod said.

"Looks that way. Anyway, Miss Tessy said Diamond would be wearing a full-length peasant dress."

"Did you recognize her right away?" Rod asked.

"No. I didn't recognize her at all. There are a lot of blondes in peasant dresses at our revivals. She actually came up to me, backstage, during the altar call. She needed to know which trailer was Jack's."

"Jack?"

"Reverend Caldwell."

"Did you show her the trailer?"

"Yes."

"And you didn't actually watch her walk to the trailer."

"That's correct," Lynnette said. "I had work to do."

"How do you know she actually made it to his trailer?"

"I don't."

Rod wrote several notes, while he nodded slowly.

"And, so, Miss Faust, you're saying that Diamond was the last one to see Reverend Caldwell alive?"

"That I couldn't say," Lynnette said. "But, she is the last one that

I know was with him. I never saw her leave and I never saw anyone else go over to his trailer. When I knocked on the trailer this morning, I assumed she was still there. When no one answered, I tried the door. It was unlocked. I entered and saw the way he was and immediately called 911." Lynnette's voice started to crack.

"Miss Faust," Rod said, placing a hand on her shoulder. "I'm sorry for your loss. But I have to ask…were you romantically involved with Reverend Caldwell?"

Lynnette started sobbing. Rod stepped back.

"No…but I loved him...I loved him so much…and now he's gone and I have to fire all these wonderful people. He was so good to me. Jack was a good man."

"So that's a 'no' on a romantic relationship?"

Lynnette nodded as she wiped her eyes with the back of her hand. A long pause followed.

"Would you like a picture of Diamond?" Lynnette asked, quietly.

"You've got one?" Rod asked, taken aback slightly.

"Sure. I've got the video from last night's revival. I'll get you a copy and point her out to you."

"That would be perfect." Rod removed a business card from his pocket. "My cellphone number is right here. I'm going to ask around to see if anyone saw Diamond leave, or if anyone saw anything else. When you get that video, give me a call and I'll come get it."

"Okay," Lynnette said, studying the card. She shook her head slightly. "I sure hope you find who did this. Reverend Caldwell was a good man."

• • •

Rod Webster tried to not kick up rocks and dirt as he tore out of the fairgrounds. In the seat next to him sat a couple of photographs of Diamond. In his coat pocket was a jump drive with the complete video of Reverend Caldwell's last revival. His little helper in the Information Technologies group was going to have a field day with the images. Rod could only imagine what information the Geek Squad could cull from a full seven seconds of his prime suspect.

As Rod turned onto Nichols Avenue, his mind was drifting on the revival and all the crying and wailing and shouting and...

His pants started vibrating. Trying to stand in the seat, he fished for his cellphone, which was buried deep in his right pocket.

"Not you again," he said, before answering. "Yeah Lieutenant, what can I do for you?"

"Webster?"

"Yes sir?"

"Where are you?"

"Well, I'm on the West Bank, just about to hit the Crescent City Connection. I was heading toward the..."

"Webster! Didn't I tell you to stay at the crime scene until Pastor Dupree showed up?"

Rod cringed. He had completely forgotten about his baby-sitting assignment.

"Yes sir," he said, trying to cover his tracks. "I was going to run some evidence over to IT and head straight back..."

"Webster, he's already there." There was an awkward pause. "If it's not too much trouble, Detective, do you think you could turn around and do exactly what I asked you to do in the first place? I swear Webster, this crap is going to be..."

"Lieutenant, I'm already turning around. I'm already headed back. I can go to IT later."

"You damn right you can!" Another long pause followed. Rod turned the cruiser around in the neutral ground. The lieutenant sounded like he was trying to catch his breath. "Now...please...take him to the fairgrounds. I just got a call from him that he is at the corner of Behrman and General Meyer at a 7-11. So, if it's not too much trouble, get him to the crime scene so we can get a read on this crap!"

"Yes sir," Rod said, hitting the accelerator. He flipped his siren on. Using his knee to drive, he grabbed the red-light from the seat next to him. "I'm almost there."

Hanging up, he tossed the phone on the floorboard.

The search for Diamond would have to wait.

CHAPTER 9

The entrance to the Whole Foods Market on Magazine Street smelled like lavender. Mary Ellen Retinoir slung the hobo bag, that carried a week's supply of cash, hand sanitizer, and post-it notes, over her shoulder, as she stepped through the automatic doors and sniffed. She loved lavender.

Facing an eight-foot-high stack of cantaloupes, she searched her "contacts" list and dialed Jarrell.

How lavender beat out the smell of the cantaloupes was a mystery. Standing in the sensor of the automatic doors, they opened and closed almost rhythmically behind her. She waited for Jarrell to answer, thumped a cantaloupe with her free hand, and read a sign advertising a sale on six-packs of organic green tea.

"The person at..." Jarrell had opted for the standard voice mail recording.

"Jarrell, it's me," Mary Ellen said. She picked up a six-pack of tea and instantly realized that it was too heavy to carry home. "Call me."

Setting the tea back into its display, she dropped her cellphone into the front pouch pocket of the peasant dress, that she purchased second-hand up the street at the Funky Monkey consignment shop.

In the foyer of the great health food store, with the automatic door behind her opening and closing in a steady beat, she tugged at the rubber band that once held her ponytail.

Cutting her hair short was a mistake. The once shoulder length, blonde hair never budged from its wrap, even pedaling through the breezeway of her apartment complex. Now it was a constant bother, always slipping out of even the tightest wrap.

Mary Ellen dropped the knotted mass of rubber band and hair into the pocket with her phone. While shaking her head, she ran her hands through her hair. Her nose directed her to a display behind the cantaloupes.

"There you are," she said to no one. She plucked a handy wipe from the canister next to the baskets and vigorously scrubbed her hands. Grabbing a basket, she used the wipe as a barrier between her hand and the green, plastic handle.

Moving into the store, she removed several lavender scented incense sticks from the display and carefully placed them in her basket.

Mary Ellen normally shopped at the Walmart on Tchoupitoulas, but they wouldn't have the specialty item she needed. If she thought the job could get done with a generic stain stick and not have an adverse effect on her sensitive skin, she would have happily biked downtown, rather than uptown. At Walmart, she could have stocked up on toothpaste, ramen noodles, and string cheese. Instead, at Whole Foods, she splurged on items normally reserved for special occasions.

Or emergencies.

Mary Ellen quickly passed the produce section, keeping her handbag pushed back with her elbow.

"Excuse me," she said, getting the attention of the teenager stocking shelves with vitamins.

"Yes ma'am?"

"Where can I find stain remover? Where's the laundry detergent and stuff?"

"Aisle 12—two that way."

"Thanks."

During her exit from the preacher's trailer, when she leapt three feet to the ground and tried to take off in a sprint, she stepped on the hem of her dress. With her hands clutching her purse tightly to her chest, she had no option but to hit the soft ground and roll a couple of times. She noticed at the bar later, that she had two enormous grass stains on her favorite dress—one near her left knee, the other at her left elbow.

The smart move would be to get rid of the dress all together. But that was a waste and the dress had proved lucky in the past.

With any luck, Mary Ellen's lucky dress could be cleaned, with a few washings and a good...

"...all organic, no phosphate, stain stick," she said, reading the label of the Tom's lavender scented stain remover out loud.

"Perfect."

• • •

Shade from the Whole Foods façade blanketed the tables and chairs placed in front for the customers who took advantage of the prepared foods. Mary Ellen took a seat at a table near her bicycle. Crossing her legs, she noticed an old man sitting on a bench in the sunlight. He wore an ancient brown cardigan, khaki pants, and a weird constant smile. He seemed to be watching her every move.

The humidity had dropped below seventy percent for the first time in six months. The air was as crisp as the lettuce on her sandwich. Unwrapping her tuna-with-dill, she spread the wax paper flat and poured a small bag of kettle-fried potato chips onto her impromptu picnic blanket.

She took a bite of her sandwich. Putting on her sunglasses, in the shade of the awning, she stared at the old man on the bench. She picked up her purse and placed her head and arm through the strap. With the sandwich in one hand, she held the purse tight to her body with her elbow.

When he stood, she uncrossed her legs and sat up very straight. She moved her legs from beneath the table. Her heart started thumping in her chest. When he made a step in her direction, she stood. Her hands tingled as she reached in her purse for her Taser. When his wife stepped past her, carrying several grocery bags, Mary Ellen felt the back of her neck burning.

"Let me get those dear," he said, smiling at his wife. She was hunched over, walking with poor posture. "I wish you would have told me you weren't getting a cart."

"Oh, it's nothing, I'm fine." She handed him the bags. "Thank you, sweetie."

Mary Ellen sat, took a few deep breaths, and returned to her lunch.

After taking another bite, she set the sandwich down and reached into the very bottom of her bag.

Pulling out the felt-wrapped object, she held it tightly. It was, after all, the most expensive item she had ever possessed.

Careful not to let it bump against the wrought-iron table, she gently laid it flat next to her sandwich. Unveiling it into the noon shadows, the mirrored finish picked up reflections from the awnings above, the trees from across the street, and the passing cars. As she picked up the end and rotated it back and forth, the kaleidoscope of colors of Uptown New Orleans seemed richer in the deep, pure gold of a two-pound cross. Greens were gold-green; blues were gold-blue. Each color looked much more expensive reflecting off of the Christian relic and into Mary Ellen's eyes.

Placing the cross back into its protective green felt bag, she placed it once again in the depths of her handbag. She finished her sandwich and lit a cigarette. Sitting, smoking, she reviewed her text messages.

After a few minutes, she crushed out a cigarette butt under her foot and spun in her seat to face the building. She sent a text message to Jarrell.

"Meet me at the Circle Bar at three."

She dropped the cellphone into the front pocket with her keys, hitched her purse high onto her shoulder, and walked to her bike.

Taking State Street to Saint Charles Avenue, she was soon pedaling downtown toward her apartment. Her bag rested safely in the front basket.

The Avenue once made Ripley's "Believe-it-or-not" for being the widest street in America. But, it still was not wide enough to safely ride a bike and send text messages. Mary Ellen steered with one hand, while typing an amazing thirty words per minute with her right thumb.

If she chose to use both hands to maneuver the bike, she could ride in the neutral ground, between the streetcar tracks. But, the ground was sandy and chewed up with National Guard Humvee tracks. The concentration needed to keep from falling into a soft patch was prohibitive. So, Mary Ellen rode on the street, dodging parked cars and distracted drivers.

The only downside of riding in the street was when she hit a patch of putrid smelling asphalt. For months after the storm, the entire Avenue smelled like spoiled food. Although the refrigerators, that had been dragged out to the curb, had been duct-taped closed, a thick, gray liquid gushed from them whenever they were loaded onto the disposal trucks. This toxic mix of rotting shellfish, meat, and condiments penetrated deep into the pavement. And on this pristine day, with the sunlight glistening through the oaks and the fresh, earthy smells of autumn filling the air, Mary Ellen passed a crack that emitted the putrid odor of rotting freezer juice, and instantly fought back a gag reflex.

Passing Napoleon Avenue, she pulled her bike over and took a break in front of Fat Harry's bar. She had a text from Jarrell.

"See you at three. What's up?"

"We need to talk about last night."

"How long did you stay at Old Point?"

"I took the 10:30 ferry."

"Have you gone by Selman's?"

"I'm going in a bit. See you at three." Mary Ellen placed her phone back in her purse after Jarrell responded with a "thumbs up" emoji.

Selman's Antiques in the French Quarter was a fifteen minute bike ride from her apartment. If she put the dress in the wash as soon as she got home, she would have just enough time to pawn the cross and then double back to meet Jarrell at the Circle Bar.

Tossing her purse into the basket, she grabbed the handlebars with both hands and took off down the center of the neutral ground.

CHAPTER 10

Tan-n-Tips was a full service beauty salon that catered to the residents of Luling, Louisiana, from a single-wide trailer facing River Road. The oyster shell covered parking lot sparkled like a million crushed pearls, as Diamond Olivet stepped onto its uneven, fluid surface. She paid the cabby with a wad of one-dollar bills.

Normally adept at keeping her balance in four-inch heels, she found it difficult to walk toward the ramp leading to the front door. The excessive brilliance of the morning sun reflecting up into her dilated pupils was disorienting.

Moving gingerly up the ramp, she held the unpainted two-by-four railing, making sure not to slide her hand along the rough wood surface. Her ankles were weak; she kept her weight shifted to the right. If she fell, she wanted to make sure she slumped over the rail. Getting up from the ground would be impossible.

Reaching the front door, she twisted the handle—locked. No sounds were coming from inside. Diamond pulled her cellphone from the back pocket of her skirt.

"You've got to be kidding me!"

The salon wasn't scheduled to open for another half hour.

Diamond plopped down. Sitting cross-legged, with her back against the front door, she pulled a pack of cigarettes from her bra strap. The sun was sheltered by an awning that ran the length of the trailer. A cool breeze brushed against her cheeks, as she smoked and waited.

Having no interest in geography, Diamond didn't know that the giant, manicured hill of land across the street was a levee. It looked like part of a golf course that ran for miles to her left and right. The grass was shaved to a half-inch; there were cart paths running along the top and up the sides. Diamond couldn't see the water hazard on the other side that was the Mississippi River.

When the door opened suddenly behind her, she fell backwards into the salon.

"What the..." Diamond said, trying to control the burning tip of her cigarette.

"Oh my god! I'm sorry darling, I didn't...let me...here." The lady that had opened the door offered her hand. In an awkward exchange, Diamond spun on the small of her back, legs akimbo, skirt sliding up her thighs, exposing her cotton panties. Reaching out with her free hand, she managed to hoist herself up.

"I am so sorry, sweetie. I didn't see you sitting there."

"It's okay," Diamond said, addled. She looked for a place to put her cigarette.

"Oh, there's no smoking inside. We have to smoke out here." She stepped past Diamond onto the porch. "You can finish that out here. We're not open for another fifteen minutes. Do you have an appointment?"

"I'm here to get a color and cut with Darlene."

"That's me. You must be the one that Miss Tessy sent."

"Yeah, she set it up."

"She told me everything and you're all paid up," Darlene said, as she shook out a cigarette. "Just let me get a quick smoke and we'll get started." Lighting the cigarette, she looked Diamond up and down. "Did she tell you about the tattoo?" She asked, squinting, as smoke trailed off into her eye.

"Yeah."

"Did she tell you what it was?"

"No."

"You're getting a bar code on the back of your neck."

"Okay," Diamond said, flicking her cigarette into the parking lot. "She said that I'm going blonde, too."

"Yeah, a different color blonde. That shouldn't take much," Darlene said, reaching for Diamond's hair. "We're going to have to take a few inches off, also. When's the last time you had color?"

"Long time." Diamond turned her back to Darlene.

Darlene lifted up the back of her hair, inspecting the back of Diamond's neck.

"It's not permanent, is it?"

"No. It's a henna."

"We'll get started on that first, but it'll probably take a few doses," Darlene said. "Miss Tessy wants it black. We're going to have to go over it a few times." She blew a lungful of smoke toward the roof of the awning.

"Whatever."

• • •

Diamond's hands started to shake, as she tried to keep her hair off of the ink of her new tattoo. The second application took too long.

"When can I sit up?" she asked, speaking toward the floor. She was bent over at the waist, seated in a beautician's chair.

"Let me take a look. Oh, it won't be long," Darlene said. "I'm going to get a quick smoke and when I get back, it should be done."

"Well, I need to smoke."

"There's no smoking in here. You have to smoke on the front porch," Darlene said, as she headed for the front door. "I'll be right back."

"But, I can move out to the front..."

"You need to just sit until it's dry. I'll be right back."

Miss Tessy had not paid Diamond enough to endure this torture. She might make it a few minutes without a cigarette, but she would never make it back to New Orleans without a fix.

Darlene had taken an excessive amount of time changing Diamond's look. Miss Tessy must have lined up a huge score to drop this kind of coin on making Diamond into the perfect escort.

After the first application of the henna tattoo, Darlene went to work on Diamond's hair color. She went much lighter on the base color, moving Diamond from dirty dishwater blonde to light blonde. The color was accentuated with three layers of highlighting. The final coloring was low-lights around her face, to bring out Diamond's high cheekbones.

The cut followed the color. A couple of inches were taken off the back; the bangs and sides were layered to frame her face with a soft, approachable style. After a shampoo and conditioning, Diamond was directed back to the chair for the second application of the tattoo.

The entire effort took two-plus hours.

"Can I sit up now?" Diamond asked when Darlene stepped back inside.

"Let me look." Darlene examined the bar code tattooed on the back of Diamond's neck by touching it lightly. "Yeah, it looks good. Hold on while I wipe it off and then you can sit up."

Diamond's hands started to shake more.

"Miss Tessy sent you something for that shaking," Darlene said, as she scrubbed crusty, dried ink residue off.

"Really?"

"Yeah, you can sit up." Darlene started brushing through Diamond's hair with her fingers. "Wow, this really turned out great."

"I know, I love it. What did you say that Miss Tessy sent?"

"It's in the back. Right back there in the storage closet on the mini-fridge."

Diamond stood and walked to the back.

"This bag?"

"Yeah, it's a nice bag," Darlene said, as she started to the front door. "Miss Tessy said to give it to you and to tell you to make sure that you have it on your date."

"What's in it?" Diamond asked. She picked up the light orange leather shoulder bag.

"I don't want to know," Darlene said, opening the front door. "I'm going to grab a cigarette."

Diamond smiled as she recognized immediately what was wrapped so neatly in a cotton handkerchief. Miss Tessy was always good to her.

CHAPTER 11

astor Cooper Dupree leaned against the passenger side door of his Toyota Camry, warming his face in the afternoon sun, like an alligator laid up against a Japanese made rock. The heat sank into his black short-sleeve shirt and black slacks.

Having eaten a king-size Kit Kat and washing it down with a 20-ounce Dr. Pepper, he allowed the satisfying sugar buzz to peak his senses.

Closing his eyes and looking toward the sun, he could feel the concrete push up against his feet. In between the sound of passing cars, he could hear flies bumping around inside a closed trash can. The bright orange of his eyelids pulsed with his heart rate. A car pulled up to the gas pumps with the windows down. Its' radio blasted a hip-hop tune.

Algiers Point, the ground beneath the black wing-tip shoes of Dupree, was first given to Jean Baptiste le Moyne de Bienville in 1719. The French governor of Louisiana and Father of New Orleans never imagined that a tiny part of his massive land grant, on the west bank of the Mississippi River, would become a convenience store parking lot.

The quarter acre plot, now owned by the 7-11 Corporation, was first sold by Bienville to Adrian de Pauger, the architect of the French Quarter. Pauger built a plantation and operated a successful holding pen for slaves and undesirables, until he lost it to the Spanish in a secret treaty made in 1762. His shock would have paled in comparison to the Acadians, who were being offloaded by the hundreds. The British—who were exiling them from Nova Scotia—promised them the parking lot would be French.

Eventually, the French took the parking lot back, just long enough for Napoleon to sell it to the Americans for less than the price of a Dr. Pepper. Undeterred and under the protection of the United States Government, the Louisiana Acadians, aka Cajuns, flourished in their bayou Babylon, differing from their Old Testament predecessors, in the way that few wanted to return to their frozen homeland.

Dupree didn't know the history of the 7-11 parking lot. The only thing he knew about the West Bank was from the movie "Black Magic". If memory served him right, the crime scene would likely have three distinct items—a voodoo doll, a chicken's foot, and some scary old black man with his front teeth sharpened into points.

The vision of an old shaman dancing around a fire and shaking gris-gris was flashing in his mind when a car pulled into the lot and honked.

"What the..."

"Are you Dupree?" A man yelled from the open window of a white Crown Victoria.

"Yes, you must be Detective Webster," he said, walking toward the car.

"That's right, we better go," Rod said. He didn't extend his hand out of the window even though Dupree was extending his. "Is that your car?"

"Yes."

"I guess it's safe to leave it here for a little while," Rod said, as he scanned the area and checked his rearview mirror. "Make sure it's locked."

"Are we far from the crime scene?" Dupree climbed into the passenger seat.

"No, but we need to get going. I don't have all day to chauffeur you around." Rod threw the car into reverse, making it difficult for Dupree to close his door.

• • •

The crime scene, a gooseneck trailer attached to a Ford 2500 pickup truck, was behind a massive tent, towering over an Algiers Point pasture. Rod Webster and Dupree pulled into the field in an unmarked NOPD cruiser, throwing up dust and hay as they circled the canvas cathedral.

"There it is."

Parked beside the preacher's portable home sat the CSI van and a vehicle from the coroner's office.

Stepping from the cruiser, Dupree took a deep breath; the smell of honeysuckle and manure mixed to give the young pastor a sense of relaxation. In the background, the metallic sounds of industry rolled in from the banks of the river.

"Look at those guys," Dupree said, pointing at a couple of horses on the other side of a barbed wire fence. "Smells like my grandpa's. He lives in Jones County Mississippi. Do you know where that is?"

"No."

"Ellisville?"

"Never heard of it."

The two stepped toward the trailer. The grass was matted down. Footprints would not be included in the collection of evidence.

Stepping into the trailer, Dupree greeted those standing in front of him. The room was well lit by the afternoon sun; it smelled like death.

"Oh jeez."

Dupree took a knee, said a short prayer, then placed a pair of latex gloves on his hands. In front of him, was a completely naked man, dead, lying on his stomach. His left arm was stretched above his head, the index finger pointing from a tight, rigid hand, as if he were giving a direction. Possibly pointing to heaven, when he fell to the floor. His right arm was down, along his side, palm up.

An odd cross protruded from his back, just below the rib cage. Blood pooled on the carpeted floor beneath the wound made by the cross.

With his head turned to the right, the man's eyes were closed. If they were open, they would be looking at a neatly coiled blue nylon cord, two sticks of stainless steel pipe, and a tennis ball.

Rod entered behind Dupree. The trailer rocked under the weight of the detective.

Dupree stood and turned to the lady standing to his right. "Cooper Dupree." He extended his hand.

"Patty Pearce. I'm the coroner." The Orleans Parish coroner was an attractive, African-American woman in her late forties with hard features. Her eyes were dark and cold; her jaw was tight. She spoke without any emotion at all. "Hey Rod."

"Good afternoon Ms. Pearce," Rod said.

"And this, Mr. Dupree is Reverend Jack Caldwell," Rod said, waving his hand toward the victim.

"Yes, yes, of course." Dupree said, as he observed the profile of the dead man's face. "I've watched him many times." Dupree took a knee and sniffed the mouth of Reverend Caldwell.

Rod Webster looked over at Ms. Pearce and made a "What the hell is this all about?" expression.

Dupree moved around the corpse like a crab. Sniffing, listening, observing the wounds from an inch away, without touching the victim at all. Finally sitting crossed legged on the floor, he picked up the rod with a tennis ball on the end.

"These have all been dusted?" Dupree asked.

"Yeah, they're clean," Rod said. "The cord was used to strangle him."

Dupree picked up the other stainless steel rods and started manipulating them, eventually sticking the handle through the base.

"The killer used this to strangle him." Dupree rolled onto his knees. He held up the device and hovered the tennis ball end over the back of Reverend Caldwell. "See the tennis ball fuzz right here. They used this to tighten the cord around his neck, by rotating it. This handle was used for leverage."

Rod removed his notebook from his back pocket and began taking notes.

"Also," Dupree said, still on his knees beside Reverend Caldwell. "The cross was inserted post mortem. There's not much blood. It looks like it's been intentionally inserted into his liver."

"All that will come out in the autopsy," Rod said, looking up from his notebook.

"Was he a drinker?" Dupree asked, standing.

"No," Rod answered. "I checked that out with the road manager. Also, there's no alcohol in the trailer."

"I wouldn't be surprised if he were drugged first." Dupree said. "His lips are chapped and his mouth smells like citrus, kind of acidic."

"Again, the autopsy will give us all these details."

Dupree closed the door behind Rod Webster and ran his hand along the flimsy door jamb.

"Who found the body? Who reported it?"

"The road manager, Lynnette Faust."

"No forced entry?"

"Correct."

"Who was the last person to see him alive?"

"We're working on that."

Dupree turned his attention to the desk positioned along the wall closest to the front of the trailer.

He flipped through a desk calendar. "Who kept up with his appointments?"

"Don't know," Rod said. "I've talked to the road manager. But she really didn't have much to offer."

"Look at this." Dupree moved his hands along the bookcase above the desk. "Nothing but doctrine, academics; it's all theological."

"So?"

"Well, there's no devotionals, no prayer books. Interesting."

"Pastor Dupree?" Ms. Pearse said, breaking Dupree's concentration. "What kind of cross is that? I've never seen one like it."

Dupree returned to the victim.

The cross was six inches tall. If it were stood upright, the arms would droop at about a 15-degree angle toward the ground, giving the cross the shape of an arrow. At the base of the cross was a threaded connection, making it look like it could be screwed into a block of wood.

"I'm not sure," Dupree said, taking a pen from his pocket and drawing the shape on the palm of his hand. "I've never seen one like it."

"So detective, what do you think?" Ms. Pearce asked Rod Webster.

"I have no idea what it is. I guess that's why they brought super-preacher in to check it out."

"No. I mean, about the murder. You've got to admit," she said. "This does look like a psycho, religious fanatic or something."

"I'm going with the 'or something'," Rod said, taking a seat at the desk. "At first glance it looks a little too weird. Almost like it's supposed to be weird. My experience tells me if it's too obvious then it's too obvious."

Dupree tightened his gloves by pulling them with his teeth. He nudged the head of the dead preacher to one side.

"Can I lift up his head?"

"Sure," Ms. Pearce said.

Dupree stretched his hands in his latex gloves and lifted the preacher's head by the hair. Straddling the preacher, Dupree followed the index finger of Reverend Caldwell's left hand to see where it was pointing. Standing quickly, he moved to a bookshelf. All the shelves were packed, except one that contained a single worn Bible, propped up with a marble book end.

Removing the Bible, he opened it to the page with the only book mark.

Circled in red lipstick was a passage in Proverbs 7.

"Look at this Detective," Dupree said.

Rod stood, moving gingerly around the trailer. With every step, his massive frame shifted the center of gravity of the dead preacher's house causing it to shift on its axles.

"What is it?"

Then out came a woman to meet him, dressed like a prostitute and with crafty intent.

Proverbs 7:10

"Maybe it's a clue from God," Rod said, looking over at Patty. She rolled her eyes.

"Yeah. Or maybe it's a clue from the killer."

• • •

Rod Webster and Cooper Dupree shot out of the toll booth at the Crescent City Connection bridge like a rocket toward the sky.

Dupree strained against his safety belt, grabbing the dash of Rod Webster's police cruiser with white knuckles. "The Proverbs verse references a prostitute and it's circled in lipstick. I wonder if Caldwell ever hooked up with…"

"Are you hungry?" Rod asked, as he made an illegal lane change.

"Uh…sure. Anyway, the passage references a prostitute with wicked intentions, so we should…"

"There is no telling how long that verse has been circled. I've got some real investigating to do before I go running down rabbit holes."

Flying over the Mississippi River at the crest of the bridge, Dupree could feel his stomach in his throat. The water seemed to be a thousand feet below them and the New Orleans skyline glistened in the afternoon sun. "This is crazy high," Dupree said, looking off to his right at the massive river.

"Yeah, it's pretty high," Rod said. He shifted lanes back to the right. The rails clipped by at sixty miles an hour. They provided little protection to keep them from plummeting to a certain watery grave, if they had a blow-out.

"Where do you start your investigation?"

"Instead of looking at the sparkly show of the crime scene and getting all giddy about weird religious symbolism and hookers, I'm going to look into who benefits the most from his death. Are there any insurance policies? Is there a will? Does he owe money to someone or does someone owe him a great deal of money?"

"Follow the money." Dupree nodded. "Basics."

Dupree's stomach fell again and a little reflux escaped into his throat. Rod slammed on the brakes to make his exit, which was over the levee below them. The cruiser pitched sharply to make the cloverleaf turn, throwing Dupree toward Rod. They slowed to a stop at the base of the exit. The big green sign in front of them read "Tchoupitoulas Avenue".

"I'm going to see if he was romantically involved with anyone. Did he have family? Is there an ex-wife, a jealous lover, a jealous husband?"

"Relationships." Dupree took his cellphone from his pocket and began typing notes.

"It's rare that someone is murdered by a stranger."

"Especially premeditated murder," Dupree said.

"Exactly. Did you say you were hungry?"

"I could eat."

"It really looks like it had a woman's touch," Rod said, drumming his fingers on the steering wheel. "The cord device? I mean, a child could have strangled someone with that thing."

"IIow do you say that?" Dupree asked, pointing toward the street sign.

"We just call it 'Chops'."

"So, what's our next step?"

"We should grab some lunch before we head back to the station," Rod said, as he adjusted the rearview mirror.

"I guess I could go for a hamburger," Dupree said. "We could drive through McDonald's."

Rod was silent.

"You know what they call a quarter-pounder in Europe?" Dupree asked, smiling.

"No."

"You're supposed to say 'They don't call it a quarter pounder?' and then I say 'no man, they got the metric system. They wouldn't know what a quarter-pound is'," Dupree said, doing his best impression of John Travolta. "Only I left out a few choice words."

"What the hell are you talking about?"

"*Pulp Fiction*, the movie? Don't tell me you haven't seen it."

"I don't watch movies," Rod said, as he guided the cruiser through a back alley. "Did you really want to go to McDonald's or were you just clowning around?"

"No, I can go for a burger."

Rod pulled the cruiser into a parking lot.

"I got a better hamburger joint than McDonald's. You can get a quarter-pounder or whatever you want to call it, and it comes with a metric ton of cheese on it." He threw the cruiser into park. "Best burgers in town."

"This is so weird," Dupree said, flipping back to his Travolta voice.

• • •

Stepping into the afternoon sun, Cooper Dupree took a huge, greaseless breath of cool New Orleans air as he exited the front door of the Corporation Bar and Grill. In the thirty minutes it took for him and Rod to order and eat, Dupree's life expectancy dropped by three months. His ears still rang with the sounds of a sizzling grill, zydeco music, and an internal swishing that he identified as his arteries beginning to clog.

Wiping the bridge of his nose with his collar, he realized he smelled like a french fry.

During the moments of conversation wedged between bites of a hamburger that was the size of his head, and an order of fries served on a plate the size of a cafeteria tray, Dupree learned that he had almost nothing in common with his new partner.

Rod Webster didn't care for mayonnaise; he didn't much like sports or television or Christmas or puppies or children or flowers or anything that Dupree brought up. In an effort to find one commonality, Dupree even asked Rod what his favorite day of the week was.

"Payday," was his response.

"So you like Friday?"

"Not really. We get paid on the last day of the month."

"So you like money?"

"Not really. I was just trying to shut you up."

Standing at the cashier's counter, Dupree found the one thing they shared.

As Rod opened his wallet, Dupree noticed the photo of a beautiful, smiling lady looking up at them, as Rod removed a few bills.

"Is that your wife?" Dupree asked.

"Was."

As they walked toward the police cruiser, Dupree waited for an opening to start a conversation on the details of Rod's loss. Once seated in the cruiser, with his seatbelt secured, he decided to jump in with both feet.

"I'm sorry for your loss. I really am."

Rod grabbed the radio. "Unit 23 to dispatch."

"How long has it been?" Dupree asked.

"Come in Unit 23."

"Yeah, Nadine, can you get a black-and-white over to South Pete's and Andrew Higgins?"

"Sure Rod."

"It's been three years for me," Dupree said. "It doesn't seem to be getting any easier."

"Are you still talking?"

"I was just asking about your wife. You don't have to be caustic."

A moment of silence followed. Dupree studied the parking lot.

"It's been a year," Rod said.

"That's a tough year. And like I said, it doesn't seem to get any easier. I just broke up with the first girl I've dated since college because I can't get Sarah out of my mind."

"...and you're not angry?"

"No. Never was."

"I don't believe it."

"It's true," Dupree said, turning toward Rod. "As bad as the circumstances were around Sarah's disappearance, I didn't run from God, I ran to God."

"Good for you," Rod said, looking out the driver's side window.

"Detective, we're living in a pretty messed up world. But, this was never God's intention. He created the world perfect, with love...and he's always loved his creation; he loves it today...and he loves you."

"What an eloquently stated pile of manure," Rod said, looking back at Dupree.

"Thanks," Dupree said, smiling. "It's sort of my thing."

"Unit 23, come in."

"Come back for Unit 23," Rod said, grabbing the radio.

"Detective, this is Dresser. What's your 10-20?"

"I see you Dresser, pull straight up," he said, stretching his hand out of the window. "Well, preacher, here's where we part ways. Enjoy the rest of your day."

"But I thought we..."

"I was told to take you to a crime scene. Dresser will take you back to your car."

"I thought we were going back to the station," Dupree said, unbuckling his seat belt.

"You can go wherever you like, but I've got an investigation and...well...enjoy."

CHAPTER 12

Regina Brandingham walked down toward the edge of the Mississippi River to spit. Holding her arms out, as if walking on a tightrope, she navigated the rip-rap used to secure the levee. With each step, she risked gashing her Gianni Bini pumps.

Her tailored jacket was bunched up around her ears. It fit better when she had bought it for one of Cecil's trade shows. Three years and ten pounds had been lost since purchasing the suit. Now, weighing in at 125 pounds, she was swallowed by the blue pinstriped coat.

Reaching the lowest dry rock, she stood for a moment staring up river toward the Crescent City Connection Bridge, listening to the water lap against the concrete chunks. The sun was casting small shadows beside her. The breeze flitted her dark hair off her shoulders; sunglasses blocked the river from looking into Regina's cool, brown eyes.

"I should have gotten my own power-of-attorney to go to the stupid closing," she said. Her voice was weak, almost silent against the massive river in front of her. If she knew any good, powerful attorneys she would have hired one, even though they were probably really expensive. "And you're strapped for cash Regina, you idiot."

The river continued to lap against its banks. It looked like it had suffered a great deal of injustices. Regina took a seat on a cold slab of broken concrete. She felt tired and old.

Her husband, Cecil Brandingham, had made a fortune on the Mississippi River. Before the hurricane, Brandingham Shipping owned a quarter mile of docks. Built in the 1920s, the massive structures were made by men who knew how to build docks to last forever. The Levee District inspectors agreed and did their inspections from the truck. If Brandingham Shipping were actually cited for repairs, they were usually completed for the cost of a couple of LSU football tickets.

Cecil made a quarter of a cent on every ton of lumber that entered the US through the port of New Orleans. The Amazon rain forest alone paid for the Brandingham home on Camp Street.

But Mother Nature gives and Mother Nature takes away.

The Mississippi River, the greatest river in the world, flooded Regina and Cecil's coffers with money. A category 4 hurricane emptied them. Seven days after the storm, the Brandingham Shipping docks floated into the dead-zone of the Gulf of Mexico, leaving Regina and Cecil with massive repairs, a class-action lawsuit, and a government investigation.

Standing once again, Regina decided on her classic goodbye scene—spit and leave town.

She scowled at the river; she shook her fist. Gulping in a lungful of sweet, wet air, she launched a spit wad twenty feet toward the center of the river.

Wiping her mouth with the back of her hand, she watched the foamy little projectile drift toward her left. Who knows? Maybe her spit could meet up with Brandingham Shipping's destroyed docks off the coast of Cuba one day.

Now, she would take her leave.

But, you still have to go to the closing!

Why didn't she wait until after the closing? If she were to direct the perfect ending to this chapter in her life, Regina would use her powerful attorney to pocket Cecil's half of the sale proceeds as well, then spit, then leave town.

Now that would have been classic!

As she watched the wad of spittle float gently toward the French Quarter, she realized she had prematurely spit; she had lost all the dramatics.

Let's do another take!

But then there was the matter of the check clearing the bank and Cecil's attorney was going to be at the closing and the movers were going to want to know a forwarding address and...

...and then there's the text message.

Balancing on the edge of her concrete lookout, she gently reached into her purse and removed her cellphone.

Lifting her sunglasses, she reread the text message from Cooper Dupree and smiled.

She couldn't close on the house, spit again, and leave town. She had to see Coop.

There was really no way to make a clean break from this town or this river.

• • •

Regina moved her head into the shade of a bronze statue and uncrossed her legs; she hiked her skirt just above her knee. Sitting alone on a metal bench, she flashed the cotton panel of her Victoria's Secret black panties toward the residents of Algiers Point. If one of them had the wherewithal to set up a telescope on the top of the levee and direct it toward the attractive woman sitting a quarter mile away on the Riverwalk, they could zero in on her crotch without anyone knowing.

Regina was in the mood to be an exhibitionist, perhaps because she showed her butt at the closing.

Cecil's attorney was not powerful. When he felt it necessary to educate Regina on what a power-of-attorney meant, he was given the middle finger. The gesture left him speechless.

The cool breeze drifting up from the mighty Mississippi gently blew up her skirt. Regina removed her coat and placed it in her lap. She picked up the draft beer resting beside her and took a long drink.

"Ahh!"

Her arms tingled. Pins and needles ran up the back of her neck. Taking another swig of beer, she smiled.

Her bank account was once again topped off. Her funds were limited, but she had enough to live comfortably, for a while.

Dropping out of society would save a bundle; Cecil was on the hook for $5,000 per month in alimony, starting in January.

A tugboat pushed a row of barges north against the current. Rounding the bend, the tugboat worked its way closer to Regina; it would soon push south against the same current.

Regina grabbed her cellphone from her purse and scanned the last few messages. She reread the text message, that she had sent to Cooper Dupree.

"OMG Cooper, please call. I would love to see you!"

Perhaps using the word "love" made her sound desperate. But, when she reviewed it, the context was similar to someone saying they would "love" a steak, or "love" to get a pedicure. Love with quotes is not real love.

Reviewing the message one last time, she dropped the phone back into her purse. Regina was glad she didn't place quotes on her love.

She took another sip of beer and watched the tugboat struggle against the river. The afternoon air had cooled a few degrees, since the sun had dropped below the buildings of downtown. The Mississippi River's tremendous cargo of water and silt rolled toward the Gulf.

Her phone began to ring in her purse; she pumped her fist when she recognized the caller as Cooper.

"Hello?" she said, trying to mask her excitement.

"Hello, Regina?"

"Yes, Cooper?" she said, sitting forward, elbows on her knees, placing a finger in her other ear, so she wouldn't miss a single word.

"Yes, oh my gosh! Regina, this is amazing. How are you?"

"Good. I'm really good." Her voice rose a little in pitch. "Busy. You know, things are good though." She regained a little composure. "How about you? I read an article on you just a few months ago. I thought of calling you but..."

"You should have."

Regina closed her eyes and pictured Cooper standing in front of her.

"Cooper, how long are you in town?"

"Just for tonight, maybe tomorrow night too. I've been called to investigate something that happened last night and...well...I'm not sure what they expect from me."

"Can you meet for dinner?" Regina blurted out. She clenched her fist tight. Her throat was dry. "My treat." She took a sip of beer.

"I'd love to, but like I said, I'm not sure what they're expecting."

"Well, I don't think they expect you to starve."

"I'm sure you're right."

Regina let an awkward pause follow.

"You know what?" Dupree said. "How about we make plans to meet around nine o'clock, you know just for a minute? Nothing big. Once I find out what's going on, maybe we can meet earlier for a bite. I'll call you later, one way or the other."

"Great," Regina said. "Nine sounds good. Come by my place. Although, oh my god, it's a mess. I'm in the middle of moving. The movers are actually coming tomorrow. Maybe we can go out for a drink."

"Yeah, sounds great."

"Okay, well I live at..."

After directions and salutations, Regina sat back and scanned the river. A mischievous smile flashed across her face. She winked at an old man walking by.

The tugboat continued to struggle against the current as the barges were navigated between the bridge abutments.

Regina would not have to struggle so hard.

Finishing the beer, her eyes continued to scan to the right. Canal Plaza One entered her peripheral vision.

Saks?

"It's a shame that they packed all my clothes and shoes," she said, standing and putting on her coat. "Looks like I may need to do a little shopping."

CHAPTER 13

New Orleans City Hall was a local architecture firm's attempt to out Stalin the Russians. They may have beaten us into space, but they knew nothing about properly designing a 20th century building. Built in 1958, functionality, and a drive to place every square inch of roofed space into efficient government service, resulted in a building that looked like it had been designed in communist Moscow. Plopped down on the first available clear cut piece of land that came available, it was a cinderblock building that was shaped like a cinderblock.

The Information Technology Department for the NOPD was located on the eighth floor. Because the chief of IT directed the use of over 1800 cameras, he was awarded the second largest office in the entire building. No one, but the chief of IT, knew exactly who, or what, was being watched at any given time.

Rod Webster flashed his badge at security as he passed, slowly dragging his left foot slightly. His left big toe had developed a crippling sprain that throbbed with every step. Placing his gun and badge in a tray, he slowly stepped through a metal detector that was barely wide enough for him to pass.

"Good afternoon detective," a young NOPD officer said. She flashed a beautiful smile as she handed Rod his gun and badge. Reaching the elevator, he breathed heavily and silently hoped he would not have to take the stairs.

Having been granted a reprieve from climbing, the elevator opened and Rod was whisked upward to the eighth floor. Stepping off the elevator, he found himself emerged in a depressingly cluttered bullpen of computer monitors, whirring machines, and manufactured lighting. The technicians milled about looking over each other's shoulders, speaking a language of acronyms.

"Is Conner around?" he asked a pasty-faced teenager, who looked as if he should be written up for truancy.

"Yeah, sure, Conner!" He yelled over the top of a row of cubicles. "Conner, you've got a detective here to see you."

Like meerkats, several heads popped up. All detectives had their favorite AV technician and vice versa. Buried in a jungle of wires and terabytes, everyone was looking out for their survival. Conner was the only one that flashed a smile, when he recognized Detective Webster.

"Detective, over here," Conner said, waving like an idiot.

"I see you." Rod made his way through the maze of cubicles.

Conner met him halfway. "Whatcha got, Detective?" Conner was as tall as Rod, but weighed only as much as Rod's beefy left leg. With his thin face and reddish hair, he looked a little like a giraffe.

"I've got a video of a church service and I need to identify a young lady in it."

"All-righty, let's see what we can do," Conner said, taking the jump drive.

After loading the file onto his computer, Rod forwarded the video to the moment when the attractive blonde looked directly into the camera.

"That's her," Rod said, stopping the video. "Her name is Diamond, probably. She works for an escort service."

"Cool. So what did she do?" Conner asked, as he typed at lightning speed on the keyboard. "Is this the preacher at the tent show revival in Algiers Point?"

"Just tell me her real, full name."

"The facial recognition software is running," Conner said, moving to another keyboard. "This may take a while."

Rod took the opportunity to make a pot of coffee.

"No match," Conner said, when Rod returned to the cubicle twenty minutes later. "I even double checked the name Diamond through the vice data base. None of them passed the facial recognition identifier."

"That thing never works," Rod said, taking a seat on a tiny chair.

"Yeah, it's a shot in the dark a lot of times," Conner said with a smile. "But, while it was running, I took the opportunity to review the rest of the video. Look at this."

Rod scooted his chair toward Conner's computer monitor.

"This is the same girl; it's a little later in the video. She's at the altar and the camera angle changes. Here she is, getting a blessing or something, and the preacher puts his hands on the side of her head. Look, he lifts up her hair just a little bit."

"Yeah."

"Okay, do you see that black dot there on the back of her neck? I thought that was an identifying mole or something. Turns out, it's even better. Look what happens when I enhance the image and blow it up a bit."

"It's a tattoo," Rod said.

"Yep, right there at the base of her skull, right on the back of the neck," Conner said, looking back over his shoulder. "A lot of girls get them there, so that when they pull their hair up you can see the tattoo, but if they need to cover it up at work or something, they can..."

"I got it," Webster said. "Can you make out what it is?"

"That's what I was going to show you next. Look. If I zoom in even closer and rotate the image and then remove the peripheral pixels by making it black and..."

"It's a barcode," Rod said.

"Very Orwellian."

"Well, Mr. Conner, as usual you've been a big help. Can I get a copy of that?"

"Right here." Conner handed him a folder. "Also, I did a quick search of all the tattoo parlors in the city that have a "barcode" category on their website and placed a copy of those in there as well. There were only two, but I'm sure any tattooist in the city could do a barcode."

"I'm sure." Rod thumbed through the folder. "Conner, I do appreciate it. I'll let you know what I come up with."

Rod started to make his exit.

"By the way Detective," Conner said. "You might want to check out Marcel's Uptown."

"Why's that?"

"Because the orange leather shoulder bag she's carrying is expensive and unique," Conner said, smiling. "Marcel's is the only store in the city that carries them."

"Nice work, Conner. Thanks."

• • •

Parallel parking was not Rod Webster's strong suit—he was never good at geometry. To keep from looking like a parking novice and blocking traffic on Magazine Street with endless iterations of back and forth, he opted to pass Marcel's and park in the Subway Sandwich lot across from Whole Foods. This decision meant that he would have to walk back to the accessory shop, but it would save him at least twenty minutes of embarrassment.

Stepping from the car, he turned toward the street and took a couple of steps, before being yelled at from behind.

"Hey, you can't park there unless you're..."

Rod flashed his badge toward a security guard, who was standing in front of the Subway, as he continued toward the street.

"Yes sir, you have a good day officer." Rod heard from behind him.

The half-block to Marcel's was a lovely stroll. The sidewalks had character. Above them were balconies, below were pavers that varied with each storefront. The vintage clothing store had bricks set at angles to the curb; the antique shop had a stained concrete walkway.

Rod slowed his pace, following an elderly couple. They were content to study the opposite side of the street as they strolled, hand in hand. The northern breeze was blocked by the buildings and the sun was warm on his face. He squinted from the glare off of the windshields of passing cars. His sunglasses rested in the passenger seat of his unmarked cruiser.

At Marcel's, the door was held open with an ash can. Rod stepped in and allowed his eyes to adjust.

"Can I help you?"

Rod turned toward a slight, young lady, wearing clothes that looked as if they were from the shop two stores over. Her dark eyes were accentuated with an eyebrow piercing; her small, sculptured nose was accentuated with a nose piercing.

"Yes, I hope so," Rod said, holding out a clipboard. "I'm looking for a girl named Diamond. I don't have her last name. This is a picture and you can see that she is carrying a bag, that I believe you sell."

"Yeah, that's one of ours," she said, studying the picture.

Rod was suddenly aware that her tongue was accentuated with a piercing as well.

"Are you a cop?"

"Yes. I'm Detective Webster." He removed his badge with his free hand.

"What did she do?"

"I didn't say she did anything. I just need to talk to her. Do you know her?"

"Yeah, I know her," the girl said. She turned and started walking toward the counter. "But it's not Diamond. It's Mary Ellen. She's in here often enough. I just saw her earlier today. She rode by the shop around...uh...I would say about 12:30."

Rod followed her to the counter. "She rode by? What kind of car does she drive?"

"She doesn't; she rides a bike. I saw her heading downtown." The girl reached in her purse and pulled out her cellphone. "You sure she's not in any trouble?"

"Well, no," Rod said. He wanted to grab the girl's phone, but held back. "I didn't say that. I said I need to talk to her."

"Here's her number," she said, holding out her phone. "I know her from the Bulldog. She's really cool and all and don't tell her you got the number from me, okay?"

"Sure," Rod said, writing down the number. "What's her last name?"

"I don't know."

"You wouldn't know where she lives."

"Nope, like I said, I know her from the Bulldog. She works there."

"Really?" Rod said, as he wrote frantically in his folder. "Well Miss..."

"Mandy. My name is Mandy."

"Miss Mandy, you've been a great help," he said, as he turned toward the entrance.

"Sure, anytime."

• • •

Rod Webster stood in front of the precinct building, contemplating his next move. His search for Mary Ellen had taken him to the Bulldog Tavern, her apartment, and finally Whole Foods. An old lady that lived in the apartment across from Mary Ellen sent him on a wild goose chase to the grocery.

The time spent navigating in his squad car through the streets of Uptown was not totally wasted. Family records, DMV information, phone records, and credit card transactions for Reverend Jack Caldwell, Lynnette Faust, and Mary Ellen Retinoir were waiting for him on his desk. Rod could literally spend the next twelve hours combing through reams of data in an attempt to find a clue or a motive.

"What's up Rod?" an officer asked, pushing a young man past him. The boy's hands were bound behind him with a tie-wrap.

"Not much." Rod's voice was flat.

"You coming in?"

"I don't know."

The thought of opening files and looking through all that crap sent a paralysis through his entire body.

Pedestrians on Canal Street moved around him like water around an enormous cypress stump. Rod stood for a moment looking at his wrists.

"What did he do?"

"Nothing!" the kid shouted.

"Shut up, you," the officer said, jerking him around and pushing him into the squad room.

Rod flipped his right hand over and back, rubbing his wrist with his left. His left big toe throbbed in its leather shoe.

The late afternoon sun was hidden; a chill was coming. Rod stepped through the double doors and was overcome by the stench of street life. Sweat, urine, and soured food combined to create a nauseating odor that stung his sinuses. He moved quickly past the entry, through the waiting area facing the desk sergeant. Slick, worn church pews served as benches.

Rod stepped past a lady in tears, begging the desk officer to release her husband immediately.

Her face was bruised.

"He will lose his job."

"I'm sorry lady. Looks like they're releasing him tomorrow morning."

She cursed the stupid law that required wife beaters to stay in jail for at least twenty-four hours.

Grabbing a cup of coffee, Rod entered his office and let out a huge sigh. The files were sitting on his chair, stacked about two feet high. Daunting.

Rod worked in humble surroundings. His office was nothing more than a desk surrounded by three and a half partitions, the missing half partition served as the entry to the cubicle. A diploma hung on one of his movable walls; it was surrounded by a couple of certificates.

An outside observer could learn a lot about Detective Rod Webster just by looking at his desk. He was married with no kids. His wife was younger than he was, unless it was an old picture. Clutter indicated that he was either very busy or very sloppy. He tinkered with science; a microscope rested on his back table. He was computer literate, he ate out a lot, he liked the New Orleans Saints, and went to Mardi Gras parades—evidenced by the fortune cookie strips, trinkets, and newspaper clippings cluttering the desk.

Picking up the stack of files, he shoved a pile of paperwork to the side, using the back of his hand, and cleared a space on his desk. His chair groaned, as he sat.

An hour of reviewing documents uncovered several things that needed a follow-up:

- Where is Alana Caldwell Foster? Does she stand to inherit the Caldwell Ministries LLC, valued at over two-million dollars?

- Whose phone number is 985-555-2765? The last number called by Mary Ellen Retinoir.

- Is Miss Tessy still available at 504-555-1104?

- Is Lynnette Faust aware that she is the beneficiary of a $250,000 life insurance policy?

A review of Reverend Caldwell's documentation uncovered a daughter from his first marriage. The marriage ended six years before he started the Houston mega-church. There was no record of him ever paying child support. However, with the absence of a will, Alana Foster would be the sole heir to whatever Caldwell had acquired.

Phone records showed that the only phone call Mary Ellen Retinoir made after ten-o'clock last night was to the unknown phone number. After dialing the number and getting no answer, Rod called Conner. The number was assigned to a "burner" cellphone bought at a Walmart in Metairie and was not registered to any name.

The number for Miss Tessy, given to him by Lynnette Faust, was another burner phone purchased in Canton, Mississippi.

And, finally, there was the beautiful Lynnette Faust.

A $250,000 life insurance policy was a little short-sighted to ruin a lucrative job.

But, directing the escort to Caldwell's trailer and then not finding him dead until 10:30 in the morning was odd.

"Why are you lying to me, Miss Faust?" Rod said, as he wrote.

CHAPTER 14

Ignatius Selman rarely opened the blinds and windows at his shop. The sun didn't accentuate his wares; it only served to overmagnify the incredible amount of dust. As he turned the rod that slowly rotated the slats from vertical to horizontal, Iggy was hit with a wave of energy, a boost of Vitamin D. The bright sunshine warmed his cheeks and brought brightness to the yellowed whites of his eyes.

Having dressed in dungarees and a T-shirt, Iggy decided, that this afternoon, he would do a 'super clean' on the shop. Antiques and relics sold better when they were covered with a light layer of dust. A polished bronze figurine of Saint Joseph, just didn't look authentic. When Iggy got a new shipment of pewter crucifixes, he would immediately dump them in a solution of baking soda and water to achieve a light tarnish But with the brutally hot summer, he had no opportunity to do anything but swish dust from one rosary or saint or candle to another. The old, tired grime, accumulated over the last six months, would be cleared out to make room for a collection of fresh winter dust.

If Iggy's shotgun apartment/business had a grass lawn, he might have purchased a leaf blower sometime in the past. By simply opening the back door and propping open the four doors that separated the back bedroom, kitchen, his bedroom, the office, and the shop, he could have cranked up the leaf blower and blasted the dust right out into Toulouse Street. The air would flow through his place like a wind tunnel. But, since Iggy had no lawn, he had no lawn equipment.

The grass in his back yard was kept down by piles of crap that

Iggy had collected from years of Saturday morning garage sales.

Placing a box fan in the entrance to his shop, he directed the air flow toward the street. The place needed airing-out. Even Iggy could tell that it smelled like his dirty clothes hamper. He cranked the fan to its highest setting and waited for it to stabilize. Carefully sliding a porcelain statue of the Madonna into one corner and moving a cardboard box filled with old rosaries with his foot, he was able to clear a spot to place his step stool. Climbing the two steps, he started working the display of icons with a feather duster. The air was instantly fogged with colonies of mites, that took up residence in Iggy's sinuses.

He sneezed so violently, he nearly blew over a collection of stained-glass panes, displayed on the shelf beside him.

Stepping down, he moved quickly, nearly blinded with tears, toward the bathroom to blow his nose.

His cellphone rang. It was Lynnette Faust.

Taking a seat at his desk, he pumped his fist a few times before answering.

"Lynnette?" he said. A huge smile flashed across his face.

"Iggy, have you heard the news?" Her voice was weak, cracking. Fear gripped Iggy, as a chill ran up his spine.

"What news?"

"Reverend Caldwell has been murdered." Iggy heard Lynnette crying on the other end of the line.

A long silence followed, as Iggy tried to process the words that shot through his brain like a bullet.

"Iggy, are you there?"

"Yes." Iggy cleared his throat, trying to regain his composure. "How? When? When did this happen?"

"Last night. We found him dead in his trailer this morning. He was stabbed or strangled or something."

"I…I can't believe it." Iggy sat forward with his forearms on his thighs. He pushed the speaker on his phone and set the phone on the floor in front of him. "Uh…how are you doing? How are you holding up?"

"It sucks, Iggy. I've got to be honest. We're getting packed up for Jackson. And…well, there isn't going to be a Jackson. I can't believe it's over. We all thought it ended when we lost the church in Houston…you know that. But then the revivals were doing so well…and…that god-damned Jack. He had to just keeping pushing and pushing and…"

Iggy sat up and looked toward the ceiling. Pressing his palms together, he pointed to the heavens, shaking his head slowly. "It's really over."

"Iggy?" Lynnette said, after a long pause. "Would you like to meet me tonight? I need to talk to you about some stuff with the ministry."

"What did you say?"

"Iggy, can you meet me tonight? There are some money issues we need to discuss. Reverend Caldwell had a substantial amount of money, that…"

"You're kidding me."

"No. And, Iggy, he took out an insurance policy when we lost the Houston church and I'm the beneficiary."

Iggy's mind raced with what the "substantial amount of money" comment meant.

"You know that puts me in the crosshairs," she added.

"But you had nothing to…"

"Iggy, it doesn't matter. Also, I think you may have been named in the will and…"

"Me? Why?"

"…I have a Zoom meeting with his lawyer at 5:00. If you are named, you'll be investigated as well. We'll be on the short list of suspects. So, tonight, where and when?"

"Hello? Is anyone back there?" A voice came from the shop. A customer was calling from the storefront.

"He named me in his will?"

"Yes. I have a strong feeling that he has."

Iggy's face went pale. He squeezed his hands, trying to keep them from tingling. He picked his phone up from the floor.

"Hello?"

"Lynnette, I need to go," Iggy said as he stood.

"Iggy? Tonight?" Lynnette asked.

"I'll call you back shortly." He hung up the phone as he stepped into the shop.

"Hello?" Iggy yelled toward the front.

A young girl stepped past the fan, struggling to keep her skirt from being pulled against the intake screen.

"Hey," she said, stepping inside a few more feet. Blonde, with a bright smile, her hair looked windswept and was sticking to her temples.

"Can I help you?" Iggy unconsciously started straightening items around him.

"Do you buy items?" She reached into the bottom of a large, leather handbag.

"Depends on what it is," Iggy said. "I'm always looking for unique collectables. What have you got?"

The girl pulled a felt-covered object from her purse.

Iggy's stomach immediately leapt into his throat, as the color left his already pale cheeks. It was the green bag.

"I recently found this," the girl said, laying the object on the counter next to the cash register. Iggy walked behind the counter. Removing the object from the bag, she exposed the cross Iggy hoped was still contained within.

"It's beautiful," Iggy said. His voice cracked a little. "Here, move it into the sunlight."

She slid the gold cross along the counter, protecting it with the felt, until she caught a dust speckled sunbeam.

"Oh, my goodness, it's beautiful. Isn't it?" Iggy ran his finger along the edges. "What is your name?"

"Mary Ellen."

"Mary Ellen," Iggy said, looking up at her. His lips curved up into a smile that displayed a full set of crooked front teeth. "Where did you get this?"

"I told you," she said, picking up the cross. "I found it."

"You're lying."

"No. I..."

"Missy, I know you're lying."

"Up yours!" Mary Ellen said, snatching the felt bag from the counter. She turned toward the door.

"I'll give $1,100 for it," Iggy said, standing upright and hitting the release button on the cash register. "That's what I paid for it eight years ago."

Mary Ellen stopped a few feet from the door. The fan was excessively loud. "Did you say $1,100? It's worth $10,000."

Iggy laughed.

"No, it's worth $1,100 and that's with the others," Iggy said, pulling the drawer from the register. He thumbed through several bills, trying to collect eleven one-hundred-dollar bills.

"The other what?" Mary Ellen asked, stepping back toward the counter.

"The grapevine crosses. This cross was sold with the set of four grapevine crosses. They go together."

"I don't have those," Mary Ellen said. She looked skeptical.

Iggy smiled.

"Without the other crosses, I can only give you...$200," Iggy said, laying a couple of one-hundred-dollar bills on the counter.

"But, this is solid gold."

"No dear. It's not," Iggy said. "It's actually polished brass."

"But, I was told it sold for $12,000…uh…recently."

"And who told you that?"

"No one," Mary Ellen said. "I researched it…on-line."

"Well, whoever paid $12,000 was a real sucker," Iggy said. "On its own, without the grapevine crosses, this is a $200 cross. I will admit, whoever you "found" it from, kept it very nice. I can give you $300." He placed another one-hundred-dollar bill on the counter.

Iggy let an awkward pause follow.

"But, hey, that's neither here nor there. I couldn't care less where you got it. The point is, it's value comes from the historical significance, not the material of construction and, without the other crosses, it's just…well it's just not that valuable."

"Okay," Mary Ellen handed Iggy the cross.

"I want the felt as well."

She picked up the $300.

"I suppose you'll pass on getting a receipt," Iggy said, as she handed him the green felt bag.

Mary Ellen exited the shop quickly.

Holding the cross in the sunlight, Iggy felt a chill run up the back of his neck as the reflection of his shop glistened in the polished finish.

Suddenly, Iggy was done cleaning for the day.

CHAPTER 15

Pastor Cooper Dupree pulled his Toyota Camry into a space reserved for "visitors" on the curb of Alix Street in Algiers, Louisiana. The enormous wooden doors marking the entrance of the Holy Name of Mary Church were to his right and seemed as high as the levees. Still buckled in tight, Dupree sat in the shade of a beautiful oak that lined the neutral ground. The air smelled like autumn, with a hint of musty Spanish moss; his shirt smelled like the fryers at the Corporation Bar And Grill.

The sexton was scheduled to meet him in twenty minutes.

With 3,000 calories of fat pulsing through his arteries, Dupree had to fight the urge to take a nap. Instead, he grabbed his laptop, opened a Word file titled "Caldwell", and began typing.

"Detective Webster is a jerk," he said, typing the same words below the notes he had written earlier. Officer Dresser had tried to change Dupree's first impression of the detective, during the ride back to his car.

"Detective Webster's all right," the officer said, driving back over the Crescent City Connection. "He just likes to do things on his own. Since his wife died, he hasn't been partnered with anyone. I think he's still working through it."

Dupree could certainly understand, but he still hated being dumped.

He picked up his iPhone.

Not a good idea Coop.

He almost dialed Kelly Mitchell.

Throwing the phone in the seat beside him, he began to scan the notes he had made concerning the cross used in the murder.

"The cross (looks like an arrow) is six inches long with the cross pieces projecting out about 2 inches. The cross pieces start at two inches from the end and are angled (not 90 degrees!) toward the base. It looks to be about 75 degrees. Extending from the end of the cross is a three inch long wood screw (3/8" in diameter with 16 threads per inch). It's as if the cross was used as a handle or to hang something from the ceiling. Cross is bronze; metal screw is iron, rusted, worn. Bronze is tarnished. Funeral cross, maybe? Search casket designs, search incense holders."

With the front windows rolled down, a light breeze blew across the front seat of the Toyota.

When the sexton finally opened the front doors of the Holy Name Church, forty minutes had passed and Dupree had made the following notes:

Grapevine Cross

Georgian Orthodox Church

British Standard Whitworth

Dr. Alonzo Morrissey

Dupree waved up to the elderly gentleman and logged off his computer. A moment later, he was ascending the marble steps toward the entry.

"Good afternoon," he said, extending his hand. The man in charge of keeping the church safe, clean, and as exclusive as a Mardi Gras Krewe looked at Dupree inquisitively. Because he was a much smaller man and was hunched over at the shoulders, Dupree found it difficult to make eye contact. Ignoring Dupree's hand, the sexton hitched his pants over his belly and turned back into the church.

"I was told you needed to get in. Is there something wrong?"

"No sir. I was just in need of a quiet place, to pray."

"A vigil, eh?"

"Well no, not really," Dupree said, following the man into the narthex.

"You can't do a mass without approval of Father Clement," he said, spinning around quickly. "You're not planning to do a mass, are you?"

"No, no, not at all. I just wanted to pray; in there would be fine. Just a quiet place."

"I can let you in there, but I need to lock up when you leave."

"That's fine. I'll come get you."

The man looked suddenly perplexed. He began thumbing through a large ring of keys. He unfastened the lock on a pair of stained-glass doors and ushered Dupree into the sanctuary.

"Here you go. I'll be out here when you're done." He stepped back into the narthex.

"You don't have to wait for..."

"I'll be fine. I'll be right here."

Dupree smiled. "Thanks."

In his past criminal cases, deep meditation in a house of prayer, any house of prayer, brought about revelation. Deep prayer, lying face down on the burgundy carpet of Christ Church in Pascagoula had led him to the whereabouts of a serial killer. Now, with the crime scene fresh in his mind, he needed to get inside a church.

The mid-afternoon sun was flooding in through several large stained-glass windows lining the western wall. Walking the aisle between sixty well-worn pews, he moved slowly toward the altar. An enormous crucifix was on the wall behind the altar, the image of Christ was at least nine feet tall. Candles on both sides of the altar were lit. It was hard to tell if they were real, or if they were flickering electric bulbs.

"Hey! Father! Please don't go up on the altar," the sexton yelled into the empty church.

"Yes sir," Dupree said. "I'm good right here."

Standing before the crucifix, Dupree took several long, deep breaths and let the weight of the moment sink deep into his soul.

Poor Reverend Caldwell.

Images of the crime scene flashed in his mind—so much hurt, pain, death.

Dupree sensed remorse—there was so much that he had done that he was sorry for.

I should have been more up front with Kelly, knowing...that...I'm sorry for hurting Kelly.

There was so much he had left undone...

Detective Webster needs you, Lord. Help me to bring your peace to him.

How easy it was for Dupree to slip into sin.

Romans, Chapter 3, came to the forefront of his thoughts.

"There is no difference, for all have sinned and fall short of the glory of God," he said, under his breath.

Minutes slipped by; his heart felt heavy in his chest. When he opened his eyes, he saw giant Jesus on the cross and smiled. Romans, Chapter 3, also told him the good news.

"You are justified freely by his grace—God's love for his creation—through the redemption that came by Christ Jesus."

He fell prostrate, burying his nose into the hardwood floor.

Thanks!

Rolling his face back and forth, he didn't worry about getting dirty or breathing in germs. As he slipped into a meditative state, ideas flashed through his mind in waves—one thought connected to another.

Stabbed in the heart. No lower. Shot with an arrow through the liver?

A young man who lacked judgment was going down the street near her corner...when out came a woman to meet him, dressed like a prostitute and with crafty intent. Come, let's drink deep of love till morning; let's enjoy ourselves with love! My husband is not at home. With persuasive words she led him astray; she seduced him with her smooth talk.

All at once, he followed her like an ox going to the slaughter, like a deer stepping into a noose 'till an arrow pierces his liver...

Proverbs 7

An arrow pierces his liver!

Dupree placed his hands on the back of his head. His forehead rolled on the floor; his elbows tap, tap, tapping as he moved back and forth.

Dupree saw the dead preacher, strangled to death with the nylon rope, with the stainless steel tubes. He saw the cross inserted into his liver.

Post-mortem.

Who circled the passage in lipstick? Who needed leverage to strangle the preacher? A woman? A child? A prostitute?

Someone with crafty intentions.

Dupree tapped the toes of his shoes on the wood flooring. His right toe struck at the same time as his left elbow. Back and forth, he squeezed his temples with his palms.

A scorned lover?

No!

This was not a crime of passion. There was no passion. This was planned—every detail was staged, calculated, premeditated.

Dupree relaxed, taking deep meditative breaths, allowing his elbows to rest on the floor.

Rahab!

With the single name, an electric shock seemed to run up his spine.

Rahab, the prostitute.

Then Joshua son of Nun secretly sent two spies from Shittim…they went and entered the house of a prostitute named Rahab and stayed there.

…the woman had taken the two men and hidden them…under the stalks of flax, she had laid out on the roof.

…she let them down by a rope through the window, for the house she lived in was part of the city wall.

Joshua 2:

Dupree rolled onto his back and spread his arms out on the floor, his eyes rolled up into his head. A tear ran down the side of his face. He opened his eyes slowly. In a vision, he saw the spies of Joshua scaling down the side of the city wall, scanning below them for their pursuers.

Heat ran up Dupree's spine. He felt a tugging in his groin.

Another exit?

Dupree rolled back over on his stomach, pushing his nose into the hardwood floors.

Who was lowered from the trailer?

Dupree's stomach knotted; he felt a little ill.

How did the prostitute leave?

Rolling over, sitting cross-legged on the floor.

"Caldwell was with a woman, who either murdered him or helped the murderer escape," he said, smiling. He rubbed his hands over his face and pushed back his hair.

Looking up at the crucifix, he shook his head slowly.

"Thank you, Lord. It's a start."

• • •

Thanking the sexton, Dupree exited the church quickly. Jogging across the street, he leapt into his car and grabbed his phone.

With a sudden surge of confidence, he made the call.

"How about we make plans to meet around nine o'clock, you know just for a minute—nothing big." The word "nothing" came out sounding like "nuth-thin".

She accepted; Dupree nodded and smiled, as he looked at himself in the rearview mirror.

Although Dupree's tongue grew fat and thick during the short conversation—having suffered a nervous reaction to making a date with a woman as beautiful as Regina, Dupree managed to mumble through. As he entered her address into his GPS, he flipped his tongue back and forth trying to gain some feeling back into it.

Tossing his phone into the passenger seat, he placed both hands on the steering wheel and began to tap his thumbs in a slow, methodical rhythm.

He pictured the crime scene—the dead preacher, the grapevine cross, the pool of blood.

He pictured Regina—wearing one of his old college sweatshirts, smiling with those full, perfect lips. Her dark eyes sparkled with mischief.

He felt a pang in his chest.

Starting the car, he pulled onto the road. He needed another look at the Caldwell crime scene before it was totally dismantled.

CHAPTER 16

Tivoli Circle, in the heart of New Orleans, was an early nineteenth century effort to develop a classical arts section of town. Museums, fountains, and an amphitheater were all on the books. Nine streets like Euterpe and Clio, named after the nine muses of Greek mythology, ran toward the river and crossed Coliseum, the main thoroughfare.

The violence and heartbreak of the Civil War derailed any plans to spend money on art. Instead, on a rainy day in the winter of 1884, a crowd of 10,000 and the ex-confederate president Jefferson Davis gathered under umbrellas and live oaks in the loop at St. Charles Avenue and Howard Avenue to dedicate their newest memorial, a 16 foot statue of Robert E. Lee atop a 60' pedestal.

Tivoli Circle was renamed Lee Circle and the great confederate general faced the north, hands folded in front of him, adorned in his grays, streaked with bird droppings until 2018. In the middle of the night, under heavy guard, city workers used a 120 foot telescopic crane to remove the statue and place it in storage along with other leaders of the confederacy. The only thing left of that wet nineteenth century morning was the name "Lee" circle and the 60' pedestal.

The Circle Bar sat at seven o'clock on the circle in what would have been the blind spot of General Lee. Mary Ellen took a seat on the barstool nearest the door. Outside, a three o'clock sun was beating down on the streetcar stop, which was a couple of iron barstools fastened to a concrete slab in the neutral ground. Inside, a midnight-like darkness blanketed the bar. Layers of filth and nicotine caked all the exposed surfaces. A Pabst Blue Ribbon sign, a string of Christmas lights strung behind the bar, and the screens of the video poker games illuminated Mary Ellen and the bartender.

"What can I get you, sweetie?" a young lady asked, smearing a damp cloth along the wooden bar. With the blue and red of the beer sign reflecting off of her eyebrow ring, the barmaid looked like she was wearing too much make-up. But, as Mary Ellen's eyes adjusted to the light, she could tell it was really two black eyes.

"I'll have a High-life," Mary Ellen said.

"Make it two," Jarrell said, coming up behind her. "You're late."

Mary Ellen spun in her chair. "I know, it's a long story." Mary Ellen offered her cheek for a kiss-hello.

"You look awesome," Jarrell said.

"Thanks."

Jarrell looked young for his age. Wearing a tight fitting, long-sleeved T-shirt and baggy jeans, he had chosen to wear a beanie over his crewcut. He had shaved, making his thin, three-day-old goatee more pronounced.

He pulled a pack of cigarettes from his front pocket.

"So what's up?" Jarrell asked, as the bartender placed the beers in front of them. He lit his cigarette.

"That'll be $6.00," the bartender said.

"I thought they were two dollars?" Jarrell asked, out of reflex.

"Happy hour ended about twenty minutes ago."

"Clever." He blew a stream of smoke toward the ceiling.

"I've got it." Mary Ellen pulled a wad of cash from her purse and placed a twenty on the bar. She counted out $140 and slid it over to Jarrell.

"What's this?"

"I found $800 dollars in the preacher's desk. I only got $300 for that stupid cross." Mary Ellen grabbed Jarrell's cigarette and took a puff. "That's your cut."

"You're kidding," Jarrell said, picking up the cash. He stuffed it in the front pocket of his jeans. "$300?"

"He was going to give me only $200."

"That asshole is so cheap. The guy's loaded and he does…"

"He said he would give me $1,100 if I had the other crosses."

"Unbelievable, that guy."

Mary Ellen took a long drink of her beer. "Sounds like he screwed Caldwell pretty good."

"He got $12,000 for the crosses. I saw the check myself." Jarrell downed the rest of his beer.

"I thought only the gold one was worth anything."

"Yeah, that's what I'm saying." Jarrell ordered another beer by waving his empty bottle at the bartender. She popped the top on a High-life and placed it in front him.

"Not for me," Mary Ellen said. "I've got work at six." She grabbed Jarrell's pack of cigarettes.

"So why couldn't you hang out at Old Point?" Mary Ellen asked.

Jarrell pulled his stocking cap off and placed it on the bar. "I told you I was working the pedicab at 10:00. Besides, you were hanging with what's-his-name from the Bulldog."

"We're co-workers," Mary Ellen said, patting Jarrell on the knee.

"Did you go home with him?"

"No. He's not my type."

"Black?"

"Married." Mary Ellen smiled. "I just had the one drink. I was back in the Quarter by 10:30."

Jarrell downed his beer, stood, and placed his stocking cap back on his head. "Got to go. Thanks for the beers. I might swing by the Bulldog tonight. You working 'til midnight?"

"Yeah." Mary Ellen stood. "Where're you heading?" She gave Jarrell a light hug.

"I've got some things," Jarrell said as he turned to the door. "I'll catch you later."

CHAPTER 17

Mary Ellen was collared as she was getting on her bicycle on Lee Circle. Because she was only wanted for questioning, the patrol cops couldn't bring her into the station without her consent. She refused.

Dispatch contacted Rod Webster at his desk.

"Webster."

"Detective, this is Nadine. They found Mary Ellen Retinoir at Lee Circle. She's refusing to come in for questioning. Would you like them to hold her until you can get there?"

"What was she doing at Lee Circle?"

"Hold."

Rod opened an e-mail sent from the law offices of Feller, Feller, and Lowenstein, the law firm that handled the bankruptcy case of Reverend Jack Caldwell. The sender, a paralegal, was reluctant to provide information on the case without the approval of one of the partners.

Rod replied. "This is a murder investigation. Confidentiality is a moot point." Rod smiled, at finally getting to write the word moot. "All I want to know is if Reverend Caldwell had a will and, if so, who was his attorney?" He was hoping one of the lawyers from Feller, Feller, and Lowenstein had been hired to prepare the will.

"She was at the Circle Bar. She's heading home to do laundry," Nadine said.

"Bring her in for operating a bicycle while under the influence."

"But…"

"Bring her in for a breathalyzer."

"10-4."

"Have the officers bring her bike. I'll impound it, if she's 0.08."

"10-4."

An e-mail reply from the paralegal pinged his computer. "Detective Webster, one of our lawyers is the attorney-of-record for Reverend Caldwell's last will and testament. I will be pleased to forward you a copy as soon as we receive a copy of his death certificate."

"Thank you." Rod responded. He picked up his phone and dialed the switchboard.

"Yes, detective?"

"Patch me through to vital statistics."

"One moment."

"This is Jada."

"Jada, this is Detective Rod Webster. Has the death certificate for Reverend Jack Caldwell been released?"

"One moment."

Rod reached in his desk drawer and grabbed two extra-large Little Debbie oatmeal crème pies from a box that looked like it had been opened by a bear. Holding the phone in one hand, he ripped the plastic off the snack with his teeth. It took three bites to consume the first pie.

"No sir, we have not received it. There's a backlog at the coroner's office."

"Thanks."

Typing with one hand, eating another oatmeal crème pie with the other, he sent an instant message to Patty Pearce.

"Patty, I really, really need the death certificate for Caldwell. Can you move it to the top of the pile? Pretty please!"

Spinning in his chair, he grabbed a pad of paper from his back desk. He only had a few minutes to prepare to interrogate pretty little Mary Ellen.

• • •

Now, seated on a metal chair in Interrogation Room #2, Mary Ellen had goose bumps on her arms. She rubbed them vigorously, trying to generate a little warmth. Blonde bangs fell across her face, masking her crystal blue eyes. She had been crying; the mascara and eyeliner, smudged in the corner of her eyes, gave her a dark, gothic look.

"Would you like a jacket?" Officer Mancini asked. "We keep it kind of cold in here."

"Maybe a cup of coffee?"

"I'll see what I can do," Mancini said. "Now, Miss Retinoir, the lead detective assigned to this case is Detective Rod Webster. He'll be here shortly to interview you so I..."

"What is this about?"

"He'll have to tell you."

"You can't just pull someone off the street and interrogate them."

"That's true, but you were drinking and operating a..."

"Oh, please, spare me." Mary Ellen began shivering. She wrapped her arms around herself as tight as possible.

"I'll be right back. I'm going to see if I can find a blanket."

Mancini stood and headed toward the door.

"After Detective Webster talks to me, then I can go?"

"I don't know," Mancini said. He paused in the door for a second. "I'm not promising anything, but if you cooperate with the detective, I have a feeling this thing might just go away. I'll be right back."

Rod watched from the room adjacent to Interrogation Room #2. Mary Ellen sat huddled in the cold steel chair, her lips taking on a slight bluish hue. She pulled her hair back and refastened her pony tail.

When the door burst open, Mancini entered, carrying a cup of coffee in one hand and a gray wool blanket in the other. Rod followed a few seconds later.

"I put a little sugar in it." Mancini set the coffee down and handed her the blanket. She immediately draped it over her shoulders, keeping her eyes on the giant man who took the seat opposite her at the table.

"I'm Detective Webster," Rod said, opening a file folder. "Miss Retinoir, do you know why we picked you up?" Rod placed his hands in front of him. His beautiful green eyes were set in a ridiculous expression of seriousness. His large, warm face did not fit the situation. If it weren't for his frown, he looked as if he might break into sudden laughter.

"It's not the bicycling under the influence?" She asked sarcastically.

"No." Rod leaned forward. His expression let her know that the situation was very serious.

"Yes sir, I believe I do," Mary Ellen said.

"Would you like to tell me?"

"Do I need a lawyer?"

"I don't know. You tell me."

Mary Ellen looked back at Mancini who was standing by the door. A camera was positioned in the corner at the ceiling. The little red dot above the lens blinked at her.

"Maybe," Mary Ellen said, after a long pause. "It depends on if I get to leave or not."

"If you answer all our questions and you've done nothing wrong, we'll release you," Rod said. "If you lawyer up, we'll tell you what we suspect you've done, read you your rights, and take you to the holding pen. Clear enough?"

"Yes sir."

"So, I ask again," Rod said, pushing away from the table slightly. "Do you know why you are here?"

Mary Ellen took a long pause. "It's about the revival preacher, isn't it? Caldwell. He sent you."

The detective furrowed his brow. His serious expression turned to confused; he looked as if Mary Ellen had just spoken in a new language. He looked over at Mancini.

"What do you mean 'He sent you'?"

"The preacher from the tent show revival, Reverend Caldwell. He sent you. It's not about that?"

"About what?" Rod asked.

"Okay, then I think I do need a lawyer, because I have no idea why you've got me here," Mary Ellen said, wrapping up tighter in the blanket. She reached for the coffee.

The detective closed his folder. He looked as if he were collecting his thoughts.

"Miss Retinoir," Rod said, clearing his throat. "You can have a lawyer, but you're correct. We want to talk to you about Reverend Caldwell."

"I knew it," Mary Ellen said, shaking her head. "They've got video." She hit her forehead with the palm of her hand. "Stupid, stupid, stupid." She paused for a moment, taking a long look at Detective Webster. "I'm not saying another word."

"You are correct. We do have video."

"What did he tell you?" Mary Ellen asked after a few seconds. "He probably thinks that lousy cross is worth twelve grand. Well, he was totally taken. I know the guy who sold it to him. He'll tell you."

"Excuse me?" Rod asked.

"This is about the cross, right? It can't be the cash."

Detective Webster remained silent.

"What did he tell you?"

Suddenly, Detective Webster jumped up, hitting his thighs on the steel table, sliding it across the floor. The noise shook the walls. Mary Ellen tried to cover her ears with her free hand. Her coffee sloshed onto the floor.

"Listen here, Miss Retinoir," Rod said, moving the table back into place and repeating the same deafening noise. "I'm not playing games. You hear me?"

"Yes, sir," Mary Ellen said, as tears welled in her eyes. "I shouldn't have done it. I'm sorry." Standing, she pointed her hands toward Mancini. "Take me to my holding cell."

"Miss Retinoir." Rod's voice softened. "Sit. We're not done here. Please, sit."

Mary Ellen took a seat and wrapped her arms around her torso tightly.

"Miss Retinoir, phone records shows the only phone call you made after ten o'clock last night was to 985-555-2765. Who is that?"

"I didn't call anyone."

"You need to check your phone."

"I don't see why," she said, removing her phone from her purse. "I can't remember the last time I called someone. I don't even call my mom or…what the…I didn't make this call."

"So you did call the number?"

"Uh…I must have pocket dialed it. Who is it?"

"That's what I'm asking you."

"I have no idea," Mary Ellen said. "I swear I didn't call anyone. Do you want me to call it?"

"Sure."

Mary Ellen dialed the number. The phone went directly to voice mail.

"The caller you have dialed…"

She held up the phone for Detective Webster to hear the message.

"Is that it?"

"Not quite," Rod said, pulling a picture from a folder. "There's still one more thing we need to talk about."

"And what is that?"

Rod slid the photo of the crime scene in front of Mary Ellen. "Maybe you can explain to me how Reverend Caldwell was strangled to death."

• • •

Rod left Mary Ellen Retinoir sobbing, shivering, with her head down on the cold metal table.

He stood outside the door of Interrogation Room #2 with Mancini.

"Take care of her," Rod said as he dialed his phone.

"Are we holding her on the theft?"

"No one's reported a theft."

"Hello? Jarrell Landry?" Rod kept Mancini from entering the interrogation room by holding his shoulder. "This is Detective Rod Webster with the NOPD. Are you available to answer a few questions?"

Rod shook his head as he listened to Jarrell.

"It would be better if you came into the precinct," Rod responded. "Yes, that would be perfect. The main one on Canal Street, near Rampart. Uh-huh, by Shirley's. That would be terrific. Ask for Officer Mancini. Thanks."

Rod released Mancini's shoulder.

"That's her alibi," Rod said. "I want to keep her here until you get a statement from him on what happened at the preachers' trailer last night."

"10-4."

"If he backs up her story, you can release her," Rod said, taking off down the corridor. "I've got to follow up with Lynnette Faust."

CHAPTER 18

As Dupree drove onto the beaten meadows of the Algiers fairgrounds, he could see the portable cathedral was stripped of its sides. Stakes were being pulled from the ground; soon it would fall in upon itself.

A flat bed tractor-trailer truck was packed with massive rolls of canvas; the driver waited anxiously for directions that might never come.

Dupree parked near Reverend Caldwell's trailer and listened to the soft sounds of nature—a bird chirping, the leaves rustling, laborers yelling at one another to quit dragging ass.

"What's the hurry, Miss Faust? We ain't got no place to go no how."

"You're not salaried workers. You're on the clock. So, unless you want to punch out now, you best move."

Grabbing his phone from the passenger seat, Dupree dialed the number for Dr. Alonzo Morrissey. The doctor was the Dean of Germanic and Slavic Studies at Tulane University.

"Morrissey," a weak voice answered after a couple of rings.

"Dr. Morrissey, this is Pastor Cooper Dupree. I'm working an investigation with the New Orleans Police Department and I was wondering if I could have a moment of your time?" Dupree asked, as succinctly as possible.

"Okay."

"Well, sir, I was wondering if you knew anything about the grapevine cross. It's a principal relic of the Georgian Orthodox Church."

"I'm familiar with it."

"I was wondering, sir, if you had come across any...recently."

"No," Dr. Morrissey said, sounding distracted. He was probably watching television or reading something on his computer. "Dupree, is that your name?"

"Yes sir."

"I need to go. Come by my office at nine o'clock tomorrow morning and I'll answer any questions you may have."

"Well...I..."

"Tomorrow, nine o'clock. Okay?"

"Yes sir," Dupree said. "You do realize tomorrow is Saturday?"

"Of course."

He took the doctor's address.

"Thanks," Dupree said, in salutation.

After grabbing a small notepad from the glovebox, he stepped out onto the beaten down turf surrounding his car. The grass had patterns of red, muddy lines running from the door of the dead preacher's home. Paths, like spokes on a wagon wheel, extended out in all directions, the widest leading directly to the back of what was left of the giant tent.

During the short trip from the church sanctuary to the fairgrounds, Rod Webster had called to say that they needed to meet at the crime scene. In their brief conversation, Dupree learned that the road manager's name was Lynnette Faust. Dupree was anxious to ask her a few questions before the detective muscled in on his investigation.

Spotting the woman that Rod Webster described as a "tall, skinny, Swedish looking woman", Dupree took the shortest path toward her, despite there being no beaten down path.

"Hey!" he yelled across the way. His slender build and long legs made him look like a gazelle, as he took uneven strides trying to dodge obstacles in the foot-high grass. Because his only free hand was needed for balance, his hair fell into his eyes and obscured his sight.

"Lynnette Faust?" Dupree waved as he picked up the pace.

"Yeah?"

"Can I have a word with you?" Dupree stopped in front of her and brushed the hair out of his eyes.

"I'm Cooper Dupree. I've been called in to help on the investigation." Dupree was slightly winded; he took big breaths in between sentences. "I was wondering if I could ask you a few questions."

"Are you working with that detective? The big black guy?"

"Yes."

"Then, take it up with him," Lynnette said, turning around. "I've told him everything."

"You're the road manager?"

"Yes," Lynnette said, turning back around. "Father, I have no idea what I can provide you that I haven't already told the detective. Don't you two talk?"

"Well, not really," Dupree said. "I just need to ask a few questions about last night? Were you the last person to see him alive?"

"No, like I told the detective, as far as I know, Diamond was the last one with Caldwell," Lynnette said, stopping and becoming more animated with her hands. "...and you would have to be blind to not know what she looks like from the video."

Dupree shook his head in disbelief.

A name? Video?

"Yes...uh...Diamond," Dupree said, writing the name down. "She's a… prostitute?" Dupree guessed.

"I think she preferred to be called an escort."

Dupree shook his head in amazement.

"Was she a small person?"

"Pardon me?"

"Petite? Was she an exceptionally small person?"

"No," Lynnette said. "She's about 5'-6", maybe 130 lbs. Just a normal sized young lady."

"How young?"

"Mid-twenties. Do I need to give you a copy of the video?"

"Uh...no, I'm sure Detective Webster will show it to me,"

Dupree said, looking up from his notepad. "Miss Faust, did you introduce her to Reverend Caldwell?"

"Pardon me?"

"Did you introduce Diamond to Reverend Caldwell?"

"No." Lynnette placed her hands on her hips and leaned in toward Dupree. "They met during the altar call. Jack pointed her out to me. I've already gone over this with the detective."

Dupree drew a line underneath the last entry in his notebook and began writing.

"Miss Faust, had you ever seen Diamond before last night?"

"No."

"Do you think that Reverend Caldwell had ever seen her before?"

"I know he hadn't. He didn't know anything about her," Lynnette said, sticking her hands in her pockets.

"Was there anybody else who may have introduced them?"

"No."

"Uh-huh." Dupree glimpsed a white Crown Victoria entering the fairgrounds. "Miss Faust, could there have been someone here last night that had a vendetta against Reverend Caldwell?"

Lynnette's face suddenly turned grim. She shook her head slowly. "Did you see him? I don't know anyone that would do that." She touched the corner of her eyes with a long pinky finger. "Jack had his faults, but..." Lynnette stopped suddenly, when Rod Webster pulled up beside them.

"Detective," Dupree said.

Lynnette turned to leave.

"One minute Miss Faust," Rod said, struggling to get out of his car. "I'm going to need you to come with me."

"I will not!" Lynnette yelled over her shoulder as she continued toward her truck.

"What's that all about?" Dupree asked, as they both watched Lynnette Faust storm off.

"I don't know. I guess she doesn't like me. Forget about all that. Pastor, I've got an assignment for you."

"Wait a minute," Dupree said. "You need to catch me up on some things. Miss Faust said that she gave you the name and photos of the woman that..."

"That's your assignment," Rod interrupted.

"What?" Dupree readied his notepad and pen.

"You won't need to write this down." Rod hiked up his britches over the front of his stomach. "I got an undercover assignment. I need you to check out Mary Ellen Retinoir."

"The girl Reverend Caldwell was with?"

"Yeah," Rod said, giving a wink. "She's really cute."

"You're kidding right?"

"Do I look like I kid?" Rod turned to get back into his car. "She works at the Bulldog Tavern on Magazine Street. She's supposed to be there at six o'clock. I want you to call me if she's not."

"Whoa. Hold on a minute," Dupree said, holding the door as Rod worked his way into the seat. "You came out here just to tell me that?"

"Well, the lieutenant wanted me to get you up to speed. Also, I need to pull Miss Faust in for some proper interrogation."

"Wait. What? How is this up to speed?" Dupree said, holding the door so that Rod couldn't close it. "You haven't told me anything."

"You're tailing our one and only suspect. I told you exactly where she is," Rod said, jerking the door out of Dupree's hands. The door slammed closed. The driver's side window slowly rolled down. "Now, I need you to investigate it. Got it?"

"Whatever." The window started to rise again. "Can I at least review the crime scene again?"

"Knock yourself out," Rod said, starting up the car and dropping it immediately into gear. He stepped on the gas and peeled off toward Lynnette Faust's truck.

• • •

At Caldwell's trailer, Dupree studied the exterior for any sign of a panel or vent or window that had been compromised. He ran his finger along edges; he stood on the hitch to examine the roof. Nothing. Lying on his back, he squirmed under the trailer examining the floor. The spare tire was dirty and undisturbed, still solidly secured to the underside. "Oh Rahab? Where did you lower yourself down?" Dupree whispered, as he inch-wormed his way along the length of the trailer.

"How did you get out, you with crafty intent? From where were you lowered?"

"What's this?" Dupree's voice reverberated from underneath.

In the floor of the trailer, two six-inch wide boards had been pried from underneath. Having been hastily replaced, light from the bathroom could be seen along the side of one board. A brand new two-inch wide slat had been placed perpendicular to the two six-inch boards and screwed into the underside of the flooring to secure them to the bottom of the trailer. When the boards were initially pried loose, with a screwdriver or small crowbar, small splinters had been flicked up along the edge. The light beige, needle sharp points had no road wear, no dirt.

Pulling himself up on his elbows, Dupree could see that several of the splintered edges were bent over, as if it had scraped along something.

"Or someone."

He moved as close as possible, being careful not to actually touch the evidence. If the splinters weren't so tiny, he might even be able to smell them emitting a fine pine odor. The tips of a few the splinters were stained a light brown.

"Blood."

CHAPTER 19

Rod Webster placed his laptop on the metal table in the middle of Interrogation Room #2. Having become completely disheveled in the trip from his cubicle, he straightened his pants and shirt sleeves. He centered his badge, which hung on a lanyard around his neck, on top of his tie that ran down the center of his massive belly.

"Miss Faust, you know this will be recorded."

"Okay."

Lynnette Faust fidgeted in the hard metal chair. With her arms crossed in front of her, her fingers constantly drummed against her triceps. She wore a blue/green flannel shirt, which made her eyes look dark. The slim cut blue jeans made her legs seem freakishly long.

"Did anyone that worked for Reverend Caldwell hold a grudge?"

"I don't think so."

"Do I need to interrogate the rest of your crew?"

"That's your call."

"Could someone have been hiding in the trailer and left after you entered? Could someone that, perhaps, worked for you, have slipped out, back into the workforce, sort of hiding in plain sight?"

"Maybe. When I found Jack, I left to call 911," Lynnette said. "No. I don't see how that could have happened. I didn't leave the outside of the trailer. I waited there until the ambulance arrived. I wanted to make sure they knew where to go. So, no. No one left the trailer after I entered."

A long pause followed as Rod typed several sentences into his investigation file.

"Miss Faust, are you aware that you are the beneficiary of a life insurance policy?"

"Yes. I believe it was for $250,000." Lynnette uncrossed her legs and sat forward. "Certainly you don't think I would kill Jack for a measly $250,000?"

"Measly? Our records show that you make $105,000 per year."

"Plus benefits," Lynnette said. "That's less than three years of pay. Like I said, measly."

"Do you stand to inherit anything from Reverend Caldwell?"

"I doubt it. He has a daughter. I assume it'll all go to her."

Rod continued to type notes. He stretched his hands.

"Miss Faust, you said you were not romantically involved with Reverend Caldwell."

"That's right."

"That's not what my investigation has discovered. According to several people working for you, there were many nights that you and Reverend Caldwell shared a room."

"That doesn't mean it was romantic."

Rod gave a questioning look.

"Jack and I fooled around a little bit. We enjoyed each other's company, but there was nothing "romantic" between us. He liked other women, much more than me."

"Did that hurt your feelings?"

"Oh yes," Lynnette said. "That's why after six years of screwing him and him screwing others, I decided to go ahead and kill him. Look, detective, you're barking up the wrong tree. I didn't kill Jack. I loved him. I needed him. You need to find Diamond. I'm sure that she either did it, or knows who did."

"I found her and she's not Diamond. The girl you pointed out as Diamond was a young lady that was there to rob Caldwell."

"But…"

"…and she did a pretty good job," Rod said. "She admitted to stealing a gold cross worth $300 and $800 in cash. Would you like to press charges?"

"I…what are you talking about? So who is Diamond?"

"We don't know if there is a Diamond at all."

"Yes, Miss Tessy said…Diamond would be…so when did the girl from the revival leave?"

"She claims she left before the revival was over. She also said she had to flee earlier than she wanted because someone else was coming into the trailer—a tall blonde."

"So that's Diamond."

"It wasn't you, was it?"

"For Christ's sake, no!" Lynnette yelled. "Have you thought for even one second that she's lying to you?"

"Yeah," Rod said. "But like I say, she's got an alibi for the time of the murder. So Miss Faust, did you ever see anyone actually enter Caldwell's trailer? At any time last night, did you see someone other than Reverend Caldwell in his trailer?"

"I did not." Lynnette sat back and crossed her legs again. She placed her arms behind her head and smiled. "You know I have an alibi too. Jack's not the only one that likes to hook-up with new born Christians."

"Perhaps, you should tell me about it."

• • •

The door to Interrogation Room #2 slammed behind Rod Webster and shook the entire hallway. Mancini was left behind to make sure Lynnette Faust found her way out of the precinct. Rod moved quickly through the tight corridor ready to bowl over anyone that stepped into his path.

Making the corner, he was stopped dead in his tracks—Lieutenant Frye and his 5' 6" frame was a wall that Webster's 350 pounds could not move.

"Webster!"

"Not now Lieutenant," Rod said, rolling his eyes toward the ceiling and breathing heavily through his flared nostrils. "Please, just not right now."

"Oh, what's wrong Detective?" the lieutenant asked, poking a tiny finger into the center of Webster's massive stomach. He stared up at his subordinate with beady, dark eyes. "Did your interrogation not go well?"

"No sir, it went fine. It's just that I was hoping to..."

"Hoping to solve this murder by interviewing a woman with no motive and a solid alibi? Jesus, Webster you've got to be the greenest detective on the force!" The lieutenant waved his hand up in front of Rod's eyes directing him to look down. "Look at me Webster! Look at me!"

"What?" Rod said, looking down. He clenched his fists trying to get circulation into his hands.

"I'm curious, Webster. What more did you learn?"

"Excuse me?"

"I'm keeping tabs on you, Webster. You just interviewed the road manager."

"Yes sir."

"Again?"

"Yes sir, again."

"Did you learn anything new?"

"No," Rod said.

"And, exactly how long did it take you to get this no-new-information?"

"I don't know."

"It took forty-five minutes."

"Okay."

"Forty-five minutes wasted," the lieutenant said. He started looking around Rod, to see if anyone was behind him. "Where's Pastor Dupree?"

"Uh...I have him verifying some information with a person of interest."

"So, you've got him tailing Mary Ellen Retinoir?"

"Yes."

"And you think this is the best use of this resource?" the lieutenant said, shaking his head back in forth slowly. "Webster, did you get his take on the crime scene?"

"Uh...well...yes. He wants the CSI unit back out to the

preacher's trailer. He thinks he may have found additional DNA evidence."

"I see," the lieutenant said. "Have you set that up?"

"Uh."

"Detective Webster, just when were you planning to do that?"

Rod hesitated a moment too long.

"Never!" Lieutenant Fry screamed. "And, do you know why? Because you've got your head up your ass! Interviewing road managers who you've..."

"Lieutenant. I was..."

"You were...nothing." The lieutenant said, looking as if he were going to take a swing at Rod.

"Yes sir," Rod said. His face became flushed. Sweat formed on this upper lip.

"When were you going to get Pastor Dupree involved with this investigation?" The lieutenant's voice became suddenly very calm.

"I was going to..."

"Right now! Do you understand, Webster? I didn't call this guy all the way over from Mississippi for the food. Now find him and get him up to speed. Got it?"

"Yes sir."

"Follow me."

The lieutenant led Rod back to his office.

"Close the door behind you."

Rod stepped in; his stomach knotted. This was the first official time he had been pulled on the carpet, since making detective.

"Webster, I want you to get to know this preacher. Do you understand?"

"Yes sir."

"This is a messed up case. I've read the crime scene report; I've seen the photos. I have to be honest, this one freaks me out. So use this guy, Dupree. From everything I've been told, he's a good guy."

"Yes sir."

"I'm serious. Three months ago he took a couple of bullets."

"Okay."

"And one other thing..." the lieutenant's voice dropped in tone. "He's also a widower."

"Sir I..."

"All I'm saying, Webster, is to use the resources that have been given to you." The lieutenant walked up next to him. He directed Rod to turn toward the door. "Use him, and keep me informed. Okay?"

"Yes sir."

"Now get," he said, directing Rod out of the office. "...and send Singleton in here."

"Yes sir."

Rod walked a few steps into the hall and caught Singleton's attention.

"What was that all about?" Singleton asked.

"I have no idea," Rod said. He looked shaken. "Oh, he wants to see you."

CHAPTER 20

Dupree stood on the corner of Louisiana Avenue and Magazine Street, window shopping for a vintage guitar. Although he couldn't even play an "A" chord, if he were to sling a 1957 Black Stratocaster over his shoulder and stroll toward the Bulldog, all the tourists would think he was a dark-haired, brown-eyed Eric Clapton. With a quick stop into the wig outlet across the street, Dupree could turn himself into Slash, or Brett Michaels, or David Lee Roth.

A small town preacher couldn't hide his identity any better.

The price of the guitar made him dump the idea of becoming a rock star. The wig shop was still an option. For fifty bucks, he could transform into a dreadlocked Rastafarian or a mullet donning redneck. Checking his look in the mirror, he decided he would go undercover as a priest. He straightened his collar. No one would suspect him of being the NOPD's new number-one operative.

Detective Webster had given him the title; Dupree smiled. Sure he was being played, but the detective, in his effort to get rid of Dupree, had given him permission to speak to the prime suspect directly.

Walking quickly past Nacho Mama's, Dupree realized that he had shaken off the lethargy that had clung to him since eating the world's largest hamburger. The sun was setting behind him; a cool breeze played with his hair. He needed to wash his face. Stopping for a moment to scan the street, he pushed on the heavy wooden door of the Bulldog and entered.

The place was practically deserted. At the bar a single patron watched Jeopardy on a television above the row of beer taps; to the right, someone was taking a nap with his head on the table. The color brown seemed to be the interior decorators motif. The paneled walls, wood tables, and hardwood floors were like a well-polished employee's lounge at a Lumber Liquidator's.

Dupree took a seat at the bar. The bartender, who was also watching Jeopardy, was seated on a cooler, about twenty feet away.

"What is Sarasota, Florida?" she said, standing.

When she turned toward Dupree and her face was suddenly illuminated by a neon beer sign, his stomach knotted.

Oh my god!

In the limited amount of light, Dupree's mind told him that Sarah was working the bar at the Bulldog. She had gone a little blonder with her hair. But, the shape of her eyes and that perfect nose and the fair complexion and the shoulders and...

"What can I do for you Father?" she said, placing a coaster in front of him on the bar.

"Uh...I...I guess."

"Take your time," she said, heading back toward the television.

Dupree watched her closely.

Sarah's walk, Sarah's hips.

He smiled, laughing to himself.

Sarah's barcode tattoo?

Mary Ellen Retinoir did favor his wife, when his wife was nineteen. Dupree studied the beer taps behind the bar.

"Okay Padre, what can I get for you?" she asked, returning when the show went to commercial.

"I'll just take a Coke."

"Coke it is. Are you going to eat?"

"I don't think so."

She poured the Coke and set it on the coaster.

"How much?' Dupree said, shifting over to get his wallet.

"Don't worry about it," Mary Ellen said. She took a seat on the cooler across from Dupree and rested her elbow on the counter. "So, what brings a nice priest like you to a bar like this?"

Dupree smiled.

"Oh, I'm not a priest."

"So you're one of those...freaks," she said, smiling. Her blue eyes were accentuated by the light from the bank of video poker machines behind Dupree.

"Wrong again," Dupree said, smiling back. "I'm a pastor, but I'm not Catholic."

"I see," she said. "Can you drink?"

"Sure," Dupree said. "I can do anything—in moderation." He let out a little laugh.

"Anything?"

"Well, no, I can't steal or murder or well…you know the list."

"Actually, I do," Mary Ellen said. "I'm sort of a Methodist."

"Cool."

"So, what are you doing here? Are you from here?"

Dupree took a sip of Coke. Mary Ellen stood and started wiping down the bar with a rag. The man sitting at the table woke up and waved toward Mary Ellen. She ignored him, giving Dupree her full attention.

"No, I'm from Pascagoula."

To Dupree's surprise and his enjoyment, he engaged in a twenty minute conversation with the prime suspect of the gruesome murder of his tent-show colleague. During their banter, that at times bordered on flirtation, Mary Ellen had to leave twice to refill an order.

"Your wife wouldn't like you being in a bar. She's probably knitting or baking a pie back in Mississippi."

"No, she doesn't like to knit."

Mary Ellen smiled and swatted the bar near his hand.

"I'm not married anymore."

"Divorced?"

"No. My wife died three years ago."

"I'm sorry," she said, grabbing Dupree's empty glass and filling it with soda.

"Let me pay for that."

"Nope. Preachers and cops drink free," Mary Ellen said, grabbing her rag again. She started wiping down the cooler that she had been sitting on. "So...what's your name?"

"Cooper."

"I'm Mary Ellen."

"Nice to meet you Mary Ellen," Dupree said, extending his hand.

"Nice to meet you." She held the handshake a little longer than customary. She flashed a beautiful smile. "I needed to meet someone like you this afternoon." She released his hand.

Dupree looked at her inquisitively.

"I guess I needed someone to talk nice to me." She continued to smile as she wiped down the bar.

"Who's been talking mean to you, Mary Ellen?" Dupree asked in a low voice, looking both ways to give the effect of a very private conversation.

"If I told you a cop, would you believe it?"

Dupree shrugged.

"It's a long story," she said, holding a finger up to a patron at the other end of the bar.

"I've got time."

The guy down the bar tapped at his glass.

"Don't go anywhere," Mary Ellen said, as she turned to attend to the customer.

Dupree checked his watch—6:20. He had less than three hours to get to his hotel, unpack, shower, and prepare to meet Regina.

"Mary Ellen...I should probably go."

She stopped abruptly and took a step back toward Dupree.

"Aren't you even going to ask me when I get off?" she asked. Her smile was warm; her eyes inviting.

"I...uh...what time do you get off?"

"Midnight."

"Thanks,...maybe...I'll..."

"Maybe you'll stop by and make sure I get home okay," she said. She gave him a wink, as she turned away. "Maybe, you can buy me a Coke on the way home."

Dupree smiled

"Maybe," he said, under his breath, as he turned to leave.

CHAPTER 21

The sun had set in the French Quarter. The horses, who pulled tourists in carriages through the streets for hours, were in their stables munching hay and drinking water. Brushed and massaged, they rested while a fresh coat of pastel polish was applied to their hooves. It was time for the tourists to sightsee under their own power.

The streets teemed with pods of tours. Haunted tours specialized in ghosts, vampires, and voodoo. Bachelorette parties booked the uncensored history tours, which went into great detail on the different sugar daddies, venereal diseases, and prostitutes. The architecture tours were small.

Jarrell prowled the streets looking for a certain clientele. A middle aged woman—overweight, wearing uncomfortable shoes, always with a friend who was equally as uncomfortable—was the perfect mark. She lagged behind on the tour and when stationary, listening to the tour guide, she removed one shoe at a time and massaged her feet.

Jarrell would swoop in, make eye-contact, and ask the friend if they would like to ride for the rest of the tour.

"Oh, that would be wonderful." The friend usually accepted the ride and offered to pay, because she was tired of listening to her friend's bitching.

Jarrell had struck out on a few tours, but eventually loaded a nice couple, celebrating an anniversary, who wanted to bar hop in a pedicab.

"Where to next?" Jarrell asked.

"Driver's choice. We still have a half-drink."

"Cool. I'm going to take you to Cosimos. They make a terrific sloe gin fizz."

After peddling to the 1200 block of Burgundy. Jarrell dropped off his fare, pocketed a nice tip, and reversed his pedicab. Five minutes later, he chained it to a telephone pole in front of Selman's Antiques.

Through the glass panel in the door, a single lamp illuminated the shop. The door between the shop and Iggy's office was closed, indicating that Iggy had closed for the evening. Jarrell punched in the code, unlocking the door in the storefront.

Immediately, the door to the office flung open.

"What do you want?"

Iggy stepped into the shop, wearing an ancient pair of olive green chinos and a Saints sweatshirt with "Bless You Boys!" printed across the front. His slicked-back gray hair and bare feet indicated that he had just showered.

"I need to use the bathroom," Jarrell said, stepping past Iggy. Through the office, into the tiny hall, between the office and Iggy's bedroom, he made an immediate left into the bathroom.

After peeling off his bicycle shorts, Jarrell finished his business and decided to shower.

Twenty minutes later, Jarrell was clean and shaved. He wore the jeans and a T-shirt that he stored in a cubby in the bathroom closet for cases just like this one. When he stepped back into the hallway, carrying the eight-ounces of clothes that made up his pedicab uniform, Iggy was in his office on his cellphone.

"…I've never had much luck getting a seat at The Carousel Bar. Yeah, yeah, I know, but if you're going to the Carousel Bar, you kind of want to sit at the carousel. What about the Royal Sonesta? The Jazz Playhouse? It's just a block down Royal from the Carousel Bar. No. It's fine. I'll meet you there at 9:00. Okay, see you then." Iggy hung up the phone.

"Who was that?" Jarrell asked.

Iggy was shocked. He spun in his chair to face Jarrell.

"None of your business." Iggy looked Jarrell up and down. "You know this isn't your own personal hotel. You can shower at your place."

Jarrell walked past Iggy into the shop. Grabbing the broom leaning in the corner, he swept the entire shop in a few minutes. He listened to Iggy make a couple more phone calls. As he rotated the candles on the main display, to ensure that all the images faced forward, he noticed the gold cross. It was resting on the green felt bag. Picking it up, he flipped it over and read the sticker price.

"$825," he said, loud enough for Iggy to hear. "You've got to be kidding me."

He heard Iggy jump up from his office chair.

"Give me that." Iggy snatched it from Jarrell.

"I see it's back," Jarrell said, returning to straightening the candles. "Where are the grapevine crosses?"

"None of your business."

"I'm just asking, because normally you display…"

"Don't you have somewhere to be?"

"I thought I owed you an hour for leaving early on Thursday?"

"You're good," Iggy said, placing the gold cross back on its green felt bag. "Just don't be late on Monday." He returned to his office. "I got a salvage shipment coming in from a burned out warehouse in Seville. I'm going to need help filtering through all of it. Now scram!"

• • •

Diamond Olivet stood in front of Selman's Antiques. Staring at the front door with one eye closed, she searched for the perfect place to apply her knuckles that would hurt the least and make the most noise.

She chose the glass window.

She reread the text from Miss Tessy, as she waited for Iggy to open the door.

"Sweetie, the package is at Selman's like you requested. I wasn't able to get you a room at the Sheraton. You're in room #515 at the Royal Sonesta. Talk to Mickey at Pat O's to meet your date. Good luck. BTW, it's $500."

"You look wasted," Iggy said, as he answered the door.

"I'm not," Diamond said, looking down at her feet. "You worry too much."

"You know, you can't come in if you're wasted. I'm not going to..."

"I'm clean, Iggy!" Diamond moved Iggy to the side with the back of her hand and stepped into the shop. She stumbled and caught her balance on the counter.

"You're stumbling around like..."

"Iggy, please," Diamond said, as she straightened her skirt. "Come here." She spread out her long, thin arms.

Iggy flashed a crooked smile. His slightly taller, much flabbier, frame moved toward Diamond's hard body. She gave him a warm hug. To keep strands of Einstein-like gray hair out of her mouth, she blew gently over the top of his head.

"Is anyone here? I'm supposed to have a package." Diamond released Iggy and started to untie her halter top. "I need to change."

The adage that you should dress for the job you want, not the job you have, held true for whores, as it did for business executives. When Diamond needed quick cash, she would wear the halter top, leather mini-skirt, and spiked heels. Standing on the corner of Rampart and Canal where the traffic was plentiful, she would be picked up within minutes and make fifty bucks.

"I've got a chance at a big score tonight, so I need to clean up," she said, as she dropped the leather skirt to her feet. She stepped through the skirt and stood facing away from Iggy wearing nothing but a black thong and a pair of stilettos.

"I know," Iggy said. "Miss Tessy left a package for you."

"Where is it?"

"Hold on." Iggy looked her up and down.

"Where is it Iggy? Seriously, don't play with me."

"I'll give it to you, but first answer me one thing. Who is this Miss Tessy?"

"It's my employer. She sets me up with dates. You know that."

Diamond waited patiently as Iggy stared at her breasts.

"I mean, what kind of person is she? Where's her office? Where did you meet her?"

"I don't know all that. Iggy, where's the package?"

"You look really good, sweetheart," Iggy said. "I like your hair." He reached out to touch the side of her face. Diamond let him play with it, while she scanned the room.

"I think it's clothes. Seriously, Diamond, who is buying you clothes?" Iggy turned and grabbed a package off of the desk. "Here you go. So, what's she look like?"

"I don't know; I've never met her. Actually, we've only communicated through texting."

"Seriously? So how did you meet?"

"I don't remember," Diamond said, opening the package. "Did she drop it off?"

"I guess. It was left out front with a note telling me to give it to you. I'm supposed to tell you to wear it tonight."

Diamond unwrapped the package.

"I'm going to shower," she said, turning to leave the room. "It'll only take me a minute."

"Are you going to shave your legs?"

Diamond bent over and ran her hands up her calf. Iggy smiled.

"Do you have a razor I can borrow?"

"Sure," Iggy said, stepping up behind her. "Do you want some company?"

"Not tonight Iggy." Diamond gave him a kiss on the forehead. "Can you make me a sandwich? It'll take me about twenty minutes."

"All I've got is peanut butter."

"That's fine."

As Diamond showered and prepared for her date, Iggy made a peanut butter and jelly sandwich and poured a glass of milk with ice. He pulled Diamond's cellphone from her purse, entered the password (which was 1234), and read the message sent to Diamond from Miss Tessy.

Room #515 at the Royal Sonesta.

• • •

Iggy locked the door to Selman's Antiques behind Diamond Olivet as she left for her date at Pat O'Brien's. Moving quickly through the shop, he took a seat at his desk and dialed Lynnette Faust.

"Hey Iggy, what's up?"

"Lynnette, I can't…just…I can't stop thinking about you. I can't stop thinking about that night in Houston. Was I wrong? Was that not what I thought it was…"

"Iggy! Stop. Iggy, it was fine. Why is this coming up now?"

"I was thinking…I was wanting more…than just sharing a drink," Iggy said, sitting back and looking up at the ceiling. He pointed up to toward heaven and just went for it. "I got a room at the Royal Sonesta. I want you to spend the night with me."

A long pause followed.

"Lynnette?"

"Iggy…we'll see."

Iggy pumped his fist and spun his chair 360 degrees.

"See you at 9:00?" Iggy asked. "One drink?"

"Yeah. One drink."

"… and you'll stay?"

"We'll see."

Iggy hung up the phone and immediately searched his web browser for the Royal Sonesta Hotel in New Orleans. Punching the "call" button, he waited through three rings for an answer.

"Royal Sonesta New Orleans, how may I direct your call?"

"Reservations," Iggy said, smiling.

CHAPTER 22

Darkness fell heavily in the Lower Garden District. On Camp Street, the oaks devoured the light from street lamps; although fully occupied, every other house on the block seemed vacant. As Regina Brandingham scanned the street from a second story window, she wished that the packers had not boxed up every clock in the house.

After coming upstairs, she moved boxes to make a clear path to the bed and fluffed up the pillows. She refreshed her make-up, brushed her hair, and sat for at least ten minutes trying to figure out what time it was. With each minute, the calculation was getting tougher, because the minutes she assumed for box moving and make-up straightening kept changing.

She watched a car drive down Camp Street; it passed her house without slowing.

"He should've been here by now." She turned from the window and walked quickly toward her bedroom. "Marta!"

It took at least fifteen minutes to do my hair.

"Yes, ma'am," Marta shouted from the kitchen. She moved quickly into the foyer.

"Marta, I absolutely can't be bothered until Mr. Dupree gets here. I've got so much to do up here. Those packers made a huge mess of my lingerie chest and..." she let her voice trail off, as she moved into the bedroom.

Sitting in a makeshift boudoir in the upstairs master bathroom, Regina brushed her hair and fought the urge to go downstairs and check the time. With her luck, as soon as she placed a foot in the foyer, he would knock on the door and ruin her chance to make a proper entrance.

Before coming upstairs to make the final preparations for Cooper Dupree's visit, Regina had pranced around the house for a solid hour in her bra and panties. Marta prepared a few appetizers. Regina placed a beautiful chardonnay on ice and rearranged the boxes in the parlor to allow access to the sofa.

It took at least twenty minutes to do my hair.

When the doorbell finally rang, Regina suddenly felt butterflies in her stomach. Years had passed since she had been excited about meeting someone, even more years had passed since she had seen Dupree.

"It'll be fine. It'll be just fine," she said, to her reflection, as she made a few final adjustments to her hair using the backs of her fingers. She smiled and checked her teeth; she kissed the back of her hand to make sure she wasn't wearing too much lipstick.

Stepping onto the landing overlooking the foyer, she could see Cooper through the front door window panes. He was facing Camp Street with his back to the door.

"Marta!"

"Yes ma'am." Marta was hiding in the parlor looking up at Regina.

"Let him in, then call for me." Regina winked.

Marta smiled and gave a thumbs-up sign.

Regina backed into the bedroom and tried not to hyperventilate.

"Good evening, you must be Mr. Dupree."

"Yes ma'am. Mrs. Brandingham is expecting me."

"Oh, yes sir. Please come in. Mrs. Brandingham!"

Regina pumped her fist a few times and took a deep breath.

When she stepped into the light of the upstairs landing, she prepared to hear Cooper Dupree's jaw hit the floor. Marta was on the ready, to mop up the buckets of slobber that were sure to flow. Instead, as she took a step toward the banister and got her first glimpse of Cooper Dupree, she nearly fainted.

He was stunning. A tailored jacket and brown slacks accentuated his athletic build. The shoulders of his jacket worked with the waist of his trousers to give his upper body a fine, inverted triangle shape. A light blue sweater drew a thousand different shades of brown from his eyes.

As she carefully descended the first several steps, his eyes seemed to look right through her. Smiling, she covered her mouth with her free hand.

"Oh my god, Coop!" she said, regaining a little composure. She hurried down the last three-quarters of the staircase and landed heavily in the foyer. "Oh my god!"

Grabbing him around the shoulders, she hugged him by pinning his arms to his side. She pressed her small, firm body against his abdomen; the fresh scent of his cologne filled her sinuses. He leaned toward her, trying to return the hug.

"Regina, you look wonderful. You really do."

"Thank you, Coop," she said, still holding the hug. "Thank you so much for coming by." She buried her face into his chest. "It is so good to see you."

"Thanks, it's really good to see you too."

Regina released him and held him at arm's length. An awkward silence followed.

"You look great, Coop."

"Thanks," he said, looking past her. "This is a really nice place."

"It's too big. I hate it," Regina said. "Come on in. Everything is packed up. I'm actually moving tomorrow as you can see." She motioned for Dupree to take a seat in the parlor. "Sit, please. Can I get you a drink? Do you drink? This is a wonderful chardonnay. I just got it this morning."

"Sure, sounds good. Let me get that."

"You do that. I'm going to grab us something to go with it. Marta made a tray earlier. Oh, that was Marta. I'm sorry I didn't even introduce you."

Regina could feel his eyes watching her as she exited the room. The little black dress she wore accentuated her hips; her legs were thin and toned. Cooper's arms were probably still numb from the hug that she had dished out.

"Here you go," she said, entering the room moments later. She placed the tray on a box next to the sofa. Sitting on the edge of the sofa, as close to Dupree as possible, she crossed her legs and bounced her bare calf in front of him. His thighs were firm. She held herself forward by keeping one hand on the back of the sofa and turning her torso toward the sexy preacher.

He sat, cradling a glass of wine in his lap.

"Cooper, I am really glad you came. When we talked, I was afraid I had made a complete fool of myself. I'm sorry I..."

"You have nothing to be sorry for." He patted her thigh and went to stand up, but she blocked him by placing her arm across his lap.

"No, please sit. I like this," she said.

A long, awkward silence followed. Dupree seemed to be intrigued by the movement of the wine in his glass.

"It's been a long time since I've had someone here I really wanted to talk to," Regina said. She placed her wine on the floor, while maintaining eye contact.

"Do you remember us, Coop?"

"I do." He kept both hands on his wine glass.

"Do you, Coop? What do you remember?"

"I remember that you were the most beautiful girl I'd ever seen," Dupree said. He moved forward to the edge of the sofa. "You're still very beautiful."

"Thank you, Coop," Regina said, as she moved closer. The words slipped out almost in a whisper.

"I remember that you broke my heart." Dupree smiled.

"Oh, I'm sorry," Regina said, grabbing his hand. She pulled it up to her face and pretended to wipe tears from the corners of her eyes with the back of his hand. "I was just a stupid kid. I never meant to..."

"Regina, please. I'm playing with you."

"Cooper?"

"Yes."

"Do you remember how much we made love that semester you were in the fraternity house?"

Cooper blushed. He smiled.

"I do."

"It's been a long time...since..." she moved closer, raising her chin, closing her eyes, waiting...waiting...

In the darkness of her closed eyes, she tasted Cooper's lips for the first time in ten years. They were as firm and moist and warm, as she had remembered. Ten years washed away in a single instant. Fortuna's wheel had rotated back to the top.

She would reign.

As she opened her lips slightly and caressed his bottom lip with her tongue, she realized that Fortuna's wheel would spin again, soon, in her bedroom, filled with boxes, with movers coming the next...

Cooper released the kiss and stood quickly.

"Regina, this may have been a mistake. I didn't come here to...uh..."

"Cooper, please. It's fine. Everything is fine." She pulled herself up using his arm.

"I'm sorry, Regina. I really am. But I need to go. I've got...."

"No, please," she said, holding his arm tightly. "Let's finish our wine."

Dupree placed his hands on her hips.

"Regina, I'm going. But we can meet tomorrow," he said, taking a soft expression. His smile eased her anxiety that he was leaving for good. "This is just a really bad time. I've got some things I have to do tonight."

Regina nodded.

"I had to see you," Dupree said softly. "I wanted to see you really badly. But I just can't start something...now...I've been called here to do some things and I really need to go."

"I understand," Regina said, giving an exaggerated frown. She hugged him tightly. "I'm just so glad to see you. We'll meet tomorrow. You promise? I'd really love to catch up."

"Of course," Cooper said, squirming gently from her embrace and turning toward the door. "Can I call you around noon?"

"Yes. I demand it." Regina rose to her tiptoes to give him a quick goodbye peck on the lips.

Dupree didn't settle for a peck. When he finally released her from his arms, every nerve in her lower body tingled and her legs were so weak that she nearly collapsed in the foyer.

CHAPTER 23

The Bulldog Tavern on Magazine Street maintained its designation as a bar (rather than a restaurant) by selling more beer than burgers each month. This allowed the patrons indoor smoking privileges. Jarrell lit a menthol cigarette and grabbed an ashtray, sliding it through a puddle of condensation. Behind the bar, Mary Ellen was a marvel of graceful bartending choreography.

After simultaneously taking another order, mixing a rum and coke, and grabbing a pitcher from the beer cooler with her free hand, she quickly spun around to place the rum back on the top shelf, tilt the pitcher under the correct tap and jerk the handle towards her.

"...and your name?"

She kicked the door to the beer cooler closed and set the pitcher upright under the tap and let it flow. She marked the tab as she took the next order—an Abita Amber.

"Draft?"

No, the customer wanted it in a bottle. She slid back the glass door, grabbed the beer, and the pitcher, which was now full. After placing the pitcher in front of the correct patron, she immediately reached into her back pocket and retrieved her bottle opener.

"Do you want to start a tab?"

She popped the top and placed the beer on the bar.

"Sure."

Taking the credit card, she placed it in the box behind the register and wrote the name on the clipboard. She smiled at Jarrell.

"You need anything?" She grabbed his cigarette.

"I'm good."

Blowing smoke toward the ceiling, she handed the cigarette back.

"What can I get you?" Mary Ellen asked the lady that had positioned herself next to Jarrell.

"Do you have Coors Light?"

Jarrell smiled.

The Bulldog Tavern was a beer bar. They served mixed drinks, but who would think to order one when there were fifty different draft beers piped up to taps right behind the bar? The selection of bottled beers exceeded one-hundred. There were Belgian Wheats, Bavarian Pilsners, and about thirty lagers.

"Yes," Mary Ellen said. "Would you like it on tap?"

The Bulldog even carried Coors Light.

The bar was dark; it smelled like cigarettes and onion rings. The crowd was typical of the New Orleans Uptown scene—law students, lawyers, people who hire lawyers, and heavily tattooed Bohemians pursuing whatever career tattooed Bohemians pursue. Those seated at the bar had to constantly fight those who pushed their way toward Mary Ellen.

"Excuse me."

Pushing in, right behind the Coors Light girl, a guy in a gray flannel suit, tie loosened, wedged his way between Jarrell and the guy seated next to him.

The anxious and thirsty patron cleverly held a twenty dollar bill in his hand to get her attention. This guy must have thought the bill was ample motivation for Mary Ellen to immediately drop what she was doing to wait on him.

"Excuse me miss!?"

Above the bar were television sets that alternated between sports programming and internet trivia games. There was a constant hum of conversation that hovered at a decibel just higher than the XM Radio playing in the background.

"Excuse me!!"

Jarrell smiled. The guy might never get served. He was a visitor, a traveler, a tourist, anything but a local.

With each exclamation, Mary Ellen would take another order from the other end of the bar.

"What is she doing?"

"Tending bar," Jarrell said as he stood. "Here you go."

"I don't need a seat."

"Whatever." Jarrell worked his way from the bar and headed for the front door. He waved at Mary Ellen.

"See you," she yelled over the din of the crowd.

Mary Ellen's work was as meticulous as a diamond cutter. She worked down the bar, from the beer cooler toward the front door, and then she started over. The suit waving the twenty was unlucky. He had approached the signal light, right when it changed to yellow—now he would have to wait the longest time possible to be served. Perhaps, if he waved a twenty and a five, she might be inclined to stop and take his order. But then the diamond would be flawed—it was best to stick with the routine.

Work down the bar toward the door; give Sal another Nola Blanc. Sal was always planted in the last seat at the bar. He timed his drafts to match Mary Ellen's work flow.

After two quick squirts of anti-bacterial hand sanitizer, she strolled back to the other end of the bar.

"What can I get you?"

"It's about time," gray flannel said. "What do you recommend in a hefeweizen? I've heard the Schneider Weisse has a smooth..."

"What can I get you, ma'am?" Mary Ellen asked the next person down the bar.

"Miss I haven't..."

"I don't have time to talk to you," Mary Ellen snapped. "Are you going to order something?"

"Well, I..."

"I'll have a pitcher of Blue Moon with extra orange wedges, please," the lady responded before the suit could speak.

"Do you have a tab?"

And, off Mary Ellen went, leaving gray suit to sit through the light cycle once again.

Sal was only a short five minutes away.

Cooper Dupree entered when she was three minutes into her

rotation. Wearing a tweed jacket and a light blue sweater, he could have passed for a Tulane Law student.

Mary Ellen recognized him immediately. She waved him toward the end farthest from the door.

"Down there! Yeah, by the guy with the tie!"

She watched out of the corner of her eye as Dupree stood, hands in his pockets, watching the display of a video poker machine.

Placing the Nola Blanc in front of Sal, she hit the Purell hand sanitizer bottle twice. Rubbing her hands vigorously, she headed toward the other end of the bar.

"Hey you, what are you doing here?" she asked, stepping out from behind the bar.

"I wanted to make sure you made it home alright," Dupree said. He shrugged. "I didn't realize this place got so busy."

"Oh yeah. The peak's over now, though. Can I get you something?"

"No thanks. I think I'll just wait out front."

"No, just stay, a seat will open up in a minute," she said, grabbing a Miller Lite from the cooler and popping the top with the ease of a skilled surgeon. She handed it to Dupree.

"You need to walk me home. My relief comes in fifteen minutes."

Dupree nodded.

"What can I get you?" she asked, addressing the suit.

The guy managed to mumble an order and left without leaving a tip.

• • •

Outside of the Bulldog Tavern, the night air was clear and cool, with a hint of soured beer. A slight breeze drifted over the dumpster sitting next to the street light where Mary Ellen had chained her bike.

"I can get that," Cooper Dupree said, holding his hand out. Mary Ellen had been fishing in her purse for a minute, trying to find her keys.

"Thanks." Shaking the keys down, she handed him the one to the bicycle lock.

Mary Ellen flashed a little grin as Dupree squatted beside her bike and started removing the chain. His shoulders were much broader than his waist; his brown cotton pants stretched tight over his haunches. She could see that he carried his wallet in his left back pocket.

"Where did you park?" Mary Ellen asked, pulling the sleeves of her navy pea-coat down over her hands. Although the coat was warm and durable, it looked like it should be thrown in the dumpster.

"I'm right over there," Dupree said, pointing across the street. He placed the chain in the handlebar basket and handed the keys back to Mary Ellen.

"Thanks. That's your Camry?"

"Yeah, that's mine."

"I like it."

Mary Ellen grabbed the handlebars.

"I don't think we're going to load this thing in your car. I guess you're stuck having to walk. Is that okay? It's only a few blocks."

"Sounds good to me," Dupree said, stepping up behind her. "Here, let me get that."

Taking the handlebars, he turned the bicycle around to follow Mary Ellen.

"You're so sweet." She hooked her arm in his for a few strides.

The walk from Magazine Street to Saint Charles Avenue was about five blocks through the middle of an upscale Garden District neighborhood. The street lights were weak; potholes were plentiful. With every seven or eight steps another dog would start barking.

"I have an old college friend that lives a few blocks up that way," Dupree said, as they crossed Camp Street. "She's actually moving tomorrow."

"She's leaving New Orleans?"

"No. She's just paring down," Dupree said. "Her divorce just finalized." He shrugged.

"My folks have been married for 35 years and…"

For three blocks they shared information about their immediate family.

"…and then there's Red," Dupree said. "He's a great dog. I mean he's like the greatest."

When they reached the front door of her apartment, Mary Ellen wished that she lived farther away from the Bulldog.

After opening the door, she turned to take the bicycle.

"I keep it inside," she said. "Thanks so much." She pushed the bike inside and leaned it against the couch. Dupree stayed outside.

"Would you like to come in?" she asked, stepping back into the doorway. "I can make some coffee."

"No thank you. I really need to get going," Dupree said, taking a step back. "It was great getting to know you, Mary Ellen."

"I really had a nice walk Cooper. If there is anything...you know...while you're here and all. If there's anything you need you can give me a call."

"I might do that. So...I guess...I'll see you around," Dupree said, turning back toward the street.

Mary Ellen waited for him to take a few steps.

"Cooper. Do you want to meet for a coffee tomorrow morning?" her voice echoed through the apartment breezeway.

He paused.

"Yeah, I guess so. What time?"

"Around ten o'clock?"

"Alright, I'll call you around nine-thirty to firm it up. Good night," Dupree said.

Mary Ellen closed and locked the door. With her back against the door, she slid down to the floor and sat cross-legged. Giving herself a big bear hug, she almost broke her face smiling so hard toward the ceiling.

CHAPTER 24

Rod Webster's dinner consisted of eight pieces of fried chicken and a half-dozen biscuits; dessert would be the tub of red beans and rice. To reduce the funny looks from the skinny people on the Canal Street streetcar, he placed the enormous mass of fried food in a brown grocery bag that he kept in his briefcase, for just this purpose. Although the unmistakable odor of Popeye's chicken and biscuits could have filled the entire streetcar, it never traveled further than Rod. He kept the bag sealed tight. If the odor did escape, Rod would breathe in heavily, taking all the salty, greasy goodness deep into his lungs.

Rod stepped off the streetcar at Broad Street and winced at the thought of making the two block trek to his apartment. Taking a seat on the bench at his stop, he reached into his brown bag of joy and pulled out a warm, moist biscuit. Two bites—gone. He milled around inside the bag for a drumstick. Pulling it out, he examined the fried chicken leg by looking up at the street lamp and rotating it slightly. The Canal Street streetcar rumbled off. He stuck the whole drumstick in his mouth and peeled off all of the meat with his front teeth. Wiping his mouth with the back of his hand, he stood and pitched the bare bone into the neutral ground. Two blocks seemed like such a long walk at this late hour.

• • •

Rod Webster had wanted Debbie to die at home.

Sitting beside her in the chair that served as his home for the last 16 days, he watched as she struggled with each breath. He grew tired of holding her hand.

The heart monitor beeped at a steady 45 beats per minute. The blinking red and white lights of the monitors and the overly illuminated call button provided the only light in her room. In one quick movement, Rod could hoist Debbie from a sterile, scratchy hospital bed and carry her to his squad car. Lights blazing, sirens wailing, he could be home in 15 minutes. Moments later, he could have her in their bed, lying beside her like they had done almost every night of their seven year marriage. She could simply fall asleep and it would be over.

Would Rod be arrested for murder?

It would be justice. He would deserve to spend his life imprisoned. He was going to suffer a life imprisoned in the memories of Debbie, anyway.

He sat forward in his chair, straining against his confining patrolman's uniform. He resisted reaching under the blankets to touch Debbie's hand. Debbie was so fair skinned and sick that she almost looked Caucasian. The thin hospital issue stocking cap covered her bald head.

Debbie coughed.

Rod's heart leapt into his throat; he quickly stood.

Debbie coughed again and began to choke. She shook violently. Rod reached over her for the call button. A trickle of blood slipped from the corner of her mouth. Rod yelled out toward the hall, as he almost pushed his thumb through the call button. Debbie opened her eyes. They were glazed over. Rod yelled again; a nurse entered; a code blue was called. Rod grabbed a piece of the blanket and wiped the corner of Debbie's mouth.

Another cough.

The nurse was barking orders; alarms were sounding. The room spun around Rod. Another nurse entered, as Rod began to float above the whole scene. He and Debbie held hands, as they floated above the hospital and Canal Street and New Orleans and Louisiana. They rose toward the skies; their hands released as Rod watched Debbie rise above him into the heavens, her dark eyes luminescent and kind.

Rod was revived with oxygen; an alcohol saturated rag was being brushed against his forehead.

"Debbie?"

"Officer Webster, Mrs. Webster is...gone. I'm sorry."

"No, please. Debbie, no."

• • •

Sweating in the cool November air, Rod looked up at his stoop. On his journey from Canal Street, he stopped only once to eat another piece of chicken. Mrs. Groff smiled at him, as he began his assent.

"Good evening, officer."

"Hey, Mrs. Groff. How are you this evening?"

"I'm not doing so well. This morning I..."

Rod drudged past—nodding, smiling, showing little empathy.

"...and wouldn't you know it, he left his oxygen on throughout..."

Rod pushed on through the door. "Good night Mrs. Groff."

"...and then my daughter wouldn't answer her phone."

He closed the door behind him.

Mrs. Groff lived in one of the downstairs apartments with her husband. Most thought she lived on the front steps with her cigarettes. Even in the rain, a passerby could see Mrs. Groff sitting under an umbrella, puffing away, while her husband sat inside hooked to an oxygen canister. The doctors had told her not to smoke around him.

"It's bad for his emphysema."

This didn't drive Mrs. Groff outside; she couldn't stand the old curmudgeon. Self-preservation (and the fact she could blow the whole building to next Tuesday, if she lit up beside her husband's oxygen tank) kept her smoking outside.

Rod had to catch his breath before going up the next flight of stairs. The hall was full of the sound of neighbors. The television was blaring through the door of the Groff's. Old man Groff was asleep, with his hearing aid turned off. Faint rumblings came from behind the door where the kids lived. It was the only apartment of the four that had children.

Although twelve-year-old Lashea and ten-year-old Darian lived there, it was apparent no adult did. The kids were left to raise themselves. Their mother was a nurse who worked nights. Rod had never seen her wear scrubs.

He listened for a moment outside their door. They were fighting. He heard something crash against the floor. The older girl screamed; the fight ended with crying and more sounds of slamming things.

Rod took a couple of steps toward the banister and looked toward the top. He wished Lashea and Darian's mother was home; he wished that she didn't have to work. He looked back over his shoulder and wished that Mrs. Groff loved her husband. Looking forward, he wished he didn't have to climb those stairs.

Taking a deep breath and hiking his bag of groceries up higher, he moved with heavy steps toward his front door. Strained wood popped and moaned under Rod's enormous frame as he took each step one at a time. The chicken couldn't mask the smell of dust, smoke, and pine-sol. The chicken's smell was all smelled out.

At the top of the stairs, Rod looked back down to the entrance, trying to admire his accomplishment. He was not impressed.

Rod's arms grew weak. Facing his door, he dropped the grocery bag and briefcase to the floor. The noise rattled throughout the upstairs landing. His neighbor across the hall was probably watching him through the peephole.

Breathing heavily with his arms hanging flaccid beside him, Rod fought the urge to collapse onto the floor and sleep in the hall. It was the only way he could avoid facing his apartment.

• • •

Sitting at his little dining table with a cold two-liter of diet Coke, he reached into the grocery bag and separated the biscuits from the chicken. He ate like a wolf, pulling off huge chunks of meat and swallowing in gulps. The biscuits were washed down with whole mouthfuls of soda.

Rod tried to stay focused on his food—first the chicken, then the red beans. But the kitchen, overrun with garbage, caught his attention. Bags of takeout food and boxes of snack cakes cluttered every square-inch of counter space. The pantry was open, displaying Rod's food staples of pop-tarts, Vienna sausages, and pie filling. The top shelf was filled with a collection of scrunched down potato chip bags.

His refrigerator contained nothing from the American Heart Association recommendation list. It was packed with pudding, cheese, and bologna. His milk was whole; his fruits and vegetables were in varying stages of rot.

Rod looked up from devouring a chicken thigh and scanned the kitchen floor, which had not been mopped in a month.

"Roaches."

It could be mice.

As Rod started on another piece of chicken, he looked into the den. There, too, he saw evidence that he was living in squalor.

Next to his lounge chair, which was permanently stuck in a reclining position, Rod saw a half-gallon of ice cream that he had tried to finish off before falling asleep in the chair last night. The cream had melted during the day and had soaked through the container, and was now making a puddle of clumped milk on the carpeting. The room was cluttered with newspapers, unread books, blankets, and shoes.

Finishing the red beans and rice, Rod rose from the table and was suddenly exhausted. He struggled into his lounge chair and fell into a euphoric fat-induced daydream. Watching the shadows of passing cars flash across the textured ceiling, Rod accepted his level of suffering. He could hardly breathe and his enormous stomach lifted and fell in sharp, rapid movements. His joints hurt and he was suffering the first signs of loss in blood circulation to his feet.

These minor inconveniences were inconsequential to the suffering he had seen.

Mr. Groff suffered with every painful breath. An enormous weight had been placed on his chest, allowing the air to exhale, but allowing nothing in. His mind was addled from the lack of oxygen and, above all, his wife was rude and unforgiving for his weakness.

The children downstairs suffered the injustice of being born to a woman with no maternal instincts. They suffered at the hand of promiscuity and the false promises of this world. The kids were pawns in the advertising games and fodder for those who devoured innocents.

Deborah suffered. She suffered so much pain, embarrassment, and...

"Rod don't go there," he said, feeling as if he had just taken his last breath.

Sitting in his apartment, ashamed of being alive, hating being separated from her, Rod's heart broke again; his enormous belly shaking with soft, gentle sobs. He placed his hands over his eyes.

Allowing himself to suffer fully, he slowly moved through the pain and grabbed a bag of Bar-B-Que flavored potato chips lying beside him on the floor. With time, exhaustion overtook him, and he fell asleep with chip crumbs littering his chest.

CHAPTER 25

Storyville, named after Alderman Sydney Story, was an altruistic attempt to corral rampant vice into a 20-block section of the French Quarter. Created in 1897, the District, as it was called by the locals, generated much needed tax dollars for over 19 years. The profits from prostitution were laundered into the New Orleans City coffers, through the daily rent charged on "cribs" that lined the streets. From inside, the ladies would solicit men, from every socio-economic background, through doors and painted windows. It was illegal for them to show their faces. However, by showing an arm or leg through a crack in the door, the prospective client could tell if the lady met his fancy.

The idea, that prostitution could be controlled, died with Storyville and the First World War. The District was soon plowed over and buried by the enormous Iberville housing projects. Now, in New Orleans, prostitution was no longer limited by space or geography, it was held within the confines of the Earth's rotation. Although it could be found on practically any street or corner, it was primarily reserved for the hours of darkness.

• • •

Diamond stepped from the storefront of Selman's Antiques, into the cool shadows of Toulouse Street. Thumping bass from a Bourbon Street bar pounded its way through two city blocks of two-hundred-year-old buildings, reaching her brain in muffled rhythmic beats. Directing her feet toward the noise and lights of New Orleans' most infamous street, she walked a few hundred feet before stopping to light a cigarette. She caught her balance by holding on to the trunk of a skinny oak tree.

A pair of legs jutted from the storefront beside her. Lying in a fetal position, covered with a newspaper, using his hand for a pillow, a homeless man lay looking up at Diamond. Grabbing a quart can of Steel Reserve, he closed one eye and took a drink with his head still parallel to the stoop.

"You're pretty," he said, as beer foam slid from the side of his mouth.

Diamond quickly lit the cigarette to cover the pungent aroma of urine and body odor cutting through the dry night air.

"Thanks."

Moving slowly through the French Quarter, circles of light, from ancient streetlamps, looked like giant stepping stones. Diamond zig-zagged from circle to circle, knowing that they led magically to her destination.

Sequins and beads worn by a group of tourists, who were bunched together beneath a balcony, reflected the neon lights from an illuminated art gallery. Their tour guide, dressed like a pirate, told a ghost story with exaggerated arm motions. Diamond hurried past, to minimize the distraction.

Turning the corner onto Bourbon, she moved gingerly through the light crowd, watching the bands of rainbow colored lights that engulfed her.

She took a puff of her cigarette. It masked the nose-crinkling smell of stale beer, Clorox, and trash cans, filled with soured milk and discarded shrimp heads.

Sensing that she was being followed, Diamond began to walk with purpose. Without swaying her hips, her arms swinging in step with her stride, she glanced back over her shoulder every time she needed to hoist her purse up higher.

One good date was all she needed to be set for the rest of the week.

Wearing skinny, tight blue jeans and a teal sweater with a loose turtleneck, she looked almost collegiate. Her blonde hair was soft and touchable. Her blue eyes were accentuated with the barest of eye make-up.

Rounding the corner at St. Peters, she could see the sign for Pat O'Brien's Bar. Stopping momentarily, she stomped out her cigarette and grabbed a twenty dollar bill from her purse. There was no way she was getting in without greasing Marshall.

As she approached quickly, Marshall started circling his finger in the air, then pointed down the street. Diamond smiled. Reaching into her purse, she removed her ID.

"Not tonight, sweetheart," Marshall said as she approached. "We've got a convention of dentists and..."

"I know, the Mick told me," she said, holding the ID with the bill underneath and flashing a pretty smile. "He's why I'm here."

"Well, the Mick ain't the one that the cops are going to collar, if they see me let you in," Marshall said, without looking at her. He was boxing a hurricane glass for a patron who was leaving.

While flashing her ID, Diamond bumped the back of Marshall's hand and, with the skill of a Vegas prestidigitator, slipped the twenty into his hand, pocketed her ID, and stepped through the entrance. Walking down the brick hallway, she glanced into the piano bar. The Mick was working the courtyard bar.

"What's up?" Diamond asked, as she stepped up to the bar.

"The four-top right of Maggie," the Mick said, as he poured a draft beer. "It's the one up-front. There's three guys at the table. Your date is the one wearing a blue suit jacket with a white shirt, that might be striped. If it is, it's really thin blue stripes. Anyway, he's wearing round glasses and he's balding."

"I'll find him."

"I already talked to him."

"Thanks."

"I told him you've got a place."

"That's right."

"So..."

Diamond removed forty dollars from her purse and placed it on the bar.

"Thanks, Mickey."

The dueling piano bar was packed. Several dozen people were

singing, some standing at their table and pumping one or two hands to *"Uptown Funk"*. As Diamond stepped into the bar, she caught the eyes of the three men, sitting at a table near the stage. They all smiled; they all had nice teeth. Diamond smiled back, turned to scan the back of the room, and waved to no one. She worked her way to the back of the bar and took a seat, hidden from the bartenders by a column.

Sitting, smoking, studying the room, she knew the waitress would not ask her for a drink order. It took less than ten minutes, before that same waitress was obliged to serve Diamond her favorite drink—a vodka and Red Bull—for free. Another minute later, she was joined by one of the men with the nice teeth.

Three drinks, a call to his buddies to tell them not to wait for him, and a casual stroll back to the Royal Sonesta Hotel at 1:00 a.m. was all it took for Diamond to close the deal on a $500-plus-expenses date.

CHAPTER 26

Ignatius Selman had no clubbing clothes and, as he walked down Toulouse Street toward Royal Street, realized, no other males had any either. Long gone were the days when men dressed for a night on the town. Fashion was lost to the wide open spectrum that ranged from basketball jerseys to fitted silk shirts, from screen-printed tank tops to bow ties. Men had freed themselves from needing to keep up with trends. Iggy was comfortable in his long sleeve blue oxford with the button-down collars unbuttoned and a pair of ironed jeans.

The women, on the other hand, were still shackled to fashion trends. Walking behind a group of young ladies, Iggy assumed that one of them had gone to H&M, purchased six of the same black mini-skirts in various sizes, and, then, bought an equal number of the same flowing cotton tops in various colors.

When he passed the doorman at the Royal Sonesta, he lamented the days in his twenties when he wore a uniform. In those long, silent days, Ignatius would rise at daybreak and don his simple brown frock and fasten it around his waist with a hemp rope. Stepping into the Jazz Playhouse, Iggy's nostalgia was instantly swept away, when he saw what had driven him from a monastic life. Sitting at the end of the bar was a beautiful woman, waving at him, smiling. He almost collapsed with joy.

A jazz trio, anchored by an upright bass and a minimalistic drum set, featured the complex improvisations of a silver-haired pianist. The music swirled around red velvet, padded chairs and booths. Iggy bent at the waist, to keep from obstructing the audience's view, as he meandered through packed tables toward the bar.

Iggy popped up when he reached Lynnette Faust, who remained seated during the hello kiss.

"Wow," Iggy mouthed, holding Lynnette's shoulders and looking at her from arms' length.

Lynnette wore a knee-length skirt that had slid halfway up her thigh when she crossed her legs. A tailored denim jacket, accentuated her broad shoulders and her thin waist. She had spiked her very short blonde hair with gel, giving her a retro, new wave look.

Taking the seat she had saved for him at the bar, he ordered a drink. For twenty minutes, they sipped their libations, held hands, and listened to the band.

"We're going to take a short break," the pianist said, after a lengthy applause.

Iggy spun in his chair to face Lynnette. His knee struck her thigh. She leaned in and gave him a light kiss.

"You look good Iggy."

"Yeah, right. People are wondering how a guy like me could be with a supermodel." He let out a little laugh. "They're trying to figure out how much money I have." Iggy smiled, as he placed a hand on her bare knee.

"Iggy, prepare to be shocked." Lynnette set her drink on the bar.

Iggy's stomach tightened, as Lynnette placed her hands on his thigh and slid them up a few inches.

She leaned in close and whispered into his ear. "Do you realize you are set to inherit $3,750,000?'"

"What are you talking about?"

Lynnette sat back and nodded.

"Jack Caldwell has left you over three-and-a-half million dollars." Lynnette spoke loud enough to be heard over the bar patrons.

"That can't be possible," Iggy said, sitting back. He searched her face for a laugh or a "psych" reaction. Her reaction was nothing of the sort. It was dead serious.

"Iggy, I'm the executor of the will. I received a copy of it this afternoon from his lawyer in Houston." Lynnette pulled her phone from her purse and pulled up a document. "See that. All assets of "Jack Caldwell Ministries LLC" are to be transferred to Ignatius D. Selman of New Orleans, Louisiana…"

"The assets of a tent show preacher? That can't be anywhere near…"

"The capital assets are about $1,250,000, when you add up tents, trucks, sound equipment, staging, etc." Lynnette said, as she returned the phone to her purse. "But the ministry had over $2,500,000 in reserves, all set in mutual funds and growth investments in the stock market. Jack wouldn't transfer them to himself, because, as part of the LLC, all gains were tax exempt. He planned to transfer the assets throughout his retirement."

"You're kidding me." Iggy went flushed. His face burned. He dipped his fingers in a glass of water on the bar and daubed his face and the back of his neck with drops of cool water. "What about his personal assets?"

"Half to his daughter and half to me." Lynnette grabbed a bar napkin from a stack and handed a few to Iggy. "Which is not insignificant. I think when it is all said and done we'll each receive around $1,500,000."

"But why me? Why did he leave the ministry to me?"

"He liked you Iggy. You might not have thought so. But you never forsook him. The money you loaned him after the Houston bankruptcy allowed him a fresh start. You believed in him, even during the scandal, when everyone else left him for dead."

"It wasn't even that much money," Iggy said, still in shock.

"I know. What's a quarter million?"

"$200,000. And he paid it all back." Iggy shook his head. "Unbelievable."

"When it comes down to it, Iggy, I think, he thought, if something should happen to him, you would do the right thing with the ministry." Lynnette took a drink of her whiskey.

"Unbelievable."

"So, Iggy, you didn't know anything about this?" Lynnette asked, as she ordered another drink by nodding at the bartender who was grabbing her empty glass. "His lawyer said that you were sent a copy when he updated it back in March."

"I never got it."

"Because it was registered mail. You would have had to sign for it."

"No. I swear."

"When the cops get word of the will, they are going to be climbing straight up your ass."

"But I had nothing to do with it. I didn't even know about the will."

Lynnette leaned in close to Iggy once again. "Well, the police are going to want to know who signed for that letter."

"I can't imagine."

The bartender placed the whiskey and water on the bar beside Lynnette.

"Well, they found out Jack had a life insurance policy, for a measly $250,000, and that I am the beneficiary and this big fat black detective interrogated me for almost an hour. It was awful. Finally, I told him I wanted a lawyer, and he let me go. So, don't be surprised if he drags you in as well." She picked up her drink and took a sip. "I can't imagine how much they're going to rake you over the coals."

"When will they get a copy of the will?" Iggy asked, getting the attention of the bartender. He smiled at Lynnette.

"Probably not until the middle of the week. They won't release it publicly until the lawyer gets a copy of the death certificate," Lynnette said, sitting back. "Just be prepared to get grilled."

"Well, we've done nothing wrong."

"Yes sir," the bartender said, wiping the bar in front of Iggy with a rag.

"Can we get a bottle of Champaigne?"

"Of course, sir. Any particular one?"

"The most expensive one you can find."

"Right away."

• • •

Lynnette Faust grabbed her denim jacket from a hanger and a robe with the "Royal Sonesta" emblem embossed on the lapel.

"Up and at 'em, stud," Lynnette said, tossing the robe onto the bed.

"Lynnette, please stay the night," Iggy said, rolling from under the sheets. "I'm begging."

"I can't, sweetie. I want to, but I've got responsibilities. Walk me to the elevator."

Iggy had spent the last thirty minutes being completely silent, watching every move Lynnette made as she prepared to go. He didn't say a word as they showered together, as he rested in bed and watched her reapply her make-up, blow dry her hair, and dress. Even when she stood, propped against the closet jamb, he was speechless watching her put on a pair of black leather pumps.

"Will I see you tomorrow?" Iggy asked. "Have lunch with me."

"Doubtful." She grabbed her purse with one hand and reached for his hand with the other. "We're probably heading back to Houston, first thing."

"Aren't I the head of it now?" Iggy grabbed her around the waist to keep her from moving toward the door. "I'll just say we're staying in Algiers Point."

"Get that approved by 10:00 tomorrow and we'll talk," she said, wrenching out of his grasp and pulling him toward the door.

As they stood at the bank of elevators, Lynnette watched the lights indicating the floor location.

"Iggy, you're a very wealthy man now."

"I suppose I am."

"Do you have a will?"

"I did, a long time ago." Iggy followed suit by watching the floor indicators. The one to the left was only a floor away.

"Well, you might want to revisit it."

The door to the elevator slid open.

Lynnette kissed him passionately before stepping into the elevator.

"I'll leave it all to you, if you stay the night," Iggy said, pleading and nodding his head back toward their room.

"You're cute, Iggy," Lynnette said, as the door started to close. "Keep in touch."

CHAPTER 27

When the clever murder device, with the mechanical advantage, was purchased, the killer didn't need to disguise their intention. At Mary's Ace Hardware on Rampart Street, no one questioned the purchase of four-feet of three-quarter inch stainless steel tubing, four-feet of one-quarter inch stainless steel tubing, a tube cutter, and twenty-five feet of blue nylon cord.

Mary's Ace hardware didn't carry tennis balls. Not one single establishment sold tennis balls in the French Quarter. They had to be purchased on Amazon Prime.

How different things might have been, if the killer had walked in and purchased a blue tarp, duct tape, muriatic acid, an axe, and the blue nylon cord? Apparently, blue nylon cord was needed for practically every murder.

"911, what is your emergency?"

"Well, I would like to report a murder that's going to happen," the cashier at Mary's Ace Hardware would have said, after completing the sale and bagging everything but the axe.

"Can you describe the assailant?"

"Of course, attractive, not at all the 'murderery' looking type. I actually didn't want to call, but I felt it was my duty."

Anyway, because of the invention of the clever murder device, the phone call never took place.

Instead, a young dentist from Nashville lay dead on a firm Royal Sonesta bed. Beside him were the 8" handle, the 8" base, the blue nylon cord, and the tennis ball.

He almost looked comfortable, lying on his stomach, lengthwise on the bed. Barefoot, arms along his side, palms up, he was clothed in white pajama pants with no shirt. However, his head was wrapped in a piece of shrimp netting and his closed, swollen eyes were directed toward the ceiling. The white pillow case looked fresh; it framed his ashen face perfectly. The janitorial staff might have been tempted to leave him alone, if it weren't for the trail of blood coming from the corner of the doctor's mouth.

CHAPTER 28

Pastor Cooper Dupree pushed through his morning run. His abdomen was tight; pain wrapped around to the small of his back. Exercising early cleared his mind and burned a few of the ten-thousand calories that he consumed the day before.

Although Dupree never dieted, he did keep a running tally of calories-in versus calories-out in the back of his mind. Yesterday, he was sure he had gained two solid American pounds, one third of that being a layer of grease coating his large intestines. Meeting Rod Webster for breakfast meant Dupree needed to go all out on his last lap around Audubon Park.

Running at a steady 8-minute-mile pace, he breathed in the cool, fresh air being filtered by the hallway of oaks lining the track. The sun peeked over Tulane University behind him. As he made the turn toward the river and Audubon Zoo, he gave a head nod to a foursome of golfers, who were milling around the dew-covered tee box to his left.

Dupree's meeting with Regina Brandingham had made for a fitful night's sleep.

"Man, she looked good," he said. His voice bounced with each stride.

His dreams were vivid and disturbing. Waking up at three in the morning and catching the last five minutes of a *Girls Gone Wild* infomercial didn't help much either. He rolled out of bed at five, took a cold shower, and put on his workout clothes. Driving around Uptown in the pre-dawn hours gave him time to reflect. Strenuous exercise forced out thoughts that were buried deep in his soul to come out in huffs.

"...and she really wants you," he said, wiping sweat from his brow. "She really does!"

"But you're not like that," he said, in a slightly different voice.

"You're a man, Dupree, flesh and bones."

"Thou shalt not commit adultery!" He said, using his deep, authoritative God voice.

"She's not even married."

"But, I tell you," Dupree said, using his softer Jesus voice. "That anyone who looks at a woman lustfully has already committed adultery with her in his heart."

"I didn't look at her that way."

Dupree started running faster; his arms pumping. His breath was being pushed out of his lungs immediately after being sucked in. He wanted to torture himself; he wanted to be punished for his thoughts.

You looked at her that way!

Dupree broke into a full out sprint; his feet thumbed heavily on the paved running track. He closed his eyes and pressed his palms into his temples, running blindly, headlong toward the finish line.

"It's wrong, man! It's just wrong."

Dupree lunged toward an imaginary tape and ran off the track into the cold, damp grass. Rolling several times, he finally collapsed, lying on his back breathing heavily, staring at the orange morning sky.

With his chest heaving, he held his side and said a silent prayer.

"I'm sorry, Lord."

Once his heart rate returned to normal, he stood and brushed himself off: his back was damp and cold. He began walking toward his car.

It's got to stop with last night.

Sometimes, the best thing to do was to avoid temptation altogether.

• • •

Having showered and dressed in his clergy uniform, Dupree looked out of the window from his booth at the Blue Moon café, trying not to laugh. Rod Webster was making his fourth attempt to parallel park in a space big enough for a limousine. The early morning sun was low; the reflection of sunlight off the blocked cars on Prytania Street made Dupree wish he had his sunglasses.

Located four blocks from Tulane and Loyola Universities, the Blue Moon was frequented by college kids and yuppie Uptowners. There were never any tourists. Rod had recommended the place because of the size of their pancakes.

As Dupree watched Rod extract himself from his car and curse at the passing motorists, he struck a pose by propping one foot up on the padded seat.

The waitress stepped up and placed her hands on her hips. She was a shapely, 40-something blonde, with hair pulled back into a bun. Her expression was stern.

Dupree dropped his foot back onto the floor.

"Thanks," she said with a smile. She took Dupree's order for coffee and placed a menu on the table.

"We're going to need one more coffee, I think."

"Oh, Detective Webster's with you?" she asked as Rod entered the café. "Hello Detective."

"Hello, Carla," Rod said. He was straightening his clothes, as he walked. Sweat had formed on his brow.

"You want your coffee with extra cream?"

"Yes ma'am I do."

"What's up, Preacher?" Rod asked, looking at Dupree in his booth. "You mind if we sit at a table?"

"That's fine," Dupree said, sliding out. "Things are good; how about you?"

"Good," Rod said, taking a seat. "How did it go last night with the girl?"

"Mary Ellen? It went fine. She worked until a little after midnight and went straight home. I got back to my hotel at about one o'clock."

"Great." Rod studied the menu. "The pancakes are great; they're big, but they're fluffy and good. They've got some good syrup, too, but you've got to ask for it."

"I'm not really that hungry," Dupree said.

Carla was placing the coffee and carafe on the table; she positioned the sugar and creamer in front of them.

"What'll it be for you?" she asked Dupree.

"I'm good with coffee."

"Detective?"

"The usual, but make my eggs fried hard this time."

"You got it," Carla said, jotting down the order and exiting quickly.

"So what are your plans for today?" Dupree asked.

"I need to follow up on a few things that shook out from the financials and phone records," Rod said, dumping a teaspoon of sugar into his light brown coffee. "I should get the ballistics report back this morning; the forensics are due this afternoon. Maybe we'll get a hit on the DNA. When are you going to get back to following our suspect?"

"Honestly Detective, I think it's a colossal waste of time. I got this thing I want to track down and I thought..."

"Whoa, cowboy," Rod said. "You need to follow this girl. That's your job. We don't need you wasting a bunch of time. I need you to keep an eye on her."

"Seriously? That's what you want me to do?"

"I'm serious." Rod took an expression that was so over-the-top serious that he looked like he was kidding.

Dupree was lost; he sipped his coffee trying to plan his next step.

CHAPTER 29

Saint Nino's cross is the primary symbol of the Georgian Orthodox Church. The cross brings a sense of penitence with its sagging, sad horizontal arms, which drop slightly toward the ground. Grace flows from its image as the penitent is directed to look upward toward the heavens.

Legend credits the "grapevine" cross as having originated from the Virgin Mary, who gave it to Saint Nino on a mission to Georgia. Having bounced through several safe-houses throughout Eastern Europe, during invasions by the Persians, Muslims, and Turks, it eventually wound up in the Sioni Cathedral in Tbilisi.

"...and then a replica turned up embedded in the back of a tent show preacher in Algiers, Louisiana," Dupree said to no one, as he made the turn into the faculty parking lot of Tulane University's main campus.

Weaving through a labyrinth of red-brick and stone covered halls that extended a mile from St. Charles Avenue, Dupree found himself buried in a depressing cave of weathered buildings. Tulane had curb appeal. Gibson Hall, a sprawling building of rock, reigned over the Avenue, with Romanesque architecture and a strong jaw. Inside the campus, however, Dupree was nestled in a collection of structures that would easily fit into a community college in the nearby town of Gretna.

Walking quickly toward the graduate studies building, Dupree noticed the landscaping that welcomed him to campus had turned into patches of dead grass. The oaks, across the way in Audubon Park, were a distant memory. Students were absent; the beautiful morning couldn't drag them from their dorm rooms and frat houses to enjoy the fresh air and sunshine.

Stepping into the building, Dupree was hit with the smell of academia—dust and stale carpet. Making his way up two flights of stairs, he soon stood in front of an open office with a gold-embossed "Dr. Alonzo Morrissey" plaque on the door.

"Dr. Morrissey?" he asked, knocking gently on the doorjamb.

"Yes, Pastor Dupree?"

Dupree passed through a small, unmanned reception area and entered the office. Books consumed the eye. Buried, in the midst of the volumes, was the doctor, who was apparently suffering a vitamin D deficiency. Pastor Dupree's first inclination was to carry the man to the front entrance and get him into the sunlight.

"Dr. Morrissey, hello. Thanks for seeing me," Dupree said, extending his hand. He took the doctor's grip; it was weak and clammy.

"My pleasure. Please take a seat."

Dupree decided to stand. "I won't take up much of your time. I'm investigating a murder that took place the night before last and there's..."

"The preacher...Caldwell?"

"Yes."

"I saw it on the news."

"Good. That's really good," Dupree said, opening his notebook. "As I was saying on the phone, I was researching something I thought was important at the crime scene."

"The grapevine cross?"

"Yes."

"Why was it important?" Morrissey asked. His tone was calm.

"Well, I'm not really at liberty to say."

Morrissey nodded.

"Anyway, studying the cross, I figured that it was British made, likely in the late nineteenth century. You see, this particular cross has an extended wood screw on the end. I was thinking it was a handle, maybe for a casket. Anyway, it had BSW threads, so I was directed to look..."

"BSW?"

"British Standard Whitworth, it was a standard fastening thread of that time period," Dupree said, referring to his notes. "Anyway, so knowing this cross is affiliated with the Georgian Orthodox Church and being British, I was wondering if you might know anything else about it or, where it might have come from."

"I do," Dr. Morrissey said.

"Really?"

"Yes, Pastor. I purchased them for a display some years ago."

"You're kidding me!?" Dupree said, falling back into a chair. "This is amazing. This is...did you say 'them'? There's more than one?"

"There are four and they're not handles for a casket. They were actually fastened to the end of a pew. Worshippers ran their hands over them, as they entered. This took the place of crossing themselves." Dr. Morrissey sat back. "I bought them in 1997 from the London Parish of St. George."

"Do you still have them?"

"No," Dr. Morrissey said, smiling. He opened his top desk drawer and pulled out an envelope. "I sold them about eight years ago. Here's the sales receipt. I made a considerable sum on them, actually."

"Who bought them?" Dupree asked, sitting forward and taking the envelope.

"A man named Selman, Ignatius W. Selman, of New Orleans Louisiana. He has a shop on Toulouse Street."

"Really," Dupree returned the smile. "Just for grins, is this the cross?" Dupree handed Dr. Morrissey his iPhone that was displaying a picture of the grapevine cross.

"That's it." Morrissey nodded. "I sold all four to him."

"...and this is his address on the receipt?"

"Yes, it was at the time. It's in the French Quarter."

CHAPTER 30

I t seemed a little touristy to meet at the Café Du Monde, but Cooper Dupree was undercover, as a small town preacher in town for a little sight-seeing. The choice was obvious.

After leaving Dr. Morrissey's, Dupree contacted Rod Webster and informed him that he was going to meet Mary Ellen and, then, head over to visit an antique dealer on Toulouse Street.

Rod seemed disinterested.

Dupree parked the Camry on Royal Street. After two blocks downriver then one block down St. Peters Street, he found himself in Jackson Square. He walked diagonally through the park. The Saint Louis Cathedral was lit up like a Christmas tree, with the orange sun barely peeking above the trees of Algiers. The green awnings of New Orleans' most famous café were only a hundred yards away, as he ducked under the limbs of a purple crepe myrtle. A homeless man resting on a bench beneath the massive weed caught his attention.

"I'll run you for a buck," the man said. Haggard and damp, petals from the crepe myrtle were all over his head and shoulders.

Dupree reached deep into his pocket and pulled out a couple of bucks.

"Here you go, friend."

"Bless you, Father."

As Dupree passed, he pulled his wallet out and removed a couple more dollars, replacing the ones he had removed from his front pocket. Exiting the park onto South Peter Avenue, he stopped to pet a Hansom cab horse and make small talk with the courier.

Looking past the giant face of the horse, he spotted Mary Ellen.

He hid behind the carriage, observing his mark.

At ten o'clock in the morning, the French Quarter was just waking. Tourists wore tennis shoes—walking, pointing, sniffing the breeze. Shops were opening; homeless drunks were pushed into the street by the stiletto heel of a clerk. Steel sheets were hoisted from store fronts. Shapely, tattooed girls shooed pigeons, as they scribbled the lunch menu on sandwich boards.

Across four busy lanes of traffic, a beautiful young lady with a thick wool scarf, waited to meet her date. She was a local; she wasn't on the clock. Surrounded by an acre of souvenir shops, Cajun food restaurants, and local art, she sat on the edge of a concrete embankment that lined a garden of magnolias and azalea bushes. Fat, dried magnolia leaves littered the ground at her feet; her coffee sat on a table, just out of her reach.

The cool November had made her cheeks a little pink and clashed with the blush she had applied in her warm apartment. Occasionally, she would glance toward her coffee. The cup smoldered with vapor and aroma; she obviously couldn't drink coffee when it was searing hot.

A seagull perched on the opposite side of the table. Taking the coffee and sipping, she smiled at the bird.

"Good morning Father," a voice said, from behind Dupree. He spun around to greet an elderly couple wearing matching sweatshirts.

"Good morning."

The greeting identified Dupree as a tourist.

In the French Quarter, when a tourist greeted a local, they were often ignored. They should have expected nothing less. The reason people flocked to this part of New Orleans was to watch the animals in their cages, to witness first-hand the eccentricities of its inhabitants.

If this couple would have passed Mary Ellen, she would have sat stoic, content to study her seagull and leave them thinking that she was deaf. In five minutes, this same couple would likely pass another young, attractive girl, wearing a similar outfit and scarf, and not smile at her. How awkward, when this young girl would greet them with an inviting glance and a warm "Good morning!"

People in the Quarter reacted in the exact opposite way as expected. Friendly to the easterners and distant to the midwesterners, they would shame the liberal West Coast tourists with their application of individual freedom and government reliance. Liberals were beaten at their own game.

God help the conservatives. If they dared to roam the streets of the Crescent City, these right-wingers were met with a blast of promiscuity that made Sodom and Gomorrah look like Kansas.

The French Quarter was indeed an equalizer. Liberals realized that there was a need for restraint; conservatives discovered a base lust that gave them a non-black/white reason for living. Tourists left with a better appreciation for those that were their opposites, because, maybe for the first time in their life, they were forced to deal with them.

"Have a nice visit Father."

"Thank you."

When they passed, he looked over to see Mary Ellen waving him over.

"Good morning, Mary Ellen." Dupree said, breathing heavily, after sprinting across the four-lanes of South Peter Avenue. He took a seat at the table.

"Hey, you. Wow, you look so official with your little collar and everything," Mary Ellen said. "I think you just sat in bird poop."

Dupree stood and wiped off the seat of his pants.

"Great, that stuff really shows up on black."

"You can sit here," Mary Ellen said, patting the concrete next to her. "You want some coffee?"

"Yeah, sure."

"You've got to go up to the window and they'll get it for you. I've got extra beignets, if you want one."

"Sure. I'll be right back."

Returning, he set his café latte, cut with a generous helping of chicory, in front of him and reached into the bag on the table.

"This place is beautiful. I parked a couple of blocks over and walked through the square. Thanks for inviting me," Dupree said, removing one of the small fried donuts from a bed of powdered sugar.

"Be careful with that."

"Why? They're not hot." Taking his first bite, he sucked in a lungful of powdered sugar. He began coughing, uncontrollably.

"That's why. You breathe in and that sugar goes right into your lungs. Take a sip of coffee."

Dupree grabbed his coffee and took a swig. His coughing immediately stopped, having been replaced with his screams.

"Oh yeah, the coffee's really hot."

"It's like lava!"

"Tell me about it," Mary Ellen said, letting out a little laugh. "Mine's just now cool enough to drink."

"I've got a lot to learn," Dupree said, standing and brushing a pound of confectioner's sugar off his all-black attire. Having cleared his lungs, he tapped lightly on his blistered lip with a damp paper napkin.

"You're doing fine."

For twenty minutes, Dupree and Mary Ellen engaged in conversation. Dupree listened intently; Mary Ellen seemed genuinely interested in him.

"Do you guys do confession?" Mary Ellen asked.

"We do what's called a corporate confession of sins during the church service," Dupree said. "That's where we confess that we are sinners, but we don't have confessional booths, like Catholics. Why? Is there something you want to confess?"

"You'd like that, wouldn't you?" Mary Ellen laughed.

Dupree nodded, smiling.

"Okay, Pastor Cooper, I did something, that I'm very sorry for, Friday night, and…well…it looks like I may be in a lot of trouble. I would like to be forgiven for that horrible mistake."

"If I may ask." Dupree sat forward, placing his elbows on his thighs and clasping his hands, as if he were preparing to pray. "Is this thing you did, something that you do often and you just got caught or called out for it?"

"I don't..."

"I guess, what I'm asking, is this thing, that you're sorry for, something you will do again and again. Is this a lifestyle choice? For instance, and just as an example, if you were a prostitute, and you suffered consequences from this lifestyle and it catches up with you and you're sorry for that, but because..."

"I get it," Mary Ellen said, tapping Dupree's knee. "No, I'm not a prostitute." She laughed. "That's just icky."

"That's not what I really..."

"No, no. I know." Mary Ellen laughed. "What I did Friday, is not a lifestyle choice. It was a stupid thing I did and I wish I never got involved. But I did it, and well, I'm sorry and I will never do anything likc it again."

"Well in that case, I would say you are forgiven and..."

Dupree's phone rang.

"I'm sorry," he said. "I've got to take this. Do you mind?"

"No, go ahead."

"Dupree."

"Pastor," Rod Webster said. "Can you talk?"

"Yes, Gregor, how are you?"

"Seriously? Are you with Miss Retinoir?"

"I am. I am."

"What antique store are you going to?"

"Selman's on Toulouse Street," Dupree said, smiling at Mary Ellen.

"Meet me there in twenty minutes. You're not going to believe this, but Iggy Selman, the proprietor of Selman's, is a huge supporter of Caldwell Ministries."

"Well, Gregor, I'll try. I'm kind of busy."

"Twenty minutes," Rod said, hanging up.

"Okay, is that all?" Dupree asked. "I'll see if they have one. Okay. Take care. Bye."

"What was that all about?"

"Nothing." Dupree took a seat next to Mary Ellen. "Just a friend wanting me to pick up something for him. Which reminds me, I really need to get going."

"Sure," Mary Ellen said. "I hate to eavesdrop, but did you say Selman's on Toulouse?"

"Uh…yes. You know it?"

"Actually, I went by there yesterday," she said. "That is so weird."

"Really? Did you buy anything?"

"No. Just stopped in," Mary Ellen said, standing. She straightened her scarf. "Well, I really should be going. It was nice seeing you, again."

"Thanks. I had a really nice time," Dupree said, taking Mary Ellen's hand in a departing handshake. "Hey, would you mind if I called you?"

"No, I'd like that."

"Because, maybe, we can go out for dinner sometime."

"Okay."

"Maybe tomorrow?" Dupree said, letting a wry smile break across his face.

"Okay, sure," Mary Ellen said. She continued to hold his hand. "I don't work tomorrow, so...call me." She moved closer and rose up on her tiptoes, giving him a little peck on the lips.

"Okay," Dupree said, smiling. "Thanks."

CHAPTER 31

Rod Webster's chair groaned as he plopped down at his desk; a four-stack of pancakes, three eggs, and a half pound of bacon almost caused the pins holding the steel frame supports to snap. If Rod could have eaten one more pancake, he would have found himself falling backwards into a filing cabinet and yelling for the Jaws-of-Life to extricate him from his metal desk, chair, and bookshelves.

Starting with financial statements from Caldwell Ministries, Rod made a list of major expenditures and major donors. He reviewed Caldwell's personal financial statements for odd purchases. He was reviewing the bankruptcy documents from the failure of the "Spirit Life" Church in Houston, when the coroner's report was delivered at 9:30. There were only a couple of sentences on the eight page report that were important.

"The cause of death was asphyxiation from strangulation. Blue nylon strands were found imbedded in the skin as deep as the hypodermis level. The nylon cord used in the strangulation created hairline fractures in the C4 and C5 vertebrae. The metal object found in the back of the victim was inserted post-mortem."

"Rohypnol was present at a level that would likely cause unconsciousness. No alcohol or drugs were present."

"Roofied," Rod said, signing off on the sheet that confirmed he had read the entire report. He tossed the file on the stack going back to 'document control'.

The search for Alana Caldwell Foster led to nothing. The only heir to Reverend Caldwell's estate had married into money, lived in Marin County, California, and, apparently thought that her biological father had died at birth.

"...do you mean died at your birth or at his...but how could he...never mind." Rod said, when talking to Miss Foster. "Thanks for your time. Sorry for waking you."

He hung up the phone and immediately dialed the forensics lab. They answered on the twenty-third ring.

"Yes Detective?"

"Hey, Sandra?" Rod cradled the phone receiver in his shoulder, using his hands to work through the stacks of folders in front of him.

"It's Sondra."

"Yeah, uh...Sondra, have you got an ETA on that DNA for the Caldwell case?" Rod asked, closing the folder containing the bankruptcy documentation. He opened the folder titled "Caldwell Ministries LLC permit applications".

"Actually, we won't have DNA results until Monday afternoon."

"Did you get the samples from yesterday afternoon?"

"The splinters?"

"Yeah."

"I've got them right here. They're going out as soon as FedEx gets here."

"Well, I kind of need them ASAP."

"All I can do is get them on the FedEx truck."

"Thanks."

Rod read a loan application that indicated Caldwell Ministries had a lien against its tent. The lien holder was a New Orleans resident named Ignatius W. Selman.

"Occupation: Proprietor of Selman's Antiques and Relics, Toulouse Street." Rod read aloud. "Huh." He dialed Cooper Dupree.

"Dupree."

"Pastor, can you talk?"

"Yes, Gregor, how are you?" Rod shook his head; Dupree was taking this undercover thing way too seriously.

"Seriously? You must be with Miss Retinoir."

"I am. I am."

"What antique store were you going to?"

"Selman's on Toulouse," Dupree said.

"Meet me there in twenty minutes," Rod said, standing.

• • •

In 1803, there were thirteen hundred free blacks in the City of New Orleans. In seven years, the number would explode to over 10,000, outnumbering their free white neighbors by three-to-one. To accommodate the massive influx, the best architects of Port-au-Prince, Haiti—the home town of most of the new inhabitants—were conscripted to address the demands.

The shotgun shack was their answer.

Brilliantly modeled after their hometown shanties, the design held the width of the house to less than 30 feet, setting the property tax at the lowest the city would levy. Porch, living room, bedroom, then kitchen were aligned in a single line, as straight as the barrel of a shotgun. This was not, however, the actual origin of the name.

"To-gun", the West African Fon word meaning 'place-of-assembly', was quickly Americanized into "Shotgun". It was immortalized into folklore, when police realized they could clear out an entire house with a single shotgun blast through the front door.

After circling the block at Toulouse Street for a third time, Rod Webster turned into a parking garage. Lieutenant Frye would just have to deal with it.

The automobile was the downfall of the shotgun shack. With no place for a driveway, curbside parking was all that was available. The advent of the two-car family forced many urbanites into the suburbs of Metairie, Lakeview, and New Orleans East.

Stepping onto Toulouse Street, Rod hiked up his pants and wiped a bead of sweat from his brow with the sleeve of his suit coat. Cooper Dupree rounded the corner at the other end of the block.

"Dupree!" he yelled, waving a giant paw above his head and drawing the attention of everyone else on the block.

Spotting the detective, Dupree started jogging toward him. Rod smiled; Dupree was so green. No one runs in the French Quarter, unless they were being chased.

Especially not a priest.

"Hey, detective." He was not the least bit winded.

Rod turned him around. "This way."

Walking back toward Selman's Antiques, Rod decided to relieve Dupree of his undercover duties.

"How did your meeting with Miss Retinoir go?"

"Good, we just met for a minute."

You really should let him off the hook.

"I'm supposed to call her later about getting together tomorrow."

"I don't know," Rod said, instantly changing his mind. They stopped in front of their final destination. "I might need you to keep closer tabs than that."

"Whatever," Dupree said. "So, what's the deal with this?" He pointed at Selman's Antiques with his thumb. "You know I wanted to talk to Selman about the…"

"You didn't say anything about Ignatius Selman. You just said an antique shop on Toulouse."

"Yeah, Selman purchased the grapevine cross that we found at Caldwell's. He bought a set of them from a professor at Tulane about eight years ago and I was…"

"How did you find that out?"

"God told me," Dupree said, smiling. "No. Actually, I lucked out. I found the grapevine cross on the internet and then tracked it down to the only person in New Orleans that would be remotely interested in it and…voila! I came up with Selman's Antiques. So why do you want to talk to Selman?"

"He's bankrolled Caldwell Ministries in the past. And, I found recent phone calls from Caldwell to this shop."

"Huh," Dupree said, pulling a notebook from his back pocket. "Bankrolling." Dupree wrote a few notes. "What's that about?"

"I guess we'll find out," Rod said, pushing on the door.

Stepping into the shop, Rod immediately realized that Dupree was not going to be able to follow him. Junk and crap were stacked to the rafters; nothing was immediately identifiable. The mass of metal and cloth and paper and glass looked like the living room of a classic hoarder. The dominant color was fifty shades of beige; dust covered every exposed surface.

"Hello!" Rod yelled toward the back of the house/shop. "You better stay there," he said, back toward Dupree who was holding the door open.

"One minute." A voice came from the back.

"Look at this place," Rod said, shifting to the side. He was careful not to knock over a stack of framed icons that were teetering on the edge of the counter.

"Can I help you?" the man said, stepping into the shop.

"Looking for Ignatius Selman."

"You got him."

"Mr. Selman, we're with the NOPD and I was wondering if we could have a minute of your time."

"Of course," Iggy said, stepping through the shop and directing Rod outside with a head nod.

The three took up positions on the sidewalk in front of the store.

"Morning Father," Iggy said, toward Dupree.

"Good morning, Cooper Dupree," he said, extending his hand.

"I'm Detective Rod Webster, Mr. Selman. I wanted to ask you about your relationship with Reverend Jack Caldwell."

"That's what this is about?" Iggy said, nodding slowly. "Relationship? None, never met the man."

"Really, our records show that you were a big supporter of his ministries."

"I helped out from time to time," Iggy said. "But, that doesn't mean I ever met him."

"You loaned him $212,500 a few months after he went bankrupt?"

"Sounds right."

"Why?"

"Let's just say I want to "promote the kingdom"."

"Uh-huh…and you've never met him?" Rod made another entry in his notebook. "Records show he called you, a week ago Thursday."

"I talk to him on the phone. I've been to his revivals. But, that doesn't mean I ever met him."

"Uh-huh."

"I liked the way he preached," Iggy said. "I watched him all the time when he was on television back in Houston."

"That was five years ago. Our records show that you gave him $35,000 just last month."

"*Loaned* him $35,000. Big difference," Iggy said. He looked over at Dupree. "I guess you want some of that action."

"What? Uh...no."

"Talk to me, Mr. Selman." Rod waved his hand in front of Iggy's face.

"What's he here for?"

"Well, sir," Dupree said. "I was curious about the grapevine crosses you purchased from Dr. Morrissey. Do you remember them?"

"Of course," Iggy said. "I was actually reminded of them yesterday. A young girl came in here and pawned the cross that was with them."

"Come again," Rod said.

"I sold the four grapevine crosses, the ones I purchased from Dr. Morrissey, to Caldwell, along with the one the girl pawned yesterday," Iggy said. He brushed a mass of gray hair from his face. "I got $12,000 for them. Caldwell probably just used part of the $35,000 I loaned him. But what do I care? I'm making money on both ends. He always paid me back, with interest. Now he's dead...I wonder how long it's going to take to get my $35,000 back now?"

"No clue," Rod said. "This girl you referred to..."

"Yesterday, a girl came in with the brass one. I bought it back for $300. It's worth at least $850. Anyway, I asked her about the grapevine crosses. She didn't know anything about them. Said she found the brass cross—found." Iggy shrugged.

"This girl, what did she look like?" Rod asked.

"Blonde, young, maybe twenty, pretty. She was on a bike," Iggy said, looking around. "She was wearing one of those peasant dresses."

Rod looked over at Dupree who was shaking his head.

"Mary Ellen told me she came by here yesterday," Dupree said, toward Rod. "Can I look at the cross you purchased yesterday?"

"Sure, let me..."

"Mr. Selman, the money that you gave Caldwell Ministries," Rod said, taking back the questioning.

"Loaned."

"It's just...odd. Are you sure there wasn't any...I mean, you weren't in some way compelled to loan the money for reasons other than 'promoting the Kingdom?'" Rod watched Iggy's reaction closely.

"No, detective. I just liked the man's work. And he always paid back his loans. Now, do you want to see the cross?"

Rod's phone rang. He held his finger up to hold Iggy.

"Yes sir," Rod said, taking a serious tone. He covered his other ear with his notebook, turning away from Dupree to get some privacy. "I see. Yes sir. We're heading that way." He stuffed the phone in his pocket. "We've got to go."

"But I thought we..."

"We've got to go! Now!" Rod snapped, stepping past Dupree.

"Where?"

"Two blocks over at the Royal Sonesta, there's been another one."

CHAPTER 32

Soft music surrounded Regina; she took Dupree into her arms. He was shirtless. Moving to kiss her, he caressed her stomach as his hand moved gently lower. As their lips touched, the back of his fingers slid under the elastic of her panties. Regina let out a soft sigh.

"Cooper, it's been so—beep, beep, beep,"

She raised her voice to cover the annoying noise that overpowered the ballad floating around the bedroom.

"Coop, I've missed you, please don't—beep, beep, beep."

When Dupree slid down the sheets to kiss her neck, the beeping became maddening.

"Cooper!" Regina yelled, as she awoke quickly and sat bolt upright in bed. "Marta!"

Regina rolled out of bed and grabbed a robe. Stepping into the hall, she yelled down toward the foyer.

"Marta, what is that noise?"

Marta hurried in from the kitchen, dodging boxes that had been shoved toward the front door. "Mrs. Brandingham, that is the moving truck."

"When will it stop? Oh my god, I cannot listen to that all day."

"No ma'am, it only makes that noise when the truck is backing up. It will stop soon."

Sure enough, it stopped just as Regina Brandingham fell back into bed and covered her head with a pillow. She groaned.

Skipping a shower, Regina did the minimum of morning preparation, opting against any make-up. She put on a pair of old Levi's jeans, a gray thermal top, and a flannel shirt. When Marta laid out her work clothes, she must have wanted her employer to look like a lumberjack.

No sooner had Regina stripped the bed than a knock came at her bedroom door.

"Come in."

"Excuse us ma'am, we need to load the mattresses," a young man said. He looked small to be lifting such a large item. His partner was twice his size.

Regina threw the sheets in the hamper with her dirty clothes and robe.

"Marta has some drinks and snacks for you. Watch your back," Regina said, backing away from the men.

"Yes ma'am. Thanks."

Regina followed them out of the room. In the kitchen, she took a seat on the counter and bumped her socked feet against the cabinet below. The kitchen table was gone. The sun was bright; the movers were getting louder, as the empty rooms began to amplify every sound.

"Marta, have you seen my phone?" Regina asked, when Marta entered.

"Here it is." It was sitting just out of arm's reach near the stove.

Regina checked her messages—four text messages from people she didn't want text messages from and three missed calls from those she didn't want to talk to.

It was nine-thirty and Cooper Dupree had still not tried to contact her. It didn't matter that he said he would call around noon.

Regina decided playing hard to get was for young girls; twenty-nine-year-olds have no shame. She dialed Dupree's number.

"Hey, this is Pastor Dupree. I can't take your call right now..."

"Cooper, it's Regina. I just wanted to call and tell you how nice it was to see you last night and...I was wondering… if you would like to go out for some lunch today? The moving guys are here now and I thought...well...I thought I would treat you to a New Orleans lunch, so call me. Okay? Bye."

CHAPTER 33

Rod Webster and Cooper Dupree were ushered into the Royal Sonesta Hotel through a back entrance that led them through the covered courtyard. The temperature was kept at a balmy 78 degrees, ensuring the livelihood of Royal Palms, bougainvillea, and a blooming bird-of-paradise. Rod had no time to admire the intricacy of the landscape architecture. If he were not rushing to review another crime scene, he might have stopped to admire the varied collection of bromeliads, flaunting leaves of green and red and purple, from their sheltered environment beneath a manicured clump of bamboo. There was no time to fill the eye with beauty; the hotel manager needed the mess in Room #515 cleaned up immediately.

Passing an ornate fountain, the centerpiece of the garden, Rod caught a glimpse of the lily pads and the reflection off the water of the dining hall adjacent to the atrium. The buffet at the Sonesta was a little pricey.

"This way gentlemen," the hotel manager said, leading them through a hall to a service elevator.

Stepping off the elevator, they hurried down a carpeted hallway, illuminated with gold lamps next to each numbered door.

"It's just around there."

When Rod turned the corner, he was greeted by the faces of three patrol officers, another man dressed liked the manager, and the frightened eyes of a Latin-American maid.

"Good morning Detective," one of the patrolmen said, stepping forward and offering his hand.

The maid looked past Rod and crossed herself when she saw Dupree. She started uttering prayers under her breath in Spanish.

"Good morning," Rod said. He made eye contact with everyone. "You guys wouldn't have some gloves?"

One of the officers asked the maid in Spanish; she quickly turned to her cart and handed a pair to both Rod and Dupree.

"Thanks," Rod said. He turned to Dupree. "Follow me."

Rod pulled one end of the yellow crime tape from the doorjamb and let it fall to the floor. The door was propped open with a chair.

"Dear God," Rod said, aloud. Dupree dropped to one knee behind him.

"You know what this means?" Rod asked, rhetorically. Dupree continued his prayer; his head was bowed low.

The first sign that Rod and Dupree had a serial killer on their hands was the optic yellow tennis ball. It stood out against the backdrop of the white comforter. Next to the tennis ball were two 8" stainless steel tubes and a blue nylon cord.

Although the room at the Sonesta was a far cry from Caldwell's trailer, the two crime scenes had a commonality of tidiness. Everything was meticulously neat.

"The bed is even made," Rod said as he scanned the room. He noted that the victim's suitcase was sitting open on a stand, with all the clothes neatly folded.

"This is bad," Dupree said, standing up and looking around Rod.

Rod walked into the room with Dupree close in tow. They moved to opposite sides of the bed and examined the victim by bending at their waists, hands behind their backs.

"Looks like shrimp netting," Rod said. "His neck's been broken."

"It looks like it's been twisted all the way around. What's keeping it so straight?"

"Look, right there. This cord is looped under his chest and it's tied off over here," Rod said, pointing the path of the cord out with his finger.

"There's not a lot of blood."

"No, just this here." Rod leaned over and sniffed the victim's mouth.

Dupree opened the drawer of the nightstand.

"This is what I was afraid of," he said. "Come look."

Rod walked around the bed and looked into the drawer.

A Gideon's Bible was opened to Proverbs 7 and, on top of the Bible, was another grapevine cross.

• • •

The chief of security for the Royal Sonesta could have been mistaken for Rod Webster's twin, except his mustache was much thicker and he was white. Rod muscled his way past the chief to gain control of the only chair in the security office. The two looked like a couple of walruses battling for the best place on a tiny ice floe.

"I'm going to need to sit there, so that..."

"Just load the tape," Rod said, settling his massive haunches deep into the desk chair.

"That's what I'm trying to tell you. It's not a tape." The security chief tried to reach around the detective to manipulate the mouse. Rod pushed himself back quickly and ran over Dupree's pinky toe.

He let out a muffled scream.

"Come on guys!" Dupree said, keeping a string of expletives buried in his throat.

"I need to load the file so that you can forward through it with the mouse."

"Let him load the file."

"Get at it," Rod said, pushing the chair back as far as possible.

Dupree pushed his back against the door and massaged his little toe with his other foot. The surveillance room was a converted janitor's closet that held a desk, a computer, one file cabinet, and a shelf stocked with cleaning supplies. Everything in the room was within arm's length, including the detective and the chief.

Dupree tapped Rod on the shoulder.

"Like I was saying," Dupree said, picking back up on a conversation started on their way to the security office. "She must not have known that Caldwell bought the cross from Selman. It makes no sense to sell it back to Selman. He would have known she stole it."

"Didn't look like Selman minded buying stolen property."

"Yeah, but if she stole the one, she must have at least seen the grapevine crosses. We need to find out if she has the other two," Dupree said.

"Selman said she didn't know anything about them."

"We need to know for sure. I find it hard to believe that she passed on a set of $12,000 crosses for a $300 one."

"She didn't know what she was looking at. A shiny, perfect gold cross versus a rusty old, weird one," Rod said, turning toward the monitor. "When are you going to finish up?"

"Hold your horses," the chief of security barked.

"I need to find out what she knows about the grapevine crosses," Dupree said, just above a whisper.

"Here it is," the chief said. "See, here they are entering. It's around 2:05 a.m. You get a really good shot of him, and this is his...uh...escort."

Rod moved his face closer to the monitor.

"...and here they are getting on the elevator. You never get a good shot of her face, but notice the sweater. That's important."

Rod nodded his head slowly.

"...this is the shot of her entering the lobby a little while later; it's time stamped at 4:48 a.m. See, same sweater, jeans, purse, again no direct shot of her face but check this out. This is going to trip you out."

Dupree bit his lower lip.

"Look in the final shot. As she's exiting, the wind blows her hair up. You see that?"

"I sure do. What's that look like to you preacher?"

"I'd say it's a barcode tattoo," the chief said.

CHAPTER 34

"You haven't met Lieutenant Frye yet, have you?" Rod Webster asked, holding the door to Interrogation Room #2 for Dupree.

"No, but I've talked to him on the phone," Dupree said, stepping into the ice-cold gray confines of the place where so many waterless water-boarding episodes occurred. "He seems like a really nice guy."

"Oh yeah, he's a real peach." Rod took a seat at the table. Sitting forward, he blew the steam from the top of his coffee. Dupree took the seat across the table from him.

"What's he want to meet about?" Dupree asked. The mirrored wall behind him hid an observation booth.

"I think he wants to ask us how the case is going and then give you your walking papers," Rod said, sitting back. He smiled; he looked intimidating in the mirror. His tie curled around his rotund belly like a snake. If he were to stand, the tie would just dangle about three feet above the ground, swaying in the breeze one solid foot away from his belt.

"What did I do?"

"Nothing, I just don't see where you're needed," Rod said, straightening his tie and then resting his hands on his belly. "The death of the preacher turned out to be coincidental. The second murder makes you useless."

"How so?" Dupree said, standing.

"You were brought here because a preacher was murdered and you might have had some insight into the motive, or you might have seen something at the crime scene or maybe, presto-bango a lightning bolt hits you in the side of the head and you tell us where to pick up the murderer."

"It doesn't work like that and I've got to tell you you're starting to piss me off." Dupree turned away from Rod. He watched Rod's reflection in the mirror.

"I apologize, but even you can see that this is not a religious thing." Rod held his pose as Jabba-the-Hutt lounging on a metal chair. "I suppose you think the Lieutenant is going to bring in an expert, crime-fighting dentist to help with the murder from last night."

Rod watched as Dupree closed his eyes and took several deep breaths. For a moment, he thought about sitting up and taking a more defensive stance. But he looked too good, too confident, to flinch. He knew he was in control of the situation, so he just sat tight.

"We're dealing with a serial killer," Dupree said after a moment. "...and we have this Proverbs 7 thing to deal with."

"What about it?"

"Well, I've been thinking and I can tell you there are going to be a total of four murders."

"Oh really, our serial killer...or should I say our lady serial killer...is going to just stop at four."

"There's no such thing as a lady serial killer." Dupree's voice rose a little in pitch.

"Mary Ellen Retinoir was with Caldwell," Rod said. "We've got her on video with the dead dentist."

"That wasn't her."

Rod gave a questioning look.

"She's not a prostitute...or escort. I've already questioned her on that. Besides, I was with her just a couple hours before she's on the video."

"So that's her on the video."

"You know what I mean."

"Sounds like you've already ruled out our prime suspect?" Rod said, smiling. "Honestly, preacher, if I didn't know better I would think..."

"I haven't ruled out Mary Ellen!" Dupree interrupted. "Completely." His cheeks turned a little red, either from embarrassment or from the air conditioning that continued blow ice-cold air into a fifty-five degree room. He walked toward the door, then began pacing in front of the detective. "She knows something about the grapevine crosses, which, in itself, will lead us to the real serial killer. There's a chance she's complicit in the murders. For what reason, I don't know. But, this is not a female serial killer."

Dupree took a seat at the table and placed his forehead on the cold metal surface. His arms crossed in front of him.

"Well, preacher, I do agree with you on one thing," Rod said, sitting forward. He gently tapped Dupree on the shoulder. "This is not a female serial killer. Frankly, I work by the numbers and that's just too weird. But, unlike you, I don't think this is a serial killer at all."

"Why not?" Dupree said, without raising his head.

"Because, the odds are against that as well. Look, there just aren't that many serial killers in the world. It's so rare, and my luck is really bad. I would never happen across a true-to-life serial killer case. So, I'm thinking there's a motive connecting the two crimes that has nothing to do with a sicko, make-Detective-Rod-rich-and-famous, psychopath roaming the streets of New Orleans," Rod said. "So...hey...look at me. What do you mean there's going to be four murders?"

"Proverbs 7, verse 22 and 23. All at once, he followed her like an ox going to the slaughter, like a deer stepping into a noose 'till an arrow pierces his liver, like a bird darting into a snare, little knowing it will cost him his life," Dupree quoted. "Caldwell was the 'an arrow pierces the liver'. Last night, Lovett the dentist, he was 'a bird darting into a snare' with the netting."

"Okay," Rod said, opening his notebook. He started writing a few notes.

"So, if this killer has any integrity, there will be only two more murders—a hanging and a slaughter, whatever that is."

"But why?" Rod asked, not really expecting an answer. "What's the motive?"

"My first thought was he has a problem with prostitution,"

Dupree said, opening his own notebook

"Caldwell?"

"A known womanizer," Dupree said. "Maybe someone in his congregation had a real problem with it. They might think of him as a whore-monger."

"Ignatius Selman?"

Dupree shrugged. "The dentist was definitely a whore-monger."

"So, in addition to putting out the APB for Mary Ellen Retinoir, we need to follow up with a public advisory warning anyone who is thinking about hiring a prostitute that they may be opening themselves up to being hanged or slaughtered...whatever that is," Rod said.

"I don't think you want to start a full scale panic."

"So...the 'why' is simply to punish Johns, up to but not exceeding the number four?" Rod asked.

"That's what I've got so far."

"The lieutenant is not going to like that at all."

• • •

Lieutenant Frye actually hated the work that his new crime fighting duo had done so far. Cursing, stomping his foot, and taking Rod's notebook and throwing it in the trash can were a few of the nicer ways he displayed his disapproval.

Rod and Dupree's ears were still ringing when the Lieutenant took a position in front of the door, leaning on the back of a chair with both hands. During his tirade, he apparently made a few decisions.

"Reverend Dupree, your services are no longer needed. Stop by the clerk's desk and he'll cut you a check for your time and per diem."

"But, I think I can still help."

"I don't think so. Detective Webster, how soon until we get Miss Retinoir back?"

"We've got cops at her apartment, at her work, Whole Foods, everywhere. They're scouring Uptown looking for her."

"The next time you interview her I want to be involved. It doesn't take a great detective to figure out that she is the commonality in the crimes. If she didn't do it, she knows who did. I do not want her released until we find that person. Okay?"

"Yes sir."

"Reverend, give my best to Detective Campbell, when you get back to Pascagoula this afternoon."

"I wasn't planning to..."

"Reverend...please...don't make me throw this chair at you," Lieutenant Frye said, as he exited Interrogation Room #2.

"You were right," Dupree said, as Rod Webster patted him on the back. "He really is a peach."

CHAPTER 35

"Marta!" Regina yelled from the study. "Marta, my bag has been stolen!"

Stepping into the foyer, Regina spun in a circle, searching every corner. The rooms were completely empty; the movers had just pulled away in the giant truck. In the parlor where Regina made an ill-attempted seduction of her college lover, the boxes, furniture, and lamp were gone. The room had freshly vacuumed carpeting. Marta obviously backed out of the room, leaving nothing but two-foot wide swaths of fine-piled carpeting, reflecting two shades of burgundy.

Moving quickly toward the kitchen, she passed what was left of the dining room. The room, with its polished oak floors and single chandelier, was so clean that you could eat off of the floors—which would be the only option, if Marta were to serve lunch.

"Marta, the movers have taken my..."

"Mrs. Brandingham," Marta said, stepping in the back door. "I have your bag. I've put it in your car with your suitcases."

"Oh Marta," Regina said, stepping past her. "I wish you wouldn't be like that. I put it in the study, so I wouldn't forget it."

"I'm sorry ma'am."

"It's okay," Regina said, as she descended to the driveway.

"It's in the passenger seat," Marta said, following.

Regina walked around the car. "It's just that my cellphone is in there and I was expecting..."

"Hey Regina," Cooper Dupree said, walking up from the front of the house.

"Oh my god, Coop," Regina said, thinking she should dive into the front seat. She looked atrocious. "I wasn't expecting you to...Marta!"

"Yes ma'am?"

"Can you...uh...get Mr. Cooper a...something to drink and show him to...oh, my god, Cooper. I really didn't expect you to stop by. The movers just left and I haven't had a chance to clean up or anything."

"Don't be ridiculous," Dupree said, stepping up next to her and pinning her to the door of the car. His expression was stoic; his eyes heavy, tired. He took her hand and gave her a kiss hello on the cheek. "You look great."

His voice was not convincing.

"Give me a break," she said. Even looking rundown, Dupree was the handsome one. His clergyman's garb and those dark eyes were assuring and peaceful. The little white square at his throat gave his soft expression an air of authority. His hand was warm, strong.

"Did you get my message?" Regina asked. She did not want to let go of his hand.

"I did." Dupree moved back a few steps, giving Regina some room.

"So are you free for lunch?" she asked. She turned to retrieve the bag; walking past Dupree, she handed it to Marta. "Can you take this back up to my room?"

"Yes ma'am."

"Would you like to grab a bite to eat? There's a nice place just around the block or we could..."

"Regina, that's why I stopped by," Dupree interrupted. "I'm sorry but I'm going to have to pass. I wanted to tell you in person, and, I guess, I wanted to see you before I left."

"You're leaving?" Regina grabbed Dupree's hand again.

"Yeah, I think so."

"Is your investigation over?"

"For now." Dupree dropped her hand.

"So, then, you do have time for lunch."

"You would think so...but, I really need to go," Dupree said, taking Regina into his arms. The hug was cordial. He didn't squeeze her tight enough to press her breasts against him. It was obvious to Regina that he was distancing himself.

What about last night? What about the kiss? What's wrong with me?

"Really?" Regina asked, pushing back on his goodbye one last time. The word almost got caught in her throat. She felt a pang of rejection.

"I'm sorry," Dupree said as he turned.

"It was nice meeting you," he said, addressing Marta as he started down the driveway.

"Coop," Regina said. He turned. "Call me sometime, okay?"

"I will."

CHAPTER 36

The intersection of Napoleon Avenue and Saint Charles Avenue was a staging area for stranded Uptowners after the hurricane. A twenty-foot storm surge compromised the levee system that protected the city from the waters of Lake Pontchartrain. Upper and Lower Garden District residents, who decided to stay home for the storm, were suddenly blocked in by flood waters. This intersection was, thankfully, a full three-feet above sea level.

The National Guard was tasked with getting the residents out, even against their will, to other staging areas in Shreveport, Dallas, and Houston. So, riding Humvees equipped with 50-caliber guns, they corralled the residents into this intersection and waited for the flood waters to fall enough to carry them to "safety".

Mary Ellen Retinoir was eventually transported to a staging area in Houston, after having spent two days milling about the inter-section, drinking warm bottled water and nibbling on MREs. More than a couple of times, she sat beneath the awning of Copeland's Steak House, wishing the can of chicken tetrazzini was a plate of crawfish etouffee.

Now, sitting inside Fat Harry's Bar, in her favorite booth, hidden from the world passing on Saint Charles Avenue, she examined the intersection. All of the water bottles were picked up; no one was keeping guard in front of the looted Rite Aid. There were no camouflaged soldiers sweating to death, hiding from the sun. The intersection was alive, fun, beautiful.

She looked at her watch.

"Hey," Jarrell said, coming up from behind her. Wearing a T-shirt and jeans, he looked like he had been working in the kitchen.

"Where did you come from?" Mary Ellen asked. Jarrell quickly took the seat next to her.

"I was in the video poker room," Jarrell said. He tried to give Mary Ellen a kiss on the cheek. She turned away, looking back toward the Avenue. "What's wrong with you?"

"Nothing," Mary Ellen looked whimsically at the intersection. She wished she had never been to New Orleans, so that she could visit it for the first time. "Thanks again for backing up my story yesterday."

"No problem. I just told the truth."

"I wonder who did it." She turned toward Jarrell.

"What?"

"Killed the preacher." Mary Ellen slid down into the booth.

"No telling," Jarrell said, patting her leg underneath the table. "You didn't do it so...they can't..."

"I know...but still...."

"Mary Ellen, you've got nothing to hide," Jarrell said. "Listen, just be honest with them."

"What if they ask how this all got started?"

"What do you mean?"

"What if they ask how I knew about the cross?"

"Tell them I told you about them. It's no secret that I work for Selman's. It won't be long before they're barking up old man Iggy's ass and you sure as hell know he's going to tell them I took the crosses to Caldwell."

"Crosses?"

"Cross."

Mary Ellen fell silent.

"Just tell the truth," Jarrell slid out of the booth. "You've got nothing to hide. You want a beer?"

"I'll take a hard seltzer."

Jarrell headed to the bar.

The streetcar stopped at the intersection and a band of tourists stepped off. Several were taking pictures of the streetcar, when it resumed its journey toward Carrollton Avenue. Jarrell returned with the drinks.

Mary Ellen slumped down further in her seat when she noticed a squad car parking on the neutral ground. "Oh my god!"

"What?"

"It's him. Oh my god! It's the big, fat detective that...hide me."

Mary Ellen slid down in the booth as low as possible. Jarrell tried to make himself big, but it was too late. One of the only men in New Orleans that could out eat Fat Harry himself was walking straight toward their booth.

"Miss Retinoir, we need to talk."

Mary Ellen sat up.

"What's this about?" Jarrell said, positioning himself in front of the detective.

"None of your business."

"This is my girlfriend; I'm making it my business."

"Oh really, okay, and what is your name?"

"Jarrell."

"Jarrell Landry?"

Jarrell nodded.

"Can I see some ID?"

"I don't have any."

"...and yet, somehow you were able to purchase that beer," Rod said, turning toward the bartender. "Hey, Mack, did you check this guy's ID before you sold him the beer?"

"Yes, sir."

"Okay, Mr. Landry," Rod said, turning back around. "It looks like you and I have gotten off to a bad start. Now can I see that ID? Officer, could you escort Miss Retinoir to the car? Make sure you get her bike."

"Yes sir. Let's go, miss."

"Now, how about telling me a little bit about your relationship with Miss Retinoir?"

CHAPTER 37

The frightening drive through the buffer zone of Stennis Space Center on Interstate 10 gave Dupree the chance to reflect on his own mortality. The highway was perfectly straight and flat; it was apparently too remote to be policed by the highway patrol. For the first nineteen miles into Mississippi, the scenery was nothing but scrub pine trees and signs for upcoming casinos. Dupree's Camry cruise control was set at 74 mph and, as a semi-trailer truck whizzed by at about 110 mph, Dupree gripped the steering wheel, said a brief prayer of thanksgiving for having lived a good life, and watched as images of his youth flashed through his mind.

Righting the Toyota back into the center of his lane, he winced at the thought of being hurled into a pine tree and the gruesomeness of his closed-casket funeral.

With only ten miles back to civilization, Dupree tried to concentrate on his sermon. However, thoughts of Regina kept interrupting him—the warm farewell hug, the feel of his arms around her waist, the firm pressing of her breast against his chest.

The paralytic's friends must have gotten pretty dirty digging through the roof.

He saw Regina descending the steps toward the foyer. He saw her knees flicking up the hem of her little black dress with each step, rhythmically providing little glimpses of her soft inner thighs. Dupree fidgeted as he blinked wildly trying to remove the image from his head.

It's so easy for us to get dirty, trying to help others. So dirty, that we too become...become dirty with...

He remembered, peeking through gently closed eyes, Regina moving her soft lips toward his. He felt her soften into his embrace. His stomach knotted, as he looked at the passenger seat, and thought about taking her hand as she rode with him to Pascagoula.

"Jeez!" he shouted over the noise of another truck trying to run him off the road.

Steadying the car, once again reminded of his mortality, he remembered Sarah. His wife was his one true love. Regina was to be desired; Sarah was to be loved. While trying to pull up a distant memory of Sarah, perhaps in the kitchen or at a restaurant, an image of Mary Ellen pouring a Coke from the bar dispenser came to mind.

Mary Ellen Retinoir, the prime suspect in a pair of gruesome murders, was being vilified. She was the femme fatale. She was…

The Samaritan Woman!

The Samaritan woman said to Jesus, "You are a Jew and I am a Samaritan woman. How can you ask me for a drink?" (For Jews do not associate with Samaritans).

...He told her, "Go, call your husband and come back."

"I have no husband," she replied.

Jesus said to her, "You are right when you say you have no husband...the man you now have is not your husband. What you have just said is quite true."

John 4: 9-15

Dupree fished his cellphone from his front pocket and dialed Rod Webster.

"Webster," he said, after the third ring.

"Hey Detective, this is Cooper Dupree."

"I know. What's up?"

"I just had a thought. We need to find out more about who Miss Retinoir is dating. I have a feeling that maybe this is the person behind the..."

"I already know who that is and I would have to disagree with you."

"Who is it?"

"Jarrell Landry, the guy who corroborated her story on what happened at Caldwell's trailer. I'm in the middle of something."

Dupree braced himself for another truck that was coming up behind him hard.

"Can you hold one second?"

The truck passed. Dupree approached the Jourdan River Bridge, which was the first indication that law and order would soon be reinstated on the roadways.

"Dupree?" Rod said, after a moment.

"Yes sir?"

"I'm interrogating Miss Retinoir and I'm under the gun here. So bye-bye."

"Detective," Dupree took the Long Beach, Mississippi, exit and slowed to a stop. "I have a feeling that the person she's dating, is not the person she's dating."

"What the hell are you talking about?"

"Press her on the boyfriend. Please. There's something else going on."

"Like I told you, I already talked to him. His name is Jarrell Landry; he was with her when we picked her up this afternoon. The kid's clean so I..."

"So, she's living with this guy?" Dupree asked.

"I didn't say that. He's her boyfriend and I checked him out and he's cool, so can I go back to real work?"

"Yeah," Dupree said. "It's just that she never mentioned him to me."

"Okay, bye now."

Dupree threw his cellphone onto the empty passenger seat.

• • •

Beneath the red, white, and blue awning of the Chevron station in Diamondhead, Mississippi, Dupree scanned the 'recent call' folder in his phone. The past twenty-four hours flashed through his mind, like a whirlwind. Caldwell in his trailer, Dr. Lovett at the Royal Sonesta, two murders in two days that turned out to be nothing more than a couple of sick photographs burned into his mind.

Switching to the Bible application on his iPhone, he reviewed Proverbs 7 for the fiftieth time.

Nothing surfaced.

He started to pray, but lost interest.

Interstate 10 roared behind him with a steady hum of road noise and diesel engines; the cool afternoon air swirled around him, carrying the sweet perfume of gasoline and diesel.

Dupree dialed Regina Brandingham.

"Hey Coop!"

"Hey Regina," Dupree grabbed his notebook from the passenger seat. "I'm sorry for leaving so abruptly. I had a pretty rough morning and I guess I was looking to get home. I just wanted to call to apologize."

"That's no problem. How about you make it up to me?"

"Okay."

"Meet me tomorrow?"

"Well," Dupree reviewed his notes. He placed his phone on speaker and ran a search on "Jarrell Landry, New Orleans."

"I'm staying at the Columns Hotel on Saint Charles Avenue. They have a wonderful champagne brunch. Please, please come. It would be so much fun…"

There were no criminal records, no Facebook page, no Twitter handle. The name appeared in a listing of graduates from Brother Martin High School. An eight year old obituary popped up with the name "Jarrell Landry" listed as the surviving son of a Donna Landry. Jarrell Landry was mentioned on a page of "Meet the Staff" on the New Orleans Premier Pedicabs website.

"I...don't...know I've got Sunday services. I'm not sure if I can make it back tomorrow."

Regina went into a detailed description of her moving adventures, the upcoming closing on a new condominium near the lake, and a lot of other items that went into one of Dupree's ears and right out of the other.

Jesus said to her, "You are right when you say you have no husband...the man you now have is not your husband."

"What's this?" Dupree said, unconscious to the conversation.

"I was saying that I'm going furniture shopping on Monday because…"

When Dupree clicked on the profile of Jarrell Landry on the pedicab website a picture popped up.

"Regina," Dupree interrupted. "I kind of need to go. Hey listen, I'm definitely going back to New Orleans tomorrow. Can we meet for brunch around two o'clock? If that works for you?"

"Oh my god, for sure. Coop, I can't wait."

"Got to go. See you tomorrow."

Dupree looked up and made eye contact with someone who was exiting the Chevron station. The fellow returned his smile with a smile and a head nod. He hid a six-pack of beer behind him, as he passed.

Dupree dialed Rod Webster.

"This is Detective Rod Webster with..."

"Detective," Dupree said, leaving a message. "You need to check on something. I'm sending you a photo of Jarrell Landry, Mary Ellen's boyfriend, and he's standing in front of Selman's Antiques. Please, please run this to ground. Call me."

Looking back at his 'recent calls' folder, he noticed that Mary Ellen Retinoir's number was in his contacts.

She never mentioned a boyfriend.

Dupree dialed Gregor Thomson.

"What…is...up...Coop?" Gregor answered.

"Hey man," Dupree said. "I need to ask you something."

"Sure, are you in New Orleans? How is it?"

"I'm heading back," Dupree said, sliding down in the driver's seat a little deeper. "I've got to tell you, it was pretty rough." Dupree's left arm rested on the window, as he held the phone to his ear.

"So, we're still on for Wednesday?" Gregor asked.

"I think so."

"Oh, come on man, don't punk out on me now. I've been practicing some of the crazier moves on Joe-Anne."

"We'll see," Dupree said. "Hey, I need to ask you something. Remember that time we talked about asking Kelly out?"

"No."

"You said that if she didn't mention a boyfriend, then she doesn't have one."

"Yeah, that's right. Not only will she mention it, she'll mention it within the first few sentences, when you start any small talk. Say you say something like 'Hey Mary, what'cha doing this weekend...'"

Dupree's stomach knotted at the mention of Mary.

"...if she doesn't say something like 'my boyfriend and I are doing something' then she doesn't have a boyfriend. It's that simple."

"Why did you say Mary?"

"What?"

"Why did you say...oh never mind."

"All I'm saying is that, if she doesn't mention a boyfriend, that means she doesn't have one."

"You're sure?" Dupree pushed back.

"Positive. Why? You got someone you want to ask out?"

"Gotta go. I'll swing by later and get Red."

After hanging up, Dupree dialed Mary Ellen's number.

"Hey, leave a message. Thanks."

"Hey Mary Ellen, it's Cooper. I was calling to see if you were available for dinner tomorrow. I had to get back to Pascagoula, but I'll be back tomorrow around four o'clock and if you're available, I'd love to get some dinner. Let me know."

Dupree hung up, tossed the phone on the seat, and buckled his seat belt.

"You better be right Gregor," he said, placing the Camry in reverse.

CHAPTER 38

Rod Webster and Officer Mancini watched as Mary Ellen paced the floor in Interrogation Room #2. The little black and white monitor, focused on the table, would only show half of her at a time. At the wall opposite the camera, only her lower body was visible. Her hips were outlined beautifully by a pair of designer jeans; her stride made the light reflect in brilliant little sparkles on the accented stitching.

As she turned and headed back toward the camera, the view moved swiftly up, taking in her torso. Her hands clasped her elbows across her front, beneath her chest.

"Is that cashmere?" Mancini asked.

"How would I know?" Rod asked, glancing back at Mancini who was breathing over his shoulder.

"I'm just saying that looks like an expensive sweater."

As she continued past the table, her face came into view. Brows furrowed, a pronounced frown, she looked as if she were about to cry. As she approached the opposite wall, she reached over her head and began to adjust her ponytail, giving them a full upper body view.

"That's definitely cashmere. What color do you think that is?"

"Christ Mancini, I think you would call that gray."

"No, I'm not talking on the monitor. I'm talking about..."

"Mancini, I don't know. I don't care. Just let me collect my thoughts so I..."

"Alright already," Mancini said, backing away. "I'm just saying that "if" it is cashmere, then it's pretty expensive and I don't think a bartender at the Bulldog makes that kind of money. I mean, especially if she was going to wear it to work. You wouldn't want to ruin a..."

"I got it," Rod said, as he stood. "Thanks for the insight. Now can you shut up?"

Mancini began to follow Rod toward the interrogation room.

Rod stopped and turned quickly. He pointed a big, beefy finger in Mancini's chest.

"I'm going at this one alone. Got it?"

"I thought Frye wanted to be in there with you."

"Me first," Rod said, smiling as he turned back toward the hall.

As soon as he pulled on the door to Interrogation Room #2, the smile disappeared.

• • •

Rod Webster entered the room, taking the seat designated for the interrogator. He motioned for Mary Ellen to sit across from him.

"Miss Retinoir," he said, slowly opening his laptop computer. "I see you've been a pretty busy little girl."

"What do you mean?" Mary Ellen asked, shrugging her shoulders. She took a seat.

"I guess you don't know why we've brought you in, again."

"I suppose you've found more things that I didn't do that you would like to charge me with," Mary Ellen said. Her voice was calm. She kept her eyes focused on Detective Webster's eyes.

"Well," Rod said. "Not exactly. We actually believe you did them."

"What is it this time?" Mary Ellen pushed her seat back a little and then stood. Turning toward the camera, she walked toward it and pointed. "Bank robbery? Kidnapping? Mary Ellen's on a rampage! She's on a crime spree. Blame the entire New Orleans rise in crime on her."

"Please sit, Miss. Retinoir, and stop the theatrics."

"Drum up whatever charges you can; I confess!" She returned to her seat. "I'll sign them all. But, do you know what?"

"What?"

"None of them will hold because no one person is to blame for everything." Her blue eyes locked onto Rod's. Tears welled up. "I'm not responsible for that preacher's death. I'm not. I swear. And I'm not going to take the blame."

Suddenly a pain pierced Rod's chest. "What?" He massaged his left pectoral muscle with his right hand. "What did you just say?"

"No one can take the fall for everything."

The pain struck again, this time deep in the muscles of his chest; pain shot through his heart. He squeezed his left hand into a fist.

"It's not my fault he's dead!"

Oh God, no! My fingers.

Rod looked down at his hand. He watched his fist clench and unclench slowly. Another sharp pain hit him. He looked up at Mary Ellen in an expression that cried for help.

A tear escaped Mary Ellen's eyes and ran down her face; she wiped it away with the back of her hand.

As Rod's left arm went limp and fell to his side, he could see that she was still speaking, but he could hear nothing except his own breathing—his own heartbeat.

Sweat broke out on Rod's lip. Pins and needles shot up his arm.

It's not my fault he's dead!

Suddenly, the conversation with Dupree flashed through his mind.

Dupree said. "That's a tough year…it doesn't seem to get any easier…I can't get Sarah out of my mind."

"…and you're not angry?"

"No. Never was."

"I don't believe it."

"It's true…as bad as the circumstances were around Sarah's disappearance, I didn't run from God, I ran to God."

"Good for you."

Rod looked dazed, like he had been Tasered. He shook his head in sharp spasms.

"…I took some money…I took that worthless cross…and…are you okay?"

It's not my fault he's dead?

Lieutenant Frye's advice surfaced.

"...three months ago he took a couple of bullets."

"Okay."

"And one other thing, he's also a widower."

"Sir I..."

"All I'm saying, Webster, is to use the resources that have been given to you."

"...do you need some water? Detective?"

Rod closed his eyes tight. He continued to clench his left hand. He saw Debbie sleeping quietly in her hospital bed.

Debbie coughed...a trickle of blood slipped from the corner of her mouth.

"I'm going to get Officer Mancini."

It's not my fault she's dead.

Mary Ellen stood, moving quickly toward the door.

"Wait. Mary Ellen, wait. I'm okay," Rod said. Her words began to slowly register. His arm regained feeling; he raised it above his head and stretched out his shoulder. "I'm fine, please sit. Could you repeat what were you saying?"

"I was talking about Caldwell. You really don't look so good. Maybe you should..."

"Tell me about Jarrell Landry," Rod said, after looking at his notes. Pastor Dupree's request was the last entry in his interrogation document.

"What about him?"

The pain left as quickly as it came. Suddenly, Rod's thoughts were directed back on task. As he continued to squeeze his fist, he stuck his tongue out to make sure he didn't have a stroke. He typed an e-mail to his personal account for reading later. The title was "It's not my fault."

"He's your boyfriend."

"Oh god no. He's just a friend. I've known him a few months."

"He knows that you're just friends?"

Mary Ellen's expression went to a more reflective tone. "He should...but...you know how boys are. I think...I think he would like it to be more."

"Tell me." Rod leaned forward. "Is Jarrell the jealous type?"

"No, Jarrell is cool. He's not like that," Mary Ellen said. "He's a really nice guy."

"Did you know he worked at Selman's Antiques?"

"Yes."

"Is he the one that told you about the cross?"

Mary Ellen took a long time to answer. "He may have mentioned it."

"Uh-huh."

Rod made a few more keystrokes before taking the interrogation to a new level.

"Have you ever met a doctor named, Keller Lovett?" Rod studied Mary Ellen's expression—nothing.

"I don't think so," Mary Ellen said. "Why?"

"Because, I have something I would like to show you." Rod uploaded the video from the Royal Sonesta. He spun the computer screen around so that Mary Ellen could see it. "You see, this is Dr. Lovett...and this is you."

CHAPTER 39

Martin Luther once stated that everyone has a god.

"Search your soul! Where you place your trust is rightfully your god. Who or what you turn to in times of distress is your god. Who or what you thank for times of good fortune is your god."

Iggy Selman was too frail to make himself a god—like most human beings. He could not be trusted to make a good decision in times of trouble. Although he loved money (and was an expert at acquiring and saving it), money was not his god; it never brought him happiness. It could not be trusted.

Iggy's god was routine, schedule, and familiarity. And like all false gods, it eventually drove him to despair. Once an activity elevated itself to the level of becoming routine, it could not be changed without something close to an exorcism. Reading the Times Picayune with his Community coffee in the morning, driving to the flea market in Canton, Mississippi on Wednesdays, hiring Diamond Olivet on Friday night, counting the money in the safe on Saturday night, watching a Reverend Caldwell DVD on Sunday morning, and eating Verti Mart fried chicken on Sunday afternoon were just a few of the activities where Ignatius Selman placed his heart.

Routine, with all its little idols, was his god.

On Thursday, Iggy had lost one of his idols, with the death of Caldwell Ministries. Last night, with the help of her new pimp, Miss Tessy, Diamond broke the routine of their Friday night tryst. As Iggy ate a butterscotch pudding cup, using his finger as a utensil (which was another routine), he thought briefly of not counting the money in the safe.

But who can just throw out a god?

After closing the blinds in the shop, Iggy moved silently, with stealthy bare feet, to a position beneath the painting of the Last Supper. The cash register sat silent behind him. In a routine practiced at 10:35 p.m. every Saturday night for over twenty years, Iggy removed the painting, placing it softly to the right and leaning it against the cabinet that had been its recipient for so many counting episodes.

Licking his fingertips, he brushed his eyebrows. He pulled his crazy gray hair back from his forehead. Wiggling his fingers, he licked his fingertips of his right hand once more before gently touching the dial of the safe.

He opened it on the first try. The first shoebox removed was always the "Operating" shoebox. He turned and placed it on the counter, leaving the safe open behind him. He bent at the waist and removed the "working" shoebox from deep under the cash register. Opening the "working" shoebox, he grabbed the stack of cash that had been collected throughout the week and placed it in the "Operating" shoebox.

He then placed the "working" shoebox back underneath the cash register.

In typical Iggy fashion, he walked back to the front door, peered through the curtains that had been drawn, and checked the lock.

He stood motionless for a moment, listening for intruders.

Returning to the "Operating" shoebox, he removed the contents and quickly counted the stacks of cash.

"$8,650," he said, as he wrote the same number beneath the last entry on the sheet of paper belonging to the "operating" shoebox. He then removed the other seven shoeboxes from the safe and counted the $25,000 that were contained in each.

Thirty minutes passed before he had completed the task, secured the safe, and hung the painting back in place. His fingers were cramping; they smelled like ammonia.

As he started toward the office to log in this week's tally, the door exploded with noise, shaking the entire structure.

"What the..." Iggy shouted, spinning quickly. The door had not been compromised and was quiet. Iggy grabbed a concrete statue from the floor and raised it over his head, as he moved quietly toward the door. "Who's there?"

No answer. Iggy moved his head back and forth trying to get a glimpse of the person that felt it was necessary to molest his front door and scare him half to death.

"I said who is it?" he yelled at the door.

As he moved close enough to look through the door, he saw a body collapsed in the storefront.

"Oh my god!"

It was Diamond.

Opening the door quickly, Iggy bent down and examined her. She was unconscious. Stripping off his shirt in the cool night, he placed it under her head as a pillow. He straightened her legs and adjusted her mini-skirt to cover her panties. Her legs were scraped and bleeding. There was a contusion on her forehead.

"Diamond, what have you done?"

Iggy rushed back inside. Grabbing a handful of wet washcloths and a blanket, he returned. After gently cleaning the scrapes, he covered her with the blanket.

"Oh Diamond, why?"

He used the washcloth to gently clean her forehead and the sides of her face.

"Iggy?" She turned her head slowly from side to side.

"I'm here Diamond." Iggy tucked the blanket beneath her to get her off of the concrete stoop.

"Iggy, I need some money," she said, confused, dazed. The blonde hair that was meticulously styled a day earlier was now a grotesque rat's nest. Her make-up was smeared. "Iggy, please."

"No, Diamond. I told you never again." Iggy placed his arm under her. "Let me help you up."

"No!" Diamond yelled. "No, let me die. I want to die right here."

"You can die inside."

"Iggy, if I come inside, will you give me some money?"

Diamond asked, looking up into Iggy's eyes. Her blue eyes were cloudy, but still drove darts into Iggy's heart.

"We'll see. Let's just get inside."

• • •

An eerie silence fell over the French Quarter every morning at 2:00 a.m. when the noise ordinance kicked in. Bands and DJs, blaring music at 120 decibels, instantly fell silent, leaving scraggly audiences with buzzing ears and sore throats. As the last shock wave of bass flew through the brick and mortar of Selman's Antiques, Jarrell Landry stood in the storefront wondering what he might do with the property if he ever owned it.

The first thing I'd do is smash that window.

The leaded glass in the double doors that welcomed patrons into the relic resale shop would be smashed into a million pieces. The word 'Selman's', scrawled half on the left door and half on the right, would be completely obliterated. In the manner that the nation of Israel feared death from uttering the name of their God, Yahweh, Jarrell would smite the public display of the name "Selman".

Then, I'd replace the mailbox.

Glued to the front of the mailbox, in 2-inch gold letters, was the most horrid of names "I. Selman".

Punching in the code, he heard an annoying beep. He didn't hear the lock disengage.

"Give me a freaking break."

Jarrell typed in the code three more times, each ending with disturbing beep.

Knocking on the panes of glass that he would smash at his first opportunity, he waited for Iggy to answer.

"Wake up, Iggy!" He yelled through the glass. He shook the handle on the door violently.

A light flipped on in the back of the house. It was bright in the bedroom, getting dimmer as the light passed through the hallway, into the office, and eventually into the darkened shop.

Iggy worked his way through the office, when he stopped suddenly. He snarled when he noticed Jarrell. He waved his hand, trying to shoo Jarrell away.

"Iggy open up or I'm going to smash this door! Open it now!"

Iggy flipped the bird with both hands.

In the cool early morning hours, the temperature had dropped to a chilly fifty degrees. Light from a distant streetlight illuminated Jarrell as he removed his sweatshirt, opting to go shirtless rather than slicing his hand open. As he configured a boxing glove out of the shirt, Iggy suddenly took off toward the door.

"That's it, old man, your ass better open up," Jarrell said, under his breath.

Iggy was yelling obscenities as he unlocked the door.

"What do you want?" Iggy opened the door enough to stick his fat, gray face out. "It's the god-damned middle of the night."

"I wanted to see you," Jarrell said, smiling. He pulled the sweatshirt back over his head. "I know I haven't been around much to help with the shop." He reached out, as if he wanted to hug.

"You're on crack!"

"No, serious, Iggy I came by to see if you need any help this week."

"Humphf!" Iggy went to slam the door; Jarrell placed his foot in the jamb.

"Can I come in?" Jarrell pushed on the door.

"If you really wanted to help, you'd go to Canton on Wednesday and help me with the load that's coming in from Catalonia." Iggy stepped back into the shop.

"Sounds good." Jarrell moved past Iggy. "I'll go with you."

"Fine. So…I'll see you then." Iggy held the door open as Jarrell circled the counter and took a stance in front of the painting of the Last Supper.

"I always loved this painting." Jarrell ran a hand along the frame.

A loud groan came from the back of the house. Iggy closed the door and moved quickly toward the office.

"Diamond's here? I thought that was Fridays?" Jarrell continued to study the painting.

"Please go," Iggy said, in the doorway to the office.

"Can I have an advancement for Wednesday?"

"You really are on drugs."

"I need some cash." Jarrell turned from the painting.

"I don't have any money," Iggy said, his voice was weak. "Now go."

"Don't lie to me. That's a sin."

"Don't you dare talk to me about..."

"Iggy! Hush!" Jarrell ran his hand along the cash register, caressing it, running his index finger around the different keys. "I'm not even going to ask if there's any money in this old thing."

"Please go."

Jarrell moved from behind the counter toward the front door. Iggy took a step into the shop.

"Don't' worry, Iggy. I'm leaving."

Jarrell stopped suddenly at the door. "Oh, I remember one thing I wanted to talk to you about."

Iggy frowned.

"A friend of mine, a pretty blonde, came in here yesterday and sold you the cross."

"I should have known you were behind that," Iggy said, as his face began to take a little color. "You're the one that swiped the grapevine crosses."

"I have no idea what you're talking about," Jarrell said. "I was going to say, that you ripped her off. $300? Really? You see, Iggy, that's the real reason you're going to rot in hell. You're a habitual hustler. You cheated her right out of $1,000."

Iggy grunted.

"Anyway, just remember that when she comes back to get the money she is owed, you need to apologize and give her the $1,000."

Iggy's expression went blank. "I won't do it."

"You will." Jarrell picked up a small framed icon from a stack by the front door and threw it like a Frisbee toward the painting of the Last Supper. When the noise of shattered glass had quieted, Jarrell opened the front door. "Iggy, just pay her the money," he said, before exiting.

CHAPTER 40

R od Webster glanced at the picture of his wife, before unwrapping his second Hostess Twinkie.

He reread the title of the e-mail that he had sent to himself.

"It's not my fault."

Looking back at her picture, Rod smiled at his wife and popped the entire cake in his mouth, wiping the inside of it with his tongue.

"I love you baby," he said, with a mouthful of sweet, yummy goodness. Looking into the drawer of his desk, he noticed that one cake remained in the box. He looked back at Debbie and closed the drawer.

Rod turned his attention to the forensic report on Dr. Lovett.

"The victim had elevated levels of alcohol and Rohypnol. The cause of death was asphyxiation from strangulation. Blue nylon strands were found imbedded in the skin as deep as the hypodermis level. The nylon cord used in the strangulation created hairline fractures in the C4 and C5 vertebrae. There are no indications of sexual abuse. No other external injuries are evident."

It appeared that the coroner did a "cut and paste" from the Caldwell murder.

Rod was completing his review of the file when the Assistant District Attorney stepped into his office. By her look, he knew exactly what she was going to say. Releasing Mary Ellen on her own recognizance seemed like a very bad idea.

"You have to cut her loose." The ADA took the seat across from Rod.

The ADA was a semi-beautiful Tulane Law graduate that should have switched to wearing contacts years ago. Her heavy glasses weighed on her nose to the point of making permanent indentations into her skin. Her complexion, while clear, would have benefited from a little foundation to even out the different shades of tan. Concealer under the eyes to hide the faint, dark circles wouldn't be a bad idea either.

"Everything you've shown me is circumstantial," she said. She opened her briefcase and placed a file on top of Rod's desk.

"She should be forced to post some sort of bail," Rod said, as he shoved a stack of files to the side to maintain eye contact.

"It doesn't work like that. If you get some hard evidence, maybe..."

"We've got her at both crime scenes."

"You've got her at one crime scene for sure and she admits to that. The video from the Royal Sonesta is inconclusive."

"You've seen the video. Right?"

"Yes and it could be any of a hundred blondes in the city."

"With barcode tattoos?"

"Inconclusive."

"We have a strand of her hair in the Lovett hotel room," Rod said.

"Yes, and that was impressive. But you also have a different strand of blonde hair. For all we know, she's being set up," the ADA said.

"I think she brought that with her to confuse the investigation."

"Well, if that's the case, it worked. You need something more."

A smile suddenly crossed Rod's face.

"What?"

"What if we get her to talk?"

"You can't interrogate her anymore. If you keep pushing her she's going to lawyer up and then we'll have to..."

"I'm not talking about interrogating," Rod said. "Is there any way that you can get an order for a wiretap?"

"I think we could probably justify it, but do you have someone close enough that would wear it?"

"I think so."

"Who?"

"A priest."

"Oh no, no, detective, that's inadmissible. That's confidential between her and..."

"No, not that kind," Rod said, pulling the phone from his pocket. He scanned his messages. "We have a pastor from Pascagoula, Cooper Dupree. He's been working undercover."

"I don't even want to know what you're talking about." She closed her briefcase. "I tell you what. I'll get the order; you set up the tap. But, I'm making it totally clear that this priest is not taking confession or something."

"No, it's nothing like that."

"When do you think this can happen?"

"I can set it up for tomorrow afternoon."

"Alright." She headed toward the door. "I'll be back in an hour."

• • •

The Canal Street streetcar was empty, except for the conductor and one exhausted NOPD detective. The deafening, high pitched whine of electric motors and metal to metal contact drowned out the growling coming from Rod Webster's stomach. Of all the things that should be running through his mind—setting up the wiretap of Mary Ellen Retinoir or Cooper Dupree's concern about the relationship between Jarrell Landry and Ignatius Selman or getting a positive ID on the woman escorting Dr. Lovett into the Royal Sonesta—Rod had only one thing on his mind, the Twinkie he had left uneaten in the desk drawer at work.

In the last year, Rod had not left a morsel of food uneaten in his desk overnight.

Before leaving his office, Rod had even opened the drawer and studied the snack cake, almost conversing with it. His mouth watered. He could feel the sting of anticipation hitting his cheeks, tasting the sweet crème filling. His blood sugar dipped in anticipation of gobbling down the little guy, before leaving for the day.

Instead, Rod closed his desk drawer.

The streetcar stopped at a red-light; Rod was suddenly immersed in complete silence—no whirring motors, no grinding wheels, just silence. The open-bulb string of lights running above the center aisle surrounded Rod with makeshift mirrors made of streetcar windows. He sat up straight and sucked in his gut. Having skipped dinner altogether, made him feel a bit slimmer and excruciatingly hungry.

The light turned green and the streetcar lunged forward. The silence was destroyed by the shrill noise of electric motors converting power through worn brushes. The streetcar lumbered on.

Rod's abdomen tightened in pain. His last full meal was over eight hours ago. As the streetcar continued on its journey away from downtown, crossing Claiborne Avenue, they passed McDonalds, Waffle House, and Dot's Po-boy's. The soul-food kitchen on the corner of Galvez was lit with neon. Rod had stopped in more than a dozen times, to eat his weight in turnip greens, cornbread, and ham.

Not tonight.

Reaching up, he grabbed the cord to signal that he wanted to get off at the next block.

"You sure detective?" the conductor yelled back at Rod.

"Yeah."

"You eating at the Pub tonight?" the conductor asked, as Rod began to exit.

"No, I just wanted to walk a little. It's a nice evening."

"You got that right. Good night brother."

"Good night," Rod said, stepping onto Canal Street. He looked across the street at the only Irish restaurant in the city. "It's bad when you're tempted by Irish food," Rod said to himself, letting out a little smile.

• • •

The Twinkie decision, as Rod Webster would one day come to understand it, was a simple decision to not eat anything until he cleaned out his refrigerator at home. As Rod opened his refrigerator door, breaking the seal with a slurping, suction sound, he realized this decision was just a sick form of self-mutilation. He was going to be forced to cut off his nose to complete the job. With the introduction of fresh air into the icebox, several pieces of exposed food instantly turned brown and released a sulfur odor equal to burning matches.

"Oh my god!" Rod said, fighting back a gag reflex. He immediately shut the door.

Exiting the kitchen, he grabbed a vanilla scented candle from a junk-drawer in the entertainment center, stopping momentarily to flip on the radio. As music filled his apartment, the smell from the refrigerator caught up with him. He quickly moved to the bedroom.

The bed was unmade; the sheets needed changing. Rod grabbed an old T-shirt from his dresser. In the bathroom, he found the Comet Cleanser and a washcloth. With a determined, stern face, he checked his look in the bathroom mirror, took a deep breath and headed back to the kitchen.

Using a pot for a bucket, he filled it with warm water and a copious amount of Comet. The room started smelling better the instant he lit the candle; now with the help of chlorine, the room smelled like a vanilla scented public swimming pool. He wrapped the T-shirt over his nose and mouth. Grabbing a fresh Hefty lawn bag, he flicked it several times to expand it with air.

"Here goes nothing," he said, reopening the refrigerator. His eyes started to water as the noxious fumes coming from the meat compartment hit him above the T-shirt.

Without thought, not trying to save a single item, he dragged everything from the top shelf—sour cream, containers of unidentifiable leftovers, jelly, and margarine—into a garbage bag. Even the baking soda had to go.

He saved the crisper for last—grabbing handfuls of rotting vegetation and slopping it into a half-full garbage bag. He slammed the refrigerator door closed, sealed the bag, and dropped the T-shirt off his face. Without delay, he carried the fifty pounds of rotting food—pickles and salad dressing, hot sauce and horseradish—down the flight of stairs to the curb.

"What's in the bag?" Mrs. Groff asked as she lit another cigarette. Apparently, her sense of smell had been lost years ago. Mr. Groff was evidence of that.

"Just doing a little housecleaning."

"It's a little late for that."

"I know," Rod said, stepping past her. "Good night, Mrs. Groff."

Rod stood in the foyer looking up at his landing. His stomach tightened from hunger. He took the stairs, two at a time, in slow methodical steps. At the top, he looked back down at Mrs. Groff who was talking to herself.

Panting heavily, legs quivering, Rod smiled.

Re-entering his apartment, he immediately covered his face with the T-shirt and made three determined strides toward the refrigerator.

Plunging his beefy hand into the greenish bath of Comet, he removed the rag, opened the refrigerator, and started wiping down the shelves and walls. Twenty minutes later, the compressor was struggling to rechill the pristine innards of a refrigerator that hadn't been this clean since the day Debbie installed the egg holder.

Rod fell back on the kitchen floor and studied the fluorescent light above him.

"Tomorrow, I'll do the freezer."

Somewhere between scraping the remnants of a knocked-over jar of maraschino cherries on the second shelf and scrubbing the black, caked on leaves of a stalk of celery above the meat tray, Rod made the connection.

"This world is full of suffering," Rod said, looking deep into the fluorescent light. "It's not my fault."

Someone else can take the blame.

"Jesus came to suffer and take the blame…for me," Rod said, as a tear ran down the side of his face.

Pulling the T-shirt up from around his neck, he covered his eyes.

"Thank you, Debbie."

CHAPTER 41

The Oak Street Café was located in the Carrolton section of New Orleans at the end of Saint Charles Avenue. Mary Ellen walked seven blocks from the streetcar end-of-the-line on weak, unstable knees. Before the storm, the streetcar could have dropped her off on Carrolton at Oak Street and saved her five blocks, but this section of the tracks had not yet been repaired. Having slept only an hour and eaten a handful of pretzels in the last twenty-four hours, she was in dire need of breakfast. Stepping into the front of the café, she could taste the air. Her stomach told her that she was consuming waffles; she nearly collapsed from hunger.

Light jazz floated beneath the conversations of about twelve patrons. The smell of chicory and bacon mixed with the notes from the piano in the bay window facing Oak Street.

Mary Ellen quickly scanned her surroundings to see if she recognized anyone. She didn't. One couple studied the menu that was scratched on a chalkboard behind the counter; an older couple sat in the shade of the upright piano sipping coffee. A family of four talked noisily over pancakes—clanking spoons in coffee, scraping knives along plates, shuffling chairs on the tiled floor.

Mary Ellen didn't need a menu; she always ordered the plantation breakfast—two eggs any style, grits or hash browns, bacon or sausage, and toast or biscuit. Standing in line, Mary Ellen studied her reflection in the glass of the donut counter. The illuminated display case added patterns of bear claws and sprinkled donuts across her oatmeal colored sweater. Her skin took an unhealthy gray tone being outshined by the freshly made delicacies of every donut variety.

When she reworked her ponytail, several strands of long blond hair clung between her fingers. She brushed them off on the seat of her blue jeans.

"May I help you?"

"I'll have a cake donut and a medium coffee," she said. There was no way she could wait for them to make her breakfast.

"Will that be all?"

"No. I'd like a plantation breakfast also."

After answering the subsequent barrage of questions, she managed to order eggs over medium, grits, bacon, and toast. She felt like she had endured another one of Detective Webster's interrogations.

Taking her donut and coffee to the only two-top near the front windows, she watched the activity outside.

Jarrell was walking up Oak Street on the opposite side. He was wearing a light brown V-neck sweater. His eyes were darker than normal. His hair had been freshly buzzed, which made his heavy brows more noticeable.

As Mary Ellen watched him navigate between a couple of parked cars, tears welled in her eyes. She wanted to crawl under the table.

Jarrell broke into a jog; he waved to her as he passed the window. Pulling on the handle to the café, the little bells hanging from the door handle seemed to ring in time with the rendition of "House of the Rising Sun" that the pianist was playing.

"Hey," Jarrell said, taking the seat opposite her. "How did it go with the detective? I'm starved."

Mary Ellen couldn't respond.

"What's wrong?" he asked, reaching across the table to grab her hand. "Did they hurt you? Oh my god Mary Ellen if they..."

Mary Ellen pulled her hand away and held up an index finger, asking for a moment.

"What?" Jarrell said, moving to pat her other hand. "What's going on?"

"I'm...being...set up...someone's out to get me," she said firmly.

"What are you talking about?"

"There's a woman out there who is out to get me," Mary Ellen said, as a tear escaped from the corner of her eye. She snatched a napkin from the dispenser in the middle of the table and wiped her eyes roughly.

"Who?" Jarrell asked. He slid his chair around the table. Resting his arm on the back of her chair, he whispered into her ear. "Mary Ellen, who is it?"

"I don't know." She blew her nose. "After we left Fat Harry's, that detective started questioning me and I did like you said. I was honest, because I thought he was still talking about that idiot Caldwell. But...they...weren't." She grabbed another handful of napkins. Her eyes were red and puffy. "There was another murder, a tourist, and they have a video of me in the hotel lobby. But, it wasn't me! I swear it wasn't me! It's total bullshit!"

Jarrell cringed. "Shh." He wrapped his arm around her shoulders and held her tight. Looking around the room, he stared down anyone who attempted to figure out what was going on. Only the old couple had the nerve to stare back.

"Mary Ellen, you've got to…calm down," he said, with his voice as low as possible. "It's going to be fine. I can help you. Just talk to me. What do you mean there's a video of you?"

"They showed me a video," she said, talking softly. "It's my bag, my hair, even my tattoo. It looks just like me from behind."

"So, they didn't have a front shot?"

"No. There's a video of her coming in through the revolving door, but her face was obscured by the guy. The shot of her leaving, clearly shows my tattoo. You can see just a little bit of the side of her face. It looks just like me. I'm totally screwed."

A waitress interrupted them as she placed Mary Ellen's breakfast on the table.

"Can I get you a coffee?"

"No, thanks."

"You want this?" Mary Ellen asked Jarrell. Her stomach was knotted; she felt like throwing the plate across the room.

"You need to eat this."

"I can't."

Jarrell picked up a piece of bacon.

"You sure?" He asked, crunching down.

"Go ahead. Anyway, like I was saying, this woman looks just like me. That's two nights, two murders...and I've been questioned for both," Mary Ellen said, gaining her composure. "Jarrell, I need to find this woman."

"What you need is an alibi," Jarrell said, blasting Mary Ellen in the face with bacon breath. "Where were you when the woman was being filmed?"

"I was at home, asleep. It was two o'clock in the morning for Pete's sake. I'd just gotten off work a couple hours earlier."

"Did anyone see you at home?"

"No."

"Did you call anyone?"

"No. Jeez, Jarrell, they already asked me all this stuff. If I had an alibi I wouldn't be so upset." She took a bite of her donut.

"Easy," Jarrell said, as he wiped a crumb off the side of Mary Ellen's mouth. "I'm on your side."

She took a sip of coffee.

Silence followed.

"I'll be your alibi," Jarrell said, after a moment. "I'll tell them I saw you. We spent the night together."

"I told them I was alone."

"Okay, I came by to see you, but I chickened out, so I saw you but you didn't see me."

Mary Ellen shook her head.

Jarrell continued to eat her breakfast.

"You know, I might actually have an alibi," Mary Ellen said, as a smile crossed her face. She then changed expressions immediately, trying to temper what she was about to say. "I didn't want to tell you because...well, I know you want a little more from me and..."

"What are you talking about?"

"I met someone."

Jarrell's face suddenly went stern. His jaws were full of eggs. He swallowed quickly.

"What do you mean?

"I've met someone I like. His name is Cooper and he's nice and I like him."

Jarrell took her hand.

"Jarrell, please," Mary Ellen said, pulling her hand back quickly. "You know we're not like that."

"I know, but...well...I'm trying to look out for you. What's his name? Cooper? Cooper what?"

"Dupree." Mary Ellen grabbed the toast off the plate in front of Jarrell.

"How did you meet?"

"At the Bulldog."

"Where's he from?"

"Pascagoula."

"Huh. What's he doing over here?"

"He's helping a friend move," Mary Ellen said, as she slipped into thought. "He walked me home from work, Friday. His friend lives on Camp near the Bulldog." A smile crossed her face, as the image of them walking through the back streets of Uptown flashed in her mind. "And, guess what? He's a preacher. Can you believe it? Just like Caldwell. Only, this guy is super nice."

"...and so what? You think this super nice preacher from Pascagoula is going to provide you an alibi?" Jarrell asked. His voice raised above the normal level of the conversation around them.

"Easy," Mary Ellen said, patting Jarrell's arm. "You never know." She gave Jarrell a mischievous wink with her tired, blue eyes. "He's still a man, flesh and blood."

CHAPTER 42

Standing in front of a full-length mirror, Pastor Cooper Dupree placed his green stole over his shoulders, allowing it to drape down his chest toward the carpeted floor of his office. Reaching behind his neck, he used both hands to fasten the button that held it to his white robe.

"Here you go," Leslie Wixon said, handing him a wireless microphone. "Fresh batteries."

Dupree checked to see that it was off.

"It's off," she said.

Dupree snaked the microphone cord from his front pants pocket up through the robe and out the neck hole. Looking straight ahead, he clipped the mic to the stole, about four inches below his chin. He used his fingers to comb his dark hair to one side, then shook his head to make it look more natural. He checked his teeth for traces of the jelly doughnut he had wolfed down before getting ready.

"You look good," Leslie said, tugging on the back of the robe so it hung properly. She moved around him, straightening the creases in the cotton garment and making sure that the white rope, used for a belt, was level with his waist. She adjusted the knot so that it aligned with Dupree's hips.

"Thanks," Dupree said. "I guess it's go time."

"Have fun," Leslie said, as Dupree walked past her into the hall.

Several people were standing in a circle outside his office, holding coffee, making small talk. Dupree nodded, as he headed toward the sanctuary.

"Gregor!" Dupree said, spotting his friend talking to a couple of guys near the entrance to the choir loft. "Gregor."

"What's up Coop?" Gregor had managed to find a pair of long pants; he still decided to wear flip-flops.

"Hey man, did you tell anyone I was in New Orleans on an investigation?" Dupree asked, pulling him to the side and keeping his voice low.

"I don't think so. I might have told Kelly. She called me. Did I tell you?"

"No," Dupree said. "How's she doing?"

"She'll be fine. Anyway, I didn't tell anyone else. Why?"

"I got a strange phone call this morning. Forget about it." Dupree placed his hand on Gregor's shoulder. "I've got to get back to New Orleans this afternoon. Can you watch Red?"

"Of course. Is the fight still on?"

"Yeah, yeah, Wednesday. Go ahead and get the ring set-up. I'll have Leslie check the busses. Okay?" Dupree opened the door to the sanctuary. "Thanks, man."

"No problem."

• • •

Jesus Heals a Paralytic
A few days later, when Jesus again entered Capernaum,...So many gathered that there was no room left, not even outside the door, and he preached the word to them. Some men came, bringing to him a paralytic, carried by four of them. Since they could not get him to Jesus because of the crowd, they made an opening in the roof above Jesus and, after digging through it, lowered the mat the paralyzed man was lying on. When Jesus saw their faith, he said to the paralytic, "Son, your sins are forgiven."

Mark 2

• • •

"Who has the faith in this passage from Mark 2?" Dupree asked, rhetorically to a congregation of about 300. His voice was clear; his sermon text lay on the pulpit in front of him. "At first, it might seem

220

that the faith Jesus talks about is that of the four, the ones lowering the paralytic down."

"They made the opening; they lowered him down."

At this statement Dupree suddenly froze.

Joshua 2:15

So, she (Rahab) let them down by a rope through the window, for the house she lived in was part of the city wall.

The story of Rahab the Prostitute flashed across his mind. The strong feeling he had at the church in Algiers made his spine tingle.

"...the scripture...then says that...Jesus saw their faith," Dupree said. His voice weakened. He wanted to stop; the words continued to flow, as his sermon was delivered a little slower than normal. "Well, we would be tempted to think that it was the four doing all the work. And indeed the four friends of the paralytic did have faith, but it is the paralytic who has faith in Jesus."

Proverbs 7:10

Then out came a woman to meet him, dressed like a prostitute, and with crafty intent.

The passage from Proverbs 7 from the Caldwell crime scene was connected with the story of Rahab from Joshua 2.

But it's not the prostitute! Rahab saved them. She had no crafty intent.

"The paralytic," Dupree said, as his voice gained strength. He tried to maintain the momentum of his sermon, but his mind was suddenly addled. "He is the one insisting to see Jesus, he is the one who has imposed on these men to get him there no matter what, it is the paralytic that Jesus tells, 'Son, your sins are forgiven.'"

Son!

An exceptionally long pause followed as Dupree's thoughts flashed through his mind at the speed of light. His groin burned; his spine tingled. His hands were numb as if he had been hit by an electrical shock.

The silence seemed to awaken the congregation. A pause meant that the next thing the preacher said was going to be important—the longer the pause, the more important the statement.

"So it's not the prostitute!" Dupree shouted, no longer able to contain his thoughts. "It's his son!"

Joshua 2:1—Then Joshua, son of Nun! Proverbs 7:1—My son, keep my words!

"It's Caldwell's son," Dupree said in a lower voice. Sunlight flooding in through the stain glass rosary window blinded him. He took a deep breath, as he clenched feeling back into his hands. Dupree slowly regained his composure. When he realized he was still standing in the pulpit, having been moved by the Spirit before, he made no apologies. His transition back to his sermon was terse.

"So, my Christian friends!" he said, feeling his face burn. "It is the paralytic that we should first emulate. Weak, helpless, in need of healing, we should seek Christ! And it is like the four men that we should emulate secondly. Strong, capable, intuitive, we should bring others to Christ!"

With the sermon ended, Dupree took his seat behind the pulpit.

With a fresh revelation swimming in his brain, his entire body was telling him to leave the church—to get in his car and immediately drive to New Orleans and scour the streets for Caldwell's son. But, there was still so much of the worship service to finish.

Offering, prayers, communion.

He looked at his watch.

Thirty minutes, at least.

Growing more anxious with every second, Dupree's knee shook vigorously. The acolyte seated next to him in the two-person pew was being vibrated enough to slide her toward the edge. Just before she slid off the end, she grabbed Dupree's thigh for balance and to get his attention.

"Sorry," he whispered, stopping his leg immediately. "Hey Lauren, can you go down the side there and tell Mr. David that I need my cellphone?"

The thirteen-year-old stood without giving a reply. Circling behind Dupree, she walked quickly toward the back of the church. One hymn later she returned and took her seat next to Dupree.

"Thanks," he said, taking the phone while keeping it from sight. He looked over at the deacon and gave him the instructions to pass out the collection plates by nodding his head toward the altar.

He quickly typed a text message to Detective Rod Webster.

"Caldwell has a son! I'm sure of it. Find him. MER or Lovett's escort will lead you to him. Search for a prostitute with a barcode, same features, etc. Trust me on this."

He hit the send button and handed the phone back to the acolyte.

"Don't forget to give that to me after the service," he whispered.

"Yes sir."

CHAPTER 43

Rod Webster stepped off the elevator on the eighth floor of City Hall into a silent bullpen of cubicles. Sundays were the computer's downtime. For twenty-four hours, the whirring machines and copiers got to recharge their batteries or cool their motherboards or whatever they did to relax. Conner was not so lucky. As soon as Rod got Cooper Dupree's text message, he called his favorite IT technician and told him to meet him immediately.

"Conner!" he yelled across the room. There was no response. As he weaved through a few cubicles, trying to remember which one was Conner's, he heard the elevator 'ding' behind him.

Conner stepped out and started scanning the office. His red hair looked like it had been combed with a washcloth; he was wearing enormous sweatpants and a wool sweater knitted by his mother. As Rod walked up, he thought he noticed pillow indentations on the side of Conner's face.

"Hey Detective," Conner said. "You got a hot one, eh?"

"Did I wake you?"

"No, I was getting up already," Conner said, moving quickly past Rod. "It's going to take a few minutes to get my computer revved up."

"I'll make some coffee," Rod said.

"That'll be super." Conner worked his way back through the cubicles.

When Rod returned with a couple cups of coffee, Conner was running an update.

"I didn't know how you take it," Rod said, putting the coffee on the desk next to Conner's 'mouse' hand. "You get to drink it black."

"Cool. So, what have you got?" Conner asked, as he typed frantically. He already had three or four windows up and seemed to be social networking on Facebook, while he talked.

"Are you on Facebook?" Rod asked, taking a seat next to him.

"Yeah, I just updated my status; we had a flag football game planned for..."

"I don't care, can you just..."

"I've got it going, Detective. What is it you want to look up?" Conner took a sip of his coffee.

"We think the girl with Lovett was a prostitute."

"Lovett was the victim on Friday night." Conner started typing.

"Yes. What are you typing?"

"Well, I'm loading up the 'vice' database. I assumed you..."

"Okay. Anyway, you know the girl we found Friday, afternoon?"

"Yes, the one with the tattoo and purse?"

"Yes, we want to see if there are any known prostitutes that have the same tattoo."

With this information, Conner started typing and mumbling and talking to himself.

"Nope," he said, after a few minutes. During the time, Rod watched as several screens appeared and disappeared. He could have sworn he saw Conner get on Facebook again, but was afraid to call him on it.

"So, there's no one with that tattoo?"

"Not on file," Conner said, turning to face the detective. "What is it you're trying to do? You think this prostitute killed Lovett and the preacher? But you know Mary Ellen was..."

"No," Rod interrupted. He tried to collect his thoughts. "I think the prostitute that was with Lovett was dressed to look like Mary Ellen—the blonde with the tattoo. Or, it might be the other way around."

"What is Mary Ellen's last name?"

"Retinoir."

Conner spun toward his computer and within seconds had Mary Ellen's photo pulled up. With another few hundred keystrokes, he had outlined several dimensions of Mary Ellen's face.

"Her eyes are blue?" Conner asked.

"Yes."

"Height is 5' 6" about 125 pounds?"

"Yes."

"Now describe her teeth."

After going through another twenty questions, some of which did not apply, Conner hit the 'enter' button and watched as the computer came to life—buzzing and groaning and feeling like crap for having to work on its day off.

"This is the best I can do," Conner said, as a list of twenty-three prostitutes appeared in front of him. "Well, I guess I can cross reference the name Mary Ellen Retinoir with them."

No matches.

"What did that do?" Rod asked, looking over Conner's shoulder.

"That's just another run you can do to cross reference a name with another. You know like if Mary Ellen lived with one of them, it might be noted, or if she bailed her out. Stuff like that. But, there's nothing."

"Can you run that report and list all the people that are connected with each one?"

"For all twenty-three?"

"Yeah."

"Sure, it might be pretty long," Conner said, as he started back to work. Rod stood to get another cup of coffee.

When he returned, Conner had run the report and printed it out. "Not so bad," Conner said, handing it to Rod. "Only thirty pages, single spaced."

Rod began to meticulously scan the list. Conner worked at his computer, searching tattoo parlor information.

"Okay," Rod said, twenty minutes into his search. "This might be interesting."

"You got something?" Conner asked, spinning toward the detective.

"Do a search for me. Tell me everything we've got on Kirstin "Diamond" Olivet and what her connection is to Ignatius Selman."

• • •

Sunday morning in the French Quarter offered Rod Webster his choice of curbside parking places. He decided not to chance getting blocked in and double parked in the middle of Toulouse Street. As Rod sat in his police cruiser, windows down, the smell of bacon drifted through the cab from a hotel kitchen. He grabbed his computer from the passenger seat and started searching for the hotel video of Lovett and his escort.

The radio was tuned to WWOZ. A commentator lamented the destruction of the rain forest and its connection to global warming. Rod stuck his beefy arm out of the window and circled it around trying to feel the air. It was a rare day in New Orleans when the humidity was low and the air was crisp. Rod smiled. He took a huge breath, tasting the air and the bacon and the beauty of the French Quarter.

For the first night since Debbie's passing, Rod had gone to bed hungry. His rotund belly was angry and growled and cramped and pitched a big hissy fit. But Rod, simply rolled over, grabbed a pillow and hugged it like it was Debbie. He also allowed himself to be hugged back. Not by the pillow, but by a warmth that seemed to cover his whole body; a warmth that generated from his heart.

Rod had woken famished. Breaking from his normal Sunday morning routine of eating at the Shoney's breakfast buffet, he walked two blocks to the corner Rite-aid, where he purchased milk, juice, a box of raisin bran, and a multi-vitamin. He had decided to eat a healthy breakfast; Dupree's text message interrupted him in the middle of his third bowl of cereal.

Rod left the car and knocked on the front door of Selman's Antiques.

"What is it now Detective?" Iggy said, sticking his greasy, pale face into the crack between the door and frame.

"Good morning Mr. Selman, I was wondering, can I have a minute of your time?"

"What is it?" Iggy refused to open the door. A groan came from behind him.

"Is everything alright in there?" Rod asked, placing his foot in the door.

"You can't come in here..."

Another louder groan.

Rod shoved the door. Iggy stumbled backwards into the shop.

"You can't..."

"I'm shopping," Rod said, stepping quickly into the store. "Who is that?"

In the next room, jutting out from behind the desk, lying on the floor, was an attractive pair of legs attached to disgustingly dirty feet.

"None of your business," Iggy said, coming up behind Rod. He made the mistake of touching Rod's shoulder.

Rod instinctively reacted by swinging his elbow, striking Iggy in the jaw and sending him flying back toward the front door. Instantly sliding the computer bag off his arm, Rod pounced. Before Iggy could catch his balance, Rod lunged toward him. Taking a quick step to the right, Rod grabbed Iggy's arm and spun him around. Using his momentum, Rod followed Iggy to the floor, sparing him his full weight by rolling toward the side.

Air gushed from Iggy like a balloon being popped.

Rod used Iggy as support to get to his feet. Iggy, crushed and heaving for air, was safely secured. Moving quickly into the office, Rod's eyes followed the legs up to the person passed out or dead behind the desk.

"Well, this must be my lucky day!" Rod said, smiling.

Iggy coughed repeatedly, trying to regain his breath.

"Mr. Selman, you haven't killed Miss Olivet have you?"

Iggy rolled onto his back and held his stomach. "She's fine." Iggy pulled up his ragged T-shirt and started rubbing his abdomen. "Which is more than I can say for me. I think you broke a rib, you big ape."

"Kirsten Olivet?" He knelt down on one knee and started rocking her by pushing on her hip. "Don't you think about touching me again," Rod said, turning slightly to face Iggy.

"I'm pressing charges. If I start spitting up blood, you'll hear from my lawyer."

"Diamond? Can I ask you a few questions?" Rod grabbed his computer bag and took a seat in a tattered desk chair. Placing the computer on Iggy's desk, he searched his files for the security footage from the Royal Sonesta.

Diamond awoke slowly. Entering the office, Iggy helped her to sit upright on the floor with her back against the side of a filing cabinet. Iggy leaned on the front of the same cabinet; he held his stomach like he had been shot.

As Rod played the video of Lovett and his escort, he found it hard to see how the beautiful blonde hair in the video could possibly be the same as the matted, disgusting mess atop Diamond's head.

"Do you have a tattoo on the back of your neck?" Rod asked.

"A temporary one," Diamond said, as she turned and lifted a clump of hair. Her voice was much deeper than Rod expected. He thought it would sound more like Mary Ellen Retinoir's. "I got it Friday."

"Friday?"

"Yeah."

"Who did it?"

"I don't know her name. Some beauty place, somewhere."

"Can you be more specific?"

"No," Diamond said. "Miss Tessy set the whole thing up. It's just a temporary."

"Miss Tessy?" The name shot through Rod like a bullet. He pulled his little notebook from his back pocket and started thumbing through it.

"She's been setting me up with dates." Diamond scratched a scab on the back of her hand. She grabbed the blanket that she was using for a pillow and laid it across her bare legs.

"So, she's your pimp?"

"I don't need a pimp." Diamond patted Iggy's leg, then reached into his robe pocket. Grabbing a pack of cigarettes, she shook vigorously, trying to free one of the crushed smokes from the pack. "She's set me up on two dates, and the first one got screwed up."

Rod turned the computer monitor to face Diamond and Iggy, while Iggy lit a couple of cigarettes.

"Is that you?"

Diamond watched the video of the couple walking into the Royal Sonesta. She took the cigarette from Iggy.

"Yeah, that's me." She blew a lungful of smoke toward the ceiling. "That's my date. He's a dentist."

"How did the date go?"

"Great," Diamond said, looking up at Iggy. "He was a really nice guy, Iggy."

"What's wrong with you?" Rod asked Iggy.

"Nothing."

"Anyway, like I was saying." Diamond continued. "He's nice. I actually texted Miss Tessy to see if she could set up a second date, but she said she couldn't."

"Did she say why?"

"No." Diamond rolled forward onto her knees and grabbed a purse from under the desk. A moment later she held her phone up to let Rod read the text messages.

Rod wrote Miss Tessy's number into his notebook—985-555-2765.

"Where can I find Miss Tessy?"

"I don't know," Diamond said, taking her phone from the detective. "I've never met her."

"What do you mean?"

"I've never met her. We've only communicated through text messages."

"I don't understand," Rod said, spinning his chair to face Diamond. He rolled forward a few inches. "You get a random text message to go meet this dentist for a date and you just…"

"No. First it was the preacher. But that got all screwed up."

Rod shook his head. "The preacher? Caldwell?"

"Yeah, that was him. But that didn't work out."

"What do you mean?"

"I think I roofied him too hard, because…"

"Diamond!" Iggy yelled.

"Hush!" Rod snapped. "Continue Miss Olivet."

"I was going to steal some crosses from him, Caldwell, after I finished our date. But I roofied him too hard and he passed out on top of me. Ain't that right Iggy? Tell him, you were there."

Rod looked up at Iggy who had turned a shade grayer than normal.

"Yeah, Iggy why don't you tell me? You were there."

"Caldwell, called me a week before the revival and told me to get him an escort. I refused, but Diamond heard about it and said she would do it." Iggy took a puff of his cigarette. He reached over to the desk and grabbed a caked over ashtray. "I told her no. I want her to get out of the business. Anyway, she found this Miss Tessy to set it up. So I took her to the revival. I stayed behind to bring Diamond home. Anyway, she comes staggering out of Caldwell's trailer and says that he's out cold, so we split."

"Did you go in the trailer?"

"No," Iggy responded. "Like I said, I've never met Caldwell."

"Did you take the grapevine crosses?"

"No, Diamond was in no shape to hang around." Iggy said. "We left as soon as she left the trailer."

Rod found the interview with Lynnette Faust in his notebook. Diamond was the actual escort. Lynnette Faust had mistaken Mary Ellen for Diamond.

Rod flipped to the initial interview with Mary Ellen Retinoir.

"Miss Olivet, when you got to Caldwell's trailer, was he already there?"

"No." Diamond looked like she was searching the furthest reaches of her brain to find the answer to the question. "There was someone there, but they ran out as soon as I stepped in. They knocked me to the floor."

"Uh-huh. Did you get a look at them?"

"No," Diamond said. "It all happened so fast."

"Uh-huh. So, Iggy, have you met Miss Tessy?"

"Me? Of course not."

"What about when she left the package for me?" Diamond asked, looking up at Iggy.

"I didn't see her for Christ's sake! Damnit, Diamond. She left the package at the door."

"Package?"

"It was the clothes I was supposed to wear on my date with the dentist."

Rod gave an inquisitive look at Iggy.

"What? I swear, I don't know her. I never heard of her before Thursday. Do you want to search my phone?"

"Actually, yes," Rod said.

Iggy exited the office, toward the shop.

"So you've never met Miss Tessy? The person that buys you clothes and tattoos and dope and..."

"I never said dope," Diamond said, pointing at him with the fingers that held her cigarette butt.

Iggy returned with his phone.

Rod searched Iggy's phone for Miss Tessy's number. As he reviewed recent calls, the number seemed familiar.

"Okay, so you've never contacted Miss Tessy," he said, handing the phone back to Iggy.

"I told you."

Rod typed Miss Tessy's phone number into his own phone.

"What the hell," Rod said, as his "recent' folder popped up. He had dialed the number yesterday morning. It was the number that Mary Ellen Retinoir had dialed at 10:00 after the Caldwell murder. "985-555-2765 is Miss Tessy's number. Iggy?"

"Yes."

"Is this the only phone you have?"

"Yes."

"You better not be lying to me." Rod dialed 985-555-2765 and listened for a ring tone. He let it ring ten times before hanging up. In his notes from the interview with Lynnette Faust, he had written down Miss Tessy's phone number as 504-555-1104. Rod dialed it and waited another ten rings before hanging up.

"So you don't have a burner phone purchased at Walmart?"

"What's a burner phone?"

CHAPTER 44

The market for pure-bred prostitutes in burgeoning 1815 New Orleans was non-existent. New Orleans' wealthiest Madams knew the taste of their customers. Rich Frenchmen demanded the exotic, the unique; they wanted the woman that no other man had ever experienced.

They wanted a Creole.

Jarrell Landry only wanted Mary Ellen.

As he parked his car under the awning of a closed gas station in the Central City section of town, he noticed a young lady selling herself on the opposite corner. With a blotchy, chocolate complexion, she displayed her wares in a tattered denim jacket and gray sweatpants. She constantly scratched her face. Squatting, then standing, she walked in circles, mumbling to herself, stopping on occasion to scratch her calf with the top of an ancient pair of Converse sneakers. At one time she was indeed attractive and exotic, an early-nineteenth century Parisian's dream.

But Jarrell's eyes were clouded with hatred for the life she had chosen.

Jarrell saw nothing worthy in her trade; he saw nothing to be admired or pitied. She was simply a picture of trauma. He saw his own childhood, filled with beatings and sleepless nights spent listening to the grunting and hellish groans of his old man.

Grabbing the gearshift, he entertained the idea of dropping the car into drive and running her over.

As the engine revved, the whore looked over at Jarrell and flashed a toothless smile. He slumped down in the seat and removed his foot from the accelerator.

Mary Ellen had never been paid for sex.

She's not a manipulator.

It was paramount that she never degraded herself like that. Mary Ellen needed to remain pure, beautiful, vulnerable, perfect.

...and she's going to ruin it with a Mississippi preacher?

Jarrell started making a few mental notes about Pastor Cooper Dupree.

Using his iPhone he searched the internet and quickly found a brief history of Mary Ellen's new love interest.

"What have we here? Have we moved up to the big leagues, Pastor Dupree?"

Jarrell read an article outlining Dupree's work with the Pascagoula Police Department involving a kidnapping and murder investigation.

"So you're not in town to move a friend? Super nice Cooper, huh, you big fat liar."

Looking up, Jarrell noticed the prostitute making a deal through the window of a late model Honda Acura. A cool, breeze blew across the front seat, as he read an article on the disappearance of Dupree's wife.

"Wonder what Mary Ellen would think if she knew you were a cop?"

Searching the website for Christ Church, Jarrell glanced at his watch and dialed the number with his thumb.

"Christ Church, this is Leslie. How may I help you?"

"Hello, this is Jason Smith with the Times-Picayune. I was wondering if I could speak to Pastor Cooper Dupree," Jarrell said, dropping his voice into a lower, more authoritative sound.

"Uh...let's see. He's scheduled to be in Sunday School, but, no wait, he just stepped in."

Jarrell listened as Leslie relayed the message that a reporter was on the line.

"Hello?"

"Hello, Pastor Dupree, this is Jason Smith with the Times-Picayune. I was wondering if I could have a moment of your time?"

"I only have a minute. What can I do for you?"

"Well, first off, I must say that I'm a fan," Jarrell said, searching back over the article written about the murder in Pascagoula. "The work you did with the Hargood case was just..."

"Mr. Smith, can you get to the point?"

Jarrell made an educated guess.

"Well, sir, I was wondering how the investigation into the murder of Reverend Jack Caldwell was going. Are there any suspects?"

"Well, the investigation is on-going and...I'm not at liberty to comment on the details of...the case and...what did you say your name was?"

"Jason Smith."

A pause followed.

"Like I was saying," Jarrell said. "I was wanting to get a statement from..."

"Excuse me, but there's no Jason Smith on staff at the Times-Picayune," Dupree said.

Jarrell hung up and smiled.

"Welcome to the big leagues, jerk!"

• • •

To sabotage Dupree's efforts to start a relationship with Mary Ellen, Jarrell would prove him to be a liar. Leaving the Bulldog, he started his search to find Dupree's imaginary "moving friend".

Driving directly toward Saint Charles Avenue from Magazine Street on Toledano, he took a right on Camp Street as Mary Ellen had stated when she described the walk back to her apartment. Three blocks down Camp Street, he was surprised to find a house that was in the process of changing inhabitants. Large ruts ran through the front yard. The front porch had no potted plants. The oak tree, shading the front walk, had been stripped of its leaves to the height of a large moving truck.

Exiting the car, Jarrell pulled his ball cap down and flipped the hood of his sweatshirt up over his head. The house he approached had a realtor's "For Sale" sign in front that had a little banner across the top—"TOO LATE!!". Jarrell entered the number for the real estate agent into his cellphone.

He quickly typed the Camp Street address into a search engine. The internet held a wealth of information on the camelback, double shotgun. The name Cecil Brandingham seemed to be a common thread.

Walking up the driveway along the side of the house, he didn't bother trying to look in the house; all of the blinds were closed. He passed several garbage bags filled to capacity. A box of cleaning supplies rested on the back stoop. Scanning his surroundings, he took a peek into the garage and studied the layout of the backyard.

As he moved back toward the front of the house, he heard the front door open.

"May I help you?"

The question reached Jarrell before he rounded the corner. The accent was Spanish. He jogged several steps and flipped the hood off of his head. Removing his sunglasses quickly, he made sure to stay in the middle of the driveway.

"Hello," Jarrell said, making eye-contact, as soon as he passed the edge of the house. "I'm sorry. Did you call for an Uber?" He held his hand out to wave off any concern.

"No sir, I did not," the woman said. She was halfway out of the door, with one hand hidden inside. "You are not to be in the back."

"Yes ma'am. I'm sorry. I was called to this address." Jarrell pulled his cellphone from his pocket. "I was to pick up Cooper Dupree."

"He's not here."

"It was scheduled last night. I was supposed to be here thirty minutes ago, but I got stuck in Marrero and I..."

"He was here yesterday, but he left," the woman said, stepping out onto the front porch. She had nothing in her hands. "There is no one here that needs an Uber."

Jarrell pretended to study his phone.

"So, Cecil Brandingham did not order a ride for Mr. Dupree?" he asked, looking at the phone, as if he were reading an entry.

"No, goodness, no," the woman said. She walked to the edge of the porch. Her plain attire and thick accent made it clear that Jarrell was dealing with a maid or nanny. "Mr. Brandingham has not been here in a long time. The padre is Mrs. Brandingham's friend. Maybe, I should call her to see."

Jarrell made a couple of steps toward the woman. "So she's not home?"

"No, the movers have taken all the furniture."

"I understand," Jarrell said. "Can you call her just to make sure? I would hate to have made the trip up here for no reason." He took a few steps toward the housekeeper. "You can use my phone."

The maid pulled a slip of paper from her coat pocket and dialed the number.

"Mrs. Brandingham, please." A long pause followed.

"Mrs. Brandingham, I'm sorry to disturb you but there is an Uber driver here for the pastor, Mr. Dupree, and I wanted to make sure..."

The maid looked at Jarrell and shrugged as she listened.

"No ma'am. He is not here. It is a driver that has come to pick him up. He said that Mr. Cecil called for one." At the mention of Cecil Brandingham, the maid (or nanny) had to hold the phone away from her ear to keep the screaming from the other end of the line from damaging her ear drums. Jarrell picked up on a few of the expletives coming from the phone.

"I don't know. Yes ma'am. Bye," the maid said. She hung up the phone and handed it back to Jarrell. "She will be here soon."

He typed the name "Mrs. Brandingham" on the phone number that the nanny had just called.

"She wants to see you."

Jarrell turned and took off in a jog toward the car.

"Tell her that I'll be right back. I've got...something...I've got another ride to pick up."

•••

Jarrell learned three things about Regina Welsh-Brandingham from his vantage point behind a large construction dumpster three houses from the Brandingham's. First, she was staying at the Columns Hotel on Saint Charles Avenue—found when he dialed the number the nanny had called earlier. Second, she drove a black 500-series Mercedes. And third, she was drop-dead gorgeous.

As the driver's side door to the Mercedes opened and one leg emerged, Jarrell's jaw dropped in anticipation of what was to follow. Mrs. Brandingham was dressed in a conservative black dress, with a liberal slit running up the thigh. Her nylons were black, shear, expensive.

Moving up the walk, she dropped her keys into a leather handbag. Her shoulder length hair shimmered in the morning sun, which streamed through the oak tree limbs above her. Every movement was deliberately slow and calculated, as if she were filming a shampoo commercial.

When Mrs. Brandingham disappeared inside, Jarrell sat down on the sidewalk and rested his back against the dumpster. The concrete was cold through his jeans. He grabbed his cellphone and typed a couple of text messages to Mary Ellen.

"Thanks for breakfast. Hope you feel better. I talked to my boss. He owes you $1,000 more for the cross. Tell him that you talked to me."

Send.

"Let me know how it goes with the preacher. BTW, what did he tell you about the "friend" he's helping move? Call me."

Send.

CHAPTER 45

Topping the Pearl River Bridge, Cooper Dupree slid down toward the swamps of Louisiana at 70 miles per hour. In the middle of a cool 65-degree Sunday, the sun was making heat waves rise from the concrete a quarter of a mile in front of him. With his elbow resting in the window, the Camry hummed with road noise; the interior pulsed with every passing car.

Since he knew how to count to two, he knew how many dates he had this afternoon.

Regina Welsh-Brandingham was expecting him for brunch at the Columns Hotel. Mary Ellen Retinoir had called, while Dupree was in church and left a message that she was expecting him around four o'clock.

Dupree looked at his reflection in the rear-view mirror as he passed the Louisiana Welcome Center. His hair fluttered around with the wind circling the interior of the Toyota. He lifted his sunglasses. His dark eyes reflected the road in front of him; his complexion, clear and tan, was made slightly darker by his navy-blue sweater.

Dupree exited toward New Orleans. As he flew through Slidell, his phone started ringing. It was Rod Webster.

"Hey, Detective," Dupree said. "What's up? Did you get my text message?"

"I got it." Background noise indicated that the detective was driving. "Thanks. That tip turned up some good stuff."

"Okay." Dupree waited for details on the 'stuff'.

"Yeah, so anyway, I called to ask a favor."

"Sure."

"I was able to get approval for a wiretap of Mary Ellen Retinoir..." Rod paused, apparently to give Dupree the chance to come to the obvious conclusion.

"...and I was wondering if..."

"What?"

"I know that you and Miss Retinoir are getting...friendly."

"We're friends, only because you insisted that I follow her around everywhere." Dupree pulled his elbow in and rolled up the windows. He placed the phone on his right shoulder and switched to driving with both hands.

"Pastor, would you wear the wire?"

Dupree shook his head in disapproval. He grabbed the phone with his left hand. Checking his rearview mirror, he frowned.

"Pastor, did you hear me?" Rod asked.

"I don't really want to," Dupree said after a long pause.

"You know, Pastor, the wiretap could clear her."

"I don't know."

"It would be a big help to get this out of the way," Rod said. "Can you maybe contact her and meet her? We'll pay for your mileage and expenses."

"I'm actually coming into town right now. I'm about to hit the Twin Span."

"Really? Can you set up a meeting with her?"

"I'm meeting her at four o'clock."

There was a long pause.

"Will you wear the wire?" Rod asked, finally.

"I'll think about it." Dupree pulled to the far-right lane and slowed, as he traversed the Twin Span Bridge toward East New Orleans. "So, you said my tip turned up some good stuff. What stuff?"

"Oh yeah. Your tip, about the prostitute, Lovett's prostitute, my IT guy scanned the vice squad database and found a woman named Kirsten "Diamond" Olivet was connected to Ignatius Selman. I went with it. I actually found her at Selman's Antiques. Seems she's a friend of Iggy Selman."

"Get out of here. So, Selman is tied to both murders. He was at the revival. He had the crosses. He has a motive. He…"

"I know and I'm working that," Rod interrupted. "Lieutenant Frye approved to stakeout Selman's until I can run down several other leads. So what are your thoughts on Miss Tessy? It looks like she was the one that sent Diamond Olivet to both victims."

Dupree shook his head trying to file the massive information dump that shot through his brain.

"Who? Miss who?" Dupree asked. Slumping down in his seat, he rested his arm on the window ledge and held the phone tight to his ear. Vibration from the window rattled his sight; the bridge in front of him was a long fuzzy, gray line.

"I haven't told you about Miss Tessy?"

"No."

"She's linked to both murders," Rod said. "The phone number Miss Retinoir called after the Caldwell murder was to a burner phone used by Miss Tessy. Also, like I said, Miss Tessy is the one who had Diamond Olivet made over to look like Mary Ellen Retinoir before she met Dr. Lovett at the Royal Sonesta."

"What?" Dupree yelled, veering into the other lane. "What the hell are you talking about? Damnit Rod, hold on a second!"

Dupree exited the Twin Span bridge and pulled off onto the shoulder of Interstate 10, in the middle of a swamp that bordered the south side of Lake Pontchartrain. He placed his phone on his lap and took a deep breath. He clasped his hands.

Allowing his mind to clear, letting his anger and emotions settle, he closed his eyes and fell into silent prayer. Emptying his thoughts, he allowed the Spirit to move him.

Vehicles whizzed by, shaking the car. The smell of swamp gases and exhaust attacked his sinuses. Concentrating on the darkness, he thought of Mary Ellen. He wanted to hold her hand; he wanted to hold her; he wanted to keep her safe.

She's in danger. Miss Tessy is going to hurt her. Lord help me; Lord protect Mary Ellen.

"Detective," he said, picking up the phone. A minute had passed. "What do you mean that Diamond Olivet was made to look like Mary Ellen?"

"I talked to a beautician named Darlene Mason; she said that Miss Olivet had a bar code tattoo and hair styling done on Friday. This was directed by Miss Tessy."

"So Mary Ellen's being framed?"

"I'm not sure," Rod said. "The problem is, no one has ever seen Miss Tessy. Many people know her, but none of them have met her."

Dupree looked out across the swamp. An egret took flight. In between vehicles passing, Dupree could hear the steady buzz of insects.

"Because she doesn't exist," Dupree said, watching the bird flap toward the horizon.

"Exactly. It's a front, a cover," Rod said. "...and I know you don't want to hear this, but the only logical choice, the only person that really needs a cover is Miss Retinoir."

Dupree shook his head.

"Miss Retinoir used Diamond to cover her tracks," Rod said.

"But I saw her just two hours before Lovett was killed. She wasn't preoccupied. She didn't have anything planned. For a moment, I thought she was going to invite me in. As a matter of fact, I think she did," Dupree said. His mind tried to relive the walk home from the Bulldog.

"We found her hair at the crime scene."

"Even the DA knows that could have been planted," Dupree said. "How do you know it's not Diamond Olivet? What if she planned this all along and is using Mary Ellen as a scapegoat?"

"You obviously haven't met Diamond," Rod said. "She's not capable of doing anything like that."

"Then it's Ignatius Selman," Dupree said. "He's the one with the crosses. He's got the connection to Caldwell. He knows Diamond Olivet. It's got to be him."

"I thought about that," Rod said. "He's got motive. I guess."

"You damn right he's got motive!" Dupree said, suddenly perking up. "Caldwell had something on him. That's it! It's Selman! The grapevine crosses were probably never even stolen. And the Lovett thing was to make it look like a serial…"

"Dupree! Stop! This isn't a guessing game," Rod said. "Pick a lane, Pastor. Just this morning, you texted me that it was Caldwell's son."

Dupree fell silent as his face flushed.

"Caldwell doesn't have a son and his daughter's in California," Rod said. "I know you're doing your best but we can't just throw darts at…"

"Detective," Dupree said, as he dropped his car into gear and started scanning his rearview mirror for an opening in traffic.

"Yes Pastor?"

"I'll wear the wire."

CHAPTER 46

The room that Regina Brandingham chose to plan her seduction of Cooper Dupree reeked of desperation and loneliness—the two most potent pheromones released by the female human. If a red-blooded male should catch a glimpse into the room, he would immediately fall prey to his ravenous, sexual appetite. Howling like a wolf, he would rip his clothes off, all the while releasing his musk into the din of pure vulnerability.

Pouncing on top of the ornate king-size bed, he would tear at the velvet shades and dive lustfully into the bucket of champagne chilling on the nightstand.

Regina had to be exceptionally careful not to let the room service guy in by mistake.

She jumped when the phone rang. Moving quickly to the other side of the bed, she answered on the second ring.

"Hello?"

"Hey, it's me. I'm down in the lobby," Dupree said. His voice was handsome, so confident.

"Uh, I'm just about ready," she said, twisting the phone cord in her fingers. "Would you, I mean, why don't you come up and wait? I won't be a minute."

"I'll just grab something in the bar and..."

"That's perfect! I'll take a Bombay Martini, extra dirty," Regina said, sitting on the bed. She was elated that Dupree wanted a drink; it would make everything so easy. "I'm in 204, just up the stairs and to the right."

"But I..."

"Just have them charge it to the room," she said quickly. "Room 204. See you in a sec." Hanging up she fell back onto the bed and examined the ceiling.

From her recollection of books and movies, it would not take much to seduce a man. Her little black dress barely touched her knees. With her feet shoulder length apart, she slowly slid the hem up toward her waist, as she glanced at the high-backed chair in the corner. Dupree would be sitting there in moments.

Her sheer black stockings were almost white at her knees and ankles; her thighs and calves were thin, dark, alluring.

Should she remove her underwear?

Too forward.

Spreading her knees slowly, her dress continued up her thigh. She slipped her left hand down and covered herself, when her panties were finally exposed.

"Uh-uh-uh," she said, waving the index finger of the other hand at the chair.

She imagined that Dupree, crazed with lust, would leap from his chair, knocking over the coffee table, spilling his scotch or beer or wine spritzer or whatever he drank as he dived headlong on to her and started to...

"Regina!" she said, jumping out of bed and straightening her dress. "You've got to be out of your mind."

She ran her hand along the top of the comforter, smoothing out the area where she sat. The material was bothersome. Her slight hand seemed to catch on tiny protrusions that made her bed of seduction to feel gritty and rigid. After turning down the cover, she fluffed a couple of pillows.

Regina felt a bite in her abdomen.

The hardest part would be the initial contact.

A noise came from the hall.

Regina's ears rang. Her heart leapt into her throat.

"Say nothing! Say nothing," she said, aloud. "Just do it, Regina, do it big."

The clock read 2:05.

Shuffling sounds from the hall worked their way under the door. Her insides crumbled.

Walking across the room, she peered through the peephole. A maintenance man was changing a light bulb in the hall. Regina nearly hyperventilated from panic and relief.

She took a few deep breaths.

Moving into the restroom, she pretended to make little adjustments to her makeup. There was nothing more to do; she looked perfect.

The plunging neckline of the dress accentuated her small breasts by allowing a slight shadow to appear between them. She wore a gold necklace that was in perfect contrast to the simple dress. Complicated in its weaving, it fell on the warm, freckled skin of her chest in an inviting manner. Dupree would want to reach for it, to caress the gold and feel its perfection, while running the back of his hand along the skin that provided the backdrop.

Regina smiled and ran her hand along the necklace.

The room exploded with sound as Dupree started knocking on the door.

Regina opened it quickly.

"Hey," Dupree said, leaning over to kiss her on the cheek. He held a tray of drinks in one hand.

"Hey, wow you look great!" Regina said, smooching the air next to Dupree.

"Here you go, one Martini, extra dirty," he said, walking into the room. "Boy, you look wonderful. You've got plans?"

"No, I don't," Regina said, taking the martini. She took a full drink. "I was just...wow that's strong...and dirty. No, I was just looking forward to you coming by and I just thought...well, it's been a while since I had an occasion to dress up."

"You look outstanding," Dupree said. He began to inspect the room. "Look at that view. Isn't that perfect?"

He moved quickly past the bed and exited to the balcony.

"This is so nice," he said, looking up into the trees.

"It is," Regina said, as she gulped down the last of her martini. She grimaced, as she put the glass on a bureau.

"I...uh...I just love sitting out here and watching the streetcar go by." She stepped up behind him as he watched the Avenue. "I've been doing it all morning." She put her hand on the small of his back. "It's nice that you've...come by...I..."

Dupree turned to face Regina and rested against the balcony railing.

"I've missed..."

Regina placed her hands on Dupree's hips. As their eyes met, something told her to go slow. She pressed closer.

They kissed.

Two nights earlier, he had moved his hands up to the side of her head. His lips had moved with hers. She had felt the heat of his breath; she had felt him relax into the kiss.

As Regina closed her eyes tighter and opened her mouth, she felt no hands on the side of her head. She felt no relaxation. As her tongue moved forward to caress his, its advancement was met by a slammed-shut pair of rigid lips.

Dupree kept his hands on the railing, returning just enough of Regina's kiss to make him a gentleman.

"Oh Cooper," Regina said, breaking off the kiss and placing her head in his chest. She hugged him around the waist, hoping he would embrace her.

"I'm sorry Regina," Dupree said, finally embracing her around the shoulders.

CHAPTER 47

"Well, what have we here?" Jarrell asked, as a man emerged onto a second story balcony of the Columns Hotel. "Isn't that Mrs. Brandingham's room?"

Parked across Saint Charles Avenue, Jarrell had a front row seat to watching Regina, pacing and prepping for her company. In the past hour he had become a pretty skilled voyeur. Mrs. Brandingham chose to wear panties but no bra; she brushed her teeth after every cigarette. If she were on the balcony, she always covered her ears when a streetcar shrieked to a stop.

And now, her guest had arrived.

Jarrell pulled the array of photos, that he had found of Cooper Dupree, to his iPhone screen and compared them to the man standing in the canopy of an oak tree only fifty feet away.

"Tall, strong jaw, brooding eyes, broad shoulders—I think there is little doubt," Jarrell said, rolling up his window. "Pastor Cooper Dupree."

• • •

After watching the stilted rendezvous between Cooper Dupree and Regina Brandingham, Jarrell quickly got out and stood leaning against the driver's side door. With each passing car, leaves rolled along Saint Charles Avenue, finding hiding places under Jarrell's car. The sun felt warm on his cheek; sunglasses blocked the glare from the windows of the antebellum bed-and-breakfast across the street.

Only a few minutes passed before Dupree exited the front entrance and quickly descended the steps to the sidewalk.

Jarrell nodded toward Dupree when he passed. Leaning back into the car, he watched as the preacher started jogging toward downtown, in the direction of Mary Ellen's apartment.

Surely, he's not passing on that for Mary Ellen?

Slipping inside the car, Jarrell quickly started the engine and waited patiently to pull onto the Avenue. Just as an opening was available, Dupree darted across the street, one full city block in front of him. As Jarrell drove slowly forward, he noticed the preacher ducking into a white, unmarked police cruiser.

"...and who might that be Cooper Dupree?" Jarrell asked as he passed the cop car. He immediately slumped down in his seat and covered the side of his face with his free hand when he realized it was Detective Rod Webster.

CHAPTER 48

R od Webster dropped the NOPD Police cruiser into drive and pulled onto Saint Charles Avenue.

"We're going to meet the IT guy to get you wired," Rod said. "You need to fasten your seat belt."

"Okay." Dupree obliged.

"I thought I would catch you up on a couple of things. First, the photo of Jarrell Landry. It was taken by Ignatius Selman. The kid works at the antique shop, along with his pedicab thing. He actually delivered four grapevine crosses and the gold cross to Reverend Caldwell on the morning of the revival. We know that Mary Ellen stole the gold cross, but we have no idea who took possession of the grapevine crosses. Mary Ellen is certainly the prime suspect on that since all five crosses were together when Landry delivered them."

"Makes sense."

Rod caught the light at the Louisiana Avenue intersection. He turned up the fan on the air conditioner.

"When you're talking to Miss Retinoir, and I don't know how you can do this, but if you can, get her talking about the crosses. Maybe, you're in the market for some. I don't know. We would like to know anything she knows about the grapevine crosses."

"Okay." Dupree nodded.

"Also, like I was telling you about Miss Tessy, if there is a Miss Tessy, we have two burner cellphone numbers for her. We want you to dial both numbers, as soon as possible when you're in there, and see if either of those phones are in her possession."

"Can do."

"Other than that, it's really just talking to her and seeing if her alibi checks out. Keep it simple."

Heading toward downtown, they made a quick left turn onto Jackson Avenue.

"This is Central City," Rod said, as they sped past Carondelet Street, approaching LaSalle Avenue. "I get a lot of business in this area. You don't want to wander off here too often."

"So this is north of Saint Charles."

Rod let out a little laugh.

"This city doesn't have a north and south. There's no east or west either. In New Orleans, everything is toward the lake or toward the river. If that doesn't get you there, it's upriver or downriver. The whole city is geographically impaired."

"I was told yesterday that the sun rises over the West Bank," Dupree said, holding on to the dashboard. Rod had picked up speed and was weaving between potholes the size of grenade craters.

"I still haven't figured that one out yet," Rod said. He slammed on the brakes to save the front-end alignment on the cruiser. Dupree flew forward; his seatbelt locked in place.

"I had to think about it," Dupree said. "At the French Quarter, I think the river is flowing north, so that means when you look from the east side of the river, toward the east, you're actually looking at the West Bank."

"Like I said, I still can't figure it out," Rod said, making a hard turn onto Claiborne Avenue.

A few minutes and seven traffic lights later, Rod made a left on to Washington Avenue. He was suddenly buried in a massive complex of deserted project housing—busted windows, electrical wires hanging from balconies, trash blown in drifts against the base of the buildings.

This world is full of suffering.

He slowed to study the dwellings; Dupree was talking, asking questions. Rod couldn't hear anything above his own thoughts.

Rod suffered with Debbie's death.

It's not my fault.

Riding along the dark bricks of the housing complex, Rod noticed moving shadows. A child appeared from behind an overgrown hedge; movement from inside flashed briefly through the open doorways.

Debbie had left Rod in good shape. He smiled.

Laundry suddenly appeared on a clothesline; an old man was rocking on a chair on a third floor balcony, smoking. As Rod continued to drive toward the edge of the sprawling mass of buildings, he came to realize that the entire projects were occupied. There were no vacancies.

This world is full of suffering.

"Is that the flood line?" Dupree asked.

Rod ignored the question.

It's not my fault.

On the lake side of the projects, farthest from the river, the water had risen to four feet. Each building was clearly marked with a reddish-brown line that was more level and straight than any of the walls or floors. A boy stepped out from a sliding glass door; during the storm, he would have been completely submerged.

• • •

"Okay, Pastor," Conner said, as he ripped off a huge piece of duct tape from a roll. "Remove your shirt. I need to secure both microphones to your pectoral muscles, just above the nipples, so that we can triangulate the sounds. You probably should have shaved that chest hair."

Rod Webster backed away, hiding a smile.

Conner stuck the edge of the two foot strip of tape to the side of the surveillance van. Ripping another piece from the roll, he tore it off with his teeth.

"We'll be securing the tape recorder to your thigh, just below the groin," Conner said, hiding his face. "If you're wearing boxers, you'll have to go commando."

"What the..." Dupree said, as he started unbuckling his belt.

Rod Webster burst into laughter; Conner doubled over, laughing so hard he dropped the roll of tape.

"What is going on?" Dupree said, holding his pants up.

Rod came up behind Dupree and slapped him on his bare shoulders.

"I'm sorry, Pastor," Conner said, wiping tears from his eyes. "The detective put me up to it."

"I get to rip it off," Rod said, grabbing the duct tape off the van. He tried to stick it to Dupree's chest.

Dupree jumped back. "Very funny."

"Oh come on, Pastor," Rod said, chasing him toward the back of the van with the tape. "You said you would wear it."

Dupree circled around and met Conner back at the driver's side door.

"Okay, Pastor, we'll get serious," Conner said, taking the duct tape from Detective Webster. He threw it in the back of the van with the tape recorder.

Conner reached in the front seat of the van and removed a black camera case. "We've spared no expense," he said. "This is the newest and most expensive piece of surveillance equipment in the NOPD arsenal. Let me tell you right now, if something should happen to this, Detective Webster and I will be looking for a new line of work."

"That's good to know," Dupree said.

"Here is the actual microphone," Conner said, removing a strip of cloth from a case. "We simply fasten it to the inside of your sweater. You see, it feels like cloth."

"That's amazing."

"Yeah, it's really undetectable, especially if we had time to match the color. Just make sure, if you take your sweater off..."

"That's what I'm talking about," Rod said, winking at Dupree.

"Whatever."

Conner continued to stick the woven microphone to the inside of Dupree's sweater. "You can see that it's a weird color. Just be careful if you have to take it off."

"Does it connect to anything?" Dupree placed the sweater over his head.

"It's wireless," Conner said. "Here's the receiver, transmitter." Conner handed Dupree a set of keys. "This key receives the messages from the microphone, and this car-fob transmits to the van. The signal is not that strong, so we'll have to be within a hundred feet to get live feed. But, the nice thing is it records for up to 24 hours on one charge and there's a GPS."

"Unit 23 to Unit 47," Rod said, from behind them.

"This records?" Dupree said, jiggling the keys.

"Yeah."

"Come back, Detective."

"How's everything going over there?"

"Quiet," the officer on the other end of Rod's radio replied.

"10-4."

"What was that about?" Dupree asked. Conner moved around to the back of the van and was running a diagnostic on the equipment.

"That's the cop watching Ignatius Selman's place."

"Pastor give me a test," Conner said, from inside the van.

"Testing one, two, three."

CHAPTER 49

Mary Ellen Retinoir lived in a 500 square foot, one-bedroom, cinderblock apartment on the ground floor of a two-story complex. Her air conditioning bills were next to nothing. Entombed in concrete and surrounded by shade, the apartment was always cool, even in the dead of summer. On this November evening, she was tempted to turn on the heat for the first time this season, but she didn't want the place to smell like burnt dust.

From the kitchen, Mary Ellen opened the door to the only closet in the apartment. It served as a pantry from the kitchen and a clothes closet from the bedroom. She pulled a quilt from the shelf and tossed it on the couch.

Stepping into the bedroom, she reached over and tugged the corners of her bedspread. The few wrinkles that were made when she was getting dressed immediately disappeared.

With three short strides, she was in the bathroom.

Mary Ellen was stunning in a rich, burgundy sweater dress and black leggings. Her shapely calves were accentuated with a pair of ankle high boots. Her make-up framed her beautiful blue eyes with a smoky, gray palette and her lips were a full, dark red.

"You look awesome," she said as she curtsied and blew a kiss toward the mirror.

A knock at the door startled her momentarily. Grabbing a tissue, she removed the excess lipstick and exited the bathroom.

Mary Ellen checked the peephole to make sure it was Cooper Dupree. She straightened her dress. Looking into the peephole again, she noticed that he was scanning the apartments across the breezeway.

"Hey, come on in," she said, opening the door. Dupree was wearing a light blue sweater over a blue oxford shirt. His eyes were dark and clear. He wore a huge smile as he leaned down and gave her a kiss hello on the side of her face. Stepping into the doorway, he tripped on the weather stripping. Mary Ellen caught him as he fell into the apartment.

"I'm so sorry," he said, holding Mary Ellen's forearm and steadying himself. He stood back and straightened his sweater quickly, repeatedly brushing over his abdomen. "Wow. Uh…Mary Ellen… you look awesome."

"Thanks, Cooper. Can I fix you a drink?"

"Uh…sure." Dupree followed her the four steps into the kitchen. "I like your place."

"It's okay. And cheap. I've got rum and vodka."

"I'll have a rum and coke," Dupree said, pulling his phone from his pocket. "But not too strong. I was thinking we would go to Vincent's for dinner. I can drive."

"I love Vincent's." Mary Ellen reached into the cabinet above the stove and pulled a bottle of Bacardi from the shelf. "They have Chianti Classico, which is my absolute favorite wine."

"Awesome, we'll share a bottle," Dupree said, without looking up from his phone. "I'm sorry. I need to call a couple people to let them know I made it safely."

"That's fine," Mary Ellen said. She finished the drink and set it on the counter in front of Dupree.

"No answer at either one," Dupree said with a big smile. "I'll just text them."

Mary Ellen poured a vodka and soda for herself.

"Cheers," Dupree said. They clinked glasses.

"Cheers," Mary Ellen returned. Taking his hand, she led him the four steps into the living room and took a seat on the couch.

"I thought you might still be wearing your collar." Mary Ellen sat back deep into the couch and crossed her legs.

"Ha…no. I might have one out in the car if you want me to get it." Dupree took a seat next to her. Mary Ellen kicked her foot, gently tapping Dupree's calf.

"If I did, would you think I was a freak?" Mary Ellen blushed. "Oh my god, Cooper, I'm kidding." She gently slapped his thigh.

Dupree laughed.

Mary Ellen relaxed as they talked forever about her morning routine, Dupree's Sunday service, grocery shopping, popular television shows, the Saints, etc.

"…one thing, I want to do, is go back to that antique shop in the Quarter," Dupree said, in response to a question from Mary Ellen. "They had a collection of crosses that I can't stop thinking about."

"Cool."

"Uh…do you think they would be open tomorrow?"

"I have no idea," Mary Ellen said, standing suddenly. "Let me freshen that drink."

Dupree handed her his glass.

Dupree went into a long, drawn-out description of the crosses and their significance as Mary Ellen poured a couple more drinks.

When she returned, Mary Ellen slid into the couch, practically sitting on Dupree's lap.

"Here you go, Coop. I'm going to start calling you Coop." She handed him the glass. She rested her free hand on his thigh. "What's this?"

"Uh...those are...my keys," Dupree said, reaching into his pocket and removing a full key chain. "I...uh..."

"That's a lot of keys," Mary Ellen said, smiling. "Are you compensating for something?"

Dupree smiled, turning a little red.

"I'm playing with you." Mary Ellen grabbed the keys and set them on the windowsill behind the couch. She rested her head on his shoulder and gently massaged his knee.

"Cooper," Mary Ellen said, after a few moments. "About Friday night? The night we met...at the Bulldog."

"Yes?" Cooper's eyes were closed. His head tilted back, facing the ceiling. He pulled her closer.

"Remember how you walked me home?"

"Yes."

"Do you remember what time you left?"

Dupree looked at her.

"It was about 1:00."

"Are you sure?"

"Yes, you got off work at 12:30. It probably took a half hour to walk here." Dupree took a sip of his drink and set it on the windowsill next to his keys.

Mary Ellen leaned in to kiss him. With the first touch of his lips, she felt a tingle run up the back of her spine. His lips were cold, then very warm; his breath was sweet. His eyes closed as his hand, moved up her back. Falling back into the couch, Mary Ellen pulled him on top of her and slowly hooked her calf around the back of his legs.

Dupree tried to brace himself to keep his full weight off of her, but soon gave in, pressing her deep into the sofa.

"Oh Cooper, I wish you would have stayed with me on Friday," Mary Ellen said, placing her face into the crook of his neck

"Me too," Dupree said. He pulled her face up to his and kissed her again.

Moving to her side, she allowed Dupree to lie next to her as they held their kiss. His hand was on the small of her back. Her thigh moved up the side of his leg, pushing the hem of her dress higher and higher.

"I don't...suppose...you could say that...you spent the night," Mary Ellen said, kissing his eyes as she spoke.

"I'll say whatever you want me to say," Dupree said, returning the kisses to her eyes. "Why? Do you need an alibi or something?" He let out a little laugh.

"Well," Mary Ellen said, raising up slowly and kissing him on the mouth. Her hand slid up the inside of his leg. "As a matter of fact, I do."

Dupree returned the kiss, moving his hand up to hold the side of her head.

His kiss ended quickly with loud banging on the door.

"What the...

Mary Ellen jumped up.

"Police, Miss Retinoir. We have a search warrant."

Mary Ellen caught a partial view of Detective Webster's face through the peephole.

"Open up, Miss Retinoir," he said.

Within seconds the room was filled with a couple of police officers and one very large detective.

CHAPTER 50

Canal Street, named after a defunct attempt to connect Lake Pontchartrain to the Mississippi River, made being a pedicab driver in New Orleans a little tricky. When a hack drove across the four-lane thoroughfare, the avenues turned into streets and changed names completely. Carondelet Avenue was suddenly renamed Bourbon Street; Saint Charles Avenue became Royal Street.

When Napoleon sold the city in 1803, the residents tried to barricade their cultured city and European style of living by building Canal Street on the upriver edge of town. The vulgar Americans would have to fend for themselves.

Years later, so much hatred served only to make peddling a pedicab more difficult.

Parked beneath a forty-foot-tall Phoenix palm lit with hundreds of white Christmas lights strung up its trunk, Jarrell Landry waited patiently for Mary Ellen Retinoir to exit the precinct that was a block ahead of him. Fifteen traffic lights, all red, all synchronized, allowed a quick exit from the French Quarter. The cool night air was crisp, fresh, and alive with music spilling out of a corner bar.

Resting his forearms on the handle bars of his pedicab, Jarrell was reading his phone when Mary Ellen texted him. He took off, peddling toward the police station.

He rang his little bell to get her attention, when he was fifty feet away.

Mary Ellen looked stunning in a burgundy dress and black leggings.

"Hey!" Jarrell said, skidding to a stop. "You got one of those for me?"

"You can have this one," Mary Ellen said, handing Jarrell her cigarette. "I'm quitting." She pulled the pack from her purse. "I'm starting a whole new life." She handed him the pack, smiling.

"What happened in there? You said you were getting arrested."

"Oh my god, I should have texted you," Mary Ellen said, grabbing Jarrell's forearm. "I think it's over. First, the search of my apartment turned up nothing. Which of course it did! I'm so glad I cleaned the place. I would have died of embarrassment. Anyway…"

"What were they looking for?"

"A whole laundry list of things." Mary Ellen pulled a folded piece of paper from her purse and handed it to Jarrell. "Check all that stuff out."

Jarrell opened a copy of the search warrant and read down the list.

"Tennis balls?"

"Yeah." Mary Ellen laughed. "Metal tubing, burner phones, blue nylon cording, shrimp netting…"

"…and those god-damned grapevine crosses," Jarrell said, folding up the paper. "So that's it?" He handed the paper back to Mary Ellen.

"Also, while I was being interrogated for the 500th time, they uncovered video footage of the prostitute that was with the doctor going into Pat O's around 1:00 in the morning." Mary Ellen climbed into the pedicab. "Cooper swears that he was with me at that time, which he was. So, they let me go."

"But wasn't the doctor killed after the prostitute left?"

"Huh…well, maybe they've got some other things they haven't told me," Mary Ellen said, sitting back into the pedicab and covering her legs with a blanket that Jarrell provided for his patrons. "All I know is I'm free! Driver, take me to a dive bar! The finest in the city. I know, I know, the Jimani!"

"You got it," Jarrell said, dropping the pedicab into low and peddling into the French Quarter. "Are you meeting your preacher friend tonight?"

"I don't see that going anywhere now," Mary Ellen said. "It doesn't make for a very good first date when you get arrested. No. I think I'll just chill tonight. I might call him tomorrow."

"Did you ever get your money from Selman's?" Jarrell asked, turning on to Toulouse.

"I have not."

Jarrell stopped the pedicab and read his phone. "Oh no, hey, I've got a paying fare. I need to take it. I've got to drop you off here. Selman's is on the next block. You should stop in. Old man Selman's expecting you anyway."

Mary Ellen climbed out of the cab.

"I might," she said, hitching her purse onto her shoulder. "Meet me at the Jimani for a drink if you can."

"Will do." Jarrell made a U-turn and started peddling the wrong way on the one-way street. "See you."

• • •

Selman's Antiques surveillance log:

10:36. Unidentified blonde, shoulder length hair, five foot six, burgundy dress, black leggings, was allowed to enter the establishment through the front door by Ignatius Selman.

11:01. Unidentified blonde, from the previous entry, exited the establishment without assistance.

CHAPTER 51

Ignatius Selman woke clutching his stomach. In the near pitch dark of his bedroom, he rolled to the edge of his bed and flipped on the bedside lamp. Grabbing the bottle of milk-of-magnesia from his nightstand, he took two large gulps.

Iggy couldn't deal with the stress, the injustice, of being strong-armed into giving the little blonde thief another $600. The half-dollar size ulcer in his stomach punished him for cowering to her demands.

Iggy grabbed his phone and texted Diamond Olivet.

"Please come by. I've got $200! All I ask is one full day. I promise."

Iggy fell back into his bed and propped his head up with a couple of pillows.

One grand for a thief was a travesty, an outrage! One grand for a prostitute was a simple transaction between two capitalists.

Thievery was an abomination. Prostitution was noble. The fact that a civilized country would not legalize it was mind-blowing. Sure, drugs were bad, murder was a crime, stealing was for cowards and cheats. But prostitution? It was capitalism in its finest form. If it weren't for the puritan undertones of a hypocritical society, Iggy could have purchased all the good, clean, sex he wanted.

Iggy grabbed the milk-of-magnesia and took another drink. He winced, as he swallowed.

A noise from the back of the house made him jump. His heart raced. His stomach burned.

"Who's there?" he yelled, toward the kitchen. Iggy rolled on his hip and grabbed the bedstand drawer.

"Easy Iggy," Jarrell Landry said, sticking his head into the bedroom. "It's just me."

"Jesus Christ, you scared the life out of me."

Iggy grabbed his stomach.

"You want money? Screw off, I already gave your little girlfriend…" Reflux backed into Iggy's throat, making him gag. Coughing profusely, Jarrell handed him a paper towel.

Jarrell dropped a small backpack on the bed.

"No, I don't need any money."

From the backpack, he first removed two stainless tubes.

"Did you give her what we agreed on?"

"I might have been a little bit short. What are you doing with a tennis ball?"

Iggy fell back into the bed and covered his head with a pillow. "Uggh…"

Jarrell removed a length of blue nylon cord.

"You're not going to punk out on me Wednesday, are you?" Iggy asked, from beneath the pillow.

"I'm not sure I'll be going to Canton this week."

"I knew it."

"So why are you here?" Iggy asked. He pulled his legs up into a fetal position.

"Well, father, I'm here to kill you."

• • •

Ignatius Selman had lost an excessive amount of blood from the wound he suffered to his abdomen. The eight-inch blade sank into his back to the heel and actually pricked the mattress. The gag that filled his mouth was saturated with spit, breathing through his clogged sinuses was like breathing through a pair of tiny straws.

"Dad, I know you did your best."

Iggy was face down on his bed. Jarrell sat on Iggy's back, straddling him with his knees on the blood-soaked mattress.

"Ahhhh… wahhhh… aahh…oohhhh."

"I'm talking now, dad," Jarrell said, as he gently laced the blue nylon cord around Iggy's neck. He ran the line through the designated hole in the base, making sure to leave plenty of slack.

"The problem is, Iggy, you were a pathetic dad." Jarrell tied the knot. "I needed you when mom died. But, well, we won't go there."

"Wahhh…ahhh…"

"I'm talking."

Jarrell placed the tennis ball at the bottom of the base. Anchoring the clever murder device between Iggy's shoulder blades, he made one complete revolution and watched, with satisfaction, as the blue nylon cord moved along the sheets.

"When I intercepted the certified letter from Caldwell's lawyer, stating that you would be the beneficiary of his ministry, well, I knew what I had to do. I think mom would have approved."

Jarrell made another rotation of the clever device. The blue nylon cord nestled up to Iggy's neck.

"Ahhh…uhhh."

"…and because you are who you are, selfish, pathetic. I'm pleased to know, that you have no will on record. And do you know what that means?" Jarrell held the clever device. "I inherit Caldwell Ministries…" He made a quarter turn.

"Ahhhh…"

"…and the $168,000 cash that's in that stupid safe of yours." Jarrell made another quarter turn. Iggy attempted to kick, but he was getting increasingly weaker as his eyeballs started to bulge.

"I guess, before I end this, Iggy, I have only one question for you. Answer it quick and your suffering will be quick." Jarrell made another quarter turn on the device. "Why did you help Caldwell? Why would you loan him so much money, when I had to beg for every nickel?"

Jarrell quickly removed the gag from around Iggy's mouth.

Iggy struggled to get air through his restricted windpipe.

"Why Iggy?"

"It wasn't me." Blood spurted from Iggy's mouth onto the mattress. "It was…your mother. She always lent him the money…behind my back…you ignorant bastard!"

"Oh, daddy, let's not get ugly."

"I'm…not…your… daddy. Idiot. Caldwell…is your fath…"

Jarrell twisted the clever device around quickly, digging the blue nylon cord deep into Iggy's throat.

CHAPTER 52

Cooper Dupree awoke before dawn, surrounded by complete darkness and snoring. His dreams were erotic, vivid, and quickly forgotten. Stretching his arms above his head, he readjusted his coarse, hard pillow. It smelled old. Stretching his legs out slowly, his toe caught the base of a lamp and slid it along the end table. Another low, guttural snore rattled the walls.

Rod Webster was in the bedroom; he sounded like he was sleeping in the lounge chair just a foot away.

Dupree curled up and stretched his lower back by wrapping his arms around his knees and trying to escape his own hold. He rolled up to a seated position in the center of Rod's couch. Flipping on the lamp, he took inventory of his surroundings.

Rod's apartment was cluttered and needed vacuuming. The walls were bare, the only decorations were a few pictures of his wife on the mantel of a non-functioning fireplace.

Dupree tiptoed to the restroom, dodging items that longed for different homes—shoes that needed a closet, clothes that needed a hamper, newspapers that needed a recycling bin.

After completing his morning toiletries, Dupree found a can of Comet Cleanser underneath the sink. Five minutes later, he had cleaned the tub, toilet, and sink, with the washcloth that he had used to shower with the night before. Washing his hands and face, he put on a pair of running shorts, a T-shirt/sweatshirt combo, and a blue stocking cap.

After putting on his running shoes and a pair of light cotton gloves, Dupree exited the apartment, making sure to lock the door behind him.

Moments later, Dupree was up to speed, running in the neutral ground of Canal Street toward the river. With each stride, he dodged soft spots, streetcar rails, and potholes. His shoes flipped up little clumps of dewy sand. The air that filled his lungs was cool and fresh.

The sun was starting to rise over the West Bank.

Dupree slipped into penitent prayer.

"I'm sorry, Lord," he said aloud, thinking of the trickery that he used against Mary Ellen.

"Thank you," he said, in response to knowing that Mary Ellen was innocent. She was not the mysterious Miss Tessy.

"Help me, Lord."

Five minutes later, Dupree slowed as he crossed Claiborne Avenue, and jogged under an elevated section of Interstate 10. It was Monday morning and the Big Easy was slowly getting up to speed. Traffic flowed smoothly into the Central Business District. In an hour, the same traffic would be a bumper-to-bumper standstill.

Picking up the pace, Dupree could feel the heat being generated by his head into his stocking cap. His hands were wet inside the soft gloves.

Caldwell doesn't have a son.

An outbound streetcar rambled toward him; he took a few quick strides toward the right to make room.

Dupree waved at the streetcar conductor as it passed; there were no passengers. With every stride the buildings lining Canal Street were growing taller and taller. Soon he would be in the valley of the high-rise hotels.

Dupree crossed Rampart Street in a full run. His breathing was heavy but steady; sweat ran down his neck into his sweatshirt.

Ignatius Selman doesn't have a son.

As Dupree stepped onto the neutral ground past Rampart Street, he noticed, in his peripheral vision, a Mercedes-Benz dropping off a young lady dressed inappropriately for the cold. Her skirt was too short; her legs were too bare.

In his mind, Dupree saw the Bible in Caldwell's trailer; he saw the Gideon's Bible in the nightstand next to Lovett's broken neck. He thought about the first verse in Proverbs 7.

I noticed among the young men, a youth who lacked judgment.

Proverbs 7: 1

Dupree thought about verses 7 and 8 in the same chapter of Proverbs.

He was going down the street near her corner, walking along in the direction of her house. Then out came a woman to meet him, dressed like a prostitute and with crafty intent.

Proverbs 7: 7-8

Dupree stopped dead in his tracks. Grabbing his knees, he took in huge breaths; sweat dripped from his nose. Turning his head to the right, he watched the lady take a few bucks from the driver. She stuffed the money in the front of her shirt.

Where is the connection between Mary Ellen Retinoir and Diamond Olivet?

Dupree made eye contact with the lady and smiled. She smiled back. He took off again, toward the river.

"My son!" he said, sprinting as he crossed Bourbon. "A youth who lacked judgment! Thank you Lord!"

Dupree was tempted to turn around immediately. Detective Rod Webster would be very surprised to know that the identity of Miss Tessy had been revealed.

• • •

With a plastic bag filled with groceries hanging from each hand, Dupree scaled the steps to Rod Webster's apartment. He knocked on the door by kicking it with his foot.

"Morning," Rod said, opening the door. He was already dressed for work, wearing a cheap suit and a tie that was too short. His badge hung around his neck and helped to keep his tie positioned in the center of his enormous belly. "What have you got there?"

"I just picked up some breakfast," Dupree said, stepping inside. His T-shirt was wet beneath the sweatshirt. The warmth of the apartment felt good on his legs. "I hope you like egg sandwiches."

"Of course."

"I noticed your refrigerator was a little bare, so I went ahead and bought some staples," Dupree said. He started to unload a tub of margarine, mayonnaise, a jar of pickles, a pack of ham, and a half dozen other items.

"You didn't have to do that," Rod said, opening the bag that Dupree had placed on the stove.

"It's the least I could do for putting me up last night."

"Hey, thanks for cleaning the bathroom. Sorry about..."

"No," Dupree said, interrupting him. "I always do that. Anyway, I wanted to talk to you about Miss Tessy."

"What about her?"

"Where's a skillet?" Dupree started looking in the underneath cabinets.

"Right there."

Dupree fired up the oven. "During my run, I figured out who Miss Tessy is."

"Okay."

"It's Jarrell Landry." Dupree cracked an egg into the frying pan.

"What makes you think that?" Rod smiled. "Other than the fact that you want me to arrest him so that he'll stop sniffing around Miss Retinoir."

"Very funny. Anyway, it's the verse in Proverbs 7," Dupree said. "Do you want your bread toasted?"

"No thanks."

"The verse is a warning from a father to his son. The father warns his son to stay away from the seductive woman. So this whole time, we've been led to believe that the crimes were committed by the seductive woman—Mary Ellen Retinoir."

"Okay," Rod said.

"You see, Jarrell's father would have been right for giving him this warning."

"But Jarrell is not the son." Rod took a seat at the kitchen table.

Dupree handed Rod his iPhone. "Check out these articles." Dupree returned to the skillet. He broke the egg yolks with a spatula.

"Donna Landry was Jarrell's mother. Uh… she died in an automobile accident three years ago. What's this? Oh my god, Ignatius Selman was his legal guardian."

"Since the accident," Dupree said.

"How did we miss that?"

"Different last names." Dupree placed the egg sandwich, sliced diagonally, in front of Rod.

"Ignatius is Jarrell's father?"

"You can ask him when you bring him in for questioning."

Rod took a bite, consuming a quarter of the sandwich.

"But we have no physical evidence connecting him to either crime scene," Rod said, with a mouthful of food. "He's got a solid alibi for Caldwell's murder."

"He's done a good job." Dupree took a seat at the table. He placed half of his sandwich on Rod's plate. "There's nothing to say that him and Selman aren't in this together."

"What's the motive?"

"I'm not sure, yet. Money, probably. I'm on board with the 'Rod Webster school of crime solving'. You're never going to catch a real-life serial killer case." Dupree took a bite of his sandwich. "For that matter, neither will I."

"I guess this is as good a time as any to tell you," Rod said, handing Dupree his iPhone back. Rod grabbed his phone. "Check out the e-mail I just sent you. Pastor, I actually came to the same conclusion. Money is the motive."

"What is this?"

"It's Caldwell's will."

"The ministry is left to Ignatius Selman?" Dupree asked.

"A ministry that's worth over three-million dollars."

"You're kidding me," Dupree said. "We need to pick up Selman."

"And Jarrell Landry. That's our first order of business this morning."

"Give me five minutes." Dupree stood quickly and took several steps toward the bathroom before stopping cold in his tracks. "Detective?"

"Yes."

"So that means, if anything happens to Ignatius Selman, Jarrell Landry will inherit the three-million dollars."

"You better make that four minutes," Rod said, standing quickly.

CHAPTER 53

Riding shotgun in Detective Rod Webster's unmarked police cruiser, Cooper sniffed his armpits. For expediency, Dupree had passed on a shower. He wore the same straight leg jeans that he had worn to Mary Ellen's apartment and the same long-sleeve black shirt, and white clergy collar, that he had worn to Sunday services.

"You smell fine," Rod said. "You've got enough cologne on to gag a donkey."

"I'll roll the window down," Dupree said. He flipped the sun visor down and checked his look in the mirror. Running in the cool air gave his complexion a wind-burned, pinkish hue. His dark eyes were clear, alert. He patted under his chin, because it felt good.

Rod parked the cruiser on Toulouse in front of a fire hydrant. He was directly behind the officer who was on stakeout.

"Let's go."

Dupree stood a few feet away, eavesdropping on the detective.

"That's it? Okay, long night, huh? Well, if everything goes as plan, that was the last night. Thanks, Burless."

"Check this out," Rod said, handing Dupree the overnight surveillance log

"You've got to be kidding me? Mary Ellen came by here last night."

"Yep."

Rod was knocking on the front door of Selman's Antiques when his phone rang.

"Open up, Mr. Selman!" He yelled, banging with the palm of his hand. "Hello?"

"Good morning, Detective, this is Conner…from IT."

"Yes, Conner, what is it? I'm kind of busy. Selman! Open the damn door!"

"Uh…sir…it seems when you returned the wiretap, the keys… the transmitter were not in the box."

"What?" Rod turned to Dupree. "Conner says the keys weren't in the box when we turned in the wiretap."

"Oh my god," Dupree said, tapping his jean pockets. "They were on the windowsill behind her couch."

"How on…"

"When we were on the couch, they were getting in the way and I put them…"

"You've got to be kidding me," Rod said. "Conner, Pastor Dupree left them in her apartment. Apparently to worm his way into another date."

"I see that sir," Conner said. "The GPS has them at her apartment. Is there any way you could go get them? Like immediately. If anyone found out that…"

"Don't freak out on me, Conner. We've got to pick up someone. We'll go get them in a little bit."

"Thanks detective."

Rod hung up the phone and banged on the door again.

"God damn it Selman, open up. We know you're in there," Rod yelled. He turned to Dupree. "Check with Burless that Selman didn't leave."

"He's in there," Dupree said when he returned.

"That's it. Step back." Rod leveled a size thirteen, black leather wingtip on the door just below the knob. The door flew open crashing into the bookshelf stacked with framed icons.

"Selman!" Rod drew his sidearm and leveled it toward the office. "Show yourself Iggy. Let me see those hands! Don't make me use this!" Dupree entered behind Rod and followed him step for step as he walked through the shop. Rod swept the office with the gun. Entering the bedroom, Rod screamed an expletive as he took several quick steps toward the kitchen.

Dupree entered the bedroom and nearly vomited. Dropping to one knee, he closed his eyes and began to pray.

In a flash, in the picture that says a thousand words, Dupree saw blood, stainless steel tubing, a tennis ball, a knife, and the lifeless body of Ignatius Selman.

"It's clear," Rod said, entering the bedroom from the kitchen. "Jesus, Pastor, this is too much."

Dupree stood and scanned the room. He walked straight to a family Bible sitting on the dresser, held open by a grapevine cross. He opened the top drawer of the dresser and grabbed a T-shirt. Picking up the grapevine cross, he showed it to Rod.

"Well, I guess we've figured out what a 'slaughter' looks like," Rod said, stepping up next to Iggy and feeling his neck for a pulse.

CHAPTER 54

Mary Ellen Retinoir struggled to remove her dirty clothes from the floor of her closet. A week's worth of clothing was packed solid in the laundry basket and her favorite jeans were wedged behind an old pet carrier.

Feeling a chill, she grabbed a dirty, long-sleeved Henley. Unbuttoning the straps of her "laundry day" overalls, she put on the shirt and refastened the buttons.

Piling all of the dirty clothes on the basket, she sat down on top to smash them flat. She cursed the sock that escaped the roundup and was still lying on the closet floor.

Mary Ellen grabbed the laundry basket and felt a twinge in her lower back as she lifted it. Placing it on her hip, she walked through the living room. As she was opening the front door, she noticed Cooper Dupree's keys sitting on the windowsill behind the couch.

"Oh my god!" She grabbed them with her free hand. She examined them briefly before dropping them in her front pocket.

Her apartment complex consisted of two long rows of apartments, that were two stories tall, separated by a breezeway. Because the laundry was on the second floor of the row of apartments across the breezeway, Mary Ellen had to climb a flight of stairs carrying the heavy laundry basket.

Breathing heavily, she didn't even bother separating the colors from the whites, when she packed in the first load.

Sitting on a bench outside of the laundry room, she watched a sliver of Saint Charles Avenue through the breezeway between apartments. Lighting a cigarette, she sat back on the bench and blew smoke toward the sky. High clouds made a gloomy, gray back drop behind the live oak branches. It looked like rain.

"...and you've got work this afternoon," she said, to no one. "It just never ends."

She dialed Cooper Dupree; his voice mail picked up.

"Hey Cooper, it's Mary Ellen. I wanted to call and let you know that you left your keys. Uh...so call me back. Maybe we can meet. I need to explain last night anyway. Call me back. Bye."

Mary Ellen hung up and stared at the phone, wishing she had been more eloquent.

Suddenly, Jarrell Landry came running toward her apartment from the street. Mary Ellen dropped the hand that was holding the cigarette down beside her and exhaled quickly.

He started knocking loudly on her apartment door. Mary Ellen looked for a place to stash the cigarette.

"Mary Ellen! Open up, it's me." His voice echoed through the breezeway.

Something told her not to respond.

"I'm up here," she thought about saying. But she had just lit the cigarette and her nerves were frazzled and...

Is that a knife?

Mary Ellen slid down lower into the bench.

What on earth is he...

"Open up Mary Ellen. I know you're in there." Jarrell knocked even louder, hitting the door with his fist. He kept looking back toward Saint Charles Avenue.

Is he being chased?

He turned, suddenly looking relaxed. Leaning against the door, he started cleaning his fingernails with the tip of the knife blade.

Once again, Mary Ellen thought about calling out to him, but then he tucked the knife under his jacket and started banging on the door again. He looked into the window, moving his head up and down to peer through the mini-blinds.

"Mary Ellen!"

Without thought, she silently slid off of the bench and pushed herself back into the laundry room, when her cellphone began to ring.

She had forgotten it on the bench.

From inside the rumbling of the hot, humid laundry room, she could hear Jarrell taking the stairs, two at a time. She stood quickly and walked out of the room onto the balcony. Jarrell was right in front of her.

"There you are," he said. Sweat was forming on his lip. She could not see the knife. "I was wondering what happened to you." He went to kiss her. She offered her cheek and then grabbed her cellphone.

"I was just getting caught up on some laundry," she said, turning away. "What's up?"

"Nothing, we just need to talk."

• • •

Jarrell paced in front of Mary Ellen, who sat quietly on her couch, hands folded in front of her. His sneakers squeaked and the knife switched hands with each 180-degree turn. Jarrell refused to look into her eyes, opting to talk to the floor instead.

Jarrell wiped his forehead with his free hand. His left eye twitched uncontrollably. The knife was steady, slicing the air beside him, as he made another three strides.

A tear escaped from the corner of Mary Ellen's eye.

"I'm scared, Jarrell," she said, wiping her eye with the back of her hand.

"You should be," Jarrell said, leaning forward with the knife. He stuck the tip under Mary Ellen's chin. Trembling, she closed her eyes and tried to stay as still as possible. Jarrell pushed her forehead with the palm of his hand, nicking her chin with the knife tip, as she fell into the couch.

He pounced on top of her lap, straddling her.

Bringing the knife beneath her chin, he moved forward and breathed gently into her ear.

Tears filled Mary Ellen's eyes as she began to shake.

Jarrell sat back. Bringing the knife down, he cut the left strap of her overalls with a quick pull upwards. Keeping a finger over Mary

Ellen's mouth, he cut the right strap and watched as the top of her overalls fell. Her cellphone and car keys fell into her lap.

He brought the knife up to the only button fastened on her shirt.

"Jarrell, please." Her voice was weak.

With a quick stroke, Jarrell cut off the button. He leapt to his feet and checked his watch.

Mary Ellen started shaking, sobbing uncontrollably.

"Quit the blubbering! Now get up and grab your stuff. I'm about to make you famous."

Jarrell motioned her toward the bedroom. Holding the knife to the center of her back, he directed her to take a seat on the bed.

"Now where is that peasant dress you love so much?" Jarrell asked, as he emptied all the clothes from her dresser.

"It's in the wash."

"Have you got another one?"

"In the closet," Mary Ellen said, still clutching her phone and keys. "I like the one with the big front pocket."

Jarrell pulled the dress from the hanger and tossed it on her lap.

"Go ahead. Put it on," Jarrell said, blocking the door. A smile crossed his face. "Take your time."

CHAPTER 55

ooper Dupree was not comfortable with the pop-in visit. Parking the Toyota next to a dumpster in Mary Ellen Retinoir's apartment complex, he tried once more to call her. Her voice mail picked up before even a single ring. Her phone was dead.

The morning was cool, even though the humidity had returned; brightness kept his eyes in a constant squint. Exiting the car, Dupree caught a whiff of the contents of the dumpster—coffee grounds with a hint of garlic chicken.

Walking quickly through the cars, he entered the breezeway. Mary Ellen's bike was parked underneath the living room window, unchained. Dupree glanced inside, as he approached the door. The blinds were closed. Opening the screen door, he knocked loudly.

"She's not home Father. A voice came from behind Dupree. He spun to face an elderly lady standing in the door across the way. "She left about an hour ago with her boyfriend."

"Her boyfriend?"

"Uh-huh." She walked across the breezeway.

"Can you describe her boyfriend?"

The lady pondered the question. Dupree waited patiently for a reply.

"You know, the constable's coming to take me to jail," the lady said, stepping up very close to Dupree. "Unless I can get things straightened out, you know, I have a son who wanted to borrow $5000 because he's got this new job in Maine, and I told him that I wasn't going to give him another dime until he pays me back the..."

Her hair was matted to one side of her head; she wore a full complement of eye make-up. Her lipstick was bright red and smeared in the creases of her mouth.

"I see. Ma'am, do you remember what Mary Ellen's boyfriend looked like?"

"It was that boy with the bicycle cart."

"Did she say where they were going?" Dupree remained standing in the screen door. He pulled his phone from his pocket.

"Aren't you freezing? My legs are bare and I can't imagine how you...have you seen what that flood water did to my legs?"

Dupree gulped as she pulled her long skirt up, unveiling a pair of blotchy stovepipes. One was clearly thicker than the other, swollen. Both shins showed countless scabs and scars.

"I'm on antibiotics, but I've been told to keep all receipts and what-have-you because a good lawyer could...oh, my god, go please put a jacket on."

Dupree slid from beside the screen door and closed it behind him. He showed the lady his phone. "Is this her boyfriend?"

"That's him," she nodded. "They said the constable is coming Monday, and they're going to make this big to-do." She swirled her crinkled index finger over her head. "...and I'm thinking about making them forcibly remove me...with handcuffs. Do constables do that? Do they handcuff people like me?"

"I wouldn't think so," Dupree said, turning toward the dumpster. "Ma'am, did Mary Ellen say where she was going?"

"Because, like I told those National Guardsmen, I will not be treated like an animal. You can't treat me like an animal."

"No ma'am, you can't allow that," Dupree said, moving toward his car. "It was nice meeting you."

"I'll walk from here on my own two legs," she said, tears welling in her eyes. "I've been here twelve years, in that apartment right there, and I've never missed a rent note and I've been a good tenant, and now I've got to go..."

"Bye-bye," Dupree said.

"She was crying, you know," the lady said, taking a cigarette from the pocket of her tattered robe.

"Excuse me?'

"Mary Ellen was crying when she left," the lady said. She lit the cigarette and wiped her own tears with the back of her hand. "I was going to call the police, but the constable's coming to kick me out, so I was scared."

Dupree took a step toward her. Taking her free hand, he held it with both his.

"Ma'am, they won't come today. I promise," Dupree said. "Did Mary Ellen tell you where she was going? Did you hear?"

"Forgive me Father for I have sinned," she said, bowing her head.

• • •

Dupree sat in his car and made a few frantic phone calls.

Mary Ellen's phone went to voice mail. He called Detective Webster.

"Webster."

"Detective," Dupree said. "I'm at Mary Ellen's. I think Jarrell Landry has taken her. A neighbor saw her leaving and she was crying."

"Mary Ellen was crying?"

"Yes. I think Jarrell took her against her will."

"Huh. Did you get the key fob?"

"No. Her apartment's locked."

"Hold on one second," Rod said. "I'm going to get Conner on the line."

"Conner Stupak."

"Conner? This is Detective Webster. I've got Cooper Dupree on the line with us."

"Good morning Pastor. What's up? Did you get the key fob back?"

"Not yet," Dupree said. "I'm at Mary Ellen Retinoir's apartment and she's not here."

"Conner, just verify the fob is still in her apartment and I'll authorize Dupree to go in and get it."

"Hold on just a second," Conner said. Dupree could hear him typing on a keyboard. "The fob is not there. It's on Convention Center drive, heading toward the French Quarter."

CHAPTER 56

Jarrell Landry prodded Mary Ellen down a hedge-lined portico. Passing between shadows, the morning sun glinted off of the gray steel of a .38 caliber pistol.

Jarrell was careful not to bruise Mary Ellen's lower back with the gun barrel.

With bare feet, they moved quietly between the columns that supported the arcaded façade of the cathedral. Since the conception of his get-rich-quick scheme, Jarrell had planned to make the sacristy of the oldest church in New Orleans the location for his finale. New Orleans' first female serial killer—Mary Ellen "the proverbs prostitute" Retinoir—would, in an act of contrition, hang herself as a reckoning for her crimes.

Jarrell smiled at the thought.

Moving silently down a corridor that he had walked one hundred times before, Jarrell sensed freedom, power, and control.

He was finally a success.

As he prepared for the coup-de-grace, the church too would share in his success. Their doctrine of guilt had driven a psychopathic murderess to commit suicide. It was ironic that their trophy would hang from the rafters of one of the most unsuccessful projects in Louisiana church history.

In March 1849, the Saint Louis Cathedral underwent a major renovation. The church was not always the sparkling white, three-pointed diadem that adorned a full city block of the French Quarter. The cathedral was humble in its infancy. But, with an exploding growth of parishioners, the church needed more space. Architecture fitting for the great King of France, Louis IX, would be the only acceptable solution to house the throngs of Catholic sinners needing redemption.

Although the antebellum renovations had been funded with charitable donations, the project itself was run more like a government job. Finishing two years late and 400% over budget, the cathedral finally opened in 1851. All were welcome to enter and pray for forgiveness, except for J. N. B. de Pouilly. The architect, in charge of the renovation, was run out of town on a rail after botching the entire revamp.

If Jarrell failed at his task as miserably as Pouilly, he wouldn't be run out of town; he would be executed by lethal injection.

"...and nobody wants that, do they?" Jarrell asked, thinking out loud.

"Jarrell, you don't need the gun. I'm not going to..."

"Shh!"

Ascending seven steps, Jarrell reached around Mary Ellen to verify that the door was locked. It was. Reaching into his pocket, he removed the key and unlocked the door.

"This way," he said, entering first and dragging Mary Ellen by the arm behind him. The door closed, leaving them in pitch darkness.

"How did you get a key?"

"Iggy left it for me," Jarrell said, guiding them along the wall to another door. "Hell of a nice guy, my pappy."

"No, he wasn't, but that doesn't mean you have to follow..."

"Shh!"

They entered a hall with a small window that reflected light from one of the stained-glass exterior windows.

"This way," Jarrell said, leading Mary Ellen through another door and closing it quickly behind them. Again, they were in complete darkness.

Jarrell flipped on a tiny flashlight and placed it in his mouth.

Grabbing her hands, Jarrell gave her a quick half spin and then bound them behind her with a tie-wrap.

"Jarrell, I don't know what you're planning, but there is no need to do this. I'm not going to tell anyone. You know you can trust me."

"I know." Jarrell stood on a folding chair and pulled the cord to an overhead light.

Mary Ellen gasped. Jarrell reached around her and put his hand over her mouth, shoving the gun into her kidney.

"Mary Ellen," Jarrell said, calmly. "It pains me to do this. But....well...I lie. You don't deserve to be lied to. Listen."

Jarrell kept Mary Ellen facing the hangman's noose fastened to the rafter high above their heads. With thirteen loops, Jarrell had spent a whole day tying and retying to make the knot just right.

"I owe you an explanation. Please step up." Jarrell pushed her toward the folding chair that he pushed below the noose. Jamming the gun even deeper into her side and wrestling with her arms, he was careful not to dislocate her shoulders.

"Jarrell, please," Mary Ellen said, in a broken voice. "Don't."

He grabbed her by the hair on the back of her neck and raised her onto the chair.

"I never liked that tattoo. Up, up you go."

Mary Ellen balanced on the chair.

Jarrell quickly placed the noose around her neck and tightened it.

"Oh my god! Jarrell! Please!"

Grabbing another folding chair, he took a seat in front of her. He crossed his legs and rested the gun in his lap.

"It won't do any good to scream. We're buried really deep in here."

"I won't, Jarrell, I promise I won't. Just look at me," Mary Ellen said softly. Tears were rolling down her cheek. "You don't want to do this!"

Jarrell rubbed his chin, as if in deep thought.

"I think I do."

"Please Jarrell, look at me. It's me, Mary Ellen. We're friends. Why would you want to hurt me?"

"Mary Ellen, I could say that I had some altruistic motive to rid the world of whores and whoremongers," he said, looking down at her feet.

"Hell, Caldwell was a sleaze bag and that dentist—god, he was the worst of all of them. Seriously, who goes on a business trip and hooks up with a dirty whore like Diamond? She's disgusting. Well, she was until she had the makeover. She looked pretty good, then."

"Jarrell," Mary Ellen pleaded. "Look at me. We're friends. You like me. Please, don't do this."

"I do like you," Jarrell said, looking up with brown puppy dog eyes. "That's why I'm going to make you the most notorious female to walk the streets of New Orleans. Quite an honor, if you ask me."

He wiped his forehead and tried to pop his neck by twisting it back and forth.

"Remember when you told me you liked me but 'not like that'," Jarrell said, making finger quotes. "Don't flatter yourself Mary Ellen. I liked you too, but 'not like that'. I liked you because you were perfectly gullible, perfectly naïve. You're like a little puppy that can be trained to speak, or beg, or play dead. Are you ready to play dead?" He let out a little laugh.

"Jarrell, I have no idea what you're talking about. Jarrell, please."

"I bet you didn't even know that your preacher boyfriend is screwing a smoking hot MILF, right under your nose. I saw it with my own eyes, playing grab-ass right on the balcony of the Columns Hotel."

Mary Ellen shook her head.

"Such a little patsy. That's you, Mary Ellen Retinoir. Anyway," Jarrell said. "Why? You ask. I'll tell you why? It's not altruistic. My motive was really very basic. The most basic of all motives— money. Can you believe it? All this for the almighty dollar!"

Mary Ellen shook, as she began sobbing uncontrollably.

"But then again, you understand that. There's not much you wouldn't do for a buck."

"I wouldn't kill my friend," she said. Her voice escaped in short, quiet bursts.

"Hell, Mary Ellen, I killed my own father," Jarrell said, standing. "Once you've done that, all else is gravy."

He kicked the chair out from under her. The line tightened quickly; Mary Ellen fell only an inch or so. Jarrell shouldn't have tested the rafter with so much weight—the pre-stretched rope didn't allow for the satisfying pop made by her neck breaking.

Jarrell stepped away from Mary Ellen's kicks and waited patiently for all movement to stop. It was surprisingly quick.

Maybe, her neck did break.

Stepping up behind her, he cut the tie wrap off her hands and stuffed it in his pocket. Pulling the typed note and a grapevine cross from his back pocket, he dropped it on the floor at Mary Ellen's lifeless feet.

"All that's left now is a quick trip to the bank," he said, dropping "Miss Tessy's" burner phone into the pocket of Mary Ellen's peasant dress.

CHAPTER 57

"**I** do like you," Jarrell said, looking up with brown puppy dog eyes. "That's why I'm going to make you the most notorious female to walk the streets of New Orleans. Quite an honor if you ask me."

Jarrell's voice was cold, unfeeling.

Mary Ellen looked down from her perch, pulling against the restraint that bound her hands. The rope around her neck was tight; she flexed her neck muscles trying to loosen the knot.

The paneled room where she would be entombed was no larger than a walk-in closet. A single bare light bulb hanging from the ceiling overhead illuminated the scene. A rack of choir robes lined the wall to her right; a book shelf filled with hymnals and missals covered the wall to her left. Behind Jarrell was another door.

Jarrell's voice rattled around in her head. Her ears filled with the sound of her heartbeat. Her brain suddenly fired on one word "notorious".

The murder of Caldwell and the murder of the dentist were going to be pinned on her.

Notorious.

And now, he planned to cover his tracks by having this notorious female hang herself in the most notorious church in New Orleans.

"I wouldn't kill a friend," Mary Ellen said, out of reflex. All of the oxygen in her body was being pumped to her brain; thoughts of ways to survive surged through her mind at the speed of light.

"Hell, I killed my own father..."

Instantly Mary Ellen became aware that her hands were still bound. There was no way someone could hang themselves with their hands bound.

Jarrell has to free my hands. He has to stay until I'm dead to free my hands.

Mary Ellen began to cry. She bent her knees to put a strain on the rope above her. Making little moves with her neck muscles, she found an area just above her vocal cords that seemed tight, strong. She weakened her knees more, pulling the slack completely out of the rope.

"...everything else is gravy."

Jarrell stood; Mary Ellen took a huge breath.

The chair was suddenly kicked out from under her. She felt her neck pop. Twisting slightly, she was able to move the knot over her left ear.

Kick! Kick! For just a moment!

Holding her neck muscles tight, she gave up any hope of breathing.

Kick! Kick! Now slowly stop. Hang, hang...

Mary Ellen closed her eyes and began to count. At twenty, she felt her hands being tugged back and the bindings let loose. Her arms dangled beside her. At forty, she heard the door close behind her.

Reaching up with her hands, she grabbed the rope above her head and strained to loosen the knot. Air passed into her lungs, as if she were breathing through a straw. Kicking, swinging, she was able to get her foot on the edge of a bookshelf. With each pull, a little more air seeped past the rope. With each pull, her arms weakened.

CHAPTER 58

"Conner are you sure?" Rod Webster asked, as he drove through a barricade onto the paved area between Saint Louis Cathedral and Jackson Square. Driving through a sea of tourists, palm readers, and artists, Rod repeatedly honked his horn, while Dupree rode with his head stuck out of the passenger side window, yelling for people to get the hell out of the way.

"You're within thirty meters. Can you take a left?"

"She's in the cathedral?" Rod yelled.

"If that's to your left."

Rod placed the car in park and worked his way out of the driver's seat.

"This way."

Dupree climbed out of the window and sprinted around the car.

"Keep an eye out for Jarrell Landry," Dupree said. He was scanning the crowd, as he ran past Detective Webster, up the steps to the sanctuary.

"Conner?" Webster yelled into his cellphone. "Talk to me, Conner!"

"Yes sir, looks like you're ten meters closer."

Dupree noticed the hedge lined portico. "This way," he said, running around the side of the building.

"You've got to stay with me," Rod said, trying to jog. His feet thundered against the marbled walkway. "Conner can't see you."

"There," Dupree said, pointing to a side entrance. "It's open." He yelled back at Rod.

"That's it," Conner said, over the radio. "You're right on top of her."

Rod drew his sidearm as he came up beside Dupree.

"We should call for back-up," Rod said.

"They're on the way," Conner replied.

"We should wait." Rod looked at Dupree.

"I can't wait. There's no time. Give me the gun. I'll go in."

Rod shook his head. His stomach was tight; sweat ran down his temples.

Stepping past Dupree, Rod took the first of seven steps leading to the entry.

The instant Rod stepped inside, a pang hit his heart, his left arm spiked with pain. With his gun raised, his knees weak, fear froze him in his tracks. The little hallway was filled with the sounds of a struggle—banging, kicking, things crashing to the floor. There was danger behind the door at the end of the hallway.

Dupree rushed past and grabbed the doorknob.

"It's locked," he said, stepping back. "Watch out."

With the full force of his 180 pounds, Dupree flew at the door with a right kick.

"Holy...!" Dupree screamed, as he fell to the floor grabbing his ankle.

Taking a quick three strides, Rod hit the door with the full force of his shoulder, shattering the door jamb.

Rod tumbled to the floor, gun drawn, aiming up at anything that moved.

Dupree scrambled to his feet and jumped over Rod trying to keep weight off his right ankle. He grabbed Mary Ellen's waist with both hands and sat her on his left shoulder.

"Where's Jarrell Landry?" Rod yelled from the floor. He rolled to his side and climbed to his feet, using a book shelf for support.

Dupree steadied himself with his right hand jammed against the wall. He held Mary Ellen tight to his shoulder as she worked the noose off her neck with both hands.

Rod stepped through the little room and opened the door to the sanctuary. Scanning the room for any movement, he followed his line of sight with the barrel of the gun.

Stepping back into the little room, he helped Dupree lower Mary Ellen to the floor.

"Is she okay?" he asked, leaning over Dupree who looked like he was trying to revive Mary Ellen.

It took only a moment for the Detective First Class Rod Webster to realize that they were holding and kissing each other in a desperate, thankful embrace.

CHAPTER 59

Two months later.

Topping the crest of the Interstate 10 High-rise Bridge, the skyline of New Orleans emerged into view. Against the backdrop of a morning sun, the Superdome rose like a flying saucer from a bed of low fog. Skyscrapers lining the Central Business District blocked its flight to the East. An endless line of brake lights guided the way to the Crescent City Connection bridge.

"That is so cool," Mary Ellen Retinoir said. "I never get over seeing the city. I've missed it so much."

"I bet you have," Cooper Dupree said, as he started braking to take his place in the line of cars feeding into the city. "You've been more than patient."

"You made it easy."

"So you're absolutely convinced that you're going to stay?"

"If it all goes as planned, and Detective Webster can get my apartment back," Mary Ellen said, looking out the passenger side window.

They moved slowly toward their exit.

"Will you come visit me?" Mary Ellen turned toward Dupree.

"I'll do my best."

Moments later they exited onto Canal Street.

"Before you head back, I need to get the Wixons something for a 'thank you' gift."

"You don't really…"

"No. No. They went out of their way to help me. And Leslie's like my best friend now."

Dupree made a right onto Rampart Street, then an immediate U-turn.

"They helped us all. Uh…you better get down. We wouldn't want to get this far and blow your cover."

"Gotcha."

Dupree followed the GPS directions to a pay-to-park lot behind Detective Webster's precinct. As he searched the aisles for a spot, Mary Ellen sunk down deep into the front seat. She pulled her hoodie over her head to hide.

After parking, Dupree grabbed a blanket from the back seat, exited the car, and went around to Mary Ellen's door.

Dupree covered Mary Ellen with the blanket and guided her, with his hand on her waist, into a door in the back of the police precinct.

"Dupree?" an officer asked once he entered.

"Yes."

"This way."

• • •

In the tiny room adjacent to Interrogation Room #2, there were no chairs, lights, windows, or soft surfaces. Nothing hung on the walls. Light filtered in from the interrogation room through the one-way mirror. Pastor Cooper Dupree studied Mary Ellen Retinoir's expression as she watched Jarrell Landry pace back and forth. Frowning, her furrowed brows hid her crystal blue eyes. Her nose, in profile, was perfect, except for the slight nervous twitching.

When Jarrell suddenly stopped and took a seat at the steel table, turning to face the large mirror that separated the two rooms, Mary Ellen grabbed Dupree's hand. She squeezed tightly.

"You're sure he can't see us?" Mary Ellen asked.

Jarrell folded his arms across his chest and looked intimidatingly toward them.

"Positive," Dupree answered, without breaking his stare.

Mary Ellen released Dupree's hand. He placed his arm on her shoulder and pulled her close.

"I'm scared."

"You'll do fine."

Jarrell began to bite his fingernails, turning his attention from the mirror.

"I thought this day would never come," Mary Ellen said.

"To be honest, I thought it would take longer." Dupree gave her shoulder a light squeeze.

Jarrell stood, walked around the steel table, and faced the giant mirror. He was inches away from Mary Ellen's face, when he smiled and picked at his front teeth. He tugged his black fleece jacket from the back and zipped it up the front.

"It's way colder in there than in here," Mary Ellen whispered. Dupree released her shoulder and placed his hand on the middle of her back.

"He can't hear us," he whispered back, smiling.

"Have you ever been in there?"

"Once."

"It's like a freezer," Mary Ellen said, wrapping her arm around Dupree's waist. She hooked her thumb in the belt loop of his standard, black, cotton preacher pants. "I've been in there several times and, let me tell you, it's no picnic. He has no clue what he's about to face."

"Let's hope so."

• • •

Interrogation Room #2 should have exploded with sound when Detective Webster entered. The door opened so violently that it rattled the walls in Dupree and Mary Ellen's hiding place. When he sat, the giant metal table was pushed forward several inches across the tile flooring.

"He looks different," Mary Ellen said. "Did he grow a mustache?"

"No, he's always had the mustache," Dupree said, taking a step back from the one-way mirror. "He's lost over twenty pounds."

"Really?"

"Yeah."

Detective Webster was still wearing the same suit he wore during the four-day killing spree back in November. However, now the jacket hung off his frame rather than constricting it. His pants were loose in the thighs. Also, he had purchased a couple of new ties, and learned to tie a half-Windsor, which allowed him to correctly adjust the length, over his still girthy midsection.

"He looks good," Mary Ellen said, as Detective Webster opened up a laptop computer and made a few opening statements. "What's he saying?"

Dupree flipped the switch on a single speaker that hung on the wall next to the one-way mirror.

"…and we should be able to close this case once and for all." Detective Webster was typing as he spoke.

"Thank god. It's like I'm never going to get dad's stuff out of probate. Anything I can do to help move this along is good for me," Jarrell said. He turned sideways in a metal folding chair and rested heavily on the back with his chin resting on his forearm.

"First things first," Detective Webster said. "For the record, can you state your full name?"

"John Jarrell Landry."

"It is my understanding at the time of the murders of Reverend Jack Caldwell, Dr. Keller Lovett, and Ignatius Selman, and the subsequent suicide of Mary Ellen Retinoir, that you were in a relationship with Miss Retinoir."

"I wouldn't say it was a relationship," Jarrell said. "We were friends."

"Were you physical? Did you have a romantic relationship?"

"No."

"Tell me about the night Reverend Caldwell was murdered."

"Like I told you, she told me that after the revival, before Caldwell made it back to his trailer, she stole some cash and a cross. I told her that I had delivered the crosses earlier that day and that they were valuable. That's all I know."

"So you weren't there when Caldwell was actually murdered?"

"No."

"You were never in Algiers Point on the night of Caldwell's death."

"No."

"You didn't meet Mary Ellen Retinoir at the Old Point Bar for a drink around 9:15 p.m.?"

"I…uh…no, I wasn't on the West Bank that day."

"I thought you delivered…"

"I was there that morning, that's it," Jarrell said, sitting back in the chair. He crossed his arms in front of him. "She was there that night. She must have waited for him and strangled him. Just awful."

"Uh-huh." Detective Webster looked up from his laptop. "…and you know he was strangled because…"

"It's common knowledge."

"Uh-huh…did she steal the grapevine crosses?"

"I don't know. She only told me of the one, the gold one."

"But she knew you delivered the grapevine crosses?" Detective Webster asked, without looking up from his laptop.

"Yeah, sure. I told her."

"I wonder. Why would she take a practically worthless cross and leave the valuable grapevine crosses behind?"

"No clue. Mary Ellen wasn't really that bright and they're kind of bulky and heavy."

"So you knew the grapevine crosses were valuable?"

"Yes. Of course."

"Did you get a receipt when you delivered the crosses to Caldwell?"

"Well, no, that would have been up to dad."

"We found no record of the sale of those crosses to Caldwell," Detective Webster said, typing on his keyboard.

"I'm not surprised."

"What would you say if I told you that we have CCTV footage of your car leaving Algiers Point at 2:30 a.m. on the night Reverend Caldwell was murdered?"

"Uh…I would say…"

"What would you say if I told you that we found trace amounts of DNA under Caldwell's trailer, DNA so small that the state forensic labs couldn't do anything with them?"

"Ok."

"But the FBI, well, they're the FBI. It took a little time, but they identified it as your DNA."

"I'd say that they made a mistake, or no...wait...that might be when I..."

"Let's move on to Dr. Keller Lovett? Did you know the doctor?" Detective Webster asked.

"No."

"What would you say if I told you that we have a person who will testify that you paid him twenty dollars to direct Kirsten "Diamond" Olivet to the table where Dr. Lovett was seated in Pat O'Brien's on the night of the murder?"

"I would say they're mistaken. I've never even been to Pat O'Brien's. And I certainly never..."

"Were you at the Royal Sonesta on the morning that Dr. Lovett was murdered?"

"No," Jarrell said. "What is this? Do I need a lawyer?"

"What would you say if I told you that we have a witness that will place you in the service area that morning?"

"Whoa...sounds like I may need a lawyer. If you're going to throw accusations that..."

"Let's move onto the death of your father."

"He wasn't much of a father," Jarrell said, taking a defensive stature. He scooted his chair and placed his elbows on the table. "He was more of a crappy caretaker."

"You know he was under surveillance when he was murdered."

"Yeah," Jarrell said, smiling. "That must have been embarrassing for someone."

"I guess," Detective Webster said. "What would you say if I told you that we had forensic accountants go through boxes of your dad's financial journals? They went through literally reams of data that pointed to some sick obsession of him counting the money in his safe. Money that is no longer there. Money that Mary Ellen Retinoir didn't have when she committed suicide."

"I didn't take it."

"Yes, you did," Detective Webster said. "Those same forensic accountants have tied every last dime to you with photos taken of you making multiple cash deposits in multiple accounts at multiple banks."

"It's not true. I have never…"

"Let's move onto the suicide of Mary Ellen Retinoir. Why do you think she killed herself after killing three people?"

"How should I know? She was a psychopath. She wanted revenge against Caldwell or whatever. My dad tried to screw her over on the cross. I get that."

"Did you steal the money from you dad's safe, because you weren't sure that he actually left a will?"

"I didn't steal the…"

Detective Webster slid a Royal Sonesta napkin, encased in a sealed plastic bag, across the table.

"What's this?" Jarrell asked, picking up the baggie.

"It's your dad's last will and testament," Rod said, without looking up from his computer. "Looks like he bequeathed his entire estate to Lynnette Faust the day before he was murdered."

"But…"

"Did you kill Lovett because 'he was the worst of them all'?"

"I didn't…"

Detective Webster hit 'play' on an audio recording on his laptop.

"Who goes on a business trip and hooks up with a dirty whore like Diamond? She's disgusting."

Jarrell went pale. His knee started shaking violently.

"Is that your voice?"

"How…I never said…"

"Did you intercept a certified letter to your dad that contained a copy of Reverend Caldwell's will?"

"I…"

"We have a copy of the signature, so be careful what you say."

"I want a lawyer." Jarrell's voice was weak.

"Good idea," Detective Webster said. "I just have a few more questions. You don't have to answer, if you don't want to. Mr. Landry, did you buy a burner phone in Canton, Mississippi on one of your frequent trips for Ignatius Selman?"

Jarrell remained silent. He drummed his fingers on the table as he looked toward the door.

"Did you buy another burner phone in Metairie, just a week before Reverend Caldwell was murdered? Be aware that we have photos of you purchasing both."

Detective Webster closed his laptop.

"I'm wondering, when you dropped the burner phone you purchased in Canton into Mary Ellen's pocket while she was hanging in the Saint Louis Cathedral sacristy, did you hear it hit a set of car keys?"

Jarrell shook his head.

"I guess you forgot Mary Ellen Retinoir didn't own a car."

At that moment the door to Interrogation Room #2 opened and Mary Ellen Retinoir walked in followed by Pastor Cooper Dupree.

"Jarrell Landry," Detective Webster said, standing. "You are under arrest."

• • •

Cooper Dupree gave Mary Ellen Retinoir a final goodbye kiss on her forehead before climbing into his Toyota Camry. She was waving as he pulled out of the pay-to-park lot. To head back to Pascagoula, he would have taken a right onto Canal Street, driven a half mile to an elevated section of Interstate 10, and merged on the East bound lanes.

Instead, he crossed Canal and headed Uptown.

For two months, he had fought the urge to contact Regina Brandingham. He returned to Pascagoula, with Mary Ellen, hiding her from the public, waiting for FBI agents and forensic accountants to collect the information needed to build a strong enough case to meet the District Attorney's wish to seek the death penalty.

Perhaps, if Mary Ellen had not have survived the hanging and the case had died with her, Dupree would have returned to New Orleans much sooner.

Turning onto Saint Charles Avenue, he passed a streetcar heading Uptown.

Regina Brandingham was the most stunning woman on the planet and Dupree wanted her desperately.

He had to let her know.

In a final, proper farewell, one that he thought about when alone, one he fantasized about when he was at his most desperate, one he had been anticipating for 62 days, Dupree would fight his desire to part as more than just friends.

The End

CRAIG S. MORGAN is a second career writer and tree farmer. Having spent 35 years working in oil refineries, he is now dedicated to improving his carbon foot print by growing hardwood trees and writing organic novels. He lives in Pike County Mississippi with his wife, Kathryn.

For more information on Craig S. Morgan, visit his website or
follow him on social media:
www.CraigSMorgan.com
Craig S Morgan Author on Facebook
CSMorganAuthor on Instagram

Other Books By Craig S. Morgan Include:

Thou Shalt Not Mysteries:
Thou Shalt Not Murder
Thou Shalt Not Escape

Satirical Fiction
Robot Tom

Historical Fiction
Three Headstones